# REDEMPTION

## ALASKA COP SERIES

## WILLIAM L. CASSELMAN

Published by Alaska Dreams Publishing
www.alaskadp.com
1st Paperback Print Edition July 2024
PAPERBACK PRINT ISBN: 978-1-956303-23-0
1st Hardcover Print Edition July 2024
HARDCOVER PRINT ISBN: 978-1-956303-24-7
E-book version available.
Visit http://www.alaskadp.com for links.

*For my lovely wife Mona Sue, my six children, and 17 grandchildren and great-grandchildren. Thank you for your loving support and prayers. To Law Enforcement officers worldwide, who often risk their lives to maintain peace in this world of ours. I dedicate this story to the more than 58,000 men and women who lost their lives in the 10-year war in Vietnam and the 100,000 plus Vietnam and Sandbox War veterans who have lost their lives to suicide, drugs, and liquor since coming home. I wish to add to this dedication by adding all service personnel and civilians who have participated in our wars in Iraq, Afghanistan, and the secret drugs wars of Africa. Thank you all for your service to our country.*

# CONTENTS


Prologue ........... 7

1. Front De Liberation Due Quebec (FLQ) ........... 13

2. A Terrorist Has No Humanity ........... 35

3. An Expensive High ........... 60

4. North To Alaska... For The Rush Is On ........... 71

5. The Big Meeting... They Call This Intelligence? ........... 87

6. Life's Little Twists ........... 104

7. Phase II Begins ........... 120

8. The Unwanted Orphan Child ........... 138

9. A Little Change In Plans ........... 153

10. Ambush! ........... 166

11. Bird Down-A Captain's Folly ........... 184

12. Natural Enemies Can Pop Up Anywhere ........... 204

13. The Game Is Afoot ........... 214

14. A Whistle-Stop Called Curry ........... 229

15. The Deadline Hour Draws Near ........... 246

16. Bold Moves & Scary Times ........... 260

17. Dodge City Alaska Style ........... 277

18. Confrontation ........... 292

Epilogue ........... 311

*About the Author* ........... 316

*Also by Alaska Dreams Publishing* ........... 317

# PROLOGUE

North Of Chu Lai, South Viet Nam
May 14th, 1969
10:13 Hours

A young and highly tanned radio operator was startled out of his chair when terrified cries of "Mayday- Mayday- Mayday!" exploded over the airwaves. Attempts to contact the caller proved negative, but a helicopter pilot radioed in that one of their helos had been hit by ground fire and going in near Chu Lai. The pilot reported, "Too much jungle; you'll have to send in ground troops!"

Only four months out of flight school, 2nd Lieutenant Brad Dills' flight suit was covered in his aircraft commander's blood. He struggled to keep his head in the game, with one trembling hand tightly grasped around the Huey's control stick. His other was busy flipping switches as he fought to keep his dying bird in the air. Dills didn't know if his communication gear was still operational or not. He shouted frantically into his helmet microphone, hoping someone could hear him. His frightened voice clearly revealed panic while he fought to control the Huey's altitude. It was a losing battle; the helicopter was headed for the jungle floor.

The Huey flew 600 feet over the thick terrain when enemy ground fire delivered the fatal blow. As the land came closer, Lt. Dills' was thinking, *this wasn't even a combat mission!* He was transporting a Special Service Unit to Chu Lai Air

Base from their coastal airfield at Marble Mountain. They were scheduled to stop for a noonday meeting with some Marine pilots, to be followed by an evening at the Danang Officer's Club. Lt. Dills' training had not prepared him for this.

The U.S. Army UH-1 Huey had come under enemy fire from a concealed machine gun position. Several bullets from a Russian .51 caliber machine gun had raked the helicopter's left side, crippled the engine, and killed the senior pilot. His skipper dead, Lt. Dills struggled to fight the dying bird. He hoped to auto-rotate to the jungle floor, but the bird's cabin filled up quickly with black smoke as they continued to take ground fire. The Huey circled like a dying falcon as it plummeted from the sky.

The pilot's windshield had taken numerous bullet hits, making it difficult to see anything. Dills frantically glanced about in hopes of finding a soft spot to make a controlled crash. He looked over his shoulder to check his passengers and saw that some had been hit. There was nothing he could do for them now; his first priority was controlling the bird's downward spiral. Dill's mind raced between managing the bird and his concern for surviving. He hoped he could keep from killing everyone, knowing they were about to smack into the ground like a fallen rock.

The passengers were in a panic as they searched frantically for handholds and were terrified. One man struggled to breathe but hyperventilated and passed out.

Dills shouted into his helmet's microphone, "This is Whiskey-Alpha-One-Niner—we're going down! I say again, we are going down! Mayday… Mayday!" There was a spurt of static in Dill's earphones, then he heard the words of a radio operator at Danang Air Force Base, "Aircraft calling mayday, repeat your call-sign!"

"This is Whiskey-Alpha One-Nine'er! We've taken fire—my AC and crew chief are dead—I'm losing her! We're goin' down!"

"Whiskey-Alpha One Nine'er, say your position!" When there was no response the Danang operator tried again, "Whiskey-Alpha One Nine'er, say your position!" The radio operator's voice was urgent, but there was no response from Lt. Dills. After several more calls, the radio operator knew the bird had gone down. He pulled out his flight schedule for the day and located Whiskey-Alpha One Nine on the second page. The list identified the aircraft as a UH-1B Huey and named two pilots. He ran his finger across the page to show who else was aboard, "Special Services Unit… what's that?" He followed procedure and advised his immediate supervisor of the mayday call and a downed helicopter. Then he made his emergency notifications.

In the thick jungle south of Chu Lai, golden rays of afternoon sun were dimmed by the dense tree canopy. Giant trees rose over a hundred feet above the jungle floor, bunched together like broccoli sprouts creating darkness in the world below. The jungle was partially surrounded by rugged mountainous terrain to the west and an ocean twenty miles to the east. It was known for its unforgiving conditions, almost suffocating humidity, and stifling heat. It was also home to venomous snakes and a human enemy with a home-field advantage.

With a commendable effort on Dills' part, the wounded helicopter behaved like a wing-shot duck before it smashed into the upper tree branches. The dying bird broke through and continued to fall. Its long rotor blades snapped off like dry kindling, forcing the helicopter into a side roll.

The shrieks and screams of the survivors were silenced when two men were impaled by tree branches that burst through the Huey's open doors. When the Huey hit open air, it dropped like a 3,500-pound lead weight for another 70 feet before crashing into the jungle floor's thick overgrowth and rolling several times. Unable to do anything, Dills and his surviving passengers rode the bird to its final resting place against a large rocky embankment. The violent fall through the trees ripped a large section of engine cowling away, along with the right skid and what remained of the rotor blades. The helicopter came to rest on its side pinned into place by an outcropping of rocks.

Inside the Huey, the sounds of screaming men were nearly drowned out by the sounds of the aircraft tearing apart as it crashed through the trees and rolled across the ground. A couple of men were thrown clear, but the others remained restrained by safety gear. As the craft settled into its last resting spot, hissing noises escaped from the hot engine, coupled with the mournful cries of the wounded. Dills was pinned in his seat, impaled through the chest by a thick branch, his throat sliced open. His dead hand clutched the control stick tightly; his last thought was to save his gallant bird from a fiery death.

Five miles east of the crash site, members of the Ninth Marines were engaged in a major operation against a large force of North Vietnamese troops. When they heard the mayday calls from the doomed pilot, several Marines watched from a distance as Whiskey-Alpha One Nine'er struck the trees.

Shortly afterward, two rescue Hueys piloted by 1st Lieutenant Ridley and Warrant Officer Jackson hovered over the site. The crash site was unreachable by helicopter, so Ridley notified the air controller of the crash location. Unable to help further and low on fuel, the crew fired off a smoke rocket to mark the spot before returning to the airfield in Chu Lai.

Word quickly went out over the airwaves, and nearby ground units were ordered into the area to search for survivors. With heavy enemy troops in the area, it was a race to see who would be the first to reach the downed bird. A Marine platoon under the command of 2nd Lt. Rudy O'Malley was the closest American unit. They pushed it and reached the crash site, but, they were not the first to arrive. The point man spotted the bodies of a squad-sized North Vietnamese patrol surrounding the dead Huey.

Lt. O'Malley, suspecting a trap, ordered three squads to fan out and encircle the crash site while 3rd squad held back to provide cover fire. He ordered his 2nd squad to approach the bird. A moment later, Sgt. Billy Burke, 2nd Squad's leader, reported, "All the Charlie's are KIA, Lieutenant. Looks like someone survived the crash, and that must've been a big surprise for the NVA troops."

"After you check the wounded crew members, secure the enemy's weapons and any intelligence they may have on them," O'Malley ordered. He had his RTO notify command of their findings. He used a dirty neck towel to wipe his sweaty face before he approached the Huey's smoldering remains. Both pilots were dead, so he walked to where Sgt. Burke was looking over the two American survivors. A Navy corpsman was busy providing first aid. He advised SSgt. Stephen Michaels, his platoon sergeant, "It's late; we'll be holding this position through the night. Get our men situated; we can probably expect more guests. Set up a couple of ambush sites. Maintain a 50-50 watch until nightfall, then we go on 100-percent alert."

With the helicopter's tail section and rotors gone, Lt. O'Malley thought the Huey resembled a dead frog. Most of its upper body was blackened from the engine fire. Some of the nearby foliage was still smoldering so he directed a few men to attend to it.

While the corpsman treated the wounded, Lt. O'Malley took a moment to observe the two dead pilots again. They would need to carry all the bodies out; Marines do not leave their dead in the field, if possible. The two pilots were crushed, and O'Malley tried to figure out the best way to extract them without damaging the bodies further. Death was still new to the young Lieutenant, and the carnage before him shocked him more than he thought possible. His traitorous stomach suddenly erupted against his desire to not get sick in front of his men. He wiped his face, feeling slightly embarrassed, and kicked a couple of the NVA bodies to get his mind off the dead pilots. He gulped water from his canteen to clean his mouth. With his composure finally reigned, Lt. O'Malley walked over to join his corpsman and get a status report on the wounded.

The Navy Corpsman, 19-year-old Eugene Brittles, knelt over one of the wounded men as O'Malley crouched beside him. "How're they doing, Doc?"

Brittles couldn't help but notice the Lieutenant's green coloring, "Give me a moment, sir, and I'll give you something for your sour stomach. Don't worry about the men, sir—we've all gone through it. Hard to get used to what we see over here."

"I'm okay, Doc," O'Malley replied. "But thanks. I've got to get used to it sooner or later. So, what's your guess?"

"Sir, besides the pilots, I've got four KIA by that large rock; three officers, including one Marine major, an Air Force light colonel, an Air Force Captain, and a Spec four Army crew chief. I'd say they died in the crash because they were pretty broken up, but they were also hit by enemy fire when the Huey was shot up. Looks like one of those Russian .51 caliber machine guns judging by the holes in that Huey. The crew chief died before the Huey hit. He took two big hits, one in the stomach and one in the heart. Instant death."

"Okay, break out some ponchos to cover 'em up. As soon as the area's safe, I'll get some stretchers built to carry the bodies out. What about the two wounded men?"

"Both are pretty bad, Lieutenant. I don't think the enlisted man, probably the door gunner, will make it. He about bled out before we got here. There's nothing I can do for him except make him comfortable." Brittles gestured to the other wounded man, "Sgt. Burke and I agree that it appears this captain did most, if not all, of the fighting. He sure didn't want to give up his M-16 when I started doctoring him. Then he passed out."

"What's his condition?" Lt. O'Malley asked as the two men stood up and walked a few feet away.

"Sir, he's taken one bad hit to the shoulder, probably from an AK-47 and both legs are broke from the crash. His face—well sir, you can see how messed up he is. Nothing I can do out here but bandage him up. I'd say he's lookin' at some serious repair work back in the States, and he'll probably lose his left eye." Brittles rubbed his hands together, a habit he developed to control adrenaline surges and to keep from shaking. "I gave both a stab of morphine to make them more comfortable when we start dragging 'em out of here. I'll give 'em another jab along the way if it gets bad." He kicked the dirt in frustration. "Sir, I'm limited to only two sticks of morphine per customer; a third would likely cause an overdose and kill them. I sure wish they'd come up with something stronger. Too bad about the officer; it looks like the captain, took on this whole bunch of NVA and came out on top. He killed eight one-eyed, with two broken legs, a bad shoulder hit, and other injuries—that's one army officer who knows how to shoot. The gunner was too messed up to return fire, and the bird's two M-60s were damaged in the crash."

Lt. O'Malley looked the scene over. *It's getting so dark that it's hard to make out the Huey's shape, and we're stuck out here for the night. One man with two broken legs shot it out with eight NVAs and took only a shoulder hit and might possibly lose an eye. The way his face is torn up, his jaw is probably broken. I'm betting the poor guy will never look in a mirror again.* He shook his head in dismay, "Check his dog tags and give me his name—in fact, get me the names of all the dead. I want to get this sent in before anything else happens out here." He called his platoon sergeant over. "Sarge, I want all enemy weapons buried, no souvenirs this trip. We have a lot to carry out. Before we leave, toss a couple grenades in that bird. I don't want to leave anything usable for the NVA. Take whatever documents you can find off the dead. I don't want anything lost before Grave and Registration at Danang have a chance to see it. And don't forget, there's an NVA-heavy weapon out here, maybe more than one. Tonight, we stay quiet and head out at first light for the nearest LZ. I'm hoping their dead were encouragement enough for them to pull out before we moved in." He started to turn away, "We'll need stretchers built to carry all these men out, including the dead, Sergeant Michaels."

"Yes, Sir, I've already got a squad working on it."

A few minutes later, Corpsman Brittles got Lt. O'Malley's attention, "Lieutenant, you ain't gonna believe this, but this captain's a chaplain!"

"What, that wounded guy's a chaplain!?" O'Malley asked in disbelief.

"Yes, sir," Brittles replied. "Captain Anthony Rogers, Chaplain, US Army."

Lt. O'Malley shook his head; he had a hard time believing a Man of the Cloth, a Holy Joe, could have done all this. But the scene clearly showed he had. *Well, I'll let the investigator figure this one out. Hopefully, this guy can survive long enough to tell them what went on out here. A weird group of people to be flying together—*

Sgt. Michaels called for him, and he left that thought hanging.

1

# FRONT DE LIBERATION DUE QUEBEC (FLQ)

Federal Parliament Building
Downtown Toronto, Province Of Ontario, Canada
Monday, May 4th

Shortly after 2:00 a.m., a dark green City of Toronto five-ton GMC trash hauler rumbled down the business district's main drag at a slow, lumbering speed. The mammoth-sized vehicle had the whole road to itself with no other traffic in the city's business center. A large green metal trash dumpster on the two eight-foot-long steel forks in front swayed back and forth with the motions of the truck. Three men, each dressed in yellow coveralls, rode in the cab scanning the surrounding area closely as the driver pulled into an access road posted, "Reserved for Official Purposes Only". The truck stopped beside the five-story Federal Parliament Building with a loud squeal of brakes.

Two men jumped out of the truck and waited patiently as the driver lowered the large dumpster to the ground. Then all three men grabbed hold and, with apparent effort, shoved the metal dumpster into place beside two other dumpsters filled to nearly overflowing. While two men held the dumpster's lid up, the third hung over the side, reached inside, and then dropped clear.

Had someone seen, they might have thought it strange how quiet these garbage men were. They worked in complete silence without casual banter back and forth. Finished, they boarded their truck and drove off without dumping the trash from the other two full dumpsters.

13

One man observed the dumpster's delivery to the Parliament Building. A Perkins Security & Alarms Company employee parked nearly a block away. Twenty-five-year-old Security Officer Jack Herbert struggled to stay awake. A high school dropout from Montreal, Jack received his high school diploma just after his 21$^{st}$ birthday with the help of night school. He made enough money to live on working the security job and flipping burgers at a local burger joint. Officer Herbert sat in the company car listening to a late-night talk show host wax eloquently over the radio and shook his head in bewilderment in response to the people who called in. What some had to say didn't make sense and he couldn't help but wonder if they were registered voters. *That's probably why we're in such a mess right now. Bunch of idiots!* Jack reached over and turned the dial to a soft rock station, "Now this is more like it; let the 90s live again!"

Jack was responsible for 21 buildings, five parking garages, and two sizable fenced-in storage spaces in area six. It took him approximately 45 minutes to check the outside of all the facilities. Then he parked for a while, drank hot coffee, and listened to the car radio. Without another thought of the disappearing trash truck, Jack sang along with an old Wings tune his father used to play on their old eight-track tape player. As the song ended, Jack rested his chin on the steering wheel and wished for the day he could patrol these streets in a real police cruiser and chase the bad guys. He sighed as he raised his head, rechecked his wristwatch, and pulled out of the alley for another round of security checks. He was bored and wished for something to happen, but the downtown area was quiet.

The morning was unusually warm for early May and Albert Higgins, a middle-aged dairyman from eastern Ontario, was not happy about making the long drive into Toronto. He was going in to voice concern over federal employees trespassing on his property. Mornings for a dairyman meant hard work, and this trip cost him money; he had been forced to bring an off-duty employee in to work overtime. He had no choice. "Those damn feds need to stay off my land! I pay my taxes; they're lucky I didn't shoot a couple of them for trespassing!" Higgins was pulled over by a city cop for running a red light, and his mood soured. It grew even darker when he looked in his side mirror and saw it was a woman who had pulled him over. Teeth clenched, eyes glaring, and knuckles white from squeezing the steering wheel tightly, Higgins looked over his shoulder and unwisely bellowed, "Get a move on it, honey! I got me some business here in town!"

Officer Mary Bryant, a 24-year-old member of the Toronto Police Traffic Enforcement Division didn't expect her first citation so early in the morning. The bright morning had her feeling pretty chipper, so she had only planned to warn the driver. That is until Higgins shouted at her in such a disrespectful way and called her "honey". She took her time walking around his vehicle, scrutinizing it for violations, and noted a taillight was out and the right rear tire was bald. She wrote the citation slowly which only worsened Higgins' foul mood. He ground his teeth and nursed thoughts of wanting to strangle the female police officer. After the citation was signed, Officer Bryant finished by adding insult to injury when she suggested Higgins have a nice day.

"Thanks!" Higgins growled as he crumbled the citation up and tossed it to the floor of his truck. "Bah! Female cops! Been a man, I'd probably gotten a warning." Higgins pulled his faded blue Chicago Cubs baseball cap down over his furrowed brow and drove away, making sure to use his blinker when he entered traffic. He cursed the wide-hipped lady cop and the government. A few moments later, he pulled into an enclosed six-story parking garage. Though it would cost him a few bucks more than the cheaper rates further in town, this one was located beside the Ontario Provincial Parliament Building. "All the taxes I pay, you'd think the government would give us free parking!" It was 7:38 a.m., and Higgins was in a feisty mood as he locked up his truck and walked to the elevator.

The Parliament Building was a massive five-story rectangular structure with an attached parking garage. Most of the 623 federal employees who worked in the building stood around espresso stands, break room coffee pots, and a few smoking rooms. They still had twenty minutes before officially starting their day. The weekend was over and there was time for post-weekend gossip. Steel and plastic in-and-out baskets heaped with government paperwork waited on desktops. Most computer systems contained a backlog of e-mails from the weekend and hundreds of forwarded government forms that needed to be printed out and filed. There were dozens of impatient civilians lined up down-stairs waiting for security personnel to begin screening them through elaborate monitoring devices at precisely 8:00 a.m. It was 7:57 a.m., three minutes before the line of people could go through.

Higgins counted each second on his watch and shook his head when the floodgate finally opened. He forgot to give his fingernail clippers and a penknife to the security officers and when the sensor alarm went off, his face turned a reddish tint. He reached into his pocket, removed the clippers and the small knife, and handed them to the female security tech. With an icy glare, Higgins was ready to lock horns with her as he complained, "Bunch of guys out there with machine guns, and you're all concerned with my penknife and clippers?"

"Yes, sir," the young Hispanic lady said in a calm neutral voice. "We have regulations to enforce, and I appreciate your cooperation, sir." Security Technician III Cindy Douglas forced a smile in hopes of satisfying the old coot.

"Are you having problems with this man?" A tall Black man asked with a French accent. He wore a matching security uniform and gave Mr. Higgins a good once over. The officer raised an eyebrow that Higgins assumed to be an expression of superiority, which only darkened his mood. He was ready to turn around, go home, and get his rifle but he only sighed deeply and walked through the scanner a second time. When the alarm didn't go off, Higgins turned to face the security officers, "Satisfied?" he asked with a hint of hostility.

"Yes, sir. You can reclaim your items as you leave, sir," Ms. Douglas advised.

"Do I need to sign anything, so you know they're mine?"

"No, Sir. I'm sure we'll remember you."

Not about to reply, he turned around and walked toward a wall of elevators. Shoving his way onto an elevator with nine other people, Higgins's temper was simmering when the elevator finally reached his floor. Storming out, he turned to the people remaining on the elevator, "You people all smell like some lady's perfume counter. You're polluting the air with that crap, and three of you are men! Grow a pair and use some Old Spice!"

"Get real, dude, you should talk—you smell like a cow," a thin-faced man responded, and several people nodded in agreement.

Fuming, Higgins stomped off down the hall, swinging his inexpensive black briefcase as if it was a weapon. He finally found the right office and stood before the door for a moment to collect his composure before entering.

For the last three months, a Canadian government survey crew had spent several hours a day surveying land for a planned roadway across several farms, an access route to reach a new government communications project. Higgins had mailed the government a dozen letters complaining about crews scaring his cows with loud vehicles, cutting fences, and leaving tire ruts in his pastures. The government finally mailed an invitation to Higgins for an early morning meeting in Toronto. *In hopes of remedying this situation to everyone's benefit,* the letter had read.

Only seconds before her meeting with Mr. Higgins, 32-year-old Bethany Sellers, a low-level government clerk, sat at her desk and brushed her long brown hair back over her shoulders with a gentle wave of her hand. Upon seeing her first customer of the day, she pushed her chair back and headed to a large wooden office counter. She checked the wall clock; it was officially after 8:00 a.m., and she felt ready to deal with the public. Unfortunately for her, that first customer would end up being Mr. Higgins, unhappy that he was facing yet another female government employee.

Mrs. Sellers sensed the older gentleman's foul mood by the sour expression on his face. She smiled pleasantly and said in a friendly voice, "Good morning, Sir. How may I help you?"

Higgins grunted in response, plopped his briefcase down on the countertop, and opened it to retrieve his official letter of appointment. Before he could show it to Mrs. Sellers, the world around them suddenly went dark and shook violently. Someone yelled, "Earthquake!"

Higgins' last thought was a feeling of flying upward as he slammed against the ceiling tiles. For a micro-second, a wave of darkness and intense pain consumed him before his mind simply blinked off. For Mr. Higgins, death came quickly.

Mrs. Sellers's broken body was thrown across the room, then flew outside as the exterior wall disintegrated, becoming part of the rubble on the ground. Shattered glass, building debris, paper, and office furniture covered the sidewalk and street below.

At precisely 8:05 a.m., an electronic timing device sent a spark of electricity through a series of coated wires to six electric blasting caps placed in six two-pound blocks of C-4 plastique explosive, surrounded by other wired blocks of C-4. The munitions were surrounded by six drums filled with diesel fuel covered by several 80-pound bags of ammonia nitrate. Several hundred pounds of ammonia nitrate added to diesel fuel in a metal trash dumpster created an explosion that tore off the front face and southern end of the House of Parliament Building.

Thick black and gray plumes of smoke, mixed with concrete dust and tons of debris, erupted into the air to form a mushroom cloud. The plumes rose over a thousand feet into the air and could be seen for miles. Orange, yellow, and red flames shot up over a hundred feet, and debris showered down on a four-square-block area. Tons of concrete rubble, broken glass, and beams of twisted steel collapsed upon stunned unfortunate pedestrians caught in the street. An avalanche of wood and metal office furniture, metal file cabinets, and other office equipment slid off uneven floors to cascade down from offices whose walls no longer existed. Fires burned out of control causing further injuries and death to passersby on the sidewalks. Three people standing by a corner light post simply ceased to exist, disintegrated by the initial blast.

Windows as far away as eight blocks were shattered from the massive blast; nearby vehicles were crushed by substantial concrete chunks from the building's outside wall. The screeching sounds of tortured rebar mixed with continued explosions as a large section of the building crumbled in on itself. Towering flames scaled the outside walls and spread quickly to nearby buildings. Most of the fire came from the structure's natural gas lines, causing great black clouds to block the morning sun. Eerie shadows created a sense of nightfall over the downtown area. Several people on the street fainted from fear of a catastrophic disaster.

Blown-out windows injured dozens of office workers in nearby buildings. Shards of glass rained down on dozens of pedestrians below. Vehicles nearest the Parliament Building and those parked inside the attached parking garage were tossed about like children's toys. Only when the building finished its terrifying dance could anyone hear the sounds of horrific screams, and dozens of frightened calls for help. As the smoke gradually cleared in front of the Parliament Building, a ghastly sight was revealed, leaving hundreds of onlookers spellbound.

A local TV news reporter, on his way to work, said it best, "Ladies and Gentlemen, it appears as if someone had used a giant buzz saw to slice off the end of the building. The blast has exposed many inner offices and left this hellish sight that has befouled our beautiful city. It's Oklahoma City and 9-11 all over again. We, the people of Toronto, have now joined the ranks of those other terrorized victims."

Cries of panic combined with the mournful wails of the injured and dying. Survivors fled the building, climbing over debris and even being callous enough to charge over the fallen in a wild stampede to escape. In the brief moments after the explosion, most people forgot about those still trapped in the building or those under the rubble outside.

Fires burned throughout the front of the structure, surprisingly untouched by the geysers of water spewing out from hundreds of broken pipes, damaged restroom fixtures, and a single drinking fountain left water running on the third floor.

Joe C. Husher, a building custodian with 14 years on the job, had the presence of mind and the courage to make his way down to the building's basement to shut off the main natural gas supply. His actions prevented further explosions from taking place and possibly saved hundreds of lives.

Ceiling tiles, office furniture, and wood wall paneling blazed unchecked. Police and Fire Department vehicles, with red and blue lights flashing, and reverberating sirens blaring, began arriving on the scene. A few government security personnel fortunate enough to escape injury directed survivors to a second enclosed parking garage behind the Parliament Building. When city inspectors found that structure damaged, survivors were moved to a shopping mall a block away.

Medical teams set up a field hospital for treating the injured outside the safety zone. Royal Canadian Mounted Police personnel and city police officers worked together questioning building occupants to see if they had seen anything suspicious before the blast.

A few brave souls remained behind to initiate rescue operations for the scores of injured trapped in dozens of smaller collapsed offices or in shredded hallways, stalled elevators, and stairwells ripped away from walls and floors. The blast hurled heavy steel file cabinets, copiers, and desks against ceilings and walls; overturned thousand-pound counters, and sent some crashing down to the growing pile of rubble outside. The air, fouled by the explosion's pungent odor, was filled with a whirlwind of floating paper of all colors, sizes, and designs. Brightly colored singed pieces of photographs, calendars, papers, and file folders drifted in the air and skittered across the ground. A wall calendar, with pictures of horses, was found on the roof of a car more than a mile away from the Parliament Building. It had landed showing the current month with a reminder note of a wedding anniversary five days away. The calendar's owner did not survive to attend the event.

With a disaster of such scale in a busy part of town, the number of bystanders multiplied, making it difficult for emergency crews to reach and care for injured people. A heavyset man on the street shouted, "Look up there!" as he pointed to a dark-haired woman in a white blouse hanging by her hands from a piece of steel rebar. Her bare legs were streaked with blood as she dangled forty feet above the ground. "Hey, someone help her!" He shouted. No one moved; there was no way to reach her. As the stunned crowd watched, she lost her grip and fell to the jagged teeth of twisted steel below.

A man was spotted sitting behind a desk in an office exposed by the blast. He behaved as if nothing had happened. He waved and smiled at the crowd below. From the ground, onlookers could not see the shock in his eyes nor the bloody wound on the back of his head. His desk sat at an angle with one corner only inches from the ledge and a four-story drop into the arms of death. One after another, rescue personnel appeared in his office doorway, pleading with him to crawl their way. If he heard them, he ignored their pleas. While horrified rescuers watched, he stood up and walked calmly over the edge without uttering a word.

Mangled bodies could be seen in collapsed offices, some only partially revealed. The blast exposed the center stairwell which vanished below the fourth floor, trapping dozens of terrified people above. Their screams and shouts for help carried through the area. A wave of a hand, a cry for help from somewhere else, indicated survivors in different locations. Some of these would die before rescuers could arrive on the scene and get to them.

The elevators were located toward the center of the building, nearly all stopped between floors. Several people were trapped inside, uninjured but temporarily deafened by the blast. One office supervisor had to be physically dragged out by rescuers. Two women inside pushed him from the other side, happy to escape the hysterical man.

Mrs. Charles Riley, a young redhead who had come to town early to seek tax assistance for her husband's new tire shop screamed wildly for her little girl. No child could be seen in the exposed office on the third floor, and rescuers feared the worst.

The horrified crowd turned away as a body engulfed in flame fell from the top floor and struck a jagged piece of concrete. The body slowly slid to the ground to vanish in a cloud of gray dust.

A man in a torn white shirt and a woman in a dust-covered dark blue dress clutched a door frame in a corner office where most of the floor was missing. Both, bleeding from wounds, refused to move in fear the floor would give way and cause them to plummet.

People, stunned or in shock, wandered or crawled aimlessly about in most of the hallways, many bleeding from injuries, unable to ask for help. Most had lost their hearing in the explosion. Some simply sat in the stairwells, embracing one another, too terrified to move until a rescuer arrived. With kind words of reassurance from those in better shape, such victims were led and assisted down the steps to where first responder teams waited.

Officer Bryant, her uniform covered in gray dust and bleeding from a nasty head wound, crawled out of her wrecked patrol vehicle, which lay on its side. She would never forget the blast and the invisible hand that swatted her patrol car aside like a child's toy. Her vehicle rolled side-over-side until it struck a stalled city bus. Wearing her seat belt, shoulder harness, and bulletproof vest had saved her life. Still, she would be feeling the massive bruising for days to come.

First responders crawled and stumbled over rubble and broken glass, struggling to see through thick, dust-filled air to look upon the faces of the injured and the dead. Countless yards of rope were called for to provide safety lines that bridged the front of the Parliament Building like a vast spider web. A rope was also used to set up a security barricade to keep bystanders, thieves, and souvenir hunters back. Yellow police tape had little or no effect on gawkers.

Specially trained rescue dogs were brought in to search the debris for victims trapped in air pockets. Cadaver dogs were used to locate bodies crushed by hundreds of tons of reinforced steel and concrete slabs. Others would not be found until heavy equipment arrived to clear away debris.

Nearly everyone was covered in fine gray dust, which resulted in several people being rushed to the nearby hospital for respiratory problems. The whole area was filled with an extraordinary noise level, mostly distorted. Police, fire, and ambulance sirens wailed incessantly often accompanied by the blast of an air horn. Hysterical screams, cries, and shouts for help were nearly drowned out by a hundred voices barking orders from just as many different directions inside and outside the building. Then the sound of jackhammers and the Jaws of Life working to free the trapped joined the mournful cries of a building being ripped apart. Sledgehammers were swung against walls; axes broke through locked doors as fire hoses spewed out thousands of gallons of water. Onlookers stood in the streets and behind the broken windows of nearby buildings. Thousands of people shared a moment in time that would haunt them for a lifetime.

Emergency Command Post (ECP)

Support crews set up the ECP quickly, as men and women were tasked with cordoning off the disaster scene using yellow rope, plastic orange and yellow cones, and wooden barriers. Police had an established perimeter to enforce as they directed bystanders out of hazardous areas or risk arrest. Within an hour, the order was given to push the perimeter back another two blocks. Three significant roadways were closed to non-emergency traffic. Large wooden and concrete barricades were moved in to keep the public back. City inspectors set out to inspect nearby buildings and discovered structural damage in several.

Additional evacuations were ordered, and within moments, another thousand people were on the streets moving to safe zones. More rope and barricades were ordered. Every city police officer, firefighter, EMS employee, and volunteer was called in. Dozens of tow trucks were brought in to remove vehicles cluttering streets in the disaster area. Toronto City Police and RCMP were on hand to handle squabbles when argumentative owners complained about vehicles being towed away. Damaged vehicles were sent to the city impound yard or another designated spot for investigators to look at. Everything within the immediate area was considered possible evidence; police would let the city's attorneys worry about complaints later.

Two vehicles that had been waiting for a green light directly in front of the Parliament Building were crushed under massive pieces of concrete. One was believed to be a red sports car, and the other, a blue Ford station wagon. Both had been occupied, but it would be some time before the bodies could be recovered. One statue of a historical figure was found with an eight-foot length of steel rebar embedded in the chest. Its photograph made the front page of a local newspaper the next day.

Rude reporters and cameraman pushed their way through crowds of rescue workers, darting from one gruesome scene to another in hopes of finding a particularly impressive graphic shot for the next news update. They interrupted emergency workers to ask foolish questions, "Do you think you'll find anyone alive down there?" "Have you found any bodies yet?" One aggressive reporter shoved his microphone into the face of the wrong man and received a left hook to the jaw. Only moments before, the worker had zipped the body of a small child into a black body bag. The reporter demanded the man be arrested, but the police ignored him; they didn't have time to deal with a foolish reporter either. Overhead, news helicopters circled the scene like vultures flying over a dying animal until ordered off by police helicopters. When national and international news services arrived, the ECP received an order from city hall to provide room for them. A large Canadian Army tent was set up adjacent to the ECP for news people.

ECP personnel were ordered to cooperate as much as possible with reporters but not to answer any pertinent questions concerning the ongoing investigation. A public information officer from city hall was sent to liaison with news services but hadn't arrived yet. The on-scene ECP Commander, Captain Sam Whitehead of the Toronto City Fire Department, was known to be a bit of a grump with news crews. An older man was once overheard remarking, "TV reporters would sell their own children for a good news story." Captain Whitehead ordered one of his lieutenants to handle all reporters until the public information officer arrived, saying, "You just keep 'em away from me!"

Mass casualty training and exercises had prepared ground crews to quickly set up four huge white canvas tents, each capable of holding thirty cots or six eight-foot-long conference tables. With mild weather conditions, the tents' sides were rolled up, allowing more room to move about. Foldable tables and chairs were delivered in the back of four two-ton flatbed trucks. With practiced precision, crews set the items up in a quick fashion. The 23 ECP workers wore orange emergency coveralls and black baseball hats with the letters "ECP" printed in white on them. Computers and communications equipment were the next items to arrive, along with radio base stations, hand-held radios, specially designated cell phones, two large generators, and extra battery packs for all the electronics. Another truck delivered two massive spools holding several hundred yards of cable. Junction boxes were connected to generators spread about the tents, with wires and cables marked in various colors, each meaning something different. Smaller wires had numbers imprinted on white plastic tags. After hours of practice, techs could quickly run cables, set up junction boxes, and attach numbered wires to required equipment in a matter of minutes. Two 55-gallon barrels of fuel were offloaded to keep the generators running for 48 hours, with one man specifically assigned to that task. Without power, the ECP would cease to function as intended. Generators and mobile lights for night operation were delivered. At night, the scene would be lit up to resemble a night game at a major football stadium's season opening.

Sixty-five minutes after the blast, all the wiring had been laid out by 12-ECP technicians, and computers were booted up and running That time beat the record from their best drill, but no one was in the mood to comment on it. A square six-foot map showing the downtown disaster area was stapled to a tent's inner wall panel.

For years RCMP, Toronto Police, Fire and EMS Departments, and the military had conducted mass casualty drills that clearly paid off. However, most supervisors had thought a large plane crash would be their first major emergency, not an explosion of this severity in the downtown area.

Captain Jean-Paul Leon & Sgt. Brady Wilkens

Captain Jean-Paul Leon, JP to his friends, from the RCMP Intelligence Division, inhaled deeply on a cheap foul-smelling cigar to cover the smell of full body bags. Normally a non-smoker, he found a cigar's stench a necessary tool when one worked so close to death. His best friend and second-in-command, Sgt. Brady Wilkens always kept a supply of stinkers available for such times.

At six feet tall and 210 pounds, JP closely resembled the actor who had played Sgt. Preston of the Mounties on the TV series, a fact he was often kidded about until he made captain. Then it was mentioned only behind his back in low whispers. JP (Jean was pronounced as John) wore his wavy black hair cut short which did not hide the gray expanding back from his temples. A knife scar nearly four inches in length marked the right side of his neck—a souvenir from a bar fight he broke up almost 14 years earlier. With broad shoulders, his once narrow waist was beginning to protrude outward at an alarming rate. According to his wife, this was the result of early morning shift hours, too many hours behind the desk, and consuming late-night sugary treats.

Sgt. Wilkens resembled, so some said, but never to his face, a city fire hydrant. Half-Northern Sioux and half-white, he stood 5'6" and tipped the scales at 241 pounds. He had large muscular hands, a very square head, and almost no neck to speak of. His somewhat flattened nose came from his mother's side of the family, but his light brown hair came from his French-Canadian father. A hint of a French accent picked up from his father was especially noticeable when he grew angry and uttered profane words in French. Wilkens, sometimes described as a bulldog with a sour disposition, was clearly built more for strength and endurance than a burst of speed. He couldn't run very fast with short, stocky legs but had set the record for bench-pressing 400 pounds at the RCMP Academy gym, a feat he wouldn't attempt to repeat. Added to his strength was the patience of a native hunter and a fine investigator's mind. JP saw how fast Wilkens grasped intelligence work, making him JP's choice for the division's number two slot.

JP wore a blue off-the-rack Saturday Sears' "special sale" suit without a vest, which had cost him $89.95 in New York City. Wilkens wore an expensive tailored dark brown suit with a vest that set him back $798.50. Wilkens was single and could afford tailored suits on his sergeant's pay. JP was married with kids and could ill afford the two suits he owned. If the need arose, he had two sets of RCMP dress uniforms and two basic RCMP uniforms.

Their RCMP shields were in full view on their breast pockets allowing them to move freely through the disaster area and reach the ECP. They arrived in time to find Captain Whitehead standing behind a hastily installed podium, which appeared barely capable of holding the dozen or so microphones attached to it. Reporters held portable tape recorders, cell phones, and microphones directed his way, Whitehead, however reluctant, was giving news people their first statistics; "Our count at this time is 123 confirmed dead, 304 injured, and 71 people still missing. With reports from nearby hospitals still coming in, those numbers will most likely increase as the day goes by— get that damn thing out of my face!" Whitehead pushed aside the hand of a woman who held a large black microphone linked to a nearby cameraman. "Look, I don't have a lot of time for this, so let's all be polite, and I'll attempt to answer a few—and I do mean a few questions. The public information officer should be here soon, and you can harass him."

"Chief, has anyone taken credit for the bombing? Do you suspect it was an attack by an international terrorist group, such as the Taliban, ISIS, or al-Qaeda?" A young sandy-haired man with large white teeth made sure his microphone was a comfortable distance from the captain's face.

"As I said earlier," Whitehead forced himself to smile, knowing he would still come off looking like some crazed old man on TV. "We're still not sure it was a bomb. We're looking at several possibilities that could have caused this explosion. Other than that, I have no comment."

"What else could have caused such a blast? Please don't tell us you suspect a broken gas line," an attractive female reporter with shoulder-length brown hair said.

*What is it with reporters and good teeth? They must all go to the same damn dentist and get a cut rate.* Whitehead shook his head, "No comment."

Another reporter moved forward, rudely pushing the female reporter aside, "Captain, was there any prior warning given?"

"Now, all of you behave, or I'll let the newspaper reporters have all the details. You'll notice they behave like ladies and gentlemen." Whitehead gestured to the crowd of reporters standing in the back, taking notes or typing. Two or three smiled for the kind recognition, one waved a salute, and the others continued writing. "Listen, folks, give us some time to do our work," Whitehead pointed to one of the body bags being carried to a waiting ambulance, "We owe it to them." He looked about the crowd, sighed, and ignored the next barrage of questions. "A public information officer from the city will be here soon, so please be patient." He was through with the press briefing, but reporters were insistent with more questions. One year shy of his mandatory retirement at 65 years of age, Captain Whitehead had medium-length, shaggy white hair. He turned abruptly away from the reporters and walked back to the ECP to meet with JP and Sgt. Wilkens.

"JP, your cursed cigars are stinking up my command post."

"My apologies, Sam," JP tossed his cigar to the ground and stomped on it. He glanced at Wilkens, but his sergeant continued puffing away to rile Whitehead. The two men had a running but good-natured feud which went back to coaching opposing softball teams. The Toronto Fire Department against the RCMP.

"So, do you think this is al-Qaeda or ISIS—maybe Iran, or Syria—and why us? What did Canada do to the Muslims?" Whitehead asked.

JP replied, "Too early to tell, but my first impression leans that way, towards a Middle East bunch. But which bunch? You got me. Officially, I'd hold off announcing a possible culprit; it'll only add to the fear factor. We sure don't want to give those clowns any credit for this. You know they would love the publicity. A number of wannabes will try to take credit for it just to see their name in the papers." JP looked over Whitehead's shoulder at the frenzy of activity inside the ECP. "You got this place running like a piece of well-oiled machinery, Sam. All those drills are paying off, but some of your people might slow down before we lose some evidence."

"I'll worry about the evidence later; I've still got people missing. They're probably under that rubble or stuck in some room up there in that mess." Captain Whitehead added, "I'll spread the word to keep an eye out for anything that might be part of an explosive device, though I doubt there's anything left. Looks like a car bomb—a massive car bomb—like maybe a moving van. I've got the ECP personnel checking out the security videos of this neighborhood. Maybe one of those cameras caught whoever did this. It would be nice if they did."

Wilkens was about to respond but felt his pager vibrating in his pants pocket. He checked the number and called dispatch on his cell phone. A few grunts and a couple of "uh-huhs" later, he put his phone away and whispered into JP's ear, "We got a tape. One of our guys is picking it up at some radio station down by the bus depot."

"Sounds like we're about to hear from the responsible party," JP whispered in return. "Wilkins, I want a summation of the tape as soon as they play it through, the best profile we can get in a short time. Transcribe the whole thing and make a dozen copies for the bosses. We'll break it down when we get back to the office."

"Right," Wilkens got back on the phone to pass on the orders.

Thirty-three minutes later, Wilkens was filling a Styrofoam cup with hot coffee in the ECP when he received another page and called in. Hanging up, he walked over to brief JP. "Not one of our more favorable radio stations, a bit on the liberal side. They said they'd play the tape at 5 p.m. tonight but decided to let us have the first crack at it."

"Nice of them," JP said sarcastically.

"You won't believe this, the voice on the tape calls themselves the Front De Liberation du Quebec, often shortening it to FLQ. The male voice and the message were entirely in French; our people said it was an educated speaker. They targeted the Parliament Building to announce the renewal of their war for a free Quebec sovereignty."

"The FLQ?" JP said in disbelief. "That group operated back in the sixties and early seventies. The last report had them fleeing to Cuba and disappearing; some say they stepped on the wrong toes and were murdered by Castro." JP shook his head. He would have been happier had it been al-Qaeda with a random attack. There was the chance of more bombings if this was indeed the return of the FLQ.

"Copies are being made, the original tape will be sent to the lab to be analyzed for background noises, prints, DNA, and such. Radio station personnel are being printed and interviewed by our people." Wilkens looked around the ECP and asked, "Do you plan to call the Toronto Police in on this now or risk taking some flak when the Colonel hears we held back?"

"The Parliament Building is federal property, this is our case, but as a professional courtesy, we'll keep the Toronto Police informed, but, at our pace. Okay?"

"You're the one who'll catch the heat. I'm only the little Indian boy who follows the white man's orders," Wilkens smirked.

"Little my foot," JP snorted. "All right, let's go. There's nothing we can do around here. I doubt we'll be able to sift through the debris for another 24 hours. Local boys have the area secured. It's not as if we'd find a smoking gun lying around." JP glanced over at the nearby aid tent, seeing a small child being treated for facial burns that would scar her forever. A fire began burning deep inside him, a thirst for revenge against those who had done this. For the moment, he only had a man's voice on a tape speaking in French, giving themselves an old terrorist organization's name. Hopefully, by tomorrow, ECP personnel and arson investigators would locate the detonation point.

JP knew this case would take time, but he was beginning to feel one of his hunches; one day, he would eyeball the scum who had done this. His one big worry, besides dealing with the Toronto Police over jurisdiction, was the FLQ's next act of terror. Like most seasoned law enforcement veterans, he knew things usually come in threes; he hoped this was not one of those times.

Intelligence Division, RCMP Headquarters, Toronto
May 4th, 11:19 a.m.

Sitting on the corner of his desk with a cup of hot coffee, disgust written across his face, JP read the message in English as he listened to the FLQ tape recording for the fifth time His French was barely adequate, and Wilkens had to help him through the first time. Translated, the message said: "Today, at 8:05 a.m., the Front for the Liberation of Quebec struck a decisive blow against Canadian tyranny. In bombing the House of Parliament, the FLQ has demonstrated its capabilities and steadfast resolve against an autocratic Canadian government. Quebec will be free. It would be careless and dangerous for the authorities to take us—or our threats—lightly. Unlike suicidal religious fanatics of the Middle East, we are not simple terrorists who find satisfaction in bombing buses or police stations. We are true freedom fighters, men and women, who will bring devastation on a far grander scale until our goal is met with a free Quebec. You will hear from us again, I assure you." As the male voice finished speaking many voices in the background, male and female shouted, "Free Quebec, Free Quebec!" over and over until the tape ended. JP rewound the tape and played it again. By the time it finished, he felt satisfied that he could recognize the man's voice if he heard it on the street.

He looked into the expressionless faces of Sgt. Wilkens and Sgt. Steve Adler. Number three on the division roster, Sgt. Adler was the oldest detective in the division and a highly trained interrogator. He had held sergeant's rank longer than anyone could remember and was satisfied with his current status. He refused to test for lieutenant stripes because he didn't want to leave the streets and get stuck shuffling papers in some office. A few pounds overweight as a result of fondness for pasta dishes, Adler stood 5'11", had hair more silver than white, and a ruddy complexion that tended to frighten most young children. He wore a dark blue pinstripe suit purchased from the same tailor Wilkens used.

JP said, "If I didn't know you two better, I'd say you were on some dealer's payroll, but you both look real sharp. If only you weren't so ugly, the gals in the office might be giving you both the eye." He respected them and trusted their judgment. He looked at them. "Any comments, gentlemen?" Wilkens had a cup of coffee in his hand, and it reminded him, "Hey, big spender, don't forget to put some coins in the cup for your coffee—it's not free, you know. Someone's got to pay for it."

The two sergeants relaxed in an old, dilapidated brown leather couch that had survived four prior captains in its 16 years of service. Used often as a bed, the sofa was covered in cigarette burns and coffee stains too numerous to count, giving the old relic a bit of character.

"Our experts don't believe the speaker used a machine to disguise his voice. He speaks flawless French, so it's probably his primary language. I'd venture to say he has a Montreal accent," Wilkens said.

"Montreal? When did you take up voice analyzing?" Adler shook his head in wonder.

JP had become used to it by now. These two challenged one another constantly over just about everything. Hard to believe they were the best of friends and, notably, one of the best investigator teams in the RCMP. Which was the primary reason they were both assigned to Intelligence.

"Do you have anything to add, Sgt. Adler?" JP asked.

"Yes, sir, I do. Young, mid 20's—probably some college. Five, maybe six people in the background. At least one is female or a guy with a very high voice. They sound deadly serious."

"Of course, they're deadly serious; they just killed a lot of people. What makes you think college education? The guy could've dropped out of high school and read a few books," Wilkens was building up steam when JP cut him off with a wave of his hand.

"What are you two, some sort of comedy act? Keep this up, and the only work you'll find is in one of those comedy clubs downtown because your current job might end abruptly."

"Sorry, Captain," Adler said. Wilkens echoed with a pout and a nod.

JP shook his head in frustration and stood up to walk around his desk. Several stacks of papers and open files lay on his desktop. On one corner was an empty tin cup with the words, "The buck stops in the next office". The weekly duty roster sat on top of a two-day-old newspaper turned to a crossword puzzle. JP pushed the papers to the side, dropped into his old high-back black and chrome office chair, set his coffee cup down, and complained, "I really need a maid."

Adler stood up and handed JP the thick file folder he had been holding while they listened to the tape. It contained a brief history of the original Front de Liberation du Quebec, dated 1963 through 1970. "This has got to be a new bunch using the name to increase terror and make us look like a bunch of idiots for never catching the old group. Otherwise, we got some radicalized senior citizens out there."

Taking the file from Alder, JP browsed through pages, then stopped to scan news clippings that detailed the kidnapping of two Canadian dignitaries. "They got a real case of stupid when they carried this off and killed one of their hostages. They lost nearly all their support after this stunt and were forced to flee or risk getting turned in for the reward." He opened the top right desk drawer and propped his feet up, "From 1963 to 1970, they were the heroes for all Quebec freedom organizations, principally the Parti Quebecois. Hundreds of members were arrested and interrogated in the manhunt to find the FLQ. They escaped and fled to Cuba and were never heard from again. A rumor circulated in the mid-1970s that Castro executed them for refusing to participate in one of his South American operations.

"I agree with you on one point, boss. If this is the original FLQ, we're looking for a lot of grandpappy anarchists," Adler said.

"Unless… unless some of them have come back to train a bunch of young freedom fighters," Wilkens said thoughtfully.

"That is a possibility," JP ignored the pains in his lower back, stood up, and carried his coffee cup over to a simmering well-used coffee maker. "Gonna be a long shift, might as well get our tanks full. Refills anyone?"

Wilkens and Adler stepped up with cups, hoping the caffeine would kick-start their think tanks.

"Let's see some coins first," JP said. "I'm not paying for you two; I've got kids to feed."

A Quiet Suburb 3 Miles Outside Toronto City Limits
May 4th, 6 p.m.

Inside the dimly lit living room of an old two-story four-bedroom wood-frame house, a single bulb hung from the ceiling illuminating a group of young men and women. They lounged on old furniture and watched a 27" television. The six o'clock news had just begun headlining the massive destruction of the House of Parliament. Unlike others sitting in homes across the world watching the news with heavy hearts and watery eyes, these people smiled as they admired their deadly handiwork.

One of the younger women, a bright bleached blonde with short curly hair and too much black eyeshadow, pulled a small plastic vial of cocaine from a vest pocket. She set her drug up and took a hit, but with a low supply, did not offer to share. As the drug surged through her, she failed to notice the disdainful look from another woman across the room.

Several members perked up when the TV anchorman mentioned the FLQ and played a copy of their tape. "We're famous!" A young man named Shawn exclaimed.

Sitting cross-legged on the floor, Steve Munroe, the group leader, reached up and turned the television off. "We're famous, all right. Every cop in the free world is looking for us—so don't get cocky! We've just begun."

"Awe, baby, don't get down on Shawn, it's party time," Janene Prouse, high on cocaine, told her boyfriend. "Lover, you gotta keep us together. Tonight, we need to party down and celebrate!"

Steve glared at her and shook his head in dismay at the woman he was sleeping with. He looked around the group. "All right—" he raised an open can of beer and toasted their accomplishment, "up the French and down the Canucks!"

"Up the French and down the Canucks!" The group echoed loudly in unison.

Leaving the rest to get drunk or stoned, Steve got to his feet, grabbed his girlfriend by the arm, and jerked her off the couch. "Come on, we're going to bed." Steve Munroe was a charismatic fellow of half-French and half-Northern Cheyenne lineage. A handsome young man of 28 years, he had dark brown eyes, a heavily tanned complexion with an oily sheen from his mother's side of the family, wore his long black hair in a single ponytail, and usually dressed in second-hand clothes Janene found for him in local thrift stores, such as the faded Grateful Dead T-shirt he wore, hoping to pass himself off as a street person. However, being from an influential family, he held a master's degree in Political Science. When it benefited him, he was a follower of Islam, other times, he was a self-proclaimed follower of Karl Marx. The only son of a wealthy industrialist from Ottawa, his mother, an alcoholic, had committed suicide several years earlier, for which Steve blamed his estranged father.

Climbing the stairs, Steve looked down to study the man sitting alone in the shadows. Hugo Rice was reading a German newspaper as he sipped from a hot teacup. Of all the people in the room, Steve knew Hugo to be the only true professional killer among them; a man to be extremely wary of. A German mercenary, Hugo had served as an officer in the East German Army. He had uncanny expertise with explosives and was well paid for his services worldwide. He was the group's intelligence officer and weapons manager.

RCMP Intelligence Section, Toronto Office
May 4th, 8:34 p.m.


JP felt like an old man at 46, two months shy of his 21st anniversary with the RCMP. Born in Whitehorse, Yukon Territory, JP had entered the RCMP following a four-year hitch in the Canadian Navy. As a law enforcement officer, he had seen most of Canada, a large part of the United States, and parts of Europe. In four years, he would be retiring.

His office held the division's classified intelligence files, some of which went back to World War II. The files held copies of reports on serial killers, serial rapists, enemy agents, kidnappers, and notorious organized crime figures, known or suspected communists, spies, and members of newer neo-Nazi organizations, all stored in locked file cabinets under JP's care. The original files were locked up at RCMP Headquarters in Montreal. When JP took over the section, he reviewed the files and shredded 211 reports of people who were no longer alive. Policy dictated the files never left the office and except for himself, only Adler and Wilkens had access to them.

JP's wife, LeAnn, was a medium-sized woman with shoulder-length black hair and green eyes. For 19 years, she had followed him from post to post, giving birth to two sons: JP Junior, about to turn 13, and John, eight years old. Having a teenager terrified JP, with such things as driving lessons, the first date, pimples, and first chest hairs not too far distant. He was dreading the first argument about why Dad was always right.

As JP drained his coffee mug, he and his two sergeants studied digital photographs of a blackened hunk of metal taken by a concerned citizen. The twisted, jagged piece of metal had smashed through the citizen's vehicle windshield and impaled the driver's seat. Had the driver been in the car, he probably would not have survived. RCMP lab technicians had managed to determine that lettering on the metal said, "City of Toronto-Department of Sanitation". Tests showed the metal was a match to the city's trash dumpsters, and the blast marks and chemical residue matched the ingredients needed for a high-volume explosive device. Lab geeks had detected C-4, ammonia nitrates, and diesel fuel. In-depth tests would be required before the evidence could be used in court. JP had rushed to their lab for answers.

At 9:16 p.m., chief arson investigator Rich Larouch notified JP that he had located the blast point at the Parliament Building and confirmed it was where the trash dumpsters were routinely placed. The Department of Sanitation later reported one of their dumpsters was missing from a schoolyard in north Toronto. Toronto Police had found one of the city's sanitation trucks abandoned in an alley two miles from the blast.

JP remained at his desk throughout the night, reviewing old FLQ files. At the same time, Adler and Wilkens checked in with their informants. Alone, JP whispered aloud, "Domestic political antagonists usually confine their game to shooting their mouths off at rallies, maybe a flag burning or blockading government buildings with a sit-in. But a paramilitary terrorist organization with access to C-4?" The phone rang. It was his private line. LeAnn wanted to remind him to eat something, "You're always such a grouch when you go too long without something in your stomach."

"Okay, honey. I'll drop what I'm doing and run out for a hamburger. Now let me get back to work. Okay? Hug the kids, and hopefully, I'll see you sometime in the morning. Good night."

"I love you," LeAnn said softly before she hung up.

"Yeah, I love you too. Sleep well." JP hung up and looked at the old couch across the room. "Looks like another night together, old friend." But right now, food and sleep had to wait. He still had to type up his initial report for the Colonel, which was due on the old man's desk by 8:00 a.m.

Police work was usually 90% boredom and 10% sheer adrenaline rush. Those percentages could change quickly with a case like this, which JP knew from long experience.

Whenever JP wished he were home with his family, watching TV and sleeping in his own bed, all he had to do was look at the pile of photographs of the disaster scene and all those body bags. He needed to catch these killers before they could strike again, but he knew he would need a break in this case.

Remote Privately Owned Hunting Lodge
North Of Montreal, May 4th, 10:50 P.M.

Unlike most hunting lodges in the Canadian wilderness, Dr. Richard Quison's 3.8 million dollar hideaway was guarded by a well-trained security force. There were no tennis courts or enclosed swimming pool. But there was a large helipad capable of handling six medium-sized helicopters within 200 yards of the lodge. The grounds were surrounded by a seven-foot-tall security fence, monitored 24 hours a day from inside the lodge with the latest in surveillance equipment.

Five guests arrived separately by helicopter and gathered in a spacious luxuriously furnished den. They sat comfortably around a handmade oak coffee table, sipped fine brandy from Quison's private stock, and enjoyed Havana Cigars. Including Dr. Quison, each was the CEO of a large industrial company in Quebec and a senior member of good standing in the Parti Quebecois. Each consented to a security screening for listening devices and weapons before entering the lodge. Personal bodyguards scanned the lodge and its rooms before leaving their employers alone for the meeting. Well-armed helicopter crews were responsible for aircraft security to prevent anyone from placing a monitoring or explosive device onboard their bird. In the kind of business these men were involved in, taking needless risks was simply foolhardy.

"Gentlemen, I called this meeting to critique Mr. Munroe's recent action in Toronto. I would sincerely like to hear your opinion of the affair," Dr. Quison dipped the tip of his cigar into the brandy and brought it to his lips.

Sir Albert Bruisse spoke first, "Too many dead. I hadn't foreseen so many casualties."

"I agree with Albie," Bradley Osmore said, "I thought the bomb was to be detonated earlier before so many people were in their offices."

"Gentlemen, we were delivering a message to the Canadian government. Those people fail to understand anything but the effective use of deadly force," Adrian Satchell replied as he refilled his glass from a crystal decanter.

"No!" Albie exclaimed. "So many dead cannot help our cause. The public will turn against us. Remember, my friends, the original FLQ gained our party's respect and lost it with only one Canadian official's death and an unlucky civilian. Now we have multiple deaths and many injured. Mr. Munroe overstepped the boundaries we set before this operation. We should rein him in before he decides to blow up a bus filled with schoolchildren. That's all I'm attempting to say here."

"Albie, I'll handle Munroe," Dr. Quison said.

"Can you truly handle this… this dangerous malcontent? He views us in the same way he views his father. We're just rich men with no sincere conscience. If he was ever to find out our true—" Robert Neils was cut off when Dr. Quison stood to his feet and glared at him.

"Robert, I said I would handle Munroe!" Dr. Quison said abruptly. "Further, I do not wish to discuss our true anything while I have so many employees wandering the estate. At this point, we are only businessmen discussing a newsworthy disaster. To go further could possibly bring someone a great reward. So much cash that even their loyalty and fear of me might be forgotten."

"My apologies, Richard," Neils offered. His icy blue eyes showed hostility toward Dr. Quison. They may be accomplices in this endeavor, but they were not all friends.

"Fine. Now is there anything else to be said at this time?" Dr. Quison looked around at the four other men. No one spoke, and Quison raised his glass for a toast, "Very well, I suggest we adjourn to the dining room where I've had the chef prepare a pleasant late dinner of game meats for you to sample. I expect to enjoy this evening, and I hope you savor this fine vintage flown over from France, an 1892 vintage. I offer this salute to our continued success."

The four other men stood to their feet, raised their glasses and Havana cigars, took a sip, and then went to dinner.

2

# A TERRORIST HAS NO HUMANITY

Captain JP Leon's Residence, Toronto
May 9th, 8:12 p.m.

Once again, JP missed dinner with his family and had to microwave a cold plate of meatloaf and mashed potatoes. He missed having time with his boys, and not making it home for dinner had become the norm since this case opened. JP looked across the room to watch LeAnn and the two boys enjoying a sitcom on television. He sighed deeply, relieved to be home as tension drained away. He placed his weapon in a lockbox on the kitchen closet's upper shelf; other firearms were in a safe in their bedroom closet.

JP disliked most television shows but enjoyed hearing his wife and children's laughter. It helped him relax, knowing his family was at home safe from the hostile world. He tried to leave that world behind when he came through the front door, attempting to make home a refuge from all that was wrong in the world outside. He changed into soft blue pajamas and a dark blue robe. When he returned to the front room, the two boys were stretched out on the carpet, dueling over a large bowl of popcorn. LeAnn sat in her favorite chair; a navy-blue corduroy-padded rocking chair given to her by her fraternal grandmother. She was working on a baby blanket for a friend's upcoming baby shower at their church. Though his own attendance was infrequent, maybe one Sunday out of six, the Leon family attended the Toronto Airport Fellowship, a large non-denominational church, where attendance was growing fast. The church conducted multiple services to handle the growing numbers.

During one of the commercial breaks, LeAnn, who heard JP come in and turn the sink water on to wash his hands, asked him to take out the trash. "The men will be here in the morning, honey… please?"

"Hey, I've got two strong sons who can take the trash out, and I'm in my robe," JP grumbled.

"They're ready for bed, and I don't want that dog digging in the trash after we go to bed."

"That's not a dog," JP muttered. A 135-pound black longhaired Newfoundland-mix lay curled up at his feet. His oldest boy had come home with a muddy stray puppy with big brown eyes. Now the beast was nearly as big as JP junior and consumed twice as much food. One of the beast's many bad habits was chewing through black garbage bags to find the treasures inside. Another bad habit was devouring JP's favorite socks; strangely enough, the beast preferred cotton over wool. Occasionally, the dog slobbered all over JP's shoes.

Grunting, JP reached down and pulled the trash bag out of the container, secured it with a wire tie and hollered, "Going outside." As he headed for the door, the canine monstrosity made his intentions known and blocked the path to the door. JP glared down at him as the dog wagged his enormous tail, a weapon with a history of knocking over things. "You are one big useless mutt," JP complained. But shaking his head with a smile, he reached for the dog's leash, secured it to the animal's metal choke chain and yelled, "Takin' the beast out!"

When the screen door slammed shut behind him, JP was nearly pulled off the porch as the dog lunged for freedom. Surviving the dash across the backyard, JP opened the wooden back gate and released the beast to run up and down the alley. He dropped the trash bag into a large trashcan. He paid $40 a month to have four cans emptied once a week by the city, which he felt was excessive, but the city was awarded the trash-hauling contract long ago. He worked it out one day and realized that 15% of the city's budget came from the trash business in addition to the city dump.

While the dog inspected his neighbor's cans, JP took a moment to stargaze. He glanced at his backyard and remembered the long hours he and LeAnn had spent landscaping it. He loved this house; a four-bedroom, two-bath, split-level with an attached two-car garage. The house which initially cost them $168,000 was now valued at $295,000, partially due to neighborhood property values and all the work he and LeAnn had accomplished over the years.

Whistling for the hound, JP's attention was drawn to the loud sound of screeching tires out front as a car traveling much too fast raced around the street corner. "Darn, kids!" JP exclaimed. He had reported racing in the neighborhood twice before. From the noise out front, he was going back inside to make a third call. "I hope they have a patrol car nearby to catch these street racers before someone gets hurt." Before he finished muttering the vehicle locked its brakes and skidded to an abrupt stop. "That sounds like they're right out front!"

JP's police antenna shot up, and his world suddenly grew heavy. Years of experience warned him that something was terribly wrong, and he needed to move fast. He forgot about the dog, yanked the gate open, and made a dash for the house. Nearing the porch steps, he heard the sound of breaking glass and began to shout a warning to his wife. Suddenly an ear-bursting thunderclap and a bolt of lightning ripped through the house. A fiery shockwave burst through the house's bottom floor, blowing out all the windows and front and back doors.

As JP grasped the back screen door handle and started to open it, the metal screen door exploded outward. A ball of flame shot out as the concussion wave ripped the screen door off its hinges. JP was caught in the blast, thrown backward, and hurled over 12 feet to land hard in the backyard. The screen door landed atop him, and more debris rained down, but JP was unconscious.

The house was engulfed in flames; fiery debris from the explosion hit neighboring homes, yards, the street and back alley. Neighbors raced to put fires out, but there was little they could do for JP's home; it was a raging inferno. Several people called the Fire Department as crowds lined the street and watched in eerie silence while the Leon home quickly burned to the ground. With the neighbors' gutsy efforts, garden hoses and fire extinguishers, the houses on each side suffered only minor burn damage.

Trucks from the nearest fire station arrived within eight minutes, a near-record for the neighborhood. When firefighters entered the backyard, they found JP lying on the ground, injured and unconscious. They carried him out of the danger zone, where paramedics treated him for facial bruising, a concussion and $1^{st}$, and $2^{nd}$ degree burns over his upper body. He remained unconscious and woke in a hospital bed several hours later.

When the fire was out, firemen gently removed the burned bodies of LeAnn and the two boys as neighbors looked on in shock. Arson investigators arrived before the bodies were placed into body bags and carried to a coroner's van. Firefighters soaked the structure with several thousand gallons of water, filling the basement with several feet of water, then the once-happy home was left in the hands of arson investigators. Because of JP position, city investigators were soon supported by Toronto Police and RCMP detectives.

Earlier That Same Afternoon

Hugo Rice knew his job well, trained in the art of surveillance; he disguised himself as a Catholic Priest. He drove a used light-colored economy-sized rental car acquired with a forged VISA card and a bogus driver's license and followed JP home from work staying at least a quarter mile behind. Fellow FLQ members; Shawn Elders, Gordon Rogers, and Claudia Minivers followed in a black Chevrolet panel van stolen earlier from the Toronto Airport long-term parking lot. Hugo and his three compatriots stayed in contact through two inexpensive palm-sized two-way radios with a range of less than two miles.

When JP arrived home, Hugo left the neighborhood and met the other three in an alley behind a 24-hour mini-mart. He left the rental car, transferred to the van, handed the car keys to Shawn, and removed the priest garb. "Park in sight of his house, but not too close—no lights—no movement," He gave directions to JP's house and made sure that Shawn understood his instructions. "Wait until the street is clear, no witnesses. You understand?"

"I got it, Hugo, no problem." Shawn drove off in the rental.

Huddled in the back of the van, Gordon and Claudia watched Hugo prepare two firebombs. Satisfied with his work, Hugo moved into the driver's seat, then waited in silence for Shawn's call. A moment later, Shawn's voice came over the radio, "I'm here… There's some kids playing basketball in the driveway next door. Lights on inside the subject's house. Standing by."

"Copy!" Hugo replied.

Twenty minutes, the next call came. "This is me," Shawn said. He did not trust open communications and refused to give his name over the air. "Street is empty, place is clear. Subject still inside."

"We go," Hugo replied. This was Shawn's signal to drive away and meet the others at an earlier designated location.

Restless and uncomfortable sitting on metal flooring in the back, Claudia told Hugo she needed some smokes and asked if she could run into the mini-mart out front. Gordon added, "Hey, I got the munchies, man."

Giving in, Hugo allowed Claudia to make a quick run inside, but only long enough to grab smokes and a couple candy bars for Gordon. "Make fast, or I'll leave you. Avoid security cameras."

"Sure thing, Hugo." Claudia opened the side door, climbed out, disappeared behind the building, and returned shortly with a plastic bag of goodies. She had purchased a cup of coffee for Hugo, who grunted appreciation, tasted the brew, and quickly poured it outside, "Taste like crap!"

"Hey, you forgot your wig, woman. "Gordon held up Claudia's long blonde wig.

"Makes my head itch, but no problem, the kid inside is a dupe! I don't think he even noticed me. He was too busy eyeing some bimbo renting movies."

Sitting on the floor in the back of the van, Gordon held the two firebombs on his lap. Simple bombs made of (2) One-quart glass jars, each containing a measure of gasoline, a dozen or so one-inch nails, and a fragmentation grenade with the pin pulled. Encased in the jar and sealed by a screw-top lid, the grenade could not explode. When the jars broke, the grenade handles were free and the bombs would explode within five seconds. Not being a trusting soul, Hugo wrapped a single piece of corded cloth, soaked in gas, around the jar. Before putting the bomb together, he coated the inside of the jars with a gelatin mixture similar to napalm to increase the explosion. The burning mixture would stick to anyone and anything once the explosion occurred.

Claudia put Gordon's candy bars on the van floor before him and prepared to light her cigarette. "What the Hell! You want to blow us up!?" Gordon shouted.

"Oh yeah… sorry." Claudia ignored Hugo's look of disdain. He was focused on the five-million dollars waiting for him when the job was done. Not just this assassination but the entire job with these amateurs. For the twentieth time, he promised himself he would never again work with such inexperienced children. He fancied the idea of shooting them and walking away, blaming it on the authorities. Hugo was concerned the three could jeopardize his own safety with their lack of discipline and acts of stupidity. Allowing Claudia to enter the store was clearly a mistake. One that might come back to bite him.

"Street is still clear," Shawn's voice came over the radio.

"Okay… On the way," Hugo started the van. "Claudia, you throw these bombs through the front window of the house. Big window, but throw hard to break glass, or you die too." Hugo's harsh German accent often made his words come out broken.

"Why me?" She asked.

"He holds bombs; you open the door and jump out. He hands you bombs, and you run fast. He covers you with gun and pulls you into the van as I drive," Hugo replied tersely and turned away from her. He pulled out and drove down the alley to the street and on to JP's house. He wanted to take a moment to admire the lovely homes and expensive vehicles. "Not like East Germany—"

"What?" Claudia asked.

"Nothin'… You do what I tell you!"

"Okay, big guy, but don't you leave me!"

"No leave, but you run fast, or bomb get you, too."

Hugo accelerated to 50 miles per hour, rounded the corner, and ignored the screeching tires. Seconds later, he slammed on the brakes directly in front of JP's house and yelled, "Go! Go! Go!"

All of them wore full-face black wool ski masks. Hugo pulled a Beretta 9-mm from a cloth bag and held it beside his right leg. Gordon, in black coveralls, watched Claudia push the van's side door open and jump out. She was dressed in a black pullover sweater and black jeans but forgot the blonde wig and the full-face mask didn't conceal her long bright red hair.

Claudia ran up to JP's front porch with the two glass jar bombs. With a bomb in each hand, she jumped, cleared the three steps, and landed on the front porch. Quickly, she pulled out her lighter and ignited the cloth fuse, knowing she had only seconds to make the delivery, or the bombs would explode in her hands.

The window drapes were half-closed, and Claudia saw the woman and her two children in the living room. She didn't hesitate; she aimed her throw for the center of the large glass pane and threw the first bomb like she was pitching a fastball. The big pane shattered, and the bomb landed between the woman and the two children. Claudia saw the startled expression on the two boys' faces as she threw the second device. The faces of the two kids burned into her memory. With only seconds left, she turned and jumped off the front porch, landed on all fours in the front yard, got to her feet, and dashed for the van.

When the first bomb smashed through the glass window, it landed on the living room floor and rolled beside LeAnn's rocking chair. The second bomb landed only a few feet away and rolled toward the kitchen. The burner on the stovetop was heating water for tea. The glass jars exploded as the fuse's flame reached the coating solution. Glass and fiery liquid struck LeAnn and the children. Seconds later, both grenades exploded, and the gas line to the stove transformed the home into an instant inferno. LeAnn and the two children were killed instantly.

Claudia pumped enough adrenaline to power an Olympic weightlifting team knowing she had seconds to clear the explosions. But shrapnel from the blast struck her lower back and drove her to the ground. She sprawled out on the driveway, with her arms in front of her.

"Get her!" Hugo ordered. Shoving his right foot down, he revved the engine, anxious to clear out before the neighbors started coming outside to see what had happened.

Gordon jumped out of the van and ran to where Claudia lay. She was semi-conscious, so he yanked on the back of her pants lifting her off the ground and shoved her into the side door of the van, and jumped in on top of her. Hugo put the van into gear, floored the gas pedal, and sped away leaving nearly 10 feet of acceleration marks on the pavement.

Seeing blood on his hands, Gordon realized Claudia was wounded. He lifted the back of her sweater and saw a two-inch chunk of glass sticking out of her back. Blood ran down her backside and stained her pants and sweater.

"She's hurt!" Gordon told Hugo in an excited voice.

"Later—we must switch cars now!" Hugo shouted at him.

Half a block away, Shawn Elders watched the Leon house burn. The entire structure was engulfed within less than a minute, and he knew no one could have escaped the inferno. He watched as neighbors poured into the street. Some dragged water hoses out to fight fires caused by raining debris and sprayed adjacent houses. Yellow and red flames shot up over the burning structure and mixed with black smoke to produce tall glowing pillars. Streetlights illuminated the scene. Within moments, the fire could be seen from several miles away.

Shawn kept the lights off and cautiously drove away. He didn't want to run into any police or fire vehicles. He was to meet Hugo and the others at the prearranged location and headed in that direction. Ten minutes later, Shawn parked the rental car in the north lot of a large shopping mall. Using a spray can of WD-40, he wiped the surfaces in the vehicle and the outside door handles to remove fingerprints. Satisfied, he left the car and threw the car keys and spray can into a trash can by the mall, then waited to be picked up by Hugo in the black van.

They drove to a quiet warehouse district where a third car was parked adjacent to an abandoned building. As with the rental car, WD-40 was sprayed over the van surfaces, and Claudia's blood was thoroughly wiped up. The trash and WD-40 canister were placed in a heavy plastic bag and dropped into the third car's trunk, an older Chevrolet Impala. One mile away, Shawn dropped the trash bag into an industrial trash dumpster, and they headed for the safe house with a semi-conscious Claudia in the back seat.

The Hospital - 2:17 a.m.

JP's head throbbed painfully with each heartbeat as consciousness returned. He had some difficulty breathing; agonizing pain spread through his battered body. When he finally opened his eyes, everything was one big blur. After blinking several times, he was able to see, but at first saw two of everything until things returned to normal. First, he saw Sgt. Adler sitting in a chair by the door. *Why am I in bed? Where am I?* He looked about the room, the sterile emptiness and the near floor-length curtains, off-white in color, and realized he was in a hospital. An IV line ran into his left arm from a chrome metal monster that stood beside the head of his bed. Sgt. Adler snored loud enough to be heard as far away as the nurse's station down the hall, but no one complained.

JP raised his hands and saw bandages, then his memory clicked. He remembered the explosion and the flames. "LeAnn... the boys!" JP shouted as he remembered the explosion of flames. He knew his family had been trapped inside that inferno. A loud mournful cry awakened Adler.

"You're awake!" Adler rubbed his eyes and saw the look of horror on JP's face. "You're supposed to remain still, Boss!" He launched from the chair and went to JP's bedside to hold him in place. "JP, you've got some bad burns and a concussion." Adler pushed the nurse's call button.

JP ignored his friend and gritted his teeth as he glanced about the room. He reached for the bed controls. Though it hurt to use his hand, he pushed down hard on the button that raised the head of the bed. With a wild-eyed glare, he looked into his friend's face. His heart raced to the rhythm of a runaway train as he recognized the sadness on Adler's face. His voice was raw, low, and painful, "LeAnn...my... boys?"

Adler's eyes and expression displayed his sorrow, "They're gone, Jean-Paul... They're all gone." It was one of the few times he called JP by his first name and cautiously added, "It was a bomb... bombs... two gasoline bombs. From all the shrapnel, investigators suspect grenades were used... probably a gasoline bomb... Arson investigators are still at your home... your family... they're downstairs in the morgue... Oh God, I'm sorry, Boss... All three... I was told it was instantaneous."

JP let loose a howl that sounded like a wounded grizzly bear. Two nurses and a uniformed RCMP officer charged in to check on their patient. Adler told them all to get out. "Give us the room!" When they saw the patient was physically all right, they left with reluctance.

A whimper escaped JP's lips as he fought for control. He used the bed sheet and wiped his eyes. JP attempted to ignore the pain in his arms and hands as he glared at Adler with an icy look radiating pure hatred. Not for his friend but for those who had done this to his wife and children. Deep down in his heart, JP knew this was not the time for mourning. Grief would have to wait. Right now, a fire burned deep inside of him. Hot anger would drive him, and a deep thirst for revenge would guide him in the days ahead. Rage became the drug to give him focus, and JP would use it to wield his own private war. Vengeance would be his driving force as he sought out those responsible for his family's deaths.

Adler stood in silence and looked on with concern as he watched JP mentally plot his revenge. He knew there would be no lawyers, no courts, and no mercy.

These people, whoever they were, had taken JP's family. Adler knew the man lying in that bed quite well and knew those people would find their fate dished out in the form of hot lead or cold steel. He knew JP had already judged them and would execute them with a violent resolve.

"Captain, we have security outside in the hall, a constable in the lobby, and Toronto Police units stationed outside," Adler advised him to break the eerie silence.

JP studied his sergeant for a moment and in a voice strained by fire trauma asked, "Has the FLQ claimed responsibility?"

Adler could not help but notice his captain's cold, threatening look. "Yes, Sir, they called our desk within five minutes of the explosion. A different voice this time. The caller spoke in English. Communications say the call was made from a cell phone, a burner-phone—our lab is analyzing the phone tape right now."

"Any witnesses?" JP asked through clenched teeth. His singed face glowed even redder from fiery rage.

Adler, amazed at JP's strength of will, hesitated. He studied his boss with grief, JP's family was almost like his own. He had watched the kids grow up, spent time with them when he could, and went at least once a month for one of LeAnn's dinners.

JP's eyes softened briefly, "Steve, I've got my whole life to mourn my loss. Right now, I want blood for blood." The icy look of a detached professional returned as he asked again, "Any witnesses?"

"Your neighbors, the Sondgers, gave us the best information so far. After the blast, Edith Sondgers reported hearing three explosions, only a second or two apart. Arson investigators believe the first two explosions were gas bombs. As I said, they suspect fragmentation grenades. The third explosion was the gas line to the stove going up. Mrs. Sondgers ran outside to see a black panel van with back and side doors and a broken left taillight. Only the right side was lit up, but she couldn't see a license plate. She saw three people—all dressed in black. A large man with a full black face mask was behind the wheel. A second man of medium height and build dragged a third suspect into the back of the van. Mrs. Sondgers believes the dragged one, possibly a woman, was injured in the blast." Adler looked at his friend quietly for a moment, but JP glared back at him waiting to hear the rest. "Mrs. Sondgers apparently has 20-20 vision Said she saw red hair sticking out from under the suspect's mask. As this one was shoved into the van, the shirt pulled up, and Edith saw a white bra strap."

"Do we have a make on the black van?" JP asked.

A nurse came in to reconnect a heart monitor on JP's chest. In his thrashing about, it had come off, but JP did not feel like having it reconnected right then and shooed the disgruntled nurse away. "I'm still breathing, so my heart is fine. Now get out!"

"We've got Edith looking at photographs of various makes for a possible match." Adler backed up when the nurse returned with a second nurse in tow. JP would not budge. He was done playing hospital and ordered both nurses out in a loud booming voice that could be heard throughout the floor. The Mountie assigned to door duty poked his head in, and Adler ordered him back to his post before JP could launch a tirade at the young man.

JP returned to the subject at hand, "Edith Sondgers is the neighborhood busybody. She'll make a great witness. I'm surprised she didn't have her binoculars out. Check the hot sheets; the van was probably stolen." JP looked around for his pants. He might hurt like all get out, but he wanted out of the hospital bed.

"Where're my clothes?"

"You don't have any, not yet anyway," Adler answered.

"Where are they?"

"What you wore was burned; What's left of them is at the lab as evidence. We've got someone buying you some new stuff since all your other clothes were… lost."

"What'd the caller say?" JP relaxed against the bed; pain overrode his desire to leave.

Adler hesitated, which angered JP, "I asked you a question, Sergeant Adler."

Adler locked eyes with his superior, "All right. The caller wanted the RCMP to know how serious they were in their fight for Quebec's independence. You were apparently chosen because of who you are, Captain. They want to strike at the RCMP and show the authorities' vulnerability."

JP studied his friend's face and said, "Give me all of it, Steve. I'll find out the rest anyway. Let's get it over with."

"They objected to the statements you made to the press, calling 'em names. They attacked you because you… because you pissed 'em off." Adler turned around and slammed his fist into the wall, making a fist-sized hole in the sheetrock. This time the young officer on duty stayed outside.

JP sat up, his fists tightly clenched causing blood to seep through the bandages; his whole body trembled. He spoke with controlled anger, "Those animals…." His teeth were clenched as he whispered, "killed my wife… my sons… because I called them names? NAMES!" JP rolled onto his side, looked away from his friend, and wept.

Sgt. Adler didn't know what to say, but he moved out of the way when a middle-aged doctor stepped into the room and asked Adler to step outside. "I need to have a private moment with my patient, please."

"Sure, Doc."

Adler wanted JP to know his neighbor had taken care of the dog, which was untouched by the blast. The dog was singed in the fire and had to be restrained. It tried to enter the burning house several times until the neighbor put it inside his garage. All night the dog howled mournfully for its youthful masters who would never come.

Word went out over all of eastern Canada and the Canadian border stations along the Eastern Canada/USA border. RCMP and Toronto Police were looking for a black Chevrolet panel van, possibly with the left taillight not working. Edith Sondgers had gone through an intensive follow-up interview with Sgt. Wilkens and identified the van as a Chevrolet from one of the photos shown to her. Over 20 traffic stops were made that first night, upsetting quite a few people. Law enforcement officers didn't care and very few offered apologies. They were looking for terrorists, people who attacked one of their own and cold-bloodedly murdered a cop's family.

Edith Sondgers became an instant celebrity after she ignored the RCMP's request to remain silent. She was contacted by the local paper, and after several hours of her phone ringing off the hook, she decided it was a mistake. She decided to spend a week with her sister, who lived out of town. It was either that or risk losing her husband who was fed up with her prying into other people's business. Not that he minded her identifying the suspect's van, but the phone calls and people knocking at the door were enough to push him over the edge. So, she went to see her sister, and he went fishing.

After the mall closed, a mall security officer reported an abandoned black Chevy van with a broken left taillight in the parking lot. The plate number provided an address on the northwest side of Toronto, and the van was secured. The owner's wife was contacted by four Toronto Police detectives, supported by a Special Weapons Assault Team. Once calmed down, she advised them her husband had left it at the airport while he was in Virginia on company business. With her permission, the van was towed to the RCMP evidence garage to be photographed and processed by highly skilled RCMP lab technicians.

Three dime-sized blood splotches were found in the side doorframe, and tests confirmed it to be type O positive. They now had a DNA structure. However, the thieves covered the rest of the van with what was later shown to be WD-40.

"I really hate those cop shows. All they do is let the criminals know how to beat us. That CSI show and all of its reruns are murdering us," One of the lab techs informed his partner.

"Yeah, the WD-40 is a new touch, though. They were using bleach. But they blew it on the doorframe. No matter how good they get, somewhere down the line, they make a mistake."

Within 18 hours of the bombing, authorities displayed photographs of the black van over all the networks, and volunteers posted flyers throughout JP's neighborhood and outlining areas. The photograph contained a vague description of the suspects; one female, possibly with long red hair, and two males, all dressed in black clothes and black face masks.

A break came in 31 hours after the attack. A convenience store employee saw the flyer when he came to work after a day off and remembered the woman with red hair and how she was all decked out in black. He remembered her because she had come in for smokes and junk food and seemed to be in a big hurry noticeably shying away from the store's security camera. He did not know if it meant much, but he called the number on the flyer and talked with an RCMP constable.

Within three hours, Sgt. Wilkens had reviewed the store's security camera tape of that evening. Sitting beside him, Leonard Hills operated the machine and waited to make the ID. When they reached the right point in the video, he pointed out Claudia. She looked right into a second unseen security camera when she poured Hugo's coffee. Her estimated height and weight matched the suspect seen by Edith Sondgers.

"They all know about the camera behind the counter, but with so many robberies in town, the owners put up a second hidden camera," Hills said. "Guess it worked big time."

Within the next few hours, various-sized copies of Claudia's photograph were sent to all Canadian and US agencies. The flyer labeled her as a possible person of interest in the bombing and murder of three people and suspected involvement in terrorism. Claudia's photograph was provided to a New York news service, and she became instantly famous —labeled a suspected member of the now-infamous FLQ.

Dr. Quison's Hunting Lodge
May 12th, 10:14 A.M.

The last to arrive was Sir Albert Bruisse, who was in a foul mood when he entered the lodge. Without any pleasantries, he handed one of the servants his trench coat, walked into the main room, and unleashed his tirade, "Munroe's attack on that Mountie was an outrageous act of foolishness. He endangered us all! Killing that man's wife and children! He's a madman who must be stopped! If we ever get found out, we'll all be spending life in prison."

Dr. Quison smiled amiably, "Albie, calm yourself down before you alarm my staff." He gestured Bruisse toward the nearest empty chair with a wave of his hand and waited for his old friend to sit down. An attractive female servant entered and provided him with a glass of brandy then quickly disappeared after making sure everyone had refreshments. "I'm sure we all agree the killing of Captain Leon's family was foolhardy. By now, Scotland Yard, the FBI, Interpol, and even the CIA are probably involved in the investigation. Everyone is out searching for our Claudia Minivers. At this moment, she's in a safe house with a wound in her back from the blast. I've been advised an infection has set in. She's running a high fever and is reportedly delirious."

"I hope she dies!" Albie exclaimed. "How could she have been stupid enough to have a photo taken?"

"Mistakes happen but nowadays, there are cameras everywhere. Miss Minivers is quite expendable." Dr. Quison glanced around the room, "We expected major law enforcement agencies to become involved eventually. As long as we keep our heads, we can use this to our benefit." Quison shot Bruisse a stern look, even though he felt like throttling Munroe himself at the moment. He planned to have words with Hugo; this was beyond an act of simple stupidity and Hugo was responsible.

As the conversation continued, two of the five members expressed a desire to halt the operation, concerned that Munroe was becoming too much of a loose cannon. However, Dr. Quison was able to sway them into a special meeting with Munroe and Hugo to discuss their concerns and go over the next phase of their plan.

"We have invested too much time and money into this. We may have to speed things up. Yet, we can and will prevail in our overall scheme," Quison said to the members. They retired to the dining room for a well-prepared lunch of wild turkey, salmon, and wild goose.

Before Dr. Quison met with Steve Munroe and the abrasive Hugo, a diabolical scheme of international proportions was already underway. Munroe and his cause-bearing freedom fighters were only simple pawns on a massive chessboard. Instruments to be used and eventually sacrificed. These five very wealthy Canadian businessmen had put this grand plan together. They only needed the new FLQ as a way to instill terror and make headlines. It was the reason for using the FLQ name. A reminder of the past and to keep Canadian authorities busy looking for dangerous Quebec terrorists. Actually, the entire operation had nothing to do with Quebec's independence. It only concerned making five CEOs a very nice profit in one of the world's oldest schemes: insurance fraud and land speculation. They were using world terrorism to cover their tracks and to protect themselves from a lengthy prison sentence. Acts of terror moved world politics in their direction, with people questioning Quebec's right to sovereignty. There was never a reason, only an excuse.

These five gentlemen were members of the Parti- Quebecois, which was mainly a business ploy. The only one involved in the day-to-day operation of their freedom-seeking organization was Dr. Quison. In 1969 he acted as a middleman between the original FLQ and the Parti- Quebecois. When the FLQ vanished in the early 1970s, he had dropped out of sight until he thought it was safe to resurface. Under his new name and using some of the funds left behind by the FLQ, he had created a mega-bucks industrial enterprise and a large real estate company.

Financing the current Canadian Prime Minister's rise to power cost the five men a significant amount of money. Unfortunately, they realized they had selected poorly. The man's popularity continued to plummet in the polls. So, deciding to take things into their own hands and make a profit along the way, they came up with this current operation.

The Parliament Building was constructed on land leased by the federal government for a 100-year lease. There was an option for another 100 years if the federal government wished. The company that owned the lease was buried deep in blind corporations owned by Sir Albert Bruisse. Downtown Toronto had become prime real estate, worth ten times what he was getting from the government lease. So, the House of Parliament became a logical target to begin their plan. The thinking was that the federal government would opt to move their offices to another structure or possibly build a new one. Being leased land, the five men did not honestly believe the Canadian Government would seek to build a monument to those who lost their lives, as was done with the 9/11 disaster.

The lease termination would give Bruisse the leeway to charge the government payments for the remainder of the lease and the cost of clearing away the debris. He could then build a new three-story shopper's paradise to provide for his retirement in France.

Dr. Quison owned the parking garage damaged in the blast, and it was losing money daily. Taxes were too heavy, and the structure's repairs caused his management company to go into the red. With insurance paying for the garage, he could clear the land and either sell it at a significant profit or build a 12-floor hi-rise office building he had been thinking about. He would then sell the offices rather than rent them, and his insurance company would be on-site to handle property insurance for each suite.

The next target was a shopping mall owned by another member of the five who needed the insurance money for other ventures. The valuable land it was on would become ultra-modern apartments and a movie complex. More housing was needed in this part of town, and fewer malls. With rising housing costs, more and more people were looking less at single dwellings and more at multiple housing complexes. With the economy in such sad shape, several of his mall stores had gone belly-up, and he could not find anyone to replace them. The mall had become a ghost town. Most of the people visiting it were senior citizens using the indoors to jog in the morning.

The city bus station also sat on leased land that had grown far too valuable to be used for a transportation hub. The owner, one of the five, wanted to replace it with a sizable international business office complex and quadruple his profits.

Each target selected had some connection to the five men sitting comfortably around the formal dining table. They sipped brandy and, having no concern for the people they had killed or injured, talked about their grand scheme. They were the real terrorists and their cause: simple greed.

International events were about to take place elsewhere, and these five men were about to find themselves in a catastrophe, one that would have a significant effect on their future plans.

Pacific Waters Off Prince Rupert, British Columbia
May 12th, 3:48 P.M.

An international news story unfolded in the blue-green waters off Western Canada. Over a hundred Canadian fishing boats of all sizes surrounded the M/V Columbia, the majestic queen of the Alaska Marine Highway System. Each week it traveled from Seattle to Skagway and back with passengers and vehicles, making several stops along the way. The ports of Haines and Skagway were connected by highways to the Alaska-Canadian Highway, also known as the Al-Can. Many travelers preferred the beautiful sea voyage through the scenic Inland Passage in Alaska's Southeast waters over a 2,000-mile drive between Alaska and Washington State. Fear of hitting and sinking one or more of the fishing boats brought the huge ferry to a halt. Fishermen had chosen to stage a protest against Alaska fishermen operating in Canadian waters. The demonstration showed how angry Canadian fishermen were over the dwindling supply of salmon in the Pacific waters. It was an opportunity to state their strong objection against US fishermen entering their waters to fish salmon, halibut, and other bottom fish while the U.S. Coast Guard and the U.S. and Alaska Fish and Wildlife prevented Canadian fishermen from doing the same in Alaska waters.

Seattle offices for the Alaska Marine Highway demanded the Department of State take action to free their ferry. A US Coast Guard cutter was sent to safeguard the American ferry. Several hours of negotiating could not persuade the fishermen to release the M/V Columbia. A Canadian navy vessel was sent in because the Canadian Navy was not happy to see a US Coast Guard vessel in their waters dictating terms to their citizens. The situation could turn explosive if one of the fishing boats chose to open fire on the US Coast Guard cutter in their waters.

For 24 hours, the situation remained stagnant. Several news helicopters flew overhead. Then suddenly, the first Canadian fishing boat pulled away, soon followed by others. The M/V Columbia was allowed to continue north. The demonstration ended peacefully, except for some irate ferry passengers who lined the deck, shook their fists, and shouted profanities at the departing fishermen. Over a hundred boat horns sounded in response to the profane words and gestures. Fishermen waved to the departing ferry and many escorted it for several miles, in a parade of sorts, with the US Coast Guard cutter and the Canadian Light Missile Cruiser making sure everyone went

Columbia's captain came out on the deck, leaned against the railing, and waved to his Canadian escorts. The old sea dog understood a man wanting to protect his fishing grounds and was glad to be underway without anyone being hurt. The United States and Canada's Department of State breathed a sigh of relief. They sought legal action against one another over what had happened and why. The matter would be taken up in the International Court, strain the relationship between the two countries, and cost several million dollars in legal fees. In the end, the only winner were the lawyers.

FLQ Safe House

Munroe and Hugo went to Quebec to meet with their oversight committee, the remaining members were confined to the safe house. They were under orders to stay off the street unless absolutely necessary. Claudia lay in bed, semi-conscious, struggling with a high fever. The members didn't want to take a chance of her seeing a doctor with her photo plastered all over Toronto. It was shown on TV every half-hour. "Have you seen this woman? Please call your local police or the RCMP if you have any information about her."

Except for aspirin and several belts of Jack Daniels Whiskey, they had nothing to give her to fight the infection and ease the pain. Several members volunteered to take turns sitting with her using cold-water compresses in an attempt to bring her some relief. The rest of them played cards, drank beer, and watched TV. Periodically, they glanced at one another, glad it was not them up there suffering.

Dr. Quison's Hunting Lodge
May 15th, 11:20 A.M.

Munroe rolled his eyes and nodded as the five men berated him for his unwise actions against JP and the death of the man's family. Occasionally between sips of brandy, Munroe glared back at them. He held his temper in check, not an easy thing to do, as he secretly wished the guards had not taken his pistol away outside. When they turned their attention toward Hugo, a smile broke out on Munroe's face. He watched the men rebuke Hugo for having allowed this insane act of revenge. They were quite upset with him for Claudia being photographed in the mini-mart.

Hugo stood by the grand stone fireplace with a frosted mug of cold German beer in his hand and listened with a neutral expression on his face. He had been interrogated and cursed at by the best, threatened, and even undergone torture at the hands of the communists in East Germany. These five wealthy amateurs were petty flies who beat their wings to move hot air around. He used mental discipline to drown them out. He could handle their petty reprimands as long as they kept the money coming. Besides, he agreed with them, he had blown it with Claudia and the hit on Captain Leon.

Dr. Quison stepped forward to get everyone's attention, "I believe we've exhausted ourselves on these subjects and should move on." He sent a harsh look at Munroe, "I think Steve and Hugo understand how we feel, our concerns for this operation. This will not happen again."

Munroe's face was a mask of mock acceptance as he pretended to kowtow to the benevolent financiers. Behind the mask, Munroe was enraged, but he was smart enough to keep his mouth shut. This was all about money, their money, and for what they were paying him; he could sit here and behave like a scolded child shown the error of his ways.

"Steve, do you have anything to say before we continue?" Dr. Quison poured another glass of brandy for himself from a crystal decanter.

"I sure do." Munroe's hands were clenched into fists as he struggled with his temper. "Look, I can deal with you slappin' my wrists for wasting that broad and her two brats. I get all that, okay? I went overboard." Munroe shared an icy glare with Hugo; he blamed Hugo for the mistake involving Claudia, and Hugo blamed Munroe for ordering the operation in the first place. Hugo had warned him that killing a high-ranking RCMP was stupid, but Monroe ignored him. "You must agree, we got the point across that even those badge-heavy federal cowboys can be hurt."

Bruisse looked at Dr. Quison, "He didn't hear a word we said, and you think you can control him? I disagree."

"Albie, Steve, and Hugo are my responsibility. We've gone over this. I do not wish to rehash it." Dr. Quison watched Munroe walk across the room to stand beside a seven-foot-tall grizzly bear mount, a hunting trophy Dr. Quison's took on a trip to Alaska several years earlier.

"Dr. Quison, you have my word... It will not happen again," Munroe said. This seemed to satisfy all but Sir Albert Bruisse, who shook his head in defiance but held his tongue. An intelligent man, he knew this was a poor location to cross swords with Dr. Quison. This was his home, and the security teams belonged to him. No love was lost between these men; only their shared greed held them together.

Albie looked at Munroe, "What will you do about the woman? Her face is known all over the world."

"I will personally take care of that problem when we return to Toronto," Munroe replied.

"Richard, maybe we should let things cool down for a time, allow the... how do the Americans say it... trail to grow cold?" An older man, Robert Neils, was cautious. His business deals in the past had brought him millions in return for taking his time and not jumping ahead of himself.

"Look gentlemen, we're all into this plan. Mishandled, we could all earn ourselves a long stay behind iron bars and cold concrete walls. Our team is tight but Claudia got stupid, I'll take care of her," Munroe promised. He walked away from the bear and picked up a pool cue from the redwood snooker table. "Relax. Let us do the hard work, and you continue worrying about your vast holdings and future plans." Dropping the pool cue, Munroe, a smirk on his face, wandered over to Quison's liquor cabinet. Opening it, he took out a very ornate glass bottle containing a costly vintage wine. Munroe poured the wine into a small brandy snifter, took a sip, swished it in his mouth longer than most people would, then swallowed it in one gulp. "My good doctor, this is an excellent wine, and I'm sure a bit more palatable than the brandy you've made available to your guests." Munroe returned the wine to the cabinet and carried the snifter back to his chair, smiling at Dr. Quison with a glare as cold as ice. He was enjoying the disgruntled expression on the good doctor's face. "No one controls me, Dr.

Quison. I work for you. I have no duty to any cause, as you well know. My only goal is the money you provide and the kick I get out of this game we're playing."

After a moment of silence, Dr. Quison raised his own glass and saluted Munroe, "As the Americans often say, 'Let us move on.'" His statement seemed to break the tension in the room as all parties took a long sip of their drinks. "Now, I believe we can shift our direction to the next phase in our… game, as Mr. Munroe so aptly called it." Dr. Quison walked over to the pool table and stood directly in front of Munroe. "Events have taken place… very recently in fact, which allows us an opportunity…" Dr. Quison gestured to the dining room, "If you gentlemen would please follow me." Leading them into the dining room, Dr. Quison asked everyone to be seated before he continued. Munroe hesitated briefly before taking a seat. A male servant brought in a large wooden bowl of sliced bread and assorted cheeses. As soon as the servant disappeared, Dr. Quison stood up, "We have decided to switch direction for our next phase. This new plan will involve some travel for you, Steve, and your associates to the interior of Alaska."

"Alaska?" Munroe asked in surprise.

"Yes, Alaska," Dr. Quison reached down behind his chair and brought up a three-fold map board displaying the State of Alaska and placed it on the tabletop. "A change in tactics, you might say. We'll let the federals concern themselves with where you may strike next while you strike a target in another country."

"We're going to hit the USA?" Hugo asked, evidently displeased with this news by the stern expression on his face. This made him uncomfortable. He knew the United States had started executing serious prisoners again, while Canada did not have the death penalty.

"Before you begin your questions, I ask that you please wait while I explain the new operation in some detail." Dr. Quison walked over to the large wooden side table and refilled his glass with brandy. He relighted his Cuban cigar, "Since your recent attack on Captain Leon, we have learned of events taking place on the western shores of British Columbia." Dr. Quison pointed out Prince Rupert on the map. "More than 100 fishing boats held an Alaska ferry boat hostage here for 24 hours." He showed a newspaper clipping to Munroe; a photograph of the M/V Columbia and the blockade. The scene had been photographed by a Seattle-based news helicopter flying overhead.

"Is this our target? Some boat?" Munroe asked.

"Please, hold your questions until I've finished. With tensions growing between Canadian and Alaska fishermen over North Pacific waters, our beloved, unfortunately, quite inept and unpopular Prime Minister is planning a trip to Alaska. He seeks to meet with Alaska's Governor over concerns about fishing rights and salmon counts. After that, he plans to travel to Seattle to meet with Washington's governor." Dr. Quison walked back to the table, opened a manila folder, and retrieved a set of old newspaper clippings held together by paper clips. "In 1970, the original FLQ made quite a few headlines when they abducted two Canadian dignitaries. Unfortunately, one of them was killed… along with his bodyguard. Both were known members of the Parti Quebecois. Things quickly fell apart after that, and the FLQ fled the country. The Parti Quebecois felt the might of the federals' resolve because of this. Over 200 arrests were made, countless homes searched, the FLQ went to Cuba it is believed most were executed." The first clipping was a photograph of the murdered dignitary and his bodyguard.

"I'm lost; what's this got to do with us?" Munroe asked, and even Hugo nodded in agreement.

"You will learn, if you'll please be silent and let him finish," Arthur Doyle of Doyle Industries said.

"Basically, we… the five of us, would like you to kidnap our Prime Minister." Dr. Quison waited, enjoying the look of disbelief come over Munroe's face. "From our sources, we've learned of the Prime Minister's planned trip to Alaska and initial schedule." Dr. Quison was again back in front of the map board, pointing to the City of Fairbanks. "The Canadian party plans to fly to Fairbanks where they are to be met by the Alaska delegation for a pleasurable train ride through the famous Denali Park. Here, the Prime Minister will meet the Alaskan Governor. Following an overnight stay, the two politicians and their party will continue by train to Anchorage, where a press conference will be held. The Prime Minister will spend one night in Anchorage before flying to Seattle to meet with the Governor of Washington… to discuss his concerns over the fishing industry." Dr. Quison stopped long enough to sip his brandy and take another puff of his cigar.

"Why?" Munroe asked. "Why are we even thinking about kidnapping this political… ass?"

"My young friend, this is a simple case of politics, which with your education, you should be able to understand," Sir Albert Bruisse said.

"Break this down for me, I seem to be lost in the clouds, and you're flying right over me." Munroe stood up and went to stand beside Dr. Quison. One of Dr. Quison's security people suddenly appeared in the dining room, a black 9mm MP5 machine gun at the ready, his icy glare on Munroe.

"It's okay, Robert. Please step outside. Mr. Munroe was not threatening me."

"Yes, sir," Robert looked around the room, gave Hugo a stern look, and vanished back through the doorway.

"Pardon my man's intrusion. He simply felt I might be endangered by Mr. Munroe's sudden approach."

"Are we being watched, Quison?" Munroe asked. "You've got surveillance cameras on us?"

"Yes, of course. This was agreed by each of us. But no microphones and the footage is not recorded." Dr. Quison pointed to the four other men. "You remember this was agreed to earlier."

"Okay… whatever!" Munroe relaxed, but only a bit, "So, why should we travel across Canada to kidnap Mr. Terry Haegens?"

"Mr. Haegens, our current Prime Minister, is likely to be voted out of office or possibly recalled if he continues making a complete buffoon of himself. And sadly enough, Mr. Haegens is important to our cause. He is, more or less, a closet Parti Quebecois member and seeks to see Quebec become a free republic. As a result, the five of us have heavily supported his campaign. Of course, our contributions were hidden behind dummy companies and organizations… We had hoped he would further the cause for independence… I cannot tell you how much money we invested in this man without sounding like buffoons ourselves."

"Why not separate yourselves from him, let him fall on his own sword." Munroe understood politics but had not followed the current Prime Minister's activities due to his father's involvement with the man.

"We cannot." Dr. Quison replied. "To lose Haegens at this time could bring a major defeat for our party and derail our future plans. His strongest opponent is almost a sure winner and a staunch federalist supporting increased taxation of major companies like ours. With the economy the way it is, we simply cannot pass those costs down to the general public."

"So, this is more than just Parti Quebecois involvement; you're worried about additional taxes. I imagine this could run into the millions for each of you." Munroe smiled, which made Dr. Quison uncomfortable.

"We need to have Haegens re-elected, and this is where you come in," Dr. Quison said. He forced a smile, nodded and returned to his own chair.

"Okay, you got us here. We're all ears." Munroe returned to his chair, then remembered the security officer at his back. He picked up his chair and moved it to the far side of the table. "I'll sit over here."

"If Mr. Haegens was to be kidnapped by the infamous FLQ and miraculously escape… say five days later, time enough for the hostage story to grow in the newspapers, he'd become a national hero," Dr. Quison said.

"We're supposed to let him escape too?" Munroe asked.

Hugo quietly observed the interplay between Munroe and Dr. Quison as he cleaned his fingernails with a small penknife.

"Yes, but you'll have to think up some way for our beloved Prime Minister to honestly believe he is escaping from terrorists and not being released as part of a plan. Mr. Haegens, though a very charismatic man, isn't a very proficient actor. If he was to be asked too many questions by reporters and law enforcement officers, he's liable to blow the whole thing up in our faces... If he was to be let in on our tactics."

"Why, Alaska?" Munroe looked over his shoulder at the map. "We could probably do a better job right here."

"No," Dr. Quison answered. "This will attract international news as the dreaded FLQ strikes in the wilderness of our neighbor."

"You're talking about a lot of travel time, complex plans, and a lot of money for expenses."

"The delegation will travel with limited security; the Alaska Governor maintains only one Alaska State Trooper bodyguard." Dr. Quison stood to his feet and walked over to Hugo. "We know Mr. Rice here has already accomplished a similar undertaking in South America with great success. Isn't that so, Hugo?"

Hugo's only response was a slight smile, a sparkle of pride in his eyes, and a single nod. He recalled the operation and the $400,000 payment to rescue a guerrilla leader held by federalist troops. 14 of his men were killed in the process, but they got the man off the train. Tragically, the man was murdered two weeks later by his brother-in-law for a substantial reward.

"Haegens would be honored as a great hero, and the fool would certainly be re-elected." Sir Albert Bruisse said.

"Right, look how many Americans favored President Reagan after he was shot," Richmond Webster added. "Had Kennedy survived, he would've won a second term. Instead, America got stuck with Johnson and the Vietnam War. Kennedy was pulling his advisors out; he knew a war in Vietnam would be a lost cause."

"It is imperative our Mr. Haegens not be harmed. We do not need a martyr. As to the others, do with them as you will. Mind you, the kidnapping must occur after the meeting at Mt. McKinley. His abduction has to occur after he's left the park on the train but before he reaches Anchorage," Dr. Quison handed a thick manila folder to Munroe. "This contains all the information you'll need; train schedules, maps, photographs of the train, and the list of security agents accompanying him." Dr. Quison handed Munroe a larger envelope, "This contains the money you'll need, most of it in American currency. If more is required, it will be provided."

"How long do we have?" Hugo asked.

"You have 14-days to put your plan into operation. Haegens is flying to Fairbanks on May 27th, and his abduction must occur on the morning of the 29th." Dr. Quison lifted an empty black leather briefcase off the floor and presented it to Munroe, "Place your paperwork in here and lock it. I'll give you the combination before you leave."

"What about us afterward?" Munroe asked. "There's a good chance the PM will see our faces; five days is a long time to wear masks or have a hood over his face if we're supposed to let him escape."

"Once this operation is completed, the FLQ will cease to exist. You'll be given five million dollars to share and safe passage to a country that does not have an extradition treaty with the USA or Canada. If members of your group do not survive the operation… the money will be divided between fewer people." Dr. Quison smiled. Munroe knew that these five gentlemen would be happy if there were no other survivors. "A couple of you, preferably you and Hugo, will have to stay close to the Prime Minister to ensure his escape. We would hate to go through all this and end up with Haegens being eaten by a bear or falling off some cliff. Once the PM is safely in the hands of the authorities, you'll catch a chartered flight to the Philippines. After that, you can make your own travel arrangements."

"What about the money?" Munroe asked.

"Five million dollars will be deposited in a special Cayman Island account, half before the operation begins and half when we hear news of the PM's abduction." Dr. Quison replied. "You can call a phone number I will provide to verify the money is deposited."

"Philippines?" Hugo asked. "I no like Philippines no more."

"The Philippines have the closest islands clear of FBI and Interpol involvement. Don't worry; you won't be there long," Dr. Quison said. "From there, you can take a flight to a location of your choice."

Over the next seven hours, the men discussed details of the operation, equipment needs, and travel. When they were sure that even the smallest detail had been settled, the men separated and headed for their helicopters. Only Dr. Quison remained for a quiet moment alone with Hugo.

"Steve, I need to discuss another upcoming operation with Hugo. Could you leave us alone for a moment? I have several adult toys about the property to entertain yourself with."

Munroe didn't like it but seeing the two security officers standing by the door, he replied, "Sure… okay." He left Hugo with Dr. Quison and wandered off to see the toys Dr. Quison had mentioned. Under the close observation of the lodge's security monitoring devices, Munroe entertained himself with one of Dr. Quison's new six-wheel ATVs, riding through a maze of trails.

Dr. Quison stood and walked to the fireplace, "Hugo, you are to ensure the Prime Minister's safety; he's to be unharmed and found in fairly good condition. I want him terrified by the ordeal… it has to look real, but not so much that he's slobbering in front of the news cameras. We have to have him come off as a heroic figure… if that's possible. Then, you are to eliminate the remaining members of the FLQ, including our young Mr. Munroe."

"Munroe will be a pleasure… But will cost you one million extra. I want funds in my Cayman Island account before I do this… You agree?"

"I agree. My people will handle the money transfers." Dr. Quison pulled a folded map from the inside pocket of his jacket, "This is the route you will take heading south staying parallel with the railroad tracks. It's about a two-day hike. That's wilderness, so be sure to keep the railroad tracks in sight so you don't get lost. I understand the forest is quite thick through there, and you'll be able to make it to a town called Cantwell without being discovered. There are many people camping in the area, so using infrared detection to search for kidnapping suspects will slow the authorities down. From there, you will blend in with the tourists and probably find a ride to Fairbanks fairly easily. I'll leave the travel to you, but in Fairbanks, you are to vanish. You'll have enough forged documents and all the money you'll need to make your escape. I see no reason why we should ever see each other again." Dr. Quison offered his hand and Hugo shook it, silently resenting the limp hand.

Munroe appeared a short time later, having been found in the woods by security officers and told that Hugo was ready to leave. "Man, I gotta get me one of those," Munroe said enthusiastically. He smiled at Dr. Quison, "How much does one of those ATVs cost?"

"One that size is about $15,000 in American money," Dr. Quison said.

"Good, I'll be able to afford it then." Munroe glanced at Hugo, "You ready?"

"Yes, we go now." Hugo headed for the helipad without looking back at Dr. Quison.

"We'll need up-to-date intelligence on this," Munroe said before leaving.

"Not a problem, Steve," Dr. Quison said. "We have a man on Haegen's personal staff."

"Great!" Munroe turned around and followed Hugo to the helicopter where another armed security officer returned their weapons.

Dr. Quison studied the two men as they left; he estimated their success at less than 50-50. Only one man, Hugo, was a true professional. The others were a bunch of thrill-seeking patriots with a deranged power-hungry egotist for a leader. Even if Mr. Haegens and all the members of the FLQ were lost in the kidnap operation, Dr. Quison knew he and the other gentlemen would profit significantly from the destruction the FLQ had already accomplished. Most importantly, there would be no trail for the authorities to follow, which might have led to either him or the other four. As the helicopter lifted off, he raised his brandy snifter and saluted Munroe and Hugo with a smile of contentment and pride in his accomplishments to date. He turned to reenter the lodge to spend leisure time in the kitchen discussing wild game recipes with his chef.

3

# AN EXPENSIVE HIGH

Downtown Toronto
May 17th, 9:24 A.M.

Janene had put in long, tedious hours taking care of Claudia and had difficulty handling the whole matron/prisoner routine. Fed up with Claudia and Munroe being gone, she abandoned her patient and slipped into Monroe's room. She took a metal box from under their bed and took over $200 from his private funds. It took her only a few moments to sneak out of the FLQ safe house. Outside, she checked up and down the street and hesitated unsure of her destination. There was one place she could score some cocaine; she hailed a taxi and headed for town.

Sitting in the back seat, she struggled with the pain of withdrawal. Her petite body showed evidence of her condition with frequent tremors, sunken eyes with black rings, and sudden jerky movements. She needed to make a connection real soon, or the crash would likely launch her into a dark abyss. With Munroe absent, there would be no net to catch her.

After the taxi dropped her off, she stumbled about and slowly wandered down a nearly deserted stretch of road near the airport cargo storage area. She hoped to find the Candy Man, a known street dealer who often hung out there for its remoteness. This was very possibly her only option. Her other dealers had suddenly dried up primarily due to recent drug raids by a joint US and Canadian law enforcement task force. They had concentrated on the many illegal border crossings, with their primary targets being cocaine, heroin, marijuana, and fentanyl—drugs coming up from New York State and New Jersey.

The taxi ride downtown had cost $24.25, so Janene went on foot in search of the Candy Man. Two of her old friends, both hard addicts, had vouched for this guy. The word on the street said he carried class junk at a reasonable price, especially for first-time customers. He was apparently trying to build up a customer base, and then the price would increase. It was common practice to hand out low-cost pharmaceuticals to swing hardliners away from previous dealers. This practice also worked well when supplies were way down. Janene was in dire need and didn't care much about a reasonable price. She would take whatever her handful of cash could buy because that was all she had. She had to do something to get the shakes under control and bring some clarity to her mind, or she might lose it and throttle Claudia to silence her.

Janene went through all the stages of withdrawal and blasted right through the stage of denial, where the user told themselves they could quit anytime. She knew that was a lie, cocaine owned her body and soul. She had shot up heroin a few times, but it had frightened her; her fear of needles had helped her escape that monkey. Cocaine, though, was different, it didn't involve needles. It wasn't long before she was a slave to the white powder and would do whatever it took to get some including hooking a few times in the past – something Munroe never knew.

Unfortunately for Janene, Munroe had ordered Lesli to keep his girlfriend under close observation. Lesli, also known as Little P, followed Janene out of the house and through the bar district and dope haunts. She was at the airport staying within sight of Janene. A petite female with short black hair worn in a page boy cut, Lesli often used make-up and clothes to give her a Gothic look. This made it easy for her to go unnoticed in doper land.

With Claudia wounded, Lesli was pulling security watch for the FLQ while Hugo was away with Munroe. Lesli knew Janene's condition and that she would leave the safe house in search of her white powder. For a few moments during the taxi ride, she lost Janene, but picked her up again as she entered a rundown hotel. From that point on, Janene had a shadow.

Lesli put time in as a political activist for several causes. She had served a two-year hitch as an officer in the Canadian Navy. At age 26, she was handed a less than Honorable Discharge for expressing unkind sentiment about the Canadian Government's treatment of the country's Indian Tribes. The fourth member Munroe had selected for the FLQ venture, Lesli, had come with recommendations from another radical group in the Quebec area: The Red Tide. This communist-backed faction had been operating around Montreal for several decades.

Letting Shawn know of Janene's disappearance, Lesli followed her to see where and who she was looking for. Shawn knew why Janene had left the house and advised Lesli, "Just let her score a line or two, then you can drag her home in a more relaxed state. We'll let Hugo or Munroe deal with her when they return."

As Lesli watched Janene stumble about, she could see the young lady was a weak link in their security network. Something drastic needed to be done. Even with Munroe's thrashings, it seemed Janene couldn't stay away from coke. Lesli knew that with the people associated with drug trafficking, the FLQ was at risk.

Candy Man was a seedy looking greasy black-haired fellow sitting in a filthy faded-blue Ford Mustang II. He was parked beside the airport storage chain-link fence. No one else seemed to be about.

Lesli stayed at least 30-yards behind Janene and hid behind a parked out-of-service airport shuttle bus and watched as she cautiously approached the Mustang. A moment passed as the Candy Man and Janene shared street pleasantries through the open car window. Then Janene walked around the car, opened the passenger door, and slid into the front passenger seat.

Unable to hear the conversation, Lesli knew Janene was making the junkie-in-need-of-a-fix-right-now-busy-talk, while the freak with the greased back black hair pretended to care. She surveyed the scene and surrounding area, then suddenly froze. A man was hiding behind a tall stack of wooden pallets inside the cargo area. He was dressed in brown slacks and a tan-colored trench coat to fend off the morning drizzle. She knew he was no cargo flunky, especially when she noticed the black wire running up to his right ear. The man held a black rifle scope and kept the Mustang under constant observation. As Lesli watched, the man opened his coat exposing a holstered automatic. He reached down to lift up an expensive-looking camera with a huge telephoto lens and began to snap photos before placing the camera back at his feet.

*Cops!* Lesli knew she had a serious problem on her hands. Either the cop was getting ready to bust this deal, probably with another officer or two hidden away, or the guy in the car was an undercover narcotics officer. Lesli suspected this was either a buy-bust operation, which involved making the arrest as soon as money changed hands, or they were developing suspects for a more in-depth investigation. The photos would be used to pressure the user to testify against a bigger fish. Either way, Lesli had to get Janene out of that car fast.

On one knee, her large leather purse on the ground, Lesli pulled out a lethal-looking compact Ingram 9mm machine pistol. Made by Israeli Arms, it was a very effective killing machine if held by someone who knew how to use it. Lesli had become quite proficient in its use and liked its feel. Such an automatic weapon was highly illegal in Canada. She withdrew a lengthy 30-round magazine, inserted it into the firearm and chambered the first round, then pulled out a second magazine and slid it into her coat pocket. Taking a couple of deep breaths to steady herself, Lesli burst out of hiding and dashed into the middle of the road where she quickly assumed a two-handed shooter's crouch and aimed at the police officer with the camera.

Before the man in the trench coat saw her, Lesli swept the gun from left to right firing off a burst. The bullets struck the ground first, then hit the observer in both legs and hips. The impact from several hits propelled him backward and slammed him against a pile of cargo bins. He landed on a hard cement floor and lay screaming, grasping his bloody wounds. His radio was thrown out of reach. The officer was in too much pain to pull his weapon.

Closing on the Mustang, Lesli kept her weapon leveled at the man behind the steering wheel and ignored the startled wide-eyed look in Janene's eyes. "Out of the car!" Lesli shouted at her.

The undercover officer in the car decided to take a chance and ducked forward in an attempt to pull a two-inch five-shot Smith & Wesson .38 caliber revolver from his ankle holster.

When Janene saw Lesli with the gun, she opened the car door and rolled out onto the curb which allowed Lesli a free shot at the officer. Lesli stepped up to the car and glared at the panicking officer as he struggled to free his weapon from its new holster. "Not your lucky day!" With an icy glare and a sinister smirk, Lesli pulled the trigger to release a burst of bullets into the officer's upper body. She backed up and used the rest of the clip to riddle the car's length, flattening both tires on her side and leaving several holes in the windshield and wear window. Lesli took a few seconds to glance up and down the street for witnesses or other officers as she popped out the empty magazine and loaded the second. She chambered the first round and fired off a few more bullets in the direction of the wounded cop with the camera then yelled at Janene, "We gotta go, now!"

Janene, was still having trouble with what just happened, nodded in agreement, but dashed back into the car. Ignoring the bloody mess in the front seat and the lifeless eyes of the undercover officer staring at her, she hurriedly retrieved several items. Then Lesli grabbed her by the shoulder and yanked her back out, "I said now! Move it!"

"I'm comin', ah jus' gotta get mah stuff," Janene replied. She made a dash for the nearest alley, where Lesli directed her to wait by a broken-down luggage hauler.

"Look, I've got to clean this up before other cops show up, so don't move from that spot!" Lesli slipped the Ingram back into her purse, along with the two magazines. Slinging it over her shoulder, she looked at Janene with disgust and pulled a Glock 9mm pistol from a shoulder holster concealed by her jacket.

First, she ran to the wounded cop lying on the ground. He was semi-conscious, bleeding from three wounds to his lower body. Wearing lightweight driving gloves, which would prevent leaving fingerprints, she knelt beside him and removed his gun. She gave it a quick glance and said, "Nice piece." Then slid it across the pavement, and... remembering the camera, hustled to where it lay. She opened the camera, exposed the film, and returned to the officer.

While Janene watched, Lesli placed the barrel end of her pistol an inch behind the man's left ear and pulled the trigger. "Bad day, guy... No witnesses allowed." The man's head jerked hard to the left as the 9mm bullet penetrated his skull and killed him instantly. Lesli thought about dropping her Ingram, but she liked how it handled, and these weapons were hard to come by in Canada. So, she decided to keep it. She needed to hurry and get Janene back to the safe house without running into any more cops. With automatic weapons fire sounding off in this part of town, Lesli knew the police would be on the scene in moments. She had no time to waste.

The two young women changed cabs twice before taking a city bus to within walking distance of the safe house. Once they entered the house, Janene ignored the others' icy glares and quickly ran upstairs to her room. She slammed the door shut and locked it with a chain.

Lesli, very much in need of something to eat, walked into the kitchen and began making a roast beef sandwich. The fact that she had just killed two Toronto Police officers didn't bother her. Her only concern was Janene and how much longer they would have to put up with her accursed drug habit. However, that decision, she was forced to leave for Munroe and Hugo. She had done her job and was satisfied with that.

Toronto RCMP Intelligence Division
May 17th, 6:59 P.M.


"I don't get it, Boss. Why do you think the FLQ hit those two Toronto cops this morning?" Adler asked JP. The two had just reviewed the written brief on the double homicide.

"Can't explain it... only a hunch. It burns deep in my gut that this was their action." JP wore several bandages on his face and hands. He had grown weary of the hospital and left without the doctor's release. "We haven't received a call for assistance from Toronto PD, but I know they have a single witness to the shootings. An airport employee who was smart enough to take cover when the first shots were fired. A Toronto detective I've worked with in the past told me this witness poked his head up in time to see two women running from the scene." JP threw his remaining coffee into the trashcan; what he really wanted was a cold beer. But that was not going to happen right now.

"So, please explain why you think this was an FLQ hit?"

"Like I said, just a hunch. Maybe because it just sounds like a professional job," JP said. "They just didn't shoot up the scene and run off. They stayed behind long enough to execute both officers and pull the film out of the camera to keep their identities hidden. No evidence and no witnesses. We got a break with this witness keeping his head down. A smart guy, or we'd have three bodies."

"The shooters could have picked all that up watching TV. There's a lot of dopers who carry automatic weapons." Adler savored the smell of his coffee before taking a sip.

"Right, but how many dopers with automatic weapons are two white females? According to the tape recording left from the dope deal, the only thing the shooter forgot to get. It sounds like everything was going down just fine, then World War III opened up."

JP had learned the undercover officer in the car was wearing a wire which was fed to a recording device hidden near the backup officer. The two officers were attempting to develop an investigation rather than making simple buy-busts. Unfortunately, it was one undercover officer's first month on the street and his last. Although the officer's microphone was destroyed during the shooting, the electronic device recorded everything right up to where the female voice said, "Not your lucky day."

"Those two officers never fired their weapons; they had no gunpowder residue on their hands. The undercover officer's ankle holster was empty, and his weapon was missing, along with the dope they were selling. Investigators at the scene believe it happened fast, by someone who knew what they were doing. One female was making a deal for coke, and suddenly the other woman jumps in to break the party up and kills the two officers. I don't know of too many dealers out there that would risk getting into a shoot-out with the cops over such a small amount of cocaine."

"Sure, but I still don't see the FLQ tie-in," Adler, coffee cup in hand, walked to the couch and sat down. It had been a long day, and he was feeling his years.

"This may be the break we're looking for. So, give narcotics a call, ask them to lean on their informants, and see what they turn up. Sooner or later, something has to give, and when it does, I'll be there." JP stared at the photograph of his family, a silver-framed print on the corner of his desk. After a moment, he reached over and lowered it to the desktop. Adler watched but didn't say a word. He sipped his coffee and waited for JP to continue. After a long moment, JP turned and glared at Adler, "I said get a hold of narcotics—that means now, Sergeant!"

Startled by JP's rudeness, Adler jumped to his feet, "Yes, Captain, Sir. I'm on my way." He set his coffee down on the table and walked out. Adler knew JP was stressed; Colonel Augustus had asked JP to take some time off, and JP had refused. With the bombings, the Colonel needed his first team on the streets, allowing JP to stay on the job. He had taken Adler and Wilkens aside and asked them to keep a close eye on JP and report any problems.

"You two are his best friends, but your job is too important to let that friendship interfere with the investigation of these lunatics. I don't want JP turning this into some personal revenge crusade. We locate them, arrest them, and let the courts try them. We do not execute them, even though right now, I wish we could!"

FLQ Safe House
May 17th, 11:02 P.M.


Janene hid in her bedroom; terrified what Munroe might do to her upon his return. She curled up under a pile of blankets like a small child trying to escape the monsters under her bed. Only in this case, Munroe was the monster. She knew what he was capable of, the pain he had already caused her, and the ugly threats he had made.

Her only bright spot came from Shawn, who stopped by to tell her the news was carrying the shooting as a police drug bust gone wrong. "No one's connecting this to us." The packet of cocaine she had retrieved from the car was soiled with the officer's blood. She barely found enough to give her a couple lines and a momentary high. But it didn't last long, and now her fear of what may happen had brought on a severe crash. The brief euphoria gave way to extreme paranoia.

The front door opened and closed. Janene heard muffled voices, immediately followed by Munroe's loud outburst of profanity. She knew Lesli had just briefed Munroe on what had gone down at the airport. Hugo's strong voice could also be heard, apparently laced with profanity spoken loudly in German, which now caused her an attack of hysterical tears. Her body began to shake, and she bit down hard on a corner of the blanket. Her right hand was under her pillow, clutching the .38 caliber revolver she had removed from the dead officer's body. She kept her eyes clenched shut, hoping to block out the loathsome beast she could hear climbing the stairs.

The bedroom door was kicked open, breaking the chain and slamming against the wall. Munroe caught the door before it could bounce back to hit him. He saw her naked feet sticking from beneath the blankets, reached out, grabbed her right ankle, and twisted it pulling her off the bed.

Janene's body trembled, her eyes grew wide in fear, and she screamed. She brought the .38 revolver up and aimed it at Munroe's face. The weapon vibrated in tune with her tremors. Munroe didn't hesitate; he grabbed the revolver and twisted it out of her hand.

"You bastard!" She yelled.

"Maybe I should just end this now, then." Monroe pointed the revolver at her as Hugo entered the room. Instead of pulling the trigger, Munroe tossed him the handgun. "Leave us alone for a moment." Hugo closed the door and stood in the hallway with Lesli, who remained silent holding her Glock in her right hand.

Munroe jerked Janene to her feet and glared down at her. She was wearing only a light t-shirt and panties, her body visibly shaking. He forced her down to her knees in front of him as her eyes pleaded with him to stop. Instead, he continued to add painful pressure to her right hand. "You were ready to shoot me but didn't have the guts to pull the trigger." With his right hand, he pulled his own pistol out of his waistband and shoved it hard into her mouth, chipping her front teeth. Her eyes filled with tears; Janene glared back at him terrified as she struggled to breathe. She recognized that frightening look of insanity in his eyes, which she had often seen of late. His eyes were open wide and filled with a glare of craziness. Janene knew she was about to die.

Slowly applying pressure to the trigger, something suddenly clicked in Munroe's brain, and the insanity began to bleed off. Looking down at her, he lowered the pistol and let her go. Janene fell to the floor, coughing up blood and retching. "So close, Janene, so awfully close," Munroe muttered. He put the weapon back inside his waistband, reached down, grabbed Janene by the hair, and drug her toward the bedroom door. Opening it, he shoved Hugo aside and surprised Lesli by continuing to drag the screaming Janene toward Claudia's bedroom. Hugo, who thought he knew what was about to take place, got ahead of Munroe and opened Claudia's door without bothering to knock. He stood aside as Munroe pulled his howling girlfriend through the doorway.

Shawn sat beside Claudia's bed reading to her from a month-old magazine. He jumped to his feet as the door burst open, "Hey, man, what's going on?"

"Object lesson time, Shawn. Move aside." Munroe dropped Janene to the floor, where she lay curled up in a fetal position at the foot of Claudia's single bed.

Munroe looked at Shawn with hard eyes and ordered, "Go get a beer!"

Not sure he wanted to leave as he really cared for Claudia, Shawn looked into Hugo's cold glare and decided it was time to go for that beer. When he walked out the door, he whispered to Lesli, "You know what's goin' on here?"

Lesli ignored him, and Shawn continued walking.

Gordon appeared in the hallway and took Shawn by the elbow, "Come on, Shawn… We're not needed here." Gordon led his buddy down the stairs and into the kitchen, where they silently opened two cans of beer. The rest of the group attempted to watch TV and ignore what was happening upstairs.

Munroe looked at the little revolver in Hugo's hand, "She wanted to use that on me. I mean, what's a guy gonna do?" He half-heartedly kicked Janene's left hip and then turned to Claudia. She was fully awake but disoriented from a mixture of booze and fever.

"Claudia, you really need a bath!" Munroe said and turned to Hugo. "Would you be so kind as to carry our precious Claudia into the bathroom and set her into the tub?"

Hugo handed the revolver to Lesli and moved to pick Claudia up. She became frightened, "What's… why… what are you doing?" Though she was fighting a high fever, she knew something was seriously wrong.

"I thought you understood, Claudia; you're going to take a bath—you stink!" Munroe reached down, grabbed a handful of Janene's hair, and dragged her out of the way. Her wailing caused him to kick her until she stopped, and only a whimper could be heard.

"Steve… Hugo, I'll go somewhere. I'll vanish! No one will ever find me. Please!" Weakened by a week of high fever and seeing all the guns, Claudia was pleading for her life, but it fell on deaf ears. She wasn't strong enough to fight off Hugo, and when he wrapped his muscular arm around her back and touched her injury, she screamed into his ear and tried to bite him. He jerked her around, and the severe pain and fever left her limp.

When they reached the bathroom, Hugo slowly lowered Claudia into the tub. Strangely enough, he was almost gentle with her which surprised Munroe, who expected Hugo to drop her into the tub. Even in her condition, she had some degree of fight, and Hugo respected that. But, not enough to let her live. He backed away as Munroe dragged Janene's limp body beside the tub by her hair. She was shrieking again, but Munroe wanted her to see everything. He hoped she might learn from the experience, or the next bath would be hers.

"Janene, you nearly blew this whole gig because of this insatiable need you have to snort that white crap up your nose. I think it's time you were given some incentive to beat this thing." Munroe looked down at Claudia, who was only semi-conscious from the pain caused by Hugo's embrace and her roaring high fever. "Claudia, you did a great job on the Leon place, but you botched it when you just had to buy those cigarettes in some stop-and-rob joint. All those places have security cameras—I simply can't believe you forgot all that." Munroe gave Hugo a stern look to remind him that he shared the blame for this, and then stared back down at Claudia. Munroe's eyes sparkled as a touch of insanity returned, "Well, they always said that smoking could kill you, and in your case, they were right." He reached into his front pants pocket and pulled out a five-inch pocketknife, then opened it to expose an extremely sharp blade. He reached down without saying anything more, yanked Claudia's head back, and with a determined firmness, slit her throat. Claudia's eyes grew wide, and she tried to speak but only sputtered as unconsciousness and then death came from lack of blood flow to the brain. Munroe looked at Hugo, "You blew this one, so, you get to clean it up. Make sure you wash the tub out when you're done."

Without saying a word, Hugo stepped forward and turned on the hot water tap. He knew from experience that hot water would help the body bleed out faster.

Munroe glared at Janene again, whose watery eyes and running black eyeliner gave her a very unattractive appearance. "This is the last time, baby—one more screw-up, and you are ONE DEAD WOMAN!" He lowered his voice to an even more threatening level, "Then it will be your turn to take a bath." Munroe shook his head in disgust as he wondered how he ever got attached to this drug-crazed female. He left her on the floor and returned to his bedroom wrestling with doubts over the success of their upcoming operation in Alaska. He had lost one member, and he knew he couldn't count on Janene. He wondered if it was wise to let her live, thinking his followers might view it as a weakness. That's one thing he couldn't handle. At that moment, Janene stumbled into the bedroom, and like a small child, pled for forgiveness. She curled up beside him on the bed and rested her head on his shoulders, her eyes and cheeks soaked in tears.

He couldn't explain it to himself, but this girl had a strange hold on him. He wrapped his arms around her and patted her as she continued to whimper. He would give her one more chance, but only one. He couldn't afford to lose control of this group with the big prize still ahead. This could prove to be their most dangerous assignment yet. He handed her a soiled T-shirt so she could wipe her face, "When Hugo's done in the bathroom, go wash up. You're a real mess." Janene reminded him of his mother at that age. In his growing insanity, he was beginning to see his mother in Janene's face, and that similarity was the only thing keeping her alive.

Three teenage boys came across a partially decomposed body two weeks later while on a cross-country bicycle ride through a densely wooded area north of Toronto. It was a naked woman with long red hair, a sight that would bring them nightmares for months. Through computer simulation, her facial features, size, and estimated weight identified her as a possible match with the red-haired suspect wanted in connection with the Leon murder case. Lab tests matched the body's blood type with the droplets left in the black van, and eventual DNA tests confirmed her identity as Claudia Jean Codel. Her criminal file identified her as a known political activist with alleged ties to several subversive groups. She had two prior arrests for civil disobedience during violent protests. Claudia's body waited in the morgue for three weeks after positive identification. No one ever came to claim her body. She was buried by the City of Toronto in an inexpensive grave with no one to mourn her.

When JP received confirmation of her identity, he smiled for the first time in weeks. His expression concerned both Adler and Wilkens. They couldn't help but notice how cold the smile was or how frightening the glare in JP's eyes. Alone in his office, JP pulled a small black leather-bound notebook out of his pocket. He wrote Claudia's full name in it and whispered, "That's one."

4

_________

# NORTH TO ALASKA... FOR THE RUSH
# IS ON

Apartment 5A, Castle Apartments, Fairbanks, Alaska
May 22nd, 6:31 A.M.

It was a beautiful spring morning in Fairbanks; the long winter was over; the snow and ice melted away. For many, the melting exposed all the mess left from last fall - a regular occurrence with spring break-up. Not that Greg W. Hansen, Special Agent for the Alaska Railroad, cared all that much about the current weather. He was in a very foul mood having woke up with a throbbing headache and a mouth that tasted like lemon flavored cotton. He would just as soon have crawled back under the blankets than have to face another hectic Monday morning at work. The uncommon ailment was caused by spending the previous night at Pike's Landing, shooting pool, and guzzling too many pitchers of beer with a couple of his cop buddies.

Greg pushed himself up slowly in bed and grimaced as his back muscles reacted painfully when he gradually stretched them out. A not-so-gentle reminder of too much nightlife and many years of being a cop. He gently wiped the sleep from his bloodshot eyes and let out a deep sigh; he hated mornings. He had worked evenings and late nights during his many years as an Alaska State Trooper. At railroad, he worked day shifts, which often extended into the evening.

Deciding he was ready to tackle the next step, he swung his legs around, planted his bare feet on the floor, and slowly stood up. The elevation change

71

caused an extra bass beat to the thumping in his brain, and he plopped back down. Hangovers were not something anyone enjoyed, and lately, Greg had seen a few too many. He chastised himself for overindulging. That shared fifth pitcher of beer had been overkill; he wondered how his friends were doing this morning. Greg glanced down at the floor and spotted his well-worn leather moccasin slippers, a gift from his son, and slid his feet into them.

Ready for a second try, he stood up, ignored the creaks in his back, and stumbled to the bathroom. He immediately gripped both sides of the sink and made the mistake of staring into the mirror. Greg was only 44, but that old geezer who glared back at him resembled a 65 to 70-year-old. He needed a shave, a haircut, some wrinkle remover, and possibly plastic surgery. Most of all, he badly needed a hot shower. Running the sink water until it was icy cold, he rinsed his face off, ran his wet hands through his thinning hair and took a second look in the mirror. He couldn't remember when gray hair appeared, but it was more gray than brown; his mustache resembled a drowned caterpillar; it needed a trim.

Greg turned the shower on, stripped off his boxer shorts and forced his 6'5" frame into a glass shower stall, apparently constructed for someone 5'7". He couldn't stand up straight, so he leaned forward with one hand on the wall for balance and let the hot water wash over him.

Greg lived in a long-term motel rental, which provided maid service. However, it didn't involve cleaning his kitchen, which commonly bordered on a stage four bacterial attack. Simply put, Greg had become a slob since his marriage ended. His ex-wife and son lived in Anchorage with a man who had once been Greg's best friend, a fellow Alaska State Trooper, and his supervisor. The affair had ended the marriage, and his family moved to Anchorage.

"Ahhh," Greg sighed as the hot water began to relieve some of the tension. In Greg's experience, there was nothing as healing as a long hot shower for a hangover. If he had a tub, he would have spent the morning soaking out his misery, but the place only came with a toy-sized shower stall.

Since his divorce, Greg spent Sunday evenings with his buddies; his only social contact with the world. Until recently, he had rarely gotten so intoxicated; the excuse was being divorced, approaching middle age, and missing his family. It was true that misery loves company, his friends had both been through divorces and relied on their job to stay relatively sane.

Having given it to his ex-wife, Greg no longer owned a car, he used taxis instead of taking on another car payment. He had a take-home Alaska Railroad (ARR) Ford Expedition, which was always parked outside his apartment when he was off duty. Like most other police officers, Greg knew one of the worst things for a cop was to be out driving drunk. It was a surefire way to end one's career and limit future job prospects.

Greg was not what he termed a 'cop' anymore. Technically, he was considered a law enforcement officer by the ARR, who had hired him as the Fairbanks Railroad investigator. But, outside of a few investigations, Greg saw himself as a highly paid rent-a-cop. Before this, he had spent 12 years as an Alaskan State Trooper, resigning as a lieutenant during the divorce proceedings. He didn't want to be reminded that his ex-wife was living with his former supervisor, Captain Daniel Potter.

His other two friends, who he sincerely hoped were feeling as bad as he did, were Lieutenant Steve Farber, a 15-year veteran of the Fairbanks Police Department, and Corporal Jack Richards, an Alaskan State Trooper with over nine years on the job.

Greg had abruptly left the Troopers following the bitter divorce from Debbie in 2019. Then he lost the custody battle for his son, John which surprised nearly everyone, especially Greg, because Debbie was the one having an extra-marital affair. However, in its benevolent kindness, the court saw fit to give Greg reasonable visitation: one weekend a month during the school year, two weeks in the summer and every other Christmas for five days. Unfortunately, John, 14 years old, lived with his mother in Anchorage, 350 miles away. One weekend a month, Greg flew down Friday night, checked into an inexpensive hotel, visited his son on Saturday and returned to Fairbanks on the late flight Sunday night.

Dozens of his friends tried to talk him out of resigning as he only had eight years before retirement, but Greg ignored them. He had risen through the ranks rapidly, proving himself to be an extremely intelligent trooper able to quickly grasp investigation techniques. He had just pinned new lieutenant bars on and was scheduled to be assistant supervisor of the Criminal Investigation Branch (CIB) when he found out about his wife.

He knew that if he stayed around AST, he would lose his temper and get fired for assaulting Potter. The State Troopers reassigned Potter to Anchorage but there remained a sour feeling in the Fraternal Order of Troopers for what Potter had done to a fellow officer.

Greg and Debbie had sold the house as part of the divorce settlement, and Greg placed most of his share in a trust for John's college fund. He had found the one-bedroom hotel, which came with maid service and a carport to keep snow off his work car.

Following his resignation from the troopers, Donald Osborn, Chief Special Agent for the Alaska Railroad (ARR) and an old friend, approached Greg and offered him this job. They had known each other for several years, and it did not take him long to talk Greg into accepting the Fairbanks position with the ARR. He was granted a Special Officer's Commission from the Alaska State Troopers, allowing him to enforce state laws on ARR property and carry a concealed weapon. Railroad tracks ran east from Fairbanks, through Fort Wainwright, and out to Eielson Air Force Base, some 22 miles and west from Fairbanks to Anchorage and then south to Seward. Alaska Railroad tracks extended over 500 miles. There were offices and massive work yards in Fairbanks and Anchorage and smaller yards in Whittier, Seward, and Nenana.

With nothing better to do, Greg often worked six days a week. During evening shift, he cruised the streets. From time to time, he assisted the Fairbanks Police or Troopers on traffic stops when other officers could not respond. Fairbanks PD's strength was 44% undermanned, an all-time low. His assistance helped build a good relationship with the Fairbanks Police Department. In return, he was awarded red-carpet treatment at the department. He often walked back into the dispatch area, grabbed a cup of hot coffee, and asked the dispatcher to run vehicle license numbers so he could identify owners or make warrant checks. He felt more comfortable with the Fairbanks department than the Trooper's Detachment offices.

Feeling better after the shower, Greg left a steamy bathroom with a damp white bath towel wrapped around his waist. His electronic alarm clock, thumped into submission, was on the floor. Picking it up, he saw 7:04 a.m. on the digital readout. "Aw, man… I'd better get a move on."

One of the bennies of working for the railroad was wearing civilian clothes. In Alaska, that did not mean a suit or even a sport coat and tie. Alaskans were a bit more relaxed in their civilian wardrobe unless a sport coat and tie was called for, as when Greg needed to appear in court.

As a trooper, he'd spent many hours polishing leather gear, giving a mirror-like finish to his boots and taking Brasso to his collar brass and badge then double check his highly starched uniform for lint and grease spots. The Detachment 1st Sergeant who often conducted uniform inspections could be more rigid than a Marine Corps drill instructor.

Gregg selected a nice pair of brown slacks, a pair of mildly scuffed black Wellington boots, and a white cotton polo shirt. His hair was long enough to hang over the collar showing the longer strands of gray. He picked up his brown basket weave holster from the top of his dresser and slid it through his belt, slapping it into place behind his right hip. Greg carried a Glock 9mm pistol, loaded with 12-rounds of Hydro-Shock hollow point ammo. Two extra magazines were stored in the small console between the front seats of his car.

Dressed and ready, Greg took a moment to gaze at the photograph of his son on the dresser top. A silver-framed 5" by 7" color photo of his boy showing off a 34-pound King Salmon he had caught. They had borrowed a friend's car and driven down to the Kenai Peninsula for a day of fishing on the famous Kenai River. Smiling from ear to ear, John was impressed with his own accomplishment of landing the salmon without his father's help. John had gotten drenched in the process of netting the fish and bringing it to shore, but the kid was happy, and so was Greg. Looking at his son's photo reminded him that his ex-wife's unfaithfulness had separated him from his son. He shrugged off the remorse and continued getting ready for work.

Bitterness toward his wife burned deep; but he also blamed God for allowing it to happen. The Hansen Family had attended church at Door of Hope Christian Center for five years. A year before the marriage ended, Lieutenant Potter started attending the services. He was second-in-command of the Alaska State Trooper Special Emergency Response Team (SERT). Greg was accepted as a team member, and somewhere Debbie got to know Lt. Potter better than she should.

One late afternoon when Greg was scheduled to be at the range running a few troopers through semi-annual qualifications, he followed his wife to a seedy South Cushman motel. Hearing rumors about Debbie seeing Potter and knowing Potter pretty well, he suspected the worst. At first, he didn't want to believe the rumors, but catching his wife and best friend in the hotel room had brought cold reality to them. In the weeks and months that followed, he realized the man he had befriended and called a Christian brother was, in fact, a louse. Greg learned that Potter preferred to chase married women and often talked about them with his non-church acquaintances. Greg's wife didn't believe it and the divorce followed. Greg kicked the hotel room door open and with his pistol drawn, entered to find Potter and Debbie in a romantic embrace, their hastily discarded clothes in disarray on the floor. Fully exposed, they stared at Gregg, utter shock on their faces.

Greg couldn't explain what happened in the intense moments that followed, but his next memory was standing outside the motel room braced against his car door. He hadn't pulled the trigger; some mental safety catch prevented him from becoming a murderer. He couldn't recall what was said in the room in that day, but it had apparently rattled Potter. Debbie had run outside wrapped in a blanket, but Greg walked away without saying a word. He never spoke to her before court and since then only if it concerned their son.

By the time it was over, Greg didn't want anything to do with Christians. A Christian brother had wronged him greatly. His wife, an admitted Christian, committed adultery and several church members had known about the affair. So, he blamed God; he didn't return to that church and hadn't spoken with the Lord since that day.

John resented his mother for what she had done that took him away from his father and he vehemently detested the man who tried to behave like his father. Like his dad, John saw through Potter's lies and arrogance and couldn't understand why his mother couldn't. Greg never spoke poorly of her or Potter around John; he figured the boy had enough on his plate for a teenager to handle.

Gregg grabbed a navy blue ARR windbreaker off a wall hook by the front door and walked out of his two-room apartment making sure the door was locked.

"Good morning, Mr. Hansen," Edith Walker said loudly to catch his attention as he walked to his car. "I see you had another late night."

*I could've gone all day without hearing that voice. Why can't that busybody just leave me alone?* Greg thought to himself. Out of ingrained politeness, he turned to face her with a pleasant but very artificial smile.

Mrs. Walker was 63 years old; an Italian American who resembled a homely toad so Greg thought. She was dressed in a blue and white floral moo-moo. Her dyed black hair, covered by a hair net, was up in pink curlers secured by multi-colored bobby pins sticking out in various directions. She was the neighborhood gossip, maintaining 24-hour surveillance over the area, acquiring the latest hearsay and backbiting scandals.

"Yes, Mrs. Walker… another hard night of catching crooks out to steal our train tracks and safeguarding those 200-ton locomotives." Greg really didn't mind Mrs. Walker all that much. However, he was still dealing with a headache. She constantly tried to corner him into dating her divorced daughter. Lucy O'Donnell was 39 and had four very loud kids, who often ran rampant throughout the motel complex whenever they visited. Lucy closely resembled her mother but with more facial hair.

"Oh, you can't fool me, Mr. Hansen; I saw you getting dropped off by taxi last night. Looked to me like you spent a good amount of time at one of our local bars." Mrs. Walker cackled, the sound shooting up Greg's back like fingernails on a backboard.

"Don't know how you do it, Mrs. Walker, but maybe I was out dancing with some beautiful blonde last night," Greg joked. Since the divorce, Greg hadn't dated anyone and wasn't looking for female companionship. Friends were always trying to set him up with blind dates: round ones, tall ones and short ones, blondes, brunettes, and redheads, from 25 to 45 years old. All he had to do was ask, but he wasn't in the mood.

"You just forget about those blonde floozies, Mr. Hansen. You take my Lucy out. She's a fine cook and could fatten you up some."

*Only after that proverbial pig flies.* "You have a great day, Mrs. Walker. I've got to run. I have an important meeting this morning," Greg lied. He made a dash for his car, cringing from the throbbing in his head.

"I don't give up easily, Mr. Hansen," Mrs. Walker screeched before Greg slid into his car.

"I know, I know," Greg said whispered. He closed the car door and started the engine. As the car came to life, the under-dash police radio spurted out, "1-D-22 in pursuit of red Honda Civic, southbound on the Steese Highway near Trainer Gate intersection, possible 10-55," the State Trooper voice was surprisingly calm. Greg's radio was set up to receive both the Fairbanks Police and State Troopers, which occasionally could get complicated to listen to during the busy summer months.

"Another drunk driver loose on the streets," Greg muttered. One of his bad habits was talking to himself from all those lonely nights out on patrol. "Well, at least someone's having a little fun this morning." Greg backed out of his parking slot and pointed his car toward Walmart. Old habits die hard; Greg was a regular morning customer at their bakery, visiting every weekday and most Saturdays. His order was always the same - two glazed twists and a large hot black coffee. With donuts and coffee in hand, he headed for his office.

Alaska Railroad Yard, Fairbanks

The Fairbanks ARR Main Office was a blue-gray two-story metal-sided building located on the southwest corner of the ARR work yard. Greg's small office on the 2nd floor overlooked the yard. His workspace was barely large enough for an ancient black metal desk, a second-hand wheeled desk chair, and two brand new four-drawer legal-sized file cabinets. He borrowed a single metal folding chair for the occasional visitor, of which there were very few. The office's size didn't matter to Greg as he did most of his work out of his vehicle.

Unlocking the office door, he pushed it open with his boot and tossed his windbreaker onto the metal folding chair. Setting his donut bag on the desktop, he carried his coffee down the hall to grab the morning paper off Mrs. Whitcomb's desk. She brought it in to collect the coupons and read the comics and left the rest for Greg to read. With the paper in hand, it was time for his morning ritual reading headlines, finishing his coffee, and munching donuts. In Greg's opinion it was the proper breakfast for armchair champions. He laid the Fairbanks News-Miner onto his desk with front page ready to read He was about to take another bite of a donut when his phone rang. Putting his coffee down, he picked up the receiver, "Alaska Railroad, Special Agent Hansen speaking."

"How's your donut?" ARR Chief Special Agent Donald Osborn asked.

"You called before I could finish it. Between you and Mrs. Walker, I think you guys have hidden cameras on me."

"Is she still after you to date her daughter?"

"You bet! So, what's up, old great and wondrous leader?"

"We're having a meeting down here on Friday, and you need to be here. I want you to fly down on the early flight and fly back that night. Or is this the weekend you get to see John?"

"No, that's next week." Greg glanced at the calendar on the wall; the weekend he had with John was circled in red. "Maybe I can schedule lunch with him at the school or something?"

"Sorry, Greg. We'll be making it a full day with lunch brought in. Got some important people coming in, and they're covering the cost of lunch. Make your travel arrangements and call me with your arrival time. I'll pick you up at the airport. Do you have anything else to report?"

"One tool shed in the yard was broken into over the weekend. I'm waiting for an inventory to see what's missing." Greg glanced over his weekly log, specifically Friday and Saturday, while Donald waited. "Oh yeah, I issued citations to a couple trespassers on Saturday afternoon. Would've given them a warning, but they had an attitude problem. Two of those, 'This here is government land, and the government works for me' taxpayer' types."

"I love those people." Donald cleared his voice, "Greg, I know you're on salary, but you need to take the whole weekend off. Speaking of which, how much money did you lose to Farber?"

"Man, I can't have any secrets around here," Greg complained. "He got me for $20.00 on the pool table, and I had to buy two pitchers of beer. Don't worry, dad, I took a taxi home."

"I can only imagine how you feel right now. Do you want my remedy for a hangover?"

"Sure."

"Don't drink."

"Oh, a funny man," Greg said sarcastically.

"I'll see you on Friday unless something else comes up. And Greg, make sure no one walks off with any rail spikes. It makes the board members unhappy," Donald laughed as he hung up.

"Comedians!" Greg looked at the receiver and hung up. Thoughtfully, he picked up his half-eaten donut. He really liked his boss, who was more of a close friend than a supervisor. If Donald hadn't offered this job, Greg thought he would probably be working in some bush department in outer Mongolia. A place where the local men carry long-bladed filet knives and hate authority figures.

Gregg's week began with a pretty dull day, the highlight of which was another citation for trespassing on railroad property and finding an ARR crossing sign north of Nenana vandalized. He could never understand the thrill some people get in shooting up a sign. Tuesday and Wednesday were much the same, except for a minor collision between an ARR work truck and an ARR locomotive. As expected, the locomotive won the contest with only a couple chips of paint while the truck's front end was smashed in. Fortunately, the locomotive was standing still at the time of the collision. The truck driver, although somewhat rattled, was unhurt. The driver made a right turn a little too sharply, spilled his hot coffee on his lap, and the next thing he knew, the truck merged with a blue and yellow steel giant. The driver received a written reprimand in his personnel file for negligent driving. ARR insurance covered the expense of repairing the vehicle.

On Thursday, Greg chased a crazy teenager riding a Honda four-wheeler through the railroad yard and might have lost him had the kid been more experienced. The four-wheeler jumped a pile of steel rails and turned over and the teenager went flying. After ensuring he was unhurt, Greg arrested him for reckless driving and trespassing, both misdemeanor offenses. He was taken to the Alaska State Trooper's office and turned over to his father. The boy would have to appear before the state magistrate for the driving charge and a juvenile probation officer for trespassing. But by the look in the father's eyes, the worst punishment awaited him at home.

Greg didn't mind a parent giving two or three swats on the hinny if the kid was young and needed it, but he thought anything further boarded on abuse. When his son was young, they used a wooden spoon, and the most he ever got was two swats, followed by a loving embrace and some counseling. When John became a teenager, Greg learned that John hadn't minded the spoon but got bored with the counseling sessions. He got another lecture on not pushing one's father too far.

On Friday, Greg left his ARR vehicle in the Fairbanks Airport parking lot and caught the 6:30 a.m. Alaskan Airlines flight south to Anchorage.

Ted Stevens-Anchorage International Airport
May 25th, 07:34 A.M.

Clearing the security checkpoint, Greg spotted Donald standing by the yogurt counter. It wasn't hard to miss him in a crowd as he stood 6'3" and weighed over 250-pounds. He was completely bald and wore thick-framed black glasses. A retired Anchorage Police Captain, he joined the ARR in 1988 and became Chief Special Agent in 1992.

"Hey, mister, can you spare a dime for a poor unappreciated railroad employee?" Greg asked.

"Away, you vagabond!" Donald laughed and shook Greg's outreached hand. In his other hand, Donald held a strawberry-flavored frozen yogurt cone "Are the tourists showing up yet in Fairbanks?"

"They'll will soon be popping up like weeds."

"You want one?" Donald lifted his yogurt.

"Ahh-hm… no. When I eat ice cream, I want real ice cream. What's this special meeting about?"

"A security meeting I don't want to discuss with so many ears." Donald finished his cone and tossed the napkin into a plastic trashcan. "Come on, let's go." Donald led the way, with Greg trying to stay beside him and not run over anyone. The way they moved through the crowd, Greg figured Donald would have made a great fullback, clearing a hole in the line for the star tailback.

Leaving the airport in Donald's car, a white Ford Expedition, Greg repeated his question, "Okay, what is this meeting all about?"

"We got a VIP coming to Alaska in June. The gentleman wants to ride our choo-choo train from Fairbanks to Anchorage, with a one-night stopover at Denali Park." Mount McKinley, named after the former President, had been renamed Denali, an Alaskan native word meaning *The Great One*, which it was initially called.

"Who's the VIP, or can I ask?"

"Prime Minister of Canada, a Mr. Terry Haegens. He's supposed to fly into Fairbanks on June 9th and stay the night at the Princess Hotel. On the morning of June 10th, his party will board our regularly scheduled train for Anchorage with our governor and some security people along to host the entourage."

"Sounds simple enough," Greg said.

"There's just the one hitch. Haegens wants to spend the night at the park to attend a formal dinner in his honor, which means keeping the VIP car on a side track at Denali to be added to the next day's train. The next day they'll board the southbound train to continue to Anchorage, where he'll spend the night at the Hilton Hotel. The next morning the Prime Minister's flies to Seattle for a meeting with Washington's governor. Apparently, this has to do with the Canadian fishermen who blocked the M/V Columbia which resulted in the arrival of

US Coast Guard and the Canadian Navy. Local news said the Canadians were upset with Alaska fishermen going into Canadian water to fish commercially. They don't mind an American sport fishing if he has the proper license, but not commercial fishing fleets. Only so much salmon to go around, and our laws prevent them from commercial fishing in Alaska waters. So, the Prime Minister hopes to talk things out with our governor and Washington's governor, or he risks losing the next election. From what I understand, he's not too popular right now."

"When they blocked that ferry, I thought we should have sent the Marines in," Greg said.

"So did a lot of other people. But that's behind us now, and like Rodney King once said, 'Can't we all just get along.'"

"Rotten impersonation, Boss," Greg chuckled. "You'd better stay with your Laurel and Hardy routine. So, who are we meeting with?"

"Canadian Secret Service, our Secret Service, local FBI, representatives from the Anchorage and Fairbanks PD, and a couple AST guys."

"So that's how you heard about my pool shellacking; you've been talking with Farber!"

"Yeah, he's their man. He flew down last night; surprised he didn't talk to you about coming down for the meeting."

"We're like two ships passing in the night. No, that doesn't sound right. Usually, we see each other on Sunday nights unless I catch him at the PD." Greg looked at Donald, "Who else is AST sending over?" He almost hesitated to ask but needed to know.

"Two guesses, and the first one doesn't count." Donald didn't wait, "Yeah, Potter will be there. He's still commanding the SERT Team, and they'll be on standby from Fairbanks to Anchorage with a visiting head of state visiting. So, he needs to be in attendance for the meeting."

"Great!" Greg exclaimed. "Maybe I'd better check my gun at the door." He hadn't brought his pistol; the airlines wouldn't let him carry it on board, and he didn't want to risk having it stolen from his baggage. Federal law required weapons to be identified in luggage, which to Greg's meant, "Here, steal me."

FAA regulations prohibited all but federal officers from carrying weapons onboard unless municipal or state officers were escorting prisoners. Or, in the Governor's case, his assigned State Trooper. When a gun is declared in the baggage, the ticket attendant places a big red tag on it which lets baggage handlers know which suitcase to hit if they were in theft mode, and firearms were easy to sell on the streets. If undeclared, he risked getting in trouble with the FAA if his bag was checked by a sniffer dog for some reason or run through an x-ray machine. Bags were often searched with the extra security since 9-11. If the bag was somehow lost, he couldn't report the weapon lost, so he wouldn't receive reimbursement from the airlines. A no-win situation, so he left his pistol secured under the driver's seat in his locked vehicle. He knew Airport Police kept a close eye on the parking lots.

"You're both professionals, and I expect you to behave yourself in front of these Canadian hotshots and our own federal boys. Maybe later, you can sneak a punch in when this is all over?"

"No sucker punch for that boy; I want it all out in the open. We'll get some bets down and tickets sold for the big match." Greg settled back in his seat and watched cars pass by. He hated Anchorage traffic. It only worsened as the years passed because the roads simply couldn't handle the growing population. The largest city in Alaska, Anchorage, was popping at the seams with over 200,000 people. Not large by lower 48 standards, but the Anchorage bowl could handle only so many people. Alaska's population, not counting tourists, was approximately 750,000 for the nation's largest state.

"Listen, Donald, I know how to behave myself and won't embarrass you. But if that law enforcement officer pops off with something about Debbie or my son, the gloves come off. Can you believe it? The man hasn't the moral sense to marry her!"

"You're getting stirred up again, Greg. Remember, you're divorced. What happens to that woman is no longer a concern of yours. And please remember that slugging Potter could take away some of those visitation rights. Unless you want John visiting you in jail. As a reminder, it's a mandatory 30-days for a conviction of assaulting a police officer in this state… and that covers troopers too. Knowing the man, he'd probably let you hit him just to see you in jail for a month."

"Okay-okay, I'll mind my manners, just for you."

"Hey, you want to stop for a donut?" Donald asked with a chuckle.

Greg glared at him, "You know, if you weren't my friend, I just might learn to hate you."

"You do that, and Kathy will use a cast iron skillet to ka-bong your head."

Kathy and Donald had been married for 28 years, and for nearly half of that time, she had been Greg's friend, too. Kathy had thought of Debbie as a good friend until the divorce. Now, she wouldn't return Debbie's phone calls, and their paths never seemed to cross.

Donald and Kathy attended Anchorage Christian Center Church, where they met Greg and Debbie during a big statewide prayer conference. Kathy continued to pray for Debbie, but she also prayed for Greg's safety and John's ability to deal with his parent's split.

ARR Main Office, Anchorage

The ARR main conference room was warmly lit, paneled in dark cedarwood, and surrounded by framed ARR art prints. Each year another ARR poster came out, becoming collectibles for train enthusiasts. Ten were displayed in the room, with other artwork showing railroad history.

Entering the room, Greg spotted Captain Blanchard, a member of the Anchorage Police Department and a heavy-set man like Donald. He was nearly as tall as Greg but had more gray hair. Lt. Farber was beside him, talking to a distinguished looking gentleman wearing a brown tweed three-piece suit.

"Greg." Farber stepped forward and shook Greg's hand. "I know you know Captain Blanchard." Greg shook hands with Blanchard, recalling they had worked on several investigations together over the years while he was with AST. "And this is Sir Jonathan Whiteburn, Senior Agent for the Canadian Secret Service."

Greg was impressed. Sir Whiteburn had hit the headlines 14 years earlier when he took a bullet meant for the Queen of England while visiting Montreal. Once healed from his wound, the Queen happily bestowed Knighthood on him. An honor few Canadians were granted these days but endorsed by Canadian authorities.

As the years passed, Sir Whiteburn worked on several details throughout Canada. He was currently Chief of Security for Prime Minister Haegens and had chosen to attend this meeting himself. While being introduced, Greg praised Sir Whiteburn for his proficiency with a firearm while under fire. "I remember reading about the attempted assassination, and I must say, Sir Whiteburn, your aim was quite something. One bullet right through the assassin's heart, a second-round only an inch off the first."

"Please, you know as well as me, I was extremely blessed, and rather a bit lucky to have even returned fire with his bullet lodged in my chest. Those kill shots were—how should I say it best—aimed by destiny." Sir Whiteburn wiped his mustache and smiled at Greg. "I've recently learned of your own exploits, Mr. Hansen. We can agree then that we, those sworn to enforce the laws and protect the innocent, must do what we are called upon to do."

Greg was suddenly embarrassed, and his face showed it; a slight tint of red came to his cheeks as he recalled those days. As a trooper, Greg survived a shootout with three drug dealers. Working with a kind-hearted senior sergeant who was 78 days shy of a 36-year retirement, they attempted to serve a misdemeanor arrest warrant when everything fell apart. Greg's sergeant buckled when the first shot fired wounded him in the leg, and Greg dragged him out of the line of fire. One side of the patrol car was riddled by shotgun fire, and before backup arrived, Greg wounded two of the gunmen and killed the third. He was decorated for saving his sergeant's life and received a promotion.

Later in his career, while assigned as a sniper for the AST- SERT Team (Alaska's version of SWAT), Greg became one of the few SERT Team snipers to be given the *kill order.* During a bungled attempted grocery store robbery, he killed one of two men holding 17 hostages. Both men were high on drugs and about to kill a hostage when Potter gave Greg the clearance to take his shot. In 12 years with AST, Greg had made 376 arrests, investigated more than 200 injury accidents, and responded to 53 SERT Team call outs.

"Cops are cops all over the world, and the pay can never cover the willies we feel afterward," Greg said.

"Quite right, sir," Sir Whiteburn replied. The other two senior officers nodded in agreement. Sir Whiteburn patted Greg gently on the arm as a token of friendship, "I was informing Captain Blanchard and Lt. Farber that my mother was French-Canadian and my father, a full-blooded Iroquois. One can imagine the degree of differences my parents had. With my mother shouting for Quebec's independence and my father screaming for all the whites to be booted out of Canada." Whiteburn smiled as everyone chuckled politely.

While Blanchard accompanied Sir Whiteburn to the extensive coffee service, Greg gestured for Farber to come closer, "When did you know about this meeting?"

"Chief told me about it yesterday, just before he put me on the plane. Caught the 5:30 flight down and spent the night with an old academy classmate. He's retired on disability now... Quite a guy... You might know him, Jim Williams. He took a bullet to the spine and now spends most of his time in a motorized wheelchair, but he doesn't let it get him down."

"Sure, I met him some time ago before he got hit. Hard way to go out, but I'm glad to know he's making out."

"He's got a great wife and four great boys. The oldest, is ready to go through the APD Academy this summer. You should see this kid, a real bruiser. He's 6'4" and carries 250 pounds of muscle... He should make a great street cop."

"What'd Jim do before he joined APD?" Greg asked.

"Construction... He helped build the pipeline."

Lt. Farber was 36 years old and divorced. A thin man, he bordered on emaciation since his wife left him; his sport jacket hung off him as if it was three sizes too big. Greg was always after him to put on some pounds, pushing fried food and pastry at him on their Sunday nights.

"Well, next time you see Jim, give him my regards," Greg said then asked, "Have you seen the guys from AST yet?"

"By that sour look on your face, I'd say Potter was to bless us with his presence."

"Right." Greg's stomach started to rumble, and Farber heard it.

"Did you forget your morning donuts again?"

"What's with the donuts? First Donald, and now you. Does everyone know my morning routine? Is there a printed handout of my schedule?"

Greg and Farber saw another stranger enter the room and watched Donald walk up to meet him. The two men shook hands. "Agent Woods, glad you could make it," Donald said. He turned to the others, "Gentleman, allow me to introduce you to Agent Brian Woods—newly assigned to the Anchorage office of the FBI."

Woods was medium height and weight with short red hair, a thin mustache, and soft brown eyes. Not what Greg imagined as your typical FBI Field Agent. "I figured him to be more of a paper pusher," Greg said. Greg would even be more surprised to learn that Woods attended USC and, in his senior year, won a silver medal in the NCAA wrestling finals in the 148-pound weight class. He also held a 2$^{nd}$-degree black belt in Kenpo Karate. Recently assigned to the Anchorage office, Woods was a specialist on the Organized Crime Task Force and intensely disliked Mafia types.

"So, who's missing?" Blanchard asked the room.

"Captain Potter and Sgt. Olsen of AST," Donald replied. "They should be here any moment."

"How come there's no one here from our Secret Service?" Greg asked.

"Unfortunately, the man assigned this detail had to take emergency leave. I've been asked to cover for him and brief him on the details when he returns in three or four days," Woods answered.

Two Alaska State Troopers, wearing the highly identifiable sky-blue uniform, walked into the room. Both were wearing Smokey-the-Bear Stetsons which they removed immediately.

"Hey, look! The golden child has blessed us with his presence," Greg whispered to Farber, a bit too loudly.

Farber quickly elbowed him, "Shush."

Greg looked over at Donald, saw his glare, and knew he had better knock it off.

"Sorry we're late," Captain Potter apologized, ignoring Greg's icy glare.

"Captain Potter and Sgt. Olson of the Alaska State Troopers, please let me introduce you to everyone," Donald offered. Introductions were conducted with an uncomfortable air of formality. Everyone in the room, except Agent Woods and Sir Whiteburn, knew of the difficulty between Greg and Potter, including a very uneasy Sgt. Olson.

Donald bypassed introducing Greg, which made Sir Whiteburn curious. Apparently, something existed between this Captain Potter and Mr. Hansen. Being an interested law enforcement officer, he wondered what it could be.

The smile the two men exchanged was as cold as death, and no one in the room could fail to notice the icy glares they exchanged. Had it been the Old West, both men would have slapped leather by this time, and bullets would be flying.

Sir Whiteburn, a man whose employment required quick personality trait analysis and profiling, decided this might be an exciting meeting after all. These two law officers were like two cocky roosters preparing to attack. First impressions were commonly the best in dealing with people and he suspected he would not be very fond of this Captain Potter. *Yes, this could turn out to be a fascinating visit after all, and we're only finishing the introductions. I genuinely love Alaska —fresh air and rowdy buckaroos.* With an amused twinkle in his eyes, he watched the two men size each other up for the coming battle.

Greg watched Donald lead Captain Potter and Sgt. Olson over to the coffee pot, and looked up at the ceiling, wishing a personal-sized meteor would crash through the roof and drill a certain Captain Potter in the skull. It didn't happen, but he kept hoping.

5

# THE BIG MEETING... THEY CALL THIS INTELLIGENCE?

Alaska Railroad Main Office Anchorage, Alaska
May 25th, 9:26 A.M. Friday

Leaving Captain Potter's side, Sgt. Olson made his way to the giant silver coffee urn to have a few words with Greg. "How's it goin', Dead Eye?" He asked his old friend. David Olson was one of the extremely few who could call Greg by his old SERT Team nickname. He offered his hand, and the two men grinned as they shook hands. Olson's behavior toward Greg didn't make Captain Potter happy, but Olson could care less, he didn't like the captain, he just had to work for him.

Turning his back to Potter, Greg placed his hand on Olson's shoulder and answered his old compadre, "Not too bad, Beer Gut." Olson's SERT Team moniker was due to his fondness for two bottles of beer after every training exercise or call-out. He told everyone it steadied his nerves and settled the stomach acids down.

"How's the wife, and that older boy of yours doing? The last time I saw him, he was running the football for Diamond High and scored two touchdowns that day, as I remember."

"I'll tell you, partner, I'm so proud I'm about to burst at the seams. We just received the news last week that he's been accepted to the Air Force Academy."

"Wow!" Greg exclaimed. "I'm happy for you and Betty." Greg patted Olson on the shoulder and then withdrew his hand to pour some liquid non-dairy creamer into his coffee. "I heard he made All-State too."

"He did okay, but even more important, Joshua's finishing the year with a 4.0 grade average, and that's where it counts." Olson accepted the sugar container from Greg and poured some into his coffee, and the two friends toasted Olson's son. "All that money we put aside for his college fund can now go toward his future."

Olson was a six year member of the SERT Team when Greg came aboard, and the two of them had formed a quick friendship. Besides working SERT, Olson, who rigidly maintained his physical conditioning with long-distance running, was assigned to Major Crimes. Only 14 months shy of his 20-year retirement, he took a brief moment to share his plans to buy a Bed & Breakfast down on the Kenai Peninsula. "I'll let Betty manage the guests, clean the place and cook; I'll be down on the river catching those big ones."

"Right, buddy." Greg shook his head. "If I know Betty, you'll be on laundry detail, followed by KP and lugging suitcases."

"You're probably right," Olson agreed. "Hey, anytime you need a get-a-way, you've always got a place with us."

"Thanks, I'll probably take you up on it. I'll need a place to lay low after I rap your boss one in the chops."

"If we can do it in the dark away from witnesses, I'll hold him for you," Olson smiled as he looked over Greg's shoulder and saw Potter glaring at him.

"That guy is something else. How he made captain is anyone's guess. He's not too well-liked, I can tell you that. I know of three complaints against him to the union by troopers who've worked for him. One of them by a member of the team… a new guy you wouldn't know. My upcoming retirement is the only reason I'm still on the team."

"Yeah, don't make any waves. Just get that pension and walk away, my friend," Greg said.

"Potter sure doesn't make it easy. Always passing the blame on to someone else when it goes wrong and taking all the credit when something goes right. His attitude has really caused problems in our relationship with APD's team. If that man ever calls for backup, I wouldn't be surprised if all the AST and APD radios suddenly went on the blink."

"Keep your temper under control, Beer Gut. Be a yes-man until it's over. You've got Betty and Joshua to think about. Potter isn't worth it," Greg said. He turned to give Potter a smile of mockery before turning back to his friend to whisper, "Keep saying to yourself, 'I gotta take my pension and walk away'. I wouldn't want to face your wife if you screwed your dreams up by knocking Potter's block off. She'd kill you."

"Oh, how right you are!" Olson agreed.

Donald Osborn addressed the room asking everyone to find a chair around an enormous conference table. "I think we'd better begin, or the day will get away from us. Nothing like getting a bunch of old cops together, telling war stories, and complaining about our benevolent court system. Not to mention our friends, the lawyers." He glanced around the table as everyone sat down. "I won't waste time with a formal welcome. We're too small of a group for that, and no more lawyer jokes." That got a round of polite chuckles because all cops loved lawyer jokes. "I think the best way to begin this morning's session is to let Sir Whiteburn advise us of his needs."

Greg's boss couldn't help but notice that Greg and Potter were seated as far away from each other as possible, which caused him a sigh of relief. When he heard that Potter would be here, he initially considered not inviting Greg but reconsidered. Greg was the Fairbanks Special Agent and needed to be here. Donald just hoped for the best.

Sir Whiteburn rose to his feet, opened a leather binder, and spread it before him. "Thank you for having me, Chief Osborn. I truly enjoy coming to Alaska and working with the federal, state, and municipal agencies." Sir Whiteburn looked out the window with a view of the Chugach Mountain Range. "Ahhh, Alaska—A living reminder of what Canada used to be before all the cities appeared, and my people outgrew the land along our eastern shores. Your smaller communities are an example of the pioneer spirit that civilized our Northern Hemisphere. I bow to your gallant nature for standing up to nature's hardships. Today, only in Canada's outer regions do we share in this grand adventure as my beloved Eastern Canada has become much like what you like to refer to as the Lower 48, a giant metropolis. Cities merge, and crime runs rampant. As in America, many criminals in Canada only receive a slap on the wrist and possibly a stint of probation because our prisons are full." Sir White-burn stopped to take a sip of coffee. "Well, enough of that. I apologize for an old man's mutterings. We're here to discuss my Prime Minister's meeting with your Governor Hughes." He cleared his throat and smiled.

"My primary team, consisting of four agents and myself, will arrive with the Prime Minister in his airplane; a DC-10 adorned in our country's glorious colors. Unlike your Air Force One, other Canadian dignitaries use it for international travel. In-country, specifically on the east coast, the Prime Minister is flown around in a much smaller aircraft or a military helicopter. Three days before our arrival, an advance team of three agents from my staff will arrive in Fairbanks to recon the airport, the city, and your railroad station. The advance team will meet with your Fairbanks people to make any suggestions. They'll leave by train for the park the next day in order to conduct a similar recon of the park and, eventually, locations in Anchorage. I'm relying on your various departments to keep my advance team informed with up-to-date intelligence on local problems, crazies, and any hate groups that may create issues. We do not expect any protests, but in any event, we'll need you to provide crowd control and outer security at the hotels, train stations, and the park. My main team will always stay at the Prime Minister's side, so personal bodyguards will not be necessary." Sir Whiteburn stopped briefly to take another sip of coffee. We're hoping there won't be any demonstrations about what happened in Prince Rupert with the Canadian fishermen. For this, I do apologize. I'm glad it ended peacefully. Mr. Osborn, could you have someone close those curtains? The glare is quite bright?"

Donald got to his feet and walked to the far wall where he closed the drapes and then returned to his seat.

"Thank you," Sir Whiteburn said. "My main concern is using the regular train, but Prime Minister Haegens insisted on not creating any ripples with your thriving tourist business. I'd like to request that bomb dogs be provided in Fairbanks, at the park, and in Anchorage. They should give the train a good going over and a walk through of both stations and the hotels. With so many tourists coming and going in all directions, I don't see how we can use metal detectors at the train depots and not hinder travel. The dogs will have to do— and our own observational skills. Your Alaska Railroad has kindly offered us the use of a private train car for Prime Minister Haegens and Governor Hughes, making these security arrangements somewhat easier to deal with." Checking over his notes, Sir Whiteburn decided he was ready for the first round of questions. "Questions?"

Captain Potter quickly raised his hand, "Where would you prefer to have our SERT Team on standby while the VIPs are in the park? This is federal land, and we probably shouldn't be in view with all the tourists and campers." Potter hesitated when he saw the curious look on Sir Whiteburn's face. He wasn't sure if Sir Whiteburn fully understood the AST SERT Teams' operations. "Sir, unlike SWAT units in the Lower 48, SERT members are assigned normal trooper duties and respond to callouts as needed. However, for this event, my men will be on stand-by in either Anchorage or Fairbanks, depending on our dignitaries' location. My only concern was the overnight stay at the park. The closest trooper station is Healy, north of the park, and a small office in Cantwell, south of the park. These smaller posts are manned by only one trooper."

"Captain, where are these team members assigned currently?" Sir Whiteburn asked.

"I have team members in Wasilla, Palmer, Fairbanks, the Kenai Peninsula, Southeast Alaska and right here in Anchorage. I'll have to get the Colonel to authorize extra overtime to pull troopers in from days off to cover for my men. I don't foresee a problem there; we've done this before for similar circumstances."

"I would, of course, prefer a response time of 30 minutes or less," Sir Whiteburn said.

Sgt. Olson responded a bit too quickly, "No way... Sir."

Sir Whiteburn appeared somewhat unsettled, "Yes, I understand you have some 350 miles of train track to cover. Can you offer some suggestions, please?"

"I apologize for my sergeant's outburst," Potter glared at Olson, "but he is correct. I can have my team standing by in Fairbanks while the train travels to the park and then fly them south to Healy or Cantwell for the night. Once the train leaves the park, I can hold at one of those locations until moving to Wasilla. Still, depending on weather conditions and where an emergency might occur, it could take us as much as one to three hours to respond by helicopter - if a full deployment is called for. We only have one Bell Helicopter, and this could involve four trips. Our bird only carries four team members with their equipment, plus the pilot. We plan on running a few training exercises for possible problems that could develop at the park or on the train. It might surprise you, Sir Whiteburn, but we've never actually had a train robbery in Alaska. This experience will be something new in our training. Most visiting VIP's fly into the state and fly back out when their visit is over."

"Why not split your response team in half?" Agent Woods asked.

Before Potter could respond, Captain Blanchard spoke up, "The AST SERT Team isn't trained that way, Agent Woods. Unlike regular SWAT Teams, such as the one APD maintains, which can split into two or three squads if required, I've noticed Captain Potter prefers to keep his team together under his direct leadership." Captain Blanchard had scored a direct hit against Potter, adding insult to injury with one of his legendary smirks, which annoyed Captain Potter.

Greg broke into a big smile, and Sir Whiteburn had to bite his lip to keep from grinning when he realized what was happening. There was a running competition between Anchorage Police SWAT and the Alaska State Trooper's SERT. To most everyone's amusement, Sir Whiteburn saw it showing its ugly face at this meeting.

Olson sat with a blank expression on his face. In fact, he was in total agreement with Blanchard, but Potter was the one who commanded SERT.

Blanchard supervised the Anchorage PD Special Weapons and Tactical Team and wanted it plainly known that APD SWAT would not be placed under SERT Team leadership while the Prime Minister was in Anchorage. He sincerely doubted his men and ladies would go for it, not without skinning their dear Captain alive and roasting him in oil first.

"No, we will not be split." Potter answered coldly.

"Sir Whiteburn, the Anchorage Police Department will have our own tactical team on 24 hours standby once you enter our area of influence," Blanchard picked up his coffee cup and hid a big smile behind it.

"I do appreciate your offer, but at the moment, my primary concern is this 300 or so miles of open country between Fairbanks and Anchorage," Sir Whiteburn said. "I mean no disrespect to your fine department, Captain; I'm sure your team will do a commendable job once we arrive in Anchorage."

"Thank you, Sir," Blanchard answered.

Donald responded to Whiteburn's concerns, "Sir Whiteburn, I can have high rail vehicles on stand-by in Healy, Cantwell, and north of Wasilla to transport Captain Potter's team into areas inaccessible by helicopter. There are several steep canyons where a helicopter couldn't deliver a team or even provide a safe location to repel from. Depending on the weather, some of the updrafts in our narrow canyons could prove dangerous to anyone attempting to repel from a helicopter."

"I'm not sure I understand what a high rail vehicle is," Sir Whiteburn said.

"It's a normal four-wheel drive passenger truck or utility vehicle equipped with regular tires and rail wheels which allows it to drive on railroad tracks. When the rail wheels are lowered a vehicle can safely travel up to 50 miles an hour, and a bit more if needed." Donald smiled at Greg. They had responded to a gun call near a trapper's cabin, where a Trooper requested back-up. They had taken Donald's Expedition up to 75 mph before chickening out and slowing down. The vehicle was getting shaky, and they thought it was about to jump the track. By the time they arrived, the intoxicated trapper was already in custody.

"Sounds interesting. What about other helicopters?" Sir Whiteburn asked.

"If you request it, we can borrow another helicopter. One helicopter can escort the train, refuel at the park and even Talkeetna if needed. It'll carry four armed men, plus the pilot. Our other helicopter must be on stand-by for a second response to the train or other emergencies that might occur throughout the interior. We have another helicopter in Juneau to handle Southeast Alaska." Captain Potter wrote a couple of notes on the sheet of paper before him.

"Can you ask the military for additional helicopters if the need arises?" Sir Whiteburn asked.

"Of course, Sir," Potter said. "If an emergency arises, we could have the Alaska Army National Guard provide us with whatever we need." Potter didn't say that he would hate to ask such a thing from the Guard because he intensely disliked working with the military.

"Unless the risk factor changes, I see no reason a helicopter would be needed to escort the train. We'll have security personnel on the train, of course. I believe having a helicopter force on standby should be enough. There'll be five of us, one State Trooper with your governor, and at least three federal agents of your own aboard the train. That would be a sizable force if a single fanatic attempted to kill either my Prime Minister or your Governor."

"Sir Whiteburn, speaking about fanatics, how soon will you be able to provide us with the names and photos of parties you're concerned about? We'll need the names and photos of your traveling team and that advance party." Agent Wood asked.

"I have them all on a computer and should be able to provide them before I leave you today. If there are any changes, you will be notified immediately," Sir Whiteburn replied.

"How many police officers and troopers will you require in Fairbanks… and, I guess, Anchorage too?" Lt. Farber asked.

"I usually request an eight-man detail around the clock for such short visits at the train terminal for crowd control, unless you wish to add to that number, of course. I would prefer four officers on foot inside the hotel lobby at the park and a roving patrol outside, with two extra officers at the Prime Minister's door at all times. All patrols will be linked with my people by radio, and we'll have a command post set up in the adjacent hotel room. The roving patrol and lobby teams can handle relief for meals and breaks as needed. If possible, we'd prefer a two-man vehicle patrol on the property, who will remain in constant sight of the hotel to provide advance notice if protests or anything else begins to take place outside. As per our security procedures, we'll request the Prime Minister be placed on an upper level in an inside room to prevent snipers from ruining our safety record for keeping our dignitaries alive."

"The park, being federal property, will have Park Rangers on hand to assist with security during the Prime Minister's stay. They are law enforcement qualified and will work hand-in-hand with my detail if we are called to respond. I respectfully ask that a senior Ranger be placed in charge of that detail to ensure things run smoothly," Captain Potter said.

Agent Wood said, "I had hoped to have a representative from the park service in attendance, but they were unable to make it. I promised to provide them with notes from the meeting."

Sir Whiteburn nodded in agreement, "We'll only be in your two cities for a short time; however, I should warn you that our Prime Minister likes to shop—he is an avid art collector. This means an escort and a mobile patrol will be needed in Fairbanks and Anchorage. When we leave the hotel, the two uniformed officers or troopers at the Prime Minister's suite will remain in position. The four foot officers will provide crowd control, with two in front of our party and two behind. I must warn you our Prime Minister is a bit of a walker and often likes to make contact with the public. So, this will involve the Fairbanks Police and the Anchorage Police Departments."

"How do you feel about private security assisting us?" Agent Woods asked.

"I'd prefer sworn officers. Private security guards can be replaced by fanatics too easily. Several assassinations around the world have been carried out by such so-called security personnel."

Agent Wood said, "I can have seven FBI agents inside the park hotel, backed up by Park Rangers. Three of our agents will work undercover as either busboys or kitchen staff. We've been training and arming some of our rangers for several years to handle law enforcement needs, and they've become quite proficient in their duties."

"That would be quite satisfactory, Agent Woods," Sir Whiteburn replied. "Again, I believe that eight rangers would be satisfactory or less if their positions are filled by tactical attired FBI agents. I want to make sure my people can quickly identify the right people in the event any shooting erupts."

Captain Potter replied "I can have whatever troopers you may need brought in from detachments to the south or from Fairbanks. I recommend the vehicle patrol be a two-man marked State Trooper unit that works in tandem with park personnel."

Agent Woods understood Potter's desire to have his Troopers visible for this visit and accepted his offer, "That would be fine. You and I can work that out later, along with the Secret Service."

Potter nodded and made a note of it. Olson sighed and wondered how many exercises his dear captain would want to run before the Prime Minister's visit?"

Sir Whiteburn looked down at his papers, "Gentlemen, as it stands right now, we're looking at Prime Minister Haegens arriving in Fairbanks on June 9th and spending one night at the Princess Hotel near the airport. Security will be handled by Secret Service, Alaska State Troopers, and the Fairbanks Police Department. We'll have an early morning breakfast with Governor Hughes in the hotel dining room. I believe Governor Hughes is flying in from Juneau and staying the night with family?"

"Yes, Sir," Donald replied. "Governor Hughes is from Fairbanks."

"Thank you," Sir Whiteburn replied. "The two parties will convoy, escorted by Fairbanks Police... two two-man marked units should be adequate: one in front and one behind. The VIP party will immediately board the special train car for the trip to Denali Park. Fairbanks Police, Alaska State Troopers, Secret Service, and Alaska Railroad security will handle this area. The train will be inspected earlier by my security people, accompanied by a railroad Special Agent." Sir Whiteburn looked up from his notes and smiled at Greg. "I understand Alaska natives named your largest mountain Denali, meaning the Great One. I prefer that name myself; it has a sound of majesty to it. I've seen several photos of it, but this will be my first time to actually see it." Sir Whiteburn glanced at his notes, "I would prefer at least two troopers onboard the train, but not in our VIP car. Only one trooper accompanying the Governor will be there. Our team and a US Secret Service agent or FBI will be aboard for the two day ride to Anchorage. I requested two uniformed troopers to conduct a continual walk-through while the train was moving. They'll be our advanced eyes and ears for any possible problems such as radicals or intoxicated individuals.

At the park, a formal dinner will be held in a private hotel dining room followed by private time for our two politicians to talk from approximately 9 p.m. until they're ready to break. They'll spend the night in personal suites. These rooms will, of course, be well-guarded and, if possible, located on each side of the shared command post.

The following day, June 11th, the party will have a quick breakfast and take a brief tour of the park in a convoy escorted by US park rangers," he pointed to Agent Woods and reminded him of his needed to verify things with the National Park Service.

"Afterward, the VIPs will board the special train car for the journey to Anchorage. At the train depot there, the two-men and their entourage will hold a photo op with news services watched over by the Anchorage Police Department, Alaska State Troopers, Secret Service, FBI, and our host, the Alaska Railroad." Sir Whiteburn smiled at Donald, "Thank you, sir."

Donald nodded and grinned at Greg, who only shook his head. *Do you have any idea what a storm will hit you if the Governor or the Prime Minister gets shot on our property?*

Sir Whiteburn continued, "My Prime Minister will spend some time shopping in downtown Anchorage, for which he will need uniformed officers on foot and the two-man vehicle patrol. These officers might be called upon to carry packages back to the hotel." Sir Whiteburn looked at Blanchard, expecting a complaint, but the APD captain only nodded. "I understand officers do not enjoy being delivery boys, but this might happen in order to prevent someone from placing a bomb in these packages. I'll attempt to have our Prime Minister arrange to have any large packages shipped home by mail.

In Anchorage we'll be at the Hilton Hotel where he'll need the same security arrangements as in Fairbanks and the park. I'll let you men work these out amongst you. We'll leave the next day by government aircraft for the flight to Seattle. When I leave here, I'll be going to Seattle to go over these same security plans with their law enforcement personnel." Sir Whiteburn took a sip from his coffee cup. It was growing cold; he checked his watch. "A formal itinerary will be provided to your agencies 48 hours before the Prime Minister arrives in Fairbanks. A news release of his official visit will be provided 24 hours before he leaves for Alaska." Sir Whiteburn glanced around the room again. "Questions?"

"Will you require security for the aircraft?" Captain Potter asked.

"Our aircraft carries a security force of six highly trained Canadian air police; elite young men supervised by a young lieutenant who seems to value the aircraft as his own. They'll work with your airport police to safeguard the aircraft in Fairbanks and Anchorage. Is this satisfactory?"

"We'll need to give airport police advance warning, as arrangements will have to be made at both airports. With your permission, I can handle that when this meeting is over and get back to you if there are any problems," Captain Potter said.

That sounds fine, Captain... I was advised that the State of Alaska would provide limo service for the Prime Minister and two rental cars for our two teams while in Fairbanks and Anchorage. This is above the security vehicle required for the PM's shopping spree. Do you foresee any problems there?" Sir Whiteburn looked over the men in attendance to see who might reply.

Donald raised his hand up, "The limo and rental cars will be arranged through the Governor's Office, but I'll verify it before you leave here today."

"What about local news coverage?" Captain Blanchard asked, typing notes into a small laptop computer.

Sir Whiteburn looked to his note sheets, "Ah-h yes, I guess I should go into further detail. On the day Prime Minister Haegens leaves for Fairbanks, a story will be provided to news services, explaining the reason behind the State visit which concerns the recent ferry boat incident and Canada's concern over fishing issues." Sir Whiteburn put his notes down and looked around the table. "My main concern, and I believe you gentlemen will agree my fear is justified, is the lone assassin moving through the crowd." Sir Whiteburn stood up and made his way over to the coffee urn. "Once the train is moving, I do not foresee a problem. It is the ground time that has me wary."

"Between all of our law enforcement agencies, military K-9, and AST, we'll have bomb dogs on hand. K-9 units loaned from the US Army or Air Force will search the train, the luggage, and the Prime Minister's vehicles and hotel rooms. His rooms will be x-rayed by your own people. I'm sure that between us, we'll have security on him so thick—well, he'll think we're an old comfortable coat he's wearing. No one will get close to the man without us knowing about it." Captain Potter promised.

"Same goes in Anchorage, Sir Whiteburn. Your man will be safe here. We haven't lost a VIP yet," Captain Blanchard said with pride.

"Well, there was that close call at the Fairbanks Airport when the Pope visited President Reagan," Agent Wood said. "Some guy tried to pose as a Secret Service agent but was picked up before he could endanger the VIPs."

"I'd forgotten about that one," Sir Whiteburn said. "Still, Alaska has an excellent record, and your law enforcement agencies are well thought of. If I recall, the news service never suspected a thing when the suspect was taken into custody without incident. Your men did their job, and that's what's important. I believe this official visit will go off without a hitch, gentlemen. Now I suggest we take a break for lunch. I know it's a bit early for you, but I am still on Ottawa time." Everyone nodded in agreement.

"Gentlemen, I've gone out on the limb and vouched for the great halibut and crab served at the Sourdough Inn. I suggest we break up and meet back down there for a business lunch in, say... 30 minutes," Donald said and waited for a response.

"Who's paying?" Sgt. Olson asked, and everyone laughed.

"I've been informed the Secret Service will be handling the bill, but he's not here, which makes me suspicious. So, I guess it falls to the Alaska Railroad to cover the lunch expense, especially since I'm naming the place to eat." Donald looked over at Greg, raising an eyebrow and glaring glance that said, *No problems at lunch, right?*

Greg nodded that he understood and would behave himself. He mouthed the words, "Yes, dad," and put his hands together as if praying, which Donald decided to ignore. Greg hoped he'd have time to give his son a call, but John was at school, and by the time this daylong meeting broke up, he'd be rushing to catch his evening flight. *Oh well, I'll see him next weekend. Besides, after this session with Potter around, I'd be in a poor mood to hang out with him.* Greg walked down the hall, glad to see that Potter was already out of the building. He wasn't sure how he would handle a face-to-face encounter with the illustrious Captain Potter, especially with so many witnesses.

FLQ Safe House, Toronto
May 25th, 2:16 P.M.

On the opposite side of North America, a very different sort of meeting was in session which also concerned Prime Minister Haegens' visit to Alaska. FLQ members discussed travel arrangements for their own journey to Alaska. To maintain security and prevent one group from knowing what the other was doing, Hugo and Munroe ran the individual groups through their paces in Munroe's bedroom. If one team was picked up by the authorities, those members wouldn't be able to provide information about the other teams.

Shawn was on the hot seat, Munroe standing directly before him. "All right let's see if you remember everything," Munroe said with a two-hand gesture at Shawn, "C'mon, fire away; repeat your instructions."

Shawn hesitated briefly, "At 6 p.m., Group one—Gregory, Sheri, and I—leave here and proceed to the nearby bus stop. We catch the 6: 12 p.m. downtown bus. At the bus station, we transfer to the airport shuttle. Using provided cash, passports, and ID, we purchase tickets to fly to Chicago on British Airlines, flight number 83 which leaves Toronto at 8:58 p.m. and arrives in Chicago at 10:40 p.m." Shawn hesitated again as Munroe stood squarely in front of him, hands on his waist, waiting for the rest. "We spend the night in a downtown Holiday Inn, pay with cash then travel by Greyhound Bus to Seattle, a two-day trip. We spend the night at the Red Lion Inn near the airport, again paying cash. Next morning, we fly out on Alaska Airlines, flight number 91 to Fairbanks." Shawn sighed nervously. "In Fairbanks, we rent a full-size car, using one of our credit cards, and get a room at the airport Best Western Motel and wait there until contacted by you or Hugo. If anything happens to you, or we hear nothing after five days, we separate and vanish."

Shawn stared at Munroe, who handed him a beer, "Very good. Do you have everything?"

"Hugo supplied us with documents and IDs to match passports. We each carry an American Express Card, a VISA Gold Card, and $1,000 in cash. As the team leader, I carry an additional $3,000 for extra expenses - all in American currency."

Sheri, who hated long road trips, asked, "Why can't we just fly all the way?"

"Claudia's mistake has the cops combing the streets, looking for her fellow FLQ members. Lucky for us, our neighbors only saw her in the blonde wig when she left the house and didn't recognize her photo on TV. But she made one costly mistake, and one of you may make another. With these plans, we'll not make it easy for them to follow us, even if they eventually trace any of us to this house," Munroe answered. Lifting his bottle of beer to his mouth, he took another swig.

Hugo stepped forward to ensure everyone could hear him, "Remember, no weapons. Not even a knife. If you have a problem, you have phone number to call."

Munroe interjected, "Advise the answering party of your group number, your current location and call back number. Do not tell the answering party your problem; they are simply a security service that is employed by our financiers, and they do not have the need to know." Munroe walked over to where Hugo was standing, "Hugo or I will check in with the service every 12 hours and get back to you immediately. Any questions?" There were none, so Munroe dismissed them and waited for the next group to file in. Jean-Luc led the other two in and waited. Munroe watched Hugo close the door, "Your turn; repeat your instructions correctly and win a beer."

"I lead Group two—Thomas, Paul, and I. We leave at 6:20 p.m., walk north for one-half mile and catch a city bus to a transfer point where we can board the airport shuttle. If we see another team, we ignore them." Jean-Luc glanced at his notes and received a dirty look from Munroe.

"You've got to have this memorized, Idiot. No notes!" Munroe stepped forward and ripped the paper from Jean-Luc's hand.

"Sorry." Jean-Luc mumbled a word of profanity and continued, "We catch Canadian Airlines flight number 85 at 9:35 p.m. to Whitehorse, Yukon. Arrive early in the morning and rent a large 4x4, preferably a newer model suburban. If unable to rent one, I call in and wait for further instructions. If we have a vehicle, we drive to Fairbanks, using our passports to enter Alaska." Jean-Luc stopped to take a breath. "I rent a three-bedroom furnished apartment for three months at a place called... called Sophia's Station. Reservations have already been made under my false identity and secured by credit card. If questioned, we're college students visiting Alaska to study the Eskimo people. Hugo supplied us with needed papers, credit cards, and $8,000 in cash. We're to stock the apartment with enough food for the entire team for two weeks." Jean-Luc thought he was finished and began to sit down, a light sweat appearing on his brow.

"Stay standing," Munroe ordered. "Your group is to recon Fairbanks while waiting for Group One to arrive. Call that phone number once you have the apartment, and Hugo or I will contact you. I don't want them meeting at the hotel if you've been arrested. I don't want them walking into a trap. They'll not know where you are until after I've heard from you and Hugo, or I arrange a meeting time and location. Go light on the booze and, NO DRUGS!" Munroe gave everyone in the room a stern look except for Hugo. "During this phase of the operation, you get drunk or stoned, and you're dead. If you get arrested, you know nothing. Basically, consider this venture as a soldier entering enemy held territory." Munroe gestured at Hugo to continue the briefing.

"Once you join up, Jean-Luc will be the leader until Munroe and I arrive. Remember, you're all college students in town for Anthropology Studies. Ask a lot of questions and take some notes. Buy a couple cameras and take a lot of photographs. Questions?" There were none.

Munroe was in a foul mood, and no one felt like dealing with his temper. He was tired of Hugo's arrogance, squinty eyes, and general overbearing presence. But he was also afraid of the man and extremely curious about what Dr. Quison had talked with him about in private. He was suspicious of Hugo, wondering if he had been ordered to silence him permanently when the operation was over.

Group two filed out with beers in hand, and a few moments later, Group three filed in.

"All right, Gordi, you're on," Munroe plopped down on the bed beside Janene, who twitched from fright when Munroe suddenly dropped beside her.

"Group three is Michael, Louis, and me. We leave the house at 7:00 p.m., walk to the 7-11 and call a taxi to take us within a half-mile of the bus station and walk the rest of the way, take a bus to Ottawa, and catch an early morning flight to New York. We stay at the Morningside Inn on the west side and after 24 hours, return to the airport and fly to Seattle on American Airlines flight number 57. Following a three-hour layover, we fly to Anchorage on Alaska Airlines flight number 89. I'll use the credit cards Hugo gave me to pay for airline tickets and hotels. If needed, I use the cash I was provided. We each carry $1,000 in cash, and I have an extra $5,000 for additional expenses. We act like tourists, purchase cameras in New York and take lots of photographs. In Anchorage, we spend one night at a hotel of our choosing, calling our provided phone number to report our location. If everything is okay, we take the train to Denali National Park the next morning. We recon the train and look for a suitable location to stop it between Talkeetna and Cantwell—preferably a deep canyon with steep walls to prevent helicopter rescue."

"What else?" Hugo asked.

"Observe train security and photograph all bridges and crossings, record the locations and any suggestions we might have into the mini-tape recorder you provided."

"Good, add this to your list." Steve waited as Gordi mentally prepared himself for the additional information. "In Anchorage, pick up enough camping and rain gear for the three of you. Instead of coming to Fairbanks immediately, spend three nights back packing south of the park. Follow the tracks, I want detailed maps and photographs showing the best possible place in your view to stop the train and show a minimum of three escape routes from that location. Once that is completed, get back on the train or walk to the highway and hitch-hike to Fairbanks. I've heard hitch-hiking is real popular in Alaska. You must arrive by June 6th, find a hotel room and call that phone number. I'll contact you within 12 hours about where you're to go next. Any questions?"

Gordi stood up, a nearly empty Pepsi bottle in his hand, "Steve, I've been to Fairbanks before, a long time ago. This puts us there right in the heart of tourist season. What if we can't get into those hotels, you've told us to go to?"

"And what about our weapons?" Michael asked.

"First off, all weapons will be with Group four, so quit worrying. If you find a hotel without a vacancy, then find another and call that phone number. I'll call you to verify your new location. Remember, you're college kids on summer break, so act like it. Take lots of pictures in front of stupid signs. You'll need a couple tents for back packing. Make them large enough for four. The camping gear will be needed later on."

"All right," Gordi said and sat back down.

"Go get something to eat," Munroe ordered. Hugo handed beers to Group three as they filed out. "Did we forget anything?" He asked Hugo, then remembered, "Other than tents, Group one and two should purchase camping gear in Fairbanks, probably at different stores."

Hugo summoned the other two team leaders in one at a time, and Munroe advised them of the need for camping equipment, "Camping gear should consist of green rain gear for each person; one rain proof backpack per person with a built-in frame; a good sleeping bag rated to minus 20 degrees, a sleeping pad and whatever else you feel you'll need in the woods. You'll also need to buy a lot of mosquito repellant."

"Everything all green or black, no bright colors," Hugo added.

"No, no bright colors," Munroe repeated.

"What about Group four?" Gordi asked.

"Group four comprises Hugo, Lesli, Janene, and me. We travel to Alaska as honeymooners—that's all you need to know." This got a laugh.

"The rest you will learn when Hugo and I meet you in Fairbanks. You'll learn the meeting location by phone the night before. Remember to keep your phones charged. Otherwise, you may not know where to meet us, which means you'll not share the rewards." Munroe checked his watch and decided it was time to eat. He reached down, grabbed Janene's wrist, and pulled her to her feet. "Let's eat!"

Hugo and Munroe had spent several hours talking about transportation to Alaska. They finally decided to fly to Whitehorse from Toronto and rent two large RVs in Whitehorse. They'd call ahead to reserve them using one of Sir Albert Bruisse's umbrella businesses not linked to his name. They'd drive the RVs to a rented warehouse owned by Bruisse where employees would install a second fuel tank on each RV large enough to conceal weapons, ammo, and explosives needed for the operation. They would alter the storage compartments under the RV's queen-size bed. Hugo had used his sources to ship large wooden crates to an associate's business address outside Whitehorse. The wooden crates contained weapons he had ordered from an underground source he had used in the past. Among the weapons would be Stinger missile devices and the particular rockets he wanted for this venture. Using funds provided by Dr. Quison, Hugo had paid $36,000 for the Stingers and $5,000 to have them delivered to Whitehorse. The Stingers were purchased from a North Dakota Militia Group, which had obtained them from an Army National Guard Armory two years prior. A Guardsmen was paid $4,000 a piece when he and a buddy removed them from an ammo bunker. Records were altered to change the number of stored Stingers to cover the theft.

"Steve, you're asking us to cover a lot of ground in three days," Gordi whispered as he walked up to Munroe in the kitchen. Janene stood beside her boyfriend as she slapped Mayo on a piece of bread.

Moving close to Gordi's ear, Munroe whispered, "Make sure you're at least 20 miles from Cantwell; rent a car if you need. But I need those woods covered, not the road. I prefer the Cantwell side over Talkeetna. According to the map, Cantwell is smaller and farther from Anchorage. That means farther from cops."

Paul walked up to Munroe, "What happens after we hit the train? They'll have cops all over us within two hours." Paul, one of the older members, was a former sergeant in the Canadian Army. He was court-martialed, dishonorably discharged and jailed for two years for striking an officer, a man who addressed Paul's girlfriend profanely during a social event. His bitterness toward the Canadian government increased when he received a "Dear John" letter in jail and suffered physical abuse at the hands of the guards.

"Phase one is getting to Fairbanks without being followed. We'll go over final details for phase two when we meet there." Munroe said. Paul accepted it with a nod and walked away.

Janene placed two pieces of sliced ham on the bread, added some mustard and another piece of bread, and handed it to Munroe. He accepted it without saying thanks and took a large bite.

After going over the plans with each team, Munroe and Hugo were satisfied the three teams knew their instructions. "Okay, get your gear ready and leave the house on schedule. The only way you'll get a share of the money is to complete this operation with a satisfactory performance. Anything less means we failed and probably head for a jail cell… or we're dead."

Janene added her two-cents worth, "Just think, people, in two weeks, we could be lounging on some faraway beach, basking in the sun and counting our money."

The group ignored her. They were weary of her antics and drug use. When the groups left, Hugo and Lesli remained sitting on the couch in the living room. Leslie turned the television off, "Can we make that long drive in such a short time?"

"We drive all night, all day, and switch drivers." He stood up, walked over to the dining room table, and gathered up all his road maps and documents before walking downstairs to the basement. Hugo needed time to record his inventory and see what else he might need. Although he had numerous connections in Canada and a few in the Lower 48, he had none in Alaska. This was one place he'd never visited. He needed to study the train book Lesli picked up for him from the library, a book on railroad cars. This job required him to know the weight, length, and other particulars about locomotives used in Alaska. He needed to know how much explosive he would need to reduce a train car to a pile of splinters if required. Another stumbling block was finding a way to stop a locomotive without the engineer sending out a cry of alarm. This would bring the authorities too quickly. He hadn't worked out this problem yet, but he was confident the operation would be a success. There was too much money at stake to think otherwise.

There was the threat of helicopters, as Hugo knew Alaskan authorities had access to them. It was the reason he had requested the Stingers.

6

# LIFE'S LITTLE TWISTS

Main Concourse Ted Stevens-Anchorage International Airport
May 25th, 6:28 p.m.

Using a pay phone on the main concourse was somewhat noisy, but Greg wanted to make another try at reaching his son. He hoped to talk with him before he caught his one-hour flight back to Fairbanks. Potter would make sure Debbie knew about Greg being in town, and John might hear. He needed to let his son understand why he had not been able to see him. No one answered the last time he called, but this time the phone was picked up on the third ring, "Hello," a female voice answered, and Greg recognized Debbie's voice.

"It's me, Greg; I'm in town and thought I could talk with John before I left… let him know why I didn't get a chance to see him today. It was a one-day trip for work." Hearing her voice brought on a sudden surge of emotion and a strange tightness in his throat. As much as he hated to admit it, he was still in love with her, which infuriated him. *Why can't I keep on hating her?*

"Yes, I heard you were in town. You might have called earlier, Greg. John is having dinner at a friend's house, and then they're going to a movie."

"On a school night?" Greg asked. His voice sounded a little harsher than he intended it to.

"It's a Disney movie, Greg, and they're going with the other kid's parents. Besides, this isn't your weekend anyway." Debbie sounded tired, "I'll tell him you called when he gets home tonight and explain why you were in town. Anything else, Greg?"

Greg thought for a moment; he had so much he wanted to say, but the divorce made things so final. Before he realized it, "I miss you," escaped his lips. Before she could reply, he angrily slammed the phone receiver down, clenched his eyes shut, and shook his head. *I cannot believe I just said that!* With a heavy sigh, he walked headed toward his gate. Then he spotted a brightly lit sign advertising "Cheers" and remembered the chain had added one of their bars to the airport and drew a lively crowd of passengers waiting for flights. *Yeah, a beer right now sounds pretty good!*

Airport regulations following 911 allowed only ticket-holding passengers to pass the metal detectors. As a result, crowds of people were jammed around the security gate, either waiting for passengers coming in or saying goodbye. There was a circle of folks standing right outside of Cheers and he was surprised to see they were praying over an elderly couple, apparently leaving town. Greg felt was it unique that the group was conducting prayer in front of the bar, and he stopped to watch. He saw the look of tranquility on their faces and remembered how many friends he had said goodbye to when he left the church. There were times, like now, he missed it, then remembered Potter. *A wolf in sheep's clothing— where were the prayer warriors when I needed them?*

He stepped around them, walked into the bar, and found an empty stool. As he silently nursed a mug of draft beer, Greg checked his watch and saw he still had 22 minutes until his flight was scheduled to board. His thoughts turned to Debbie. *Why'd she leave me for that jerk? Being married to a cop is tough, but the woman left me for another cop! Can't she see through his line of crap? I mean, that clown has all the heart of a sewer rat.* Disgusted, Greg took another sip of suds. *Man, I gotta knock this off.* He knew that if he didn't stop thinking about Debbie, he'd be turning to heavy booze quickly. By the time he got back to the apartment, they'd probably have to pour him out of the cab after a stop at his favorite bar. "Why can't I just stop loving her? Why can't I stop caring?" Greg roared and slammed his beer mug on the wooden countertop.

The female bartender looked at him with curiosity, "Are you okay?" She wiped up the spilled beer, her eyes filled with concern for an apparently angry customer. Disturbances were rare in this bar, which was one reason she took the job. Her last employment had been at a country western bar, where there were half a dozen fights every night. She'd been struck more than once by an intoxicated patron.

Greg stared at the girl for a moment, thinking she looked young enough to be in high school, "Sorry… sorry." He pulled out a few bar napkins and wiped the splattered beer off his sleeve.

When the bartender walked away, Greg looked up at the TV and watched a segment of the nightly news, "…and the latest incident in these so-called Salmon Wars erupted earlier today in international waters off British Columbia where several Seattle-based fishing boats heading north, were reportedly ambushed by Canadian fishing boats. Some so-called *bumping* occurred between some fishing vessels, and heated words were exchanged. There's now a report of an exchange of gunfire during the incident. The US Coast Guard reported that one American fisherman was wounded, and two Canadian fishermen were thrown overboard during the brief disturbance. These men were rescued from the icy waters by others. We hope to have further details for you on the 10 o'clock news." The newscaster with bright teeth was replaced by a car insurance commercial.

"Those Canuks just don't learn," a slightly intoxicated loudmouth shouted for everyone in the bar to hear. "They keep messin' wit' us, an' the ol' Pres' will sen' in duh Navy ta keep 'em in line. We otta' jus' sink a couple ah their boats an'—"

The boisterous man was abruptly silenced when a rather large woman pushed him off his stool with enough force to drive him over one table and onto the floor. "Listen, big mouth, I'm a Canadian and proud of it. You wanna sink something? You just try taking on me." Ms. Canada was well over six feet tall and probably outweighed the loudmouth by a good 50 pounds, and it certainly was not all fat.

When the bartender, all 95 pounds of her, moved in to separate them, Greg thought it would be a good time to leave the premises. He knew the airport police would be en route and didn't need to stay around to fill out a witness statement.

Looking back over his shoulder, he saw the Amazon doll hit the loudmouth in the face with a fist the size of a ping-pong paddle. Sure enough, the airport police were coming in, and by the looks of the Amazon, they were going to have their hands full.


Pike's Landing Bar, Fairbanks
May 27th, 9:12 P.M. – Sunday


"Hey, old buddy, either get your mind on the game or make it easy on yourself and just hand me the price of a pitcher of beer. You're shooting like a beginner, Greg," Lt. Steve Farber leaned on his pool cue.

"Sorry, I had my mind on a case I'm working on," Greg replied.

"Yeah, the same case you've worked on for more than a year. Saw it in your eyes when I walked in here tonight. You've got those ex-wife blues. I recognize 'em 'cause I still get 'em a time or two," Jack Richards added from his nearby stool.

"Let's play pool before we start crying in our beer." Farber picked his beer mug off the table and guzzled down nearly a third of it, letting out a resounding burp to everyone's displeasure.

Greg made his shot, bouncing the seven ball off the pocket and leaving Farber with a good shot at the 14 ball. "I talked with her on the phone while I was in Anchorage. Made the ultimate mistake of telling her I missed her."

Farber nearly dropped his cue, "You told her that? Oh, man, big mistake, old buddy. Debbie's liable to hold that one over you for a while. Make you squirm like a fresh worm on a hook."

"Yeah, I know," Greg agreed.

"Don't feel alone, buddy, I made the same mistake and told Reana I still loved her. The woman laughed… LAUGHED in my face. I could've throttled her right there and then, but the kids were watching. I didn't come back for a month, and she still had that stupid smirk on her face," Farber said. Pool cue in hand, he lined up a shot.

"Steve, you were the one who fooled around with that adolescent topless dancer from the Showboat. Greg's case is slightly different. He's the injured party here," Jack said.

Steve made his shot, sunk the 14-ball, and frowned at Jack. "I don't care what you say, women are all the same. If they have something to hold over you, they'll use it every time. Either pay out the child support, or they'll have you before a judge so fast you can't blink! And by the way, that chick you're talkin' about, the one I only visited a few times, was twenty-three years old." Farber shifted position and lined up to shoot.

"Yeah, and you're twice her age," Jack shot back.

"What does her age have to do with it? She was over 21," Farber said defensively.

"Let's change the subject," Greg reached across the table and tapped Farber on the shoulder, "By the way, thanks for telling Agent Woods about my pool playing. Between you two and my neighbor Mrs. Walker, I have no private life anymore. You should recruit her as an informant." Greg winced as Farber sunk the 12-ball and followed up with the eight-ball into the corner pocket to win another pitcher of beer.

"How do you know we haven't?" Farber smiled. "Next game for another pitcher of beer… anyone?"

Greg nodded, "I should just stay home and watch reruns, save my money for a vacation to Hawaii." He bent over to pull out the ball rack and began setting the pool balls inside.

"You know, guys, this is technically illegal gambling we're doing here," Jack said.

"A pitcher of beer between friends. No big deal and the way you're playing, it's not real gambling," Farber replied.

"Yeah, besides, you two are the only real cops here. I won't lose my railroad job for a gambling arrest. And besides, who would arrest you two anyway?"

"Forget it, Greg," Jack said. "You're still one of us. These Sunday nights make up our social life, and it's no different than some penny ante poker game if we were home."

"Yup," Farber agreed.

"Remember that when you take your next polygraph test," Greg replied.

Farber smirked, "We see our kids when we can and spend the rest of the time on the job, lookin' out for John Q Citizen." He set the pool cue into a rack and walked over to put some change into the jukebox.

"This is turning into another cryin' jig like last week. I can't handle another hang-over like I had last Monday morning," Greg complained. He waited for Farber to select his tunes and return to the pool table to break.

The next game went fast; Greg won when Farber sunk the eight-ball attempting a bank shot on the two-ball. Afterward, they grabbed a table and watched the reruns of the afternoon's Indy 500 Race speed trials. One car, a favorite, blew an engine during the first lap and lost its try for the pole position.

Sitting his mug down, Greg asked his friends if they'd been monitoring the activities on the fishing grounds of British Columbia. He told them about his experience at the Cheer's Bar at the airport, which got a chuckle from both of them. "I'm telling you, that woman would make a great Mountie."

"I heard it was getting kind of rough out there," Jack replied. "Coast Guard will probably watch the area closely."

"Well, I hope this big meeting between the Prime Minister and Governor Hughes quiets things down before they start sinking boats," Greg whispered. He didn't want to be overheard by the bar crowd and have the news of the Prime Minister's arrival all over town by tomorrow. "I worked a fishing strike out in Bristol Bay long ago. Fishermen can get pretty violent when their livelihood is at risk. A lot of gunplay and boat fires—some homes were lost too."

"What meeting?" Richards asked.

"Sorry, I spoke out of turn. I forgot lowly corporals aren't in on the secret stuff." Greg looked at Farber, who just shrugged his shoulders.

"Well, you can do a better job than I just did and keep this secret under your hat. You'll get the word soon enough." Greg looked around to ensure no bad guys were listening, "The Canadian Prime Minister is coming to Fairbanks for a meeting with our beloved Governor. They'll ride the train to the park, spend the night, and go on to Anchorage. Then the PM goes to Seattle to work out this fishing problem with Washington's governor."

"Sounds cool. The elected officials really need to do something… I mean, there's got to be enough fish out there for everyone. Don't you think?" Richards poured himself another mug of beer, "Maybe they could have a big beer bust, and invite all the fishermen from both countries."

"There's not enough beer in the world for that party," Greg laughed, "I only hope the train doesn't derail. We've had a few problems with a section of track north of Trapper Creek; dropped box cars off the track last month. No big thing, really, they just jumped the track—no one to blame. We got 'em back in operation the same afternoon. No one was hurt, but it would be bad for foreign relations to have it happen with the Prime Minister on board."

"How come you didn't say anything on Friday?" Farber asked.

"Donald was there," Greg turned his beer mug around in his hands, unsure of whether or not he wanted to refill it. "If he wanted to share it, he would've, and like I said, it's no biggie."

"Can you imagine the security snafus we'll have?" Farber asked his friends. "Remember the fiasco when the Pope met President Reagan at the airport? They had Secret Service Agents crawling out of the woodwork."

"Yeah, and they had us waxing our cars the day before, just in case the Pope or the President wanted a ride around in a real police car," Jack said sarcastically.

"Strange how the press never picked up on that whacko that got within 10 feet of the President with a gun," Greg said. He was enjoying a mild buzz from the beer but promised himself this would be the last pitcher because he didn't want to face Mrs. Walker in the morning with another 10-point hangover. He might just shoot her if she came at him with that screechy voice and another offer of her daughter.

"What guy with a gun?" Jack asked. "I've never heard that story."

Richards looked from Greg to Farber and back to Greg. "C'mon, spit it out."

"You never heard this?" Greg asked in disbelief.

"No. So give out with the details."

"This clown got dressed in a nice dark suit, had the shades, and somehow—this is the embarrassing part; he got a hold of one of those Secret Service pins. You know, the ones they wear on their lapels and change daily or maybe every week? The President wears one, and maybe his has a locator beacon in it?" Greg took a drink of beer and licked his wet lips. "So, somehow, this guy's got one on and has a fake radio wire running into his ear to make him look all official. He gets by the first security team, and he's within shooting range when the real Secret Service agents spot him and recognize that he's a phony. Probably a mess-up between the Pope's security staff and the President's. Secret Service dudes usually know each other like brothers, but somehow, in the crowd at the terminal, this dude got too close. Well, they simply stepped in and swept him out of there before anyone could be the wiser. Not a shot was fired, and they vanished into a side room. Never heard of a trial and the news hounds never said a word. I sometimes wonder what really happened to that guy?"

"The gunman?" Richards asked.

"No, the Pope—Yeah, the gunman!" Greg replied. "I guess he's off pounding little rocks out of big rocks, or maybe his face is on some milk carton."

"Never mess around with the Feds; they can make you disappear… fast." Jack Richards said. He nodded until he got dizzy and had to stop.

"You're drunk," Farber accused Richards.

"So? Who have I got to go home to except an overweight cat that hates me and two dead goldfish?"

"You haven't gotten rid of those dead fish yet?" Greg asked.

"Naw. They keep the cat happy. He sits up there for hours, trying to figure out how to get into the tank. I'll get rid of 'em when I can get to the pet store and get some more."

"You're a sick man!" Farber said as he poured himself another mug of beer.

"Try feeding them this time," Greg said. For the next few moments, the three sat in silence listening to tunes on the jukebox, a collection of country hits where the singers lost wives, trucks, and dogs but finally got the trucks and dogs back. The night ended on a happy note.

It was another late night when Greg stumbled through his doorway relieved to see that Mrs. Walker's lights were off but figured that was because she probably had an infrared scope to watch the parking lot. Not bothering to turn the lights on, he made his way into the bedroom and stripped off his clothes, letting them pile up on the floor before setting his alarm and falling into bed. Within minutes, he was sound asleep, a mild nasal snore escaping as the digital clock flashed 02:02 a.m.

The Reindeer Lodge, Cantwell
May 29th, 11:58 P.M. –Memorial Day Weekend

The somewhat dilapidated Reindeer Lodge wasn't really a lodge; there were no rooms to rent. It was more of a tavern with a very relaxed atmosphere: one of two bars in the sleepy little community of Cantwell.

Located along the Parks Highway 150 miles south of Fairbanks and roughly 200 miles north of Anchorage, the town had less than 200 people. Besides a few homes alongside the highway, there were two gas stations, each with a small café and a couple of tourist shops. Most travelers passing through on the two-lane highway thought Cantwell was just a group of buildings along the main road. But the town itself was two miles west of the Parks Highway, along a hard-packed dirt road hidden by multiple stands of tall spruce trees. This is also where the US Post Office building was located and the almost famous Reindeer Lodge.

As summer solstice approached, the sun only hid briefly behind the towering mountains to the west. On June 21$^{st}$, the midnight sun would quickly reappear. Farther north, mountains did not obscure the sun; it stayed high providing 24 hours of daylight. However, it worked just the opposite in winter months, with only a few hours of daylight during the winter solstice on December 21$^{st}$.

Vehicle traffic on the Parks Highway was sparse, and most citizens of Cantwell were already tucked in for the night. The only people out on the town were three men hanging out inside the Reindeer Lodge; two customers and one extremely hairy old bartender with fat arms and a sour disposition. One customer was playing a game of gin with the aged bartender, and the other was quietly reading a book with an open long-neck bottle of root beer at his right elbow. The aged bartender, who was also the owner, was known as Old Man Taylor.

Old Man Taylor was the bartender, cook, and bottle washer. On a busy night, he kept the bar open until 5:00 a.m., but those were few and far between anymore. He often closed down when he got sleepy, or arthritis made it too painful to sling drinks any longer. A true Alaska sourdough, Taylor had arrived in Alaska in 1946. A former Marine, he'd seen a lot of action on most island battlefields in the Pacific Campaign of WWII. After the war, he toured Alaska and did about any job that put food on his plate and a beer in his hand. He worked on a sternwheeler that hauled freight up the Yukon and Nenana Rivers, ran numerous trap lines along the Lower Brooks Range, and spent one summer netting salmon in Bristol Bay as a deckhand. For a while, he cooked for a man who ran a guide service to hunt grizzlies, and later, for the men who built the Trans Alaska pipeline. He'd even been a patrolman for the Anchorage Police Department for two years and was in Anchorage during the Good Friday earthquake of 1964. That day, he was shaken, rattled, and rolled across the floor of a downtown bar and ended up battered and bruised at a shelter for the homeless where he spent the night handing out blankets.

At 88 years old, Taylor still had a sharp mind and a clever wit and could out-talk most people visiting his bar. His plentiful stories were varied and mostly true. He liked most people but wouldn't tolerate pushy salesmen unless they were invited or offered to buy a round of drinks for the house. When it came to the US Marines or Alaska trivia, few could hold a candle to him. In fact, the lodge maintained several versions of the Trivia Game, including one in German, a sports trivia game a German tourist sent him after the man passed through a few years back. No one who knew Taylor would bother to play with him; he had nearly every question and answer memorized.

A portly man, Taylor's head was large, round, and completely bald, with a light bulb-shaped red nose from years of sampling his goods. During Christmas, he was kidded for having a nose like Rudolph the Reindeer. His huge, fat hands were covered in thick calluses. He had a long full white beard and most of his body was well insulated by dense patches of hair. Taylor usually wore wide blue suspenders and a wide brown leather belt. Behind the bar, he wore size 13 4E black leather slippers. He had a pair of Sorrel boots for winter and a pair of black Wellington boots for summer.

Nine years earlier, Taylor won half ownership in the lodge with a full house of queens over tens. He put a bunk upstairs and never left, except to make a food and liquor run to Fairbanks twice a month. The loser of the card game, who held a full house of three eights and two sixes, kept his half of the owner-ship but moved to Phoenix. He returned every other year for a couple of weeks in the summer to check on the property and do a bit of fishing. Taylor sent him a copy of the books every quarter with his share of the profits, an arrangement that seemed to work for both of them.

On winter nights when the arctic wind was blowing hard, and the furnace quit working, he wondered if winning that game was such a fortunate thing. Chopping wood was a young man's chore and paying to have it done left him extra grumpy.

Each spring, he told anyone who would listen this was his last winter, but come September, he was still behind the bar with downcast eyes and a frown. Some people said he was sticking the profits into a Cayman Island account; others thought it might be a Swiss account. Everyone agreed he wasn't putting money back into the business because the lodge was losing the battle to time, weather, and general lack of care. The furniture hadn't been replaced in years, the artwork was ancient, and even the glassware had an aged look. One of the bar stools was supported by a 2x4. The front door looked to have weathered a flood or a tornado, and parts of the bar's wooden surface was stained with dried blood splatters from a nasty brawl.

Taylor liked comfort and could play a mean game of hearts, canasta, or spades, but only played poker with close friends who could tolerate his ranting or cheating a time or two. Sam Watterson, a local man, and a frequent card-playing enthusiast was in a heated game that Taylor seemed to be winning. At 62, Sam was a pretty fair mechanic, a sour-faced alcoholic, and a poor card player.

"Last call, boys," Taylor muttered. "Finish this game, and I'm hittin' the sack. Tomorrow's the big race, an' I spent a fortune on that TV over there to make sure I can see it in style." Taylor pointed to a large 62-inch TV and a complete satellite system sitting in the corner, the only new piece of furniture in 10 years. He had placed a big sign on top of the TV, which read, "YOU BREAK IT—YOU BOUGHT IT." He kept the remotes behind the bar, beside his Smith & Wesson Model 29 .44 caliber revolver. He often told his friends it was for bears and troublemakers alike.

Not really a rowdy bar anymore, the Reindeer did have an occasional bar fight on Friday and Saturday nights. Taylor kept a Louisville Slugger handy and was not reluctant to use it if needed. As long as the guys paid for the damages, never mistreated a lady, and never pulled a weapon, he let them return the next night.

The last guy to pull a knife in the Reindeer was found 30 miles south of Cantwell, running around without clothes and covered in mosquito bites. Trooper Bosley, a 16-year veteran of AST, responded to the call of a naked man trying to stop cars on the Parks Highway. He thought the man, covered in blood from scratching bug bites, was clearly a mental case. The man raved about how four real angry dudes had dropped him off without his clothes, and that was after some old dude knocked him around with a baseball bat. They transported him to Fairbanks, where he was placed on a 72-hour mental hold on the third floor of the hospital: the psych wing.

Trooper Bosley, who knew Old Man Taylor quite well, made a call at the Reindeer Lodge and got the whole story in graphic detail. Apparently, the man got rather upset over a pool game and pulled out a wicked-looking Bowie knife to slash a local's arm. Taylor disarmed him with his baseball bat, and some locals Taylor couldn't identify due to bad eyesight whisked the man out of the bar, and that was all he knew. Handing Trooper Bosley, the man's knife, Taylor smiled and went back to his bartender duties, as Bosley shook his head in wonder and walked out.

Sam Watterson declined another drink, an unusual event, but the man who was reading held up his index finger, gesturing one more for the road. "You know where it's at, Tony. Get it yourself. I'm about to whip ole' Sam here," Taylor said.

Nodding, Tony slid off his stool and walked behind the bar to the beer cooler. He retrieved a bottle of A&W Root Beer and returned to his stool without saying a word.

"Last of the big spenders," Taylor complained. With a mug of lukewarm coffee in his hand, he watched Tony unscrew the cap off the bottle. Taylor remembered when A & W required a bottle opener and wondered if the taste had changed over the years. He couldn't drink sugary carbonated drinks anymore, as they were too tough on his stomach.

Ten minutes later, Sam was whipped, and Taylor announced it was closing time. A disgruntled Watterson was already weaving out the door when Tony closed his book and drained the last ounce of root beer from his bottle.

"See yuh here for the race?" Taylor asked.

Tony nodded that he would be in attendance as he headed for the door.

Taylor was used to Tony's silence. The man rarely ever spoke a word unless absolutely necessary. The few words he did speak were slurred through a face covered in ugly scars that prevented him from opening his mouth normally. As a result, he was too embarrassed to speak in public. If there were more than a couple of people in the bar, he sat alone and never uttered a word. In the nine years Taylor had known Tony, he had probably heard less than a hundred slurred words come out of Tony's mouth. Not that he minded his friend's quiet; he preferred to do all the talking anyway. Tony was a good customer, never giving Taylor a problem, and always treating fellow customers politely.

No one in Cantwell knew much about Anthony Rogers except Taylor who knew he was a voracious reader, enjoyed hunting and trapping north of the Denali Highway, and lived off the land he had homesteaded. Tony was probably the best shot in the valley despite having only his right eye. Besides Taylor, Cantwell Postal Clerk Sally Brichard was the only other person in town who knew Tony received a monthly check from the Veteran's Administration. Other than junk, the only mail he received was books he ordered from three different book clubs.

A fellow veteran, Taylor agreed to cash Tony's checks at the Reindeer Lodge. Having fought his own war, Taylor understood Tony's scars were not only physical but also mental. If a new customer tried to engage Tony in conversation, Taylor steered them away, so Tony could sit peacefully and enjoy his books. He knew Tony came to the bar simply for the sound of human voices, a bit of news, and ice-cold root beer. Occasionally, Tony entered into a game of cards with

Taylor or shot some pool with other locals, but never with strangers which he avoided whenever possible, often leaving the bar if an influx of customers showed up for a weekend snow machine run or a large group of hunters stopped by for one last beer before heading into moose country.

No one remembered when Tony showed up in Cantwell or where he built his cabin. He preferred to keep the location hidden, not wanting visitors. During winter, Tony traveled on a Polaris snow machine, and once the snow melted, rode a red Honda ATV four-wheeler. He walked with a noticeable limp, and with his facial scars, approximate age, and government checks, Taylor knew Tony was trying to live peacefully. Alaska, with its vast wilderness, was home to a large number of Vietnam vets, men who had left civilization to hide in the openness of the far north.

Alaska provided Tony a quiet place to escape the shocked expressions and wide-eyed looks from horrified strangers, who gawked at his facial scars and black eye patch. They never asked, but Tony walked away from questioning eyes. Early on, the stares and whispered jokes were too hard to take, which caused him to flee the Lower 48 to find solace in the quiet mountains of Alaska, a land he read about when he was young and always wanted to see. He refused plastic surgery when doctors talked about it, mainly because he was tired of the pain. He had done a fair amount of reading about the procedures and decided against it, preferring to live like a hermit much of the time.

In the mid-1960s, Tony was ordained by the Assembly of God Church and volunteered for Chaplain service in Vietnam. He turned away from God following his experience at the helicopter crash site. The killing of eight North Vietnamese soldiers still haunted him. His parents and siblings had not heard from him since his release from the hospital over 30 years before. In Tony's mind, he was dead, and God had killed him. He lived alone in a one-room cabin, surrounded by miles and miles of rolling hills and sporadic patches of tall spruce and alder. To the north, Denali and its neighboring peaks towered above the land. This was where he felt safe. Only 320 yards from the ARR tracks, his cabin stood where he could hide behind trees and watch passenger or freight trains pass by every day in summer months and as often as three to four days a week in winter. Sometimes, he got close enough to see the faces of tourists but remain hidden from them. In winter, he listened to the blue and yellow painted locomotives pulling heavy loads of freight and coal between the Healy Coal Mines and Anchorage. Except for the Reindeer Lodge, this was as close to civilization as he ever wanted. He bought groceries from Taylor, who picked the food up in Fairbanks when he needed supplies for the bar. For meat, he hunted or trapped.

In over nine years, he'd suffered through several bitter cold winters and had been frostbitten numerous times shoveling through deep snow. In summer, he trudged across murky marshes filled with blood-seeking mosquitoes. Tony had become a true outdoorsman. Tacked on the side of his cabin were numerous animal pelts: including one coal black bruin that tried to break his door down one night; two-silver wolves he caught in traps that first year when he still hadn't learned to work the hides and pretty much made a mess of things. There was also the pelt of a golden lynx, which he had taken two years ago. He loved the color of the hide and kept it. Otherwise, Old Man Taylor sold or traded Tony's pelts for him.

Like other trappers, Tony learned his trade from another man, Jake Baker. Jake was a quiet man, much like Tony, who wanted nothing to do with the real world anymore. Half Athabascan and half white, the son of a Fairbanks trader, Jake was born in Alaska in 1915. As a child, he had lost two siblings to the Spanish Flu epidemic of 1918-19; as an adult, he'd lost two sons to a strange sickness called polio and then his wife to another man.

Out checking trap lines one evening, Jake came across Tony inadvertently setting up camp close to one of Jake's traps. Heavy snow was falling, and Jake didn't want to be responsible for the white man's death. He had Tony follow him home to his winter cabin. By the end of winter, they were great friends, and Jake mentored Tony in surviving the Alaskan wilderness. That was long ago; Jake died of cancer years earlier. He left everything he owned to Tony; 112 traps of various sizes, two rifles—a Winchester 30-30, and a Winchester 7mm with a mounted Leopold Scope. He also left Tony the land where he had built his cabin, one of the few parcels in that area not owned by federal or state governments. Homesteading was still allowed at that time as long as the land wasn't owned by anyone, and all requirements were met.

Stacked in one corner of Tony's cabin was a towering pile of large-print hardback novels. Reading small print paperbacks was difficult with his impaired vision and he liked the weight of a good hardback in his hands. He spent most summers gardening, cutting wood, and building up his trap line, with an occasional hunt for small game. Winter months were devoted to trapping. On off moments when he had time, he read for hours. Tony simply loved the great outdoors surrounding his home.

During winter, oil kept his lights burning; during summer, he relied on the sun. For heat, he was forced to rely on sheer muscle to drop trees, limb them, and cut them up for firewood. A four-wheeler came in handy to drag his eight-foot sled loaded with lengths of cut wood back to his cabin. There he stacked them until he was ready to cut them into 14-inch lengths (stove size) and split them with an eight-pound maul. His disabilities made it challenging work, but he had the time, and it was just him to be concerned about. He used only standing or fallen dead trees, as they were dry enough to burn right off. Spruce beetles had gone through the state and killed millions of trees, giving him and many others an ample supply of firewood.

Fuel for two lamps, a chainsaw, and vehicles was purchased from Taylor. It concerned Tony that Taylor was getting older; he wondered who would take over the lodge when it became too challenging for Taylor to maintain. There were other people in Cantwell to deal with, but he was uncomfortable with making new arrangements.

Glad to be home, he turned his four-wheeler off and carefully dismounted. He kept a shotgun secured to his four-wheeler and handed it over to Taylor when he entered the bar. He didn't want it stolen, his shotgun could handle a bruin, especially with a one-ounce slug round but his first round was always .00 buck. He tried to chase a bear off with a round in the air first, and then if he had to, dropped the bear with the slug.

His legs hadn't healed right from the helicopter crash, so he was forced to wear steel support braces between his knees and ankles. They fit under his jeans, and other than Taylor, no one knew about them.

Within moments, Tony had a lamp lit and the wood stove going. He sat back in an over-stuffed brown leather chair that he'd hauled in several years before. The old relic had belonged to Jake but was still in reasonable condition. He put his feet up on a handmade wood stool, lighted the oil reading lamp, and returned to the book he had begun at the bar.

Sitting comfortably, with the soft glow of a wood fire and the shadows dancing about from two kerosene lamps, he felt content. This was his castle. There were no mirrors in the cabin as he couldn't stand the sight of himself and didn't need any reminders. He cut his own hair with scissors using touch and feel. Not the greatest of jobs, but he had no one to impress out here in the wilderness. He wore a black Navy watch cap during winter and a black baseball cap in the summer.

He was engrossed in a novel about cops in Philadelphia.

When he checked his watch, Tony was surprised to see it was approaching 2:00 a.m., but the lateness of the hour didn't bother him as much as how awake he felt. Sleep wasn't his friend either. Too often, nightmares left him soaked in sweat as he relived the crash and the horrifying moments that followed. He saw the faces of the enemy soldiers screaming as they charged and all he could do was hold the trigger down on the crew chief's M-16.

Tony looked up at the presentation box hanging over the doorway, a walnut case with a glass cover to keep dust off his Captain bars, and the Silver Star and Purple Heart awards. They often troubled him, yet he couldn't take them down and wondered what the medals held over him. He still remembered the three-star general who presented them to him while he was hospitalized in Hawaii. He didn't see them again for over a year when they spilled out of his duffle bag in a sleazy hotel room in Los Angeles. He'd nearly tossed them in the trash.

Suddenly, he heard the sound of clanking metal outside. Tony was out of his chair, cussing as he strained against his leg braces and grabbed his loaded Winchester 7 mm. Cautiously, he opened the door and peeked out. In one hand, he held the rifle, and in the other, his kerosene lamp. A crisp night was lit with the brilliance of an early morning sunrise. Beautiful gold rays of sunlight breached the horizon and another day was born early in the wilderness. Alaska was gaining seven minutes a day, which meant the sun rose earlier and went down later every day. Had he left the lodge at 3:00 a.m., he would not have needed his four-wheeler's headlight to ride the trails home.

There were no car sounds, no barking dogs, no neighbors fighting, no gang warfare or police sirens, and no other irritating sounds of civilization. Only the high-pitched buzzing sounds of mosquitoes heading for the open cabin door. Tony closed the door quickly behind him and walked toward his woodpile.

His four-wheeler and snow machine were parked in a two-stall lean-to shed; everything looked all right there.

Hearing the clanking metallic sound again, Tony lifted the rifle to his shoulder and glanced in the direction of the burn barrels. A dear old friend was beside one of the barrels, playing with the lid. *I should've figured it was you. About time you woke up.* Tony shook his head, smiling at the old scarred black bear as it rummaged through his trash and gave him no mind. Knowing full well not to trust this bruin too much, Tony backed away with his rifle leveled at the bear just in case it decided to be inhospitable and charge for a bite or two of fresh meat.

For the last three years, Old Blue as Tony called him because of the bluish tint to his fur, had visited the cabin, each year a little bigger, Tony estimated him to be about 300 pounds now, and hungry after just waking from his winter nap.

Tony thought about shooting him a couple of times, but he disliked bear meat and hated the thought of shooting a beast just for sport. Animals he trapped were used; pelts were sold or used for clothing; meat was used as bait and large critters ended up cooked. He killed one bear in self-defense and gave Taylor the meat as it was illegal to sell. So, over the last three years, the bear and the man had learned to adjust to one another. The cabin was closed up tight when Tony was away so Blue couldn't break in and rummage through the cabinets. When Tony came across him or any other bear, he gave them a wide berth or fired a shot into the air.

Tony watched Blue toss an empty tuna can on the ground and grunt before going back to digging. A moment later, Blue scored a quart of spoiled soybean milk that Tony threw out. Without power to run a refrigerator, soybean milk was the only kind Tony liked in his oatmeal. He smiled as he watched the bear lap up the milk. *Good night, Blue... don't make too much of a mess.*

Bolting the cabin door with a heavy metal crossbar, Tony spent the next few moments killing mosquitoes. He slept under a mosquito net during the spring and summer because it was the only way to survive in this country. Screen material was tacked over the windows, which had metal bars to keep bears and other foragers out. Still, the occasional mosquito got in. After a bout with malaria in Vietnam, any mosquito gave him the willies; he couldn't sleep if one was buzzing around the cabin. This had given his old partner, Jake, a good laugh, so screens were put up to help.

Deciding it was time for bed, Tony braced the rifle against the log wall and blew out the last lamp to let the early morning sunshine come in. He swallowed a few pain pills the Veterans Hospital mailed to him every month, washing them down from a canteen hanging by his bed. He laid back and was asleep within moments, but it didn't last. A bad nightmare woke him two hours later. Unlike other nightmares, this one had him leading two men through the woods... two strange men who were not experienced woodsmen. The dream scene jumped ahead to a shootout with the same two men standing with him. Strangers, he wondered why they showed up in his nightmare.

He wiped sweat off his neck and shoulders with a t-shirt and sat up to put another chunk of wood into the stove. Sitting on his bunk, he tried to catch the nightmare before it faded away. *Who were the two men? I've never seen them before. Can it mean something? I don't remember reading a story like that, but that's probably what it is. Can't imagine me ever leading men into the woods; I don't guide anyone. I don't like people, especially strangers.*

He climbed out of bed, put his boots on, and went outside, rifle in hand to see if Old Blue had left. He had, but he'd left quite a mess for Tony to clean up. A while later, Tony returned inside and made an early breakfast. He needed to rebuild a wooden bridge across one of the streams on his trap line to the south and decided today was a good day to start that project. The stream flowed with spring runoff, and he couldn't get across it anymore. He'd have to drop some trees across to make a rough bridge for his four-wheeler to cross on. It would end up being a long day's work, especially for one disabled ex-Army chaplain.

7

———

# PHASE II BEGINS

Alaskaland Park, Fairbanks, Alaska
June 9th, 2:34 P.M.


Irritable after the long tiresome drive from Whitehorse, Steve Munroe, his brown button-down shirt open, stepped out of his RV and shook his head when he saw the amount of road grime on its side. He looked around, sweeping his hair back with both hands. A new sign showed the historic park in Fairbanks once called Alaskaland had been renamed "Pioneer Park".

Janene stepped out and looked around for some sort of food stand as she needed sugar to calm her jitters. She wandered toward the park entrance with Lesli at her side. Both RVs were parked together. Hugo was outside checking his RV for road damage from gravel.

The front of the park displayed a map showing streets of cabins and old wooden buildings from the early 1900s. They were either log or wood-sided homes and businesses from some of Fairbanks's earliest residents. The buildings were moved to the park in order to preserve a bit of early history for visitors when it opened in 1969 to celebrate the purchase of Alaska from Russia in 1869. Several of the buildings were rented to small businesses selling souvenirs.

Munroe walked over to Hugo's RV where the large-framed German was lying underneath rechecking welds on the fake fuel tank. Hugo routinely inspected them for fear the tank might come loose and spill weapons and explosives on the road. After Munroe checked his watch, the foursome walked to the nearby bus stop to check the schedule. The next bus would be arriving soon. He looked at the two girls, "I see the bus coming now; our people should be on it."

Hugo grunted out a reply in German that Munroe couldn't understand.

"Everything okay?" Munroe asked.

"My RV okay, need to check—" Hugo pointed at Munroe's RV.

"It can wait. Our guys should be on this bus."

Anxious to get things going because they had so little time left before the Prime Minister arrived in Alaska, Munroe was relieved when he saw his FLQ associates step off the city bus. He had to admit that they looked like tourists with cameras and shopping bags. Several of his men were dressed in recently purchased flowery Hawaiian-style shirts and brown or black shorts. One wore a dark-colored T-shirt with a big brown bear on the front. More than half had various colored baseball caps, and all wore dark sunglasses. "And these are my highly trained terrorists?" Munroe whispered over his shoulder to Hugo.

With his normal sour-faced East German Army drill instructor expression, Hugo replied, "You tell them to play tourist… they tourist!" In truth, he had thought them a bunch of rank amateurs since the beginning of this affair.

Munroe stepped forward to look at Gordi, who had strange-looking bumps over most of his face and arms. He saw the same thing on two men in Gordi's group, "What'd you three walk into?"

"Killer mosquitoes," Gordi answered. "We're covered in 'em."

"Didn't you buy any repellant?" Munroe asked, knowing the answer from the evidence.

"We forgot it," Gordi said through clenched teeth. "We each thought the other guy was going to pick it up. Then we ran out of time. Didn't know it was going to be so bad." Gordi gave his teammates a disgusted look, shaking his head in frustration.

"You learn lesson—do own work," Hugo said.

Janene and Lesli approached with paper plates, eating a large pastry. Hugo asked what it was as he didn't recognize it.

"They call it an elephant ear," Lesli answered which confused Hugo who knew what an elephant ear looked like. The doughy thing on the plate covered in white powder was definitely not an elephant's ear.

Seeing the confusion on Hugo's face, Lesli said, "They only call it that because of its shape. Its fry bread covered in melted butter and powdered sugar. It's really quite good. You want a piece?"

"We don't have time for this," Munroe snapped, giving Janene a stern look as he watched her consume a single elephant ear. "You're going to get fat eating like that."

"Sure… yeah, right." Janene turned to toss the paper plate into a trashcan and smiled at the others. "Like your shirts, real classy."

"Okay, split up and climb into the RVs. I've seen a lot of tourist groups since this trip began; no one's going to suspect anything of our bunch." Munroe looked at Janene and lightly slapped her arm with the back of his hand, "Get up front!"

"Yes, sir!" Janene assumed a military stance and marched toward the RV. Hugo watched, shook his head, and frowned. This operation would be over soon, and all these people dead, and he looked forward to it. Hugo planned to spend a couple of months basking in the sun alone on a beach in Southern Greece. His only regret would be killing Lesli whom he had come to know on this trip and grew to like but knew he would have no trouble popping a cap on her if it meant millions of dollars. The whole sentiment thing was fine, though unusual for him and certainly not worth that kind of money.

During the next hour, they gathered up all their hotel gear and food, refueled the RVs, and headed south on the Parks Highway. They had a small convoy of four vehicles; two RVs and the two rental vehicles the teams obtained.

Lesli was assigned to stay behind to confirm the arrival of the Prime Minister in Fairbanks and then board the same train for the trip south. She was to find a seat close to the engine and recon the train cars for security teams. She planned to stay in cell phone contact with Hugo as long as possible, suspecting the mountainous terrain of Denali National Park would cause transmission problems. A satellite phone for such instances had been purchased from Hugo's contacts in Canada. And, just in case, Lesli was armed with a Glock 9mm pistol which had been smuggled into Alaska inside the weapons cache of their RV.

Gordi drove the RV while Hugo sat at the table reviewing all the photographs taken by the groups. Fred Meyer's convenient one-day photo service had all the pictures ready quickly. Spread out with them were hand-scribbled reports detailing observations made by team members.

Later that evening, their convoy pulled into an RV park a few miles north of the park entrance to wait for Lesli's call confirming the Prime Minister's plane was on the ground in Fairbanks. They would not travel south until the Prime Minister's arrival was confirmed.

Munroe assigned Shawn and Paul to KP duty, and they went to work preparing the evening meal of sausages, scrambled eggs, and buttered toast. Meanwhile, Munroe and Gordi sat with Hugo, reviewing photographs again, and talked about the woods Gordi's group hiked through.

By late evening, Hugo and Munroe had made their decision. Based on available intelligence, they felt the best place to stop the train would be a steep embankment well south of a massive highway bridge that spanned Hurricane Gulch. Gordi told them the train slowed down at that spot due to numerous rockslides in the past and moved along at what he estimated to be about 15 miles per hour as it moved up the rising incline.

Gordi had left the train at the park, rented a Ford Expedition at a hotel, and drove his group down the road. They had seen a suitable spot for the ambush during the train ride, they just had to find it again. It took them the better part of the day to cross streams, ford a wild stretch of river, and locate the railroad tracks which they followed back south for several miles. At one point along the way, they had to give a sizable brown bear a wide berth. They spent that first night camped beside the tracks, fearful the bear was still in the area. It was strange for them to sleep in daylight at 3:00 a.m. They learned that the sun only set for an hour in Fairbanks but not long enough for any degree of darkness, tipping the horizon on summer solstice-June 21st, before climbing back up again.

The next day was spent trying to find a way up the steep hillsides and plan the three escape routes Munroe wanted. A rope would be needed to climb steep embankments; Gordi knew hauling heavy climbing rope out there would be no easy task.

Fortune smiled upon them when they struggled over a crest of rocks and came upon a clear summit surrounded by thick trees. Checking out the area, they eventually came upon a small rundown cabin that looked as if it hadn't been used for some time; Gordi told Hugo it appeared to be an excellent place to hold the hostages. "That's where the mosquitoes really found us. We ran off and made our way north until we found the tracks again. It's a good eight, maybe nine miles off the highway. It's rough country, and we've got water to cross along the way. This whole place is packed with streams, creeks, and rivers. Lots of waterfalls and marshes, too."

"Are the trees thick enough to keep a helicopter from landing?" Munroe asked.

"No problem, we take it out if one comes," Hugo replied.

"There's a thick forest of trees all over, and it looks like it goes for miles to the west and south. From the north, maybe a half-mile at best, that's when those mountains start. The cabin looked sound enough, only a few holes in the roof." Curious about Hugo's remark, Gordi wondered what Hugo had in mind for taking out a helicopter. None were aware of the Stingers but would be soon when they had to lug the two crates out to the ambush site.

Munroe gave Gordi a disheartening glance, "We'd better have a gallon of bug repellant. sure hope you took care of it this time?"

"Got it covered," Gordi replied reaching up to scratch one of his bites. Most had healed, but a few were bothersome holdouts. "Those things are almost the size of parakeets! They come in swarms and suck out a quart of blood before you know they're there. And there's tiny ones you can barely see called 'no-see'ums.' And then there's the bears! These things are huge! We saw one that had to go more than a thousand pounds or more."

"Don't worry; you'll be armed this time." Munroe dismissed Gordi with a wave of his hand and continued to study the photographs.

At midnight, the group sat in a tight circle around a campfire between the two RVs. Hugo and Munroe kept their voices low as they explained how Phase II of the operation would go down. Louis and Gregory were on guard duty, both armed with pump shotguns. Everything was on hold until Lesli confirmed Prime Minister Haegens had arrived and boarded the train in Fairbanks.

Club Detour, Fairbanks

On her own for a change, Lesli decided to leave her hotel room and sample the nightlife of the Golden Heart City. Leaving her phone and pistol stashed under the mattress in her room, she hit Club Detour's dance floor with near-wild abandon. Picking out a wide assortment of young men for dance partners, Lesli enthusiastically released some of her pent-up energy.

Short haircuts, youthful boisterousness, and he-man come-on lines that dripped with arrogance told Lesli she had found herself among young American servicemen. Club Detour was one of the main hangouts for single men assigned to Fort Wainwright. The post's main gate was located within a mile of the club.

Lesli didn't want to get involved with anyone; she had no time for that. So, she flirted a little with each guy and moved on leaving in her wake several young men who resembled whipped puppies. From a tall skinny young man with two left feet to a short, muscular fire hydrant of a guy who moved effort-lessly across the floor. The soldiers enjoyed her French accent and offered to buy her drinks. She declined them all and drank only cola to ensure she stayed sober. As she danced, the sweat poured off, and she could feel the tensions of the last couple of weeks drain away. At 11:30 p.m. Lesli said goodbye to several disappointed young GIs and caught a Yellow Cab outside the club and headed for Fairbanks International Airport.

As she walked through the air terminal's narrow concourse, Lesli observed dozens of people lined up before Alaska Airlines' long blue counter. Travelers were buying tickets and receiving seat assignments for the last flight of the night. Lesli enjoyed people-watching as a training exercise for personality identification. Being able to pick out law enforcement authorities dressed in civilian clothes was essential. She stayed clear of womanizers, suspected drug carriers, and ordinary troublemakers who could bring attention from the law. Lesli quickly identified professionals: doctors, dentists, and company white-collar pawns who serve the *Man.* Military personnel in civilian attire were easy, with haircuts shaved to the skull. She found difficulty separating local middle-class people from what she termed the low class.

More than a dozen men and women lined up before the counter traveling in extremely casual clothing, untypical for travelers on the east coast. Blue jeans, camouflage pants, running shoes, T-shirts, and pullover tops. These Alaskans troubled her; she hadn't been around such carefree people before, making her somewhat uncomfortable. Lesli shied away from children running about the concourse; she didn't like kids and resented parents who couldn't keep their young ones in line.

Since her job was to ensure Prime Minister Haegens' airplane arrived as scheduled, she tried to find a window looking out over the tarmac and taxiway. However, such a view from the terminal was restricted to ticketed passengers following the 9-11 disaster. Since she had no desire to purchase a plane ticket, she left the terminal and wandered around to the west side of the building where she came up against a seven-foot-high chain-link fence that gave a view of the taxiway and tarmac. Her walk rewarded her, Haegens' unique Canadian plane with a colossal maple leaf painted on the tail, was parked in the VIP area. Two police vehicles with rooftop light bars were parked by the aircraft. One was marked as an Airport Police vehicle, but the other surprised her. A dark blue US Air Force Security Forces sedan was by the stairwell leading up to the aircraft. Two Air Force security personnel dressed in full camouflage and carrying M-4 rifles slung over their right shoulders guarded the moveable stairs. Alaska daylight made it possible for her to see everything.

Lesli suspected Munroe hadn't counted on US military involvement guarding the Prime Minister. This made her wonder whether or not military troops might also be on the train as well.

She returned to the cabstand and hired a Yellow Cab to take her back to the hotel. In her room, she called Munroe to verify Haegens' arrival and report the Air Force troops. Next, she took a hot shower to wash away sweat from an evening of dancing. Lesli disliked Americans, especially the military, but she got a thrill dancing with them. Knowing the danger and being a terrorist especially one partially responsible for the death of so many people, including police offi- cers, heightened the night's enjoyment. She wondered how many of the soldiers would remember her face if things turned sour and she was arrested or killed.

For the next half-hour, Lesli sat at the table and reviewed photographs group one took of the Fairbanks train depot from various angles. Photos of Governor Hughes and his AST bodyguard were provided by a source not identified to her or the other underlings of the FLQ.

Knowing she had an early train to catch, she set her travel alarm and turned the lights off. Sleep didn't come easy; her mind was filled with old memories of running from the police and living in squalor. There were faces of the dead, fellow activists, and victims she had killed or helped kill. The most recent was the haunting memory of Claudia's brutal murder. Lesli hated Steve Munroe and hoped someday to have the opportunity to express her feelings by killing him. She looked forward to the day—the moment when it was Munroe's turn to feel the sharpness of the blade sliding along his throat. Lesli hoped it was her hand holding it. She believed Hugo had misgivings of the group leader but thinking about Hugo gave her a troubled feeling. Since traveling west with him, Lesli felt an animal-like longing for the strange German. She knew it wasn't love, she had realized long ago that she was incapable of that emotion. When sleep claimed her, Hugo's face faded away.

The Bluff RV Park, Parks Highway - Denali
June 10TH, 02:12 A.M.

The small convoy pulled out of the parking area as quietly as possible, leaving headlights off until entering the highway. They traveled for over an hour before pulling off at a secluded spot found by team three and followed a dirt road for almost a half-mile, ending at an earth berm across the road. Here, the false gas tanks were carefully removed, and the weapons and ammo unwrapped. Guns were handed out with ammo. Hugo placed the explosives in two large black backpacks with enclosed frames for easier carrying. He pulled out his toolbox and dismantled each of the RVs' built-in queen-sized beds and removed large elongated dark green boxes with stenciled military-style black letters and numbers.

Hearing a noise behind him, Hugo quickly pulled his Beretta pistol from a brown leather shoulder holster and aimed it at the intruder, only to find a wide-eyed Shawn standing there. Hugo relaxed and holstered his pistol.

"Sorry, but Steve told me to come in and help you," Shawn had both hands up, so Hugo would know he was no threat.

"Grab one end." Hugo and Shawn picked up the long green metal box and carried it outside to sit on the ground.

"What's this?" Shawn asked.

"For helicopter," Hugo replied as they removed a matching box from Munroe's RV, surprising the others with the containers' size and military script.

When the first box was opened, Gordi exclaimed, "Stingers! You got us Stingers!?" Gordi let out a mournful groan, knowing how far they would have to lug them. "There's got to be an easier way to make five million bucks."

"For the cause, baby!" Janene said.

A couple others waved a closed fist in the air, echoing her statement, "For the cause!"

"For the cause… great!" Gordi exclaimed. "You can carry some of this rope, Janene—for the cause."

Janene replied by lifting her right hand and presenting Gordi with the center finger salute.

A significant part of this operation weighed heavily on Hugo's shoulders. They had to get the weapons, ammo, food, water, equipment, and themselves to the cabin Gordi's group had found. Only then could the trap be prepared, and the FLQ had just over 24 hours to get everything ready.

"Steve, why don't we leave Janene here with the RVs? In her condition, she's gonna get one of us killed," Paul said.

"Look, you take care of your end, and I'll take care of her, okay?" Munroe glanced over at Janene, who was using a stick to make weird etchings in the dirt. He almost agreed with Paul, yet he could not part with her. *Not yet anyway.*

Michael, his backpack in place and a well-used, fully automatic M-16 draped over his shoulder, walked up to Munroe, "Steve, you really think taking Haegens hostage is going to help Quebec?"

Munroe was tired of all the questions and glared at Michael. "Only time will tell." Munroe hoisted his own pack. "We're freedom fighters, Michael. Our job is to take the war to them, to prove our resolve, and show the Canuks this will not end until Quebec has the freedom to stand on its own."

Not completely satisfied with Munroe's answer, Michael shrugged and walked back to join his group. Hugo assigned additional pack-carrying duties to each group until everyone had something to carry. Moving all the equipment, including the two Stinger boxes, would not be an easy trek. Gordi wanted to unpack the stingers and leave the boxes behind. Hugo disagreed, "Safer to carry this way."

Before they left the RVs, they sprayed WD-40 down the insides of the RV to blur any fingerprints. Doors and windows, engine compartments, and the fake gas tanks were also sprayed.

Munroe placed Janene in front of him to ensure she kept pace as the FLQ headed into the Alaskan bush. Gordi was in the lead as scout; Hugo held down the position of tail-end Charlie. Although everyone doused themselves heavily with bug, dope a squadron of blood-seeking insects surrounded them as the group ventured into the woods.

Governor Hughes' Office - Juneau, Alaska
June 10th, 5:50 A.M.

Unable to escape Juneau's wearisome political games and spend an enjoyable night with his family, Governor Hughes was forced to remain in Juneau for a late-night session with the state's Committee for Natural Resources. He caught the early morning flight which was scheduled to leave at 6:45 a.m. and arrive in Fairbanks at 8:14 a.m. Hughes would miss the planned early breakfast with Prime Minister Haegens at the Princess Hotel.

Rather than fly in a chartered aircraft, Governor Hughes flew back and forth from Juneau to Anchorage or Fairbanks on scheduled airline flights which saved the state a vast fortune. To the voters' delight, the small jet aircraft purchased by one Alaska governor was sold by the following one. Hughes was not about to make that mistake; he enjoyed the people he met on the flight. His trooper bodyguard was always in a heightened state of alert and sincerely missed that private jet where he could nap once the plane was in the air.

Surprisingly wide awake, Governor Hughes walked out of his office to find Bob Rexault, his Chief of Staff, awaiting him. Rexault was doing a final once-over of the Governor's briefing papers for the upcoming meeting with Prime Minister Haegens. Having to leave the Governor's mansion early in the morning, Governor Hughes had caught the private security guards unaware. They scrambled to their posts as the Governor walked past them with a smile on his face. "Seems you gentlemen forgot the Boy Scout motto of 'Be Prepared'."

Enjoying the growing light of a new day, Governor Hughes decided to walk to his office rather than drive. He knew it meant another security lecture from his Chief of Staff and possibly his AST bodyguard for being alone on the streets. But the Governor enjoyed the feeling of being out on the empty streets. He waved to the officer driving by in a Juneau Police car, who immediately notified the dispatcher to report the Governor was again out on the streets by himself. The Officer remained in the area to ensure the Governor was safe.

Like many other people, Rexault felt the Governor should have rattled a saber when the Canadian fishing fleet blockaded the ferry in Prince Rupert. Several times he warned his boss, "We have to meet force with force, Sir. Put the Air National Guard on alert, have the jets make a few flyovers, and fire a few shots across their bows."

"Bob, we're talking about fishermen, not Barbary pirates! This concerns the livelihood of hundreds of Canadian fishermen and their families. They're angry, and so far, except for some strained nerves, no one's been hurt. So, let's try to work this out like civilized people," Governor Hughes said.

"They'll see you as weak, Governor," Bob replied, and Hughes smiled.

Two pots of coffee were brewed for the Governor and his party and served with a box of freshly baked pastries. Bob Rexault was already on his second cup when Alaska State Trooper Sergeant John Niles appeared with a disgruntled look on his face.

"Is he here? Or did some culprit whisk him away?"

"Not funny, Sergeant," Rexault said. "Yes, our exalted leader has made it here without a kidnapping or mugging."

"Talk to him, Rexault. He's gotta stop these early morning adventures. He isn't in the state senate anymore—he's the Governor of Alaska, for god's sake!" Niles smiled coolly as Governor Hughes walked back into the outer office with an empty blue handmade ceramic mug in hand.

"I know," Governor Hughes said to Sgt. Niles. "Consider me lectured, and let's get down to business." And refilled his coffee cup.

Assigned to the Governor as a bodyguard. Niles had watched over the two state leaders before him. Along the way, Niles had formed a personal friendship with the man he was sworn to protect.

A friendship Bob Rexault envied, so he had come to detest Niles. An emotional man and a former US Air Force major, Rexault, a thin rail of a man with a long sad face topped by thick black hair, was gifted in the area of finance. That gift had made him extremely wealthy investing in the stock market. He attended the University of Alaska-Fairbanks with Governor Hughes, where the two became good friends. Rexault was the man behind the candidate, as Hughes rose from Fairbanks' city councilman to State Senator and then Governor of Alaska. When his second term ended, Rexault hoped the Governor would run for U.S. Senator and take Rexault to Washington DC with him.

Having made numerous enemies in political circles, Rexault was a man who could slice and dice with the best of them. He also knew that when Governor Hughes left politics for good, he would need to make himself scarce.

With his best political smile firmly in place, Rexault offered a Styrofoam cup of hot coffee to Sgt. Niles. "Hot coffee, Sergeant?"

"Why, thank you, Mr. Rexault." Niles took the coffee and added a single packet of sugar and a drop of cream. He thought about checking it for poison but thought it might be rude.

"Do you foresee any problems on this trip, Sergeant?" Rexault asked.

"The Colonel ensures I am kept up to date with security arrangements for this meeting. Based on the amount of security provided by the Feds and our Canadian friends, I don't believe Governor Hughes is in jeopardy. Troopers and FBI intelligence keep their eyes and ears open. It being fishing season; Intel doubts Canadian fishermen would come to Alaska to stage a protest."

"Do we have everything, Bob?" Governor Hughes asked.

"Yes, Governor," Rexault set his coffee cup down and checked his watch, "Sir, I think we'd better be leaving. I don't believe Alaska Airlines would hold their plane for the Governor."

"No. Not with their corporate headquarters in Seattle. You ready, John?" Governor Hughes asked Sergeant Niles.

"All ready to go, Governor."

Sergeant Niles stepped over to Rexault's desk. Without asking the Chief of Staff for permission, he picked up the phone and called the private security post on the first floor of the state office building. Hanging up after a few words, Niles turned to Governor Hughes, "Your car is ready, Governor."

"Thank you, John." Governor Hughes understood why his Chief of Staff and bodyguard didn't get along but wished they did. Both Class A personalities, they often butted heads to best serve their leader. The Governor believed it would make things much easier if they became friends. He had thought about replacing Niles to smooth things out, but the Commissioner of Public Safety advised him that could affect Nile's chance of further promotion. So, he put up with their disagreeability and played the role of the referee when needed.

Sergeant Niles was a flaming red-haired Irishman with NFL linebacker-sized shoulders, deep brown eyes, and a square jaw. The 15-year veteran of AST was a former Juneau Police Officer who had known the Governor through his early days in the state senate. The two had shared a few fishing charters before Hughes was elected to the Governor's office. After being voted in, Governor Hughes immediately requested Niles continue as his bodyguard.

An Alaskan Governor rarely has his life threatened but was known to receive some rude letters. More than 75% of the citizens owned personal firearms, and carrying concealed weapons was legal in most public areas. AST assigned only one man as the Governor's bodyguard, but Niles maintained liaison with other law enforcement departments. He also oversaw the private security for the capitol and the Governor's Mansion.

Most often in uniform, Niles occasionally traveled in civilian clothes at the discretion of the Chief of Staff. On this trip, Rexault requested Niles travel in civvies, so he wore a dark blue three-piece suit with a navy blue tie and a light blue button-down shirt. His Model 22 Glock pistol was in a shoulder holster on his left side. He used federally provided credentials to carry a concealed weapon on public aircraft. Niles sat behind the Governor using a palm-sized mirror to keep an eye on the aisle behind him—a trick learned from the previous body-guard who had retired when his Governor was voted out of office after only one term.

Niles was aware that he would meet fellow troopers, FBI Agents, US and Canadian Secret Service Agents, and the Fairbanks Police Department in Fair-banks. There was no mention of Special Agent Greg Hansen. Unfortunately, there existed a general feeling that railroad cops were only good for ensuring no one carried off any railroad tracks or possibly hijacked a freight train.

The Alaska Airlines 737 took off on schedule for the non-stop flight to Fair-banks. The Governor, his Chief of Staff, and Sgt. Niles traveled by coach to save a couple of thousand dollars on what three round-trip first-class tickets would have cost. Hughes traveled in a rented limo from the airport to the train station where he met Prime Minister Haegens for the first time.

The train station held approximately 400 tourists, all waiting for the scenic ARR train ride through the Alaska wilderness—a security nightmare for officers brought in to safeguard the Governor and Prime Minister. It was believed that no one on the train, other than security personnel, knew of the VIPs traveling with them.

However, waiting to board the train was an attractive member of the FLQ, whose assignment, following notification from Munroe, was to take out the engine crew to keep them from using the radio. This would not occur until after the one-night stay at Denali National Park.

Fairbanks Police Department
June 10th, 3:14 A.M. (Same Day)


Unable to sleep over the coming VIP excursion, Greg Hansen left his apartment at 3:00 a.m. and drove to the Fairbanks police station where he shared a cup of coffee with FPD Sgt. Mike Warner. The midnight shift super-visor, Warner, had pulled the 12:00 a.m. to 8:00 a.m. shift for the last three years. When Greg showed up, he had just finished giving a verbal reprimand to a young rookie officer. "What'd he do? Forget to bring a note from his mom to be out after curfew?" Greg asked. The young recruit looked like a high school senior; Greg had trouble getting used to seeing kids like this out on patrol.

"Yeah, we get older, and they get younger-looking," Warner poured Greg some coffee. "Don't tell me you're actually out investigating a crime at this hour?" He asked with a note of sarcasm. Cup in hand, he sat back in his chair and took a sip.

Yeah, I'm missing one of my choo-choos," After adding extra sweetener, Greg sat in a green metal folding chair and sipped his hot coffee.

"Don't fret, Greg; I've got my men doing drive-bys at the Princess Hotel all night, and we have four men guarding our VIP. They wanted eight, but we haven't got that many men to spare." Warner propped his feet up on the desk's top drawer, glanced at the dispatcher, and looked back at Greg. "Chief promised them constant patrols, AST provided a man or two in the lobby. If you ask me, our Secret Service should've coughed up some more agents for this detail. This is really their bag, not ours. Our overtime budget is taking a serious hit for these men to be brought in on their days off to pull a 12-hour shift babysitting."

"Anything else going on?"

"Only a couple arrests for DWI and a few domestics. Nothing concerning your precious railroad." Warner stood up leaving his coffee cup on the desk and escorted Greg out of his office. "You know, I remember back when police officers had the discretion of whether or not to make an arrest at a domestic. Under the new law, we have to pinch either the husband or wife, maybe both, to prevent a callback. If the phone gets knocked off the wall, we've got to arrest the one who did it."

"Yeah, I liked it the other way too. Usually, a good counseling session or taking the old man to a buddy's house handled it. Now you have to hit one of them with a criminal charge. In another ten years or so, the police will probably be told to shoot one of them. Or worse, the cops will be told to stay out of it completely, and some shrink-trained counselors will be sent to remedy the situation. I give that about three months. After enough counselors are beaten up or shot, the police will be back handling the situation again." Greg waved at Cindy Webber, the dispatcher.

"Hey, couples are going to fight. Now we have to slap them with a night in jail, lawyer fees, and a criminal record. It's no good, and it breaks up a lot of marriages. But, at the same time, what are we gonna do with the rise in serious harm from these kinds of beefs," Warner said in disgust.

"I'm betting the lawyers changed it just to get more fees. They're always messing with people's lives. You ever notice how many politicians are former lawyers?" Greg stepped outside, taking a deep breath of the cool morning air. "Those law geeks write the laws so only a fellow lawyer can read them—job security."

"Kill all the lawyers and save civilization. Saw it on a T-shirt and almost bought it to wear into court but lost my nerve." Warner slapped Greg on the back and watched his friend head for his cushy ARR vehicle.

"Be careful out there. I'll give you a holler if I see your missing choo-choo."

"Thanks!" Greg shouted back.

Over a year ago, Sgt. Warner got into a wrestling match with three intoxicated soldiers at a traffic stop on South Cushman. His nearest backup officer was a good three minutes away, and he was deeply concerned he might have to shoot one or more of the guys. Hansen drove up at that point and jumped into the pile. They got the three men into handcuffs just as the FPD backup officer arrived on the scene. Since that night, Warner made sure all of his officers knew who Greg was and provided him with whatever services he needed as a professional favor to a fellow officer of the law.

Greg drove by the train station, which was completely deserted. By 6:00 a.m., people would be arriving, and the train depot would end up being one of the busier locations in Fairbanks for three hours.

Eielson Air Force Base's Security Forces would bring two K-9 units to check the area for bombs. Greg thought it might be a technical violation of the Possee-Comitatus Act, which prevented the military from being used against civilians unless under martial law, but he doubted anyone would complain. Most passengers would enjoy watching the K-9 units work, especially the kids. E By 6:00 a.m., representatives from the FBI, AST, and Secret Service, along with a private security company and Sgt. Warner's FPD crew would be at the station on security detail.

Leaving the depot, Greg drove through the ARR yard and stopped beside the passenger cars which came in on the late afternoon run from Anchorage. Cleaning crews worked through the night to get the cars ready to go by 5:45 a.m. sharp for the trip south. Greg inspected each car, spending a few more moments in the baggage and VIP car. The car designated for the dignitaries was a regular passenger car. The only difference was that some seats had been removed to allow additional legroom for the special guests. One set of seats was turned around so the two VIPS could face each other during the ride. A beverage cart with snack trays provided by the Princess Hotel was to be placed in the car and an ARR hostess would offer service during the trip.

Greg looked out a window to see a familiar black Chevrolet Trailblazer pull up outside. Smiling to one of the cleaning crew and commenting on their dedication, Greg stepped out to meet his old friend, AST Corporal Jack Richards. "Hey, Jack." Greg waved and walked over to Jack who was with a stranger and introductions were made.

"Greg, this is Tod Loury, Canadian Secret Service." Richards gestured to

Greg, "And this is my good friend, Special Agent Greg Hansen with the Alaska Railroad; A former Trooper who went rogue."

Both men shook hands, and Greg said, "I see we had the same idea, making a walkthrough of the cars before leaving the yard."

"Yes, standard procedure. Are you acquainted with the workers on board, Greg?" Tod Loury asked.

"No. I know the cleaning service that's handled cleaning the cars for several years but employees change nearly every summer. This isn't a high-paying job; most of these are college students working through the summer."

"It's possible one of them could place an explosive device on board during their duties?" Richards asked.

"Yes, I suppose so." Greg looked back at the cars where 14 young men and women were finishing up their chores.

"I guess that's the main reason the K-9 units will search each car," Jack said. "Only so much we can do without putting guards on the workers and then guards on those guards, and so on.

"I apologize if I sound paranoid, but it comes with the job," Loury said.

"Don't worry, I understand completely. You can't let your guard down," Greg agreed. "Would you like a tour of the cars?"

"Yes, please, and if possible, I'd like to check the locomotive. One of my duties is to see what access there is to the engineer during the journey. Much like we inspect access to pilots when the Prime Minister uses an aircraft other than our own."

"This way for one free tour." Greg walked toward the cars with both men at his side.

Tod Loury chatted with several cleaning crew members after the inspection and paid particular attention to the baggage car.

Greg led them back to their vehicles. "The engineer and his locomotive will be here soon to hook up and pull the train to the station. I'll leave you two now; I want to inspect the tracks and the rest of the yard."

"Thank you, Greg, for your kindness," Loury shook hands with Greg again.

Waving at Richards, Greg drove away. He was very impressed with Tod Loury and how observant the man was. Nothing seemed to escape him, from slippery floor plates to loose cables in the baggage car. Greg noticed that Loury wrote nothing down and suspected the man might be one of those with near total recall, or he walked around with a hidden tape recorder.

Another thing Greg noticed as he drove away was that his ARR vehicle was beginning to look more and more like his apartment; it was a mess inside. Pizza boxes, bakery bags, Pepsi cans, candy wrappers, and even a pair of smelly white socks. *I wondered where those socks went to. I gotta clean this mess up before Donald comes up and wants a ride. He'd never let me live it down.*

At 6:05 a.m., Greg parked his vehicle in the parking slot reserved for him at the depot. The first tour bus was already in sight, and several baggage handlers were standing around with hands in their pockets. Their job was to transfer baggage from bus to train without losing or breaking anything. They were all young men dressed in Princess Tours' pullover blue shirts and blue shorts or ARR coveralls. A growing number of young women were baggage handlers. *Times keep changing, and I keep getting older. More women going into the labor area.*

By 6:30, four uniformed AST, four FPD officers, and several private security guards in brown uniforms were walking about the depot. And there were men in dark sunglasses and dark suits—stone-faced federal agents with a radio cord behind the ear. These elite men and two women avoided the uniformed officers as they inspected the growing crowd of travelers and some who came to see someone off. Law enforcement personnel saw the ever-increasing crowd as a nightmare. If a shooting or bombing were to occur, these professionals knew it was very probable some innocents would be hurt.

As promised, the ARR would hold the train until the VIPS were prepared to depart, which was not mentioned to the groggy-eyed train passengers standing about in crowds, snapping photos of nearly everything around them. Unfortunately, the Fairbanks depot was not located in the more attractive part of town. It was located on the north side of the Chena River tucked at the end of a dead-end road that gave access only to the depot. A turnabout road in front of the depot allowed limited customer parking. A thick natural stand of trees and bushes separated it from the Johansen Expressway on the north. A wide rail yard and tracks where the train parked for boarding and departure were directly behind the building. The most advantageous point for a sniper would be the woods in front of the depot. And that kept officers constantly on the alert.

Lesli stood in the crowd, attempting to look like a tourist, wearing new tan shorts and a dark blue summer top. A black fanny pack was wrapped around her hips, and a Cannon 35mm camera hung from her neck. Her concealed 9mm pistol was in the back pocket of her fanny pack, along with one extra magazine of 14-hollow point rounds. There was bound to be an officer who might recognize the bump of a shoulder holster, a mistake she couldn't afford. Lesli hoped they weren't searching passengers' personal belongings. She was ordered to make herself scarce and call Munroe by satellite phone if that happened.

Watching other passengers board without any difficulty, Lesli got in line. She purchased a one-way ticket to Anchorage for $159.00 and proceeded toward the train. She was about to board when two men suddenly appeared on each side of her.

"Excuse me, miss, may I see your ticket and some form of ID," Corporal Richards asked.

"Uhm… sure. Could you tell me what this is about?" Lesli tried to hide her French accent.

Corporal Richards, in civilian clothes, presented his AST credentials.

Fighting fear, she fiddled with her fanny pack and opened the front compartment for her wallet. She pulled it out and presented it to Richards.

"Would you pull your ID out, please?"

Richards accepted her forged Alaska Driver's License and handed it to Tod Loury. He gave it a thorough once-over and studied Lesli's face again as he compared it with the one pictured on the driver's license. After a brief moment, he handed it back to her. "Thank you, Ms. Wakefield. I do hope you enjoy your train ride," Loury said.

"Can you tell me why I was stopped, Officer?" Lesli asked. She recognized Loury, having seen him before when Prime Minister Haegens visited a shopping mall in Ottawa.

"Only a random check, Ma'am. We're stopping a few people due to some problems with immigration. That's all," Richards replied. "Thank you again."

Lesli put her license away, smiled, and boarded the train as the two men walked off.

"Well, what do you think?" Richards asked when they were out of earshot.

"She looks familiar, but I can't remember where or why. I'll have to let Sir Whiteburn know, but it's probably nothing," Loury answered.

"In your line of work, you can never be too careful. We'll keep an eye on her, just in case."

Both VIPs finally aboard the special car, dozens of hands were shaken, polite smiles offered, and words of diplomacy exchanged, the train was finally loaded and slowly started to pull out 42 minutes late. Lesli was in the third car back from the locomotive. Her assignment would not be called for until tomorrow, so she sat back and enjoyed the view of Alaska's countryside.

In the ninth car back from the engine, Governor Hughes and Prime Minister Haegens faced each other. Governor Hughes had his back to the front of the train out of courtesy to his guest. US Secret Service had a direct radio link with a two-man AST vehicle traveling the Parks Highway. Captain Potter's temporary command station was set up in Healy's trooper station. The team flew from Fairbanks to Healey early that morning using two helicopters but only one stayed with the team until transportation was needed the following morning to jump to the Trapper Creek AST Station.

Sir Jonathan Whiteburn stood at the front of the train VIP car, chatting with Agent Loury. "We won't bother the Prime Minister with this, but I'd like us to take a walk through the train, and you can point this woman out to me."

"Yes, sir," Loury replied.

Twenty-five minutes later, they returned to the VIP car, "Well, she's either very good at what she does, or she's who she says she is. But you're right; she does look familiar," Sir Whiteburn said to Agent Loury. "Let's keep an eye on her, especially during our stop at the park. Assign a couple of men to her if she decides to spend the night."

After a second once over, Lesli was extremely nervous, especially after recognizing Sir Whiteburn when he walked by and smiled at her. Pulling on all her courage, she smiled back and returned to her book. *Apparently, they suspect me, but they aren't sure; otherwise, they would have grabbed me by now.* She was in a quandary, wondering how they might know her. To the best of her knowledge, no photographs had been taken of her since leaving the Navy, and then she was known by another name. Lesli was unaware that several photographs were taken at a so-called secret gathering of individual political activists several years earlier by a Montreal Police Department informant, and they eventually reached the RCMP. They, in turn, provided a copy to their Secret Service. Lesli, then known as Karla White and a strong activist for Indian rights, stood with several other known political activists in one of the photographs, a group already labeled as a danger to the Canadian Government.

She was also unaware of her photograph being taken at the Alaska Customs Station. Those photographs were funneling through departmental red tape. Identified as a known terrorist for her connection with the Red Tide, Sir Whiteburn would be sent this information. Unfortunately, it would arrive too late to prevent the implementation of Phase II. The FLQ would be striking at the heart of Alaska where citizens had little experience involving international terrorism, and the following events would shock many people.

8

—————

# THE UNWANTED ORPHAN CHILD

June 10th, 9:04 a.m.

Only three newspaper reporters were allowed to travel in the VIP train car for the trip south. For once, newspaper people would have the edge over television crews, who all too often shoved newspaper reporters to the back of the room. Newspaper reporters came at the request of Prime Minister Haegens who preferred newspapers to television and radio. A television reporter once caught the Prime Minister in an embarrassing moment, exposing his balding head and allowing the entire world to see him without his expensive toupee. The three newspaper reporters chosen by the Governor's Office were Brad Thompson of the Fairbanks Daily News-Miner, Larry Ogden of the Juneau Empire, and Cindy Meyers of the Anchorage Daily-News. All three were under the close supervision of Bob Rexault who kept them at arm's length from Prime Minister Haegens and Governor Hughes until the two VIPs were prepared to address them.

Traveling with Prime Minister Haegens was James Riley, Interior Secretary to the Prime Minister and a close friend of many years. An avid jogger and outdoorsman, Riley was of average height topped off with a near-razor cut of short gray hair. He was an accredited lawyer with a sharp mind, a watchful eye, and a constant problem for Sir Jonathan Whiteburn, often demanding and behaving as if Whiteburn worked for him, much the same way Bob Rexault treated Sgt. Niles.

Special Agent Hansen was gently shoved off into the shadows during the elaborate welcoming ceremony, where everyone connected to the meeting of state was introduced. Not that Greg minded, he had his own job to do. Uniformed FPD officers and AST troopers formed an outer ring of protection, keeping the crowds of curious civilians back. Closer in, US and Canadian Secret Service agents remained alert with their backs to the politicians as they studied the public for that lone assassin. Only Sgt. Niles remained at Governor Hughes's backside, never letting the Governor more than three feet away. Canadian Secret Service placed two sniper teams on the roof of the depot. Their job was to size up anyone seen as a threat to the PM and governor and if necessary, 'shoot to kill.'

Working with the Canadians, Captain Potter positioned two of his SERT Team long rifles on nearby ARR building rooftops to keep the immediate area under observation. The AST helicopter, with two other SERT Team members aboard, monitored the scene from 500 feet above. The rest of the team was already standing by in Healy. Potter relied on Fairbanks PD for support if something significant went down.

AST and FPD marked patrol vehicles kept vehicle traffic from approaching the train by way of the tour bus entrance and limited traffic through the roundabout to taxis, small buses, and private vehicles dropping off passengers. Army K-9 explosive dogs searched baggage as it entered the receiving area on the east end of the building. Overly curious tourists shoved each other to get a photo of the dogs and increased security. Governor Hughes and Prime Minister Haegens' presence had become known, which increased the nervousness of the protection detail, as they had been trained that a camera could quickly become a firearm.

Prime Minister Haegens and Governor Hughes shook hands with friendly enthusiasm, said a few polite words, and hustled aboard their assigned train car. The train was already running late. The disgruntled conductor had a few testy words with Bob Rexault until ARR dispatch was given the word from Agent Woods that it was okay for the train to depart.

Feeling much like the unwanted orphan child, Greg leaned against a light blue painted steel pillar and casually waved at the departing tourists. No one bothered to ask him questions about the trip. Captain Potter made it clear he wasn't needed with a quick rebuff, "We won't need your services here, Mr. Hansen. Maybe you could assist in loading baggage after the K-9 unit has cleared it."

It took all of Greg's willpower to keep from twisting Potter's head off. In the end, he turned around, went inside the depot to be away from everyone, and clenched his teeth in private.

The AST could only get one K-9 bomb dog from Eielson Air Force Base and two dogs from Fort Wainwright. USAF Security Forces Sgt. Miller and his dog, *Patches,* were busy sniffing rows of suitcases lined up before the baggage car. Other dogs were inside the train cars doing a second walk-through. Patches had already searched all the train cars, spending a few extra moments in and outside the VIP car. The dog was severely in need of a break. But again, everything and everyone was being rushed to get the train out of Fairbanks before the middle-aged train conductor suffered a nervous breakdown or strangled Bob Rexault. Sgt. Niles was rooting for the conductor, of course.

Lt. Farber witnessed the exchange between Potter and Greg but had his hands full with traffic and crowd control. He could only offer his friend a look of understanding.

Corporal Richards was on the train and hadn't seen Greg or would have asked for his assistance. The Wakefield woman bothered him for some reason, maybe it was only a cop's hunch, but he felt she was bad news. Had he found Greg, he might have asked him to ride along, sit near her, and play tourist. Greg had police powers on board and carried a gun if action was needed.

Feeling his self-esteem crashing against some imposing rocks of pride, Greg shuffled back to his car like a man who'd just been fired or told his winning lottery ticket was a fraud. He drove slowly back to his office, cutting through the ARR yard to call Donald. Greg knew his boss was waiting for a detailed report on the celebrated fanfare of the VIP's departure. Then he planned to go to the pistol range and put a hundred rounds through a man-shaped silhouette he envisioned as Captain Potter of the Alaska State Troopers. *Maybe 200 rounds if the silhouette holds up.*

On Board The Special VIP Car

Prime Minister Haegens traveled with a small party consisting of James Riley, Sharon Marbles, his personal secretary; Lloyd Bruce, his personal assistant and communications officer; Brig. General Arthur Ridley, his military advisor; and Sir Jonathan Whiteburn, with his four Canadian Secret Service Agents.

Hoping to make this an intimate meeting, Governor Hughes traveled with only Bob Rexault and Sgt. John Niles. Agent Woods of the FBI and US Secret Service Agent William Tensley III also accompanied the VIP passengers because of the Prime Minister's presence.

As Captain Potter's onboard eyes and ears, Corporal Jack Richards of AST was assigned to this detail. Richards volunteered for the duty after hearing about it from Greg. He thought it might be fun playing Nursemaid to some political big shots. He'd already formed a quick friendship with Agent Tod Loury and was getting to know Sir Jonathan Whiteburn.

Richards expected Greg to ride along since this was his train, and the line was, in effect, under his jurisdiction. After seeing him early that morning at the train yard, he hadn't laid eyes on Greg.

The Honorable Nancy Sterns, U.S. Senator for Alaska was added to the guest list. Half-Aleut, she was raised in Dillingham, a daughter, and granddaughter of Bristol Bay fishermen. Sterns was quite the political tigress when it came to state and federal fishing issues. When she learned of the meeting between Haegens and Hughes, she invited herself along and in doing so, nearly drove Bob Rexault to the point of resigning. During one phone call, he went so far as to hang up on her which caused the Governor to apologize to Sterns on Rexault's behalf, who refused to talk with the "loudmouthed woman." Rexault and Sterns avoided each other at the train station as much as possible, but both tossed the evil eye back and forth after they boarded the VIP car.

Accompanying Senator Sterns was Walter Brown, Special Assistant to the Senator and always at her elbow. Young, idealistic, and a young Brad Pitt look-a-like, Brown had recently been admitted to the Alaska Legal Bar. Bob Rexault, having a dirty mind, suspected more was going on there than just a working relationship. In truth, there was, but not the way Bob imagined. Brown was the oldest son of Stern's younger brother. Alone, he often referred to her as Aunt Nancy, a fact they kept secret, so she wouldn't be accused of nepotism by news people. She was grooming him for political office in hopes that he would become a state senator to represent both the Independence Party and the people of Bristol Bay when she retired.

In total, the VIP train car held 23 people which included the three newspaper reporters and a service attendant named Carlos, a second-generation Alaskan-Philippine. There was ample room to move about, sip soft drinks, bottled water, coffee, and tea, and select a pastry as they enjoyed the fantastic Alaska scenery. In hopes of scoring points with the Governor, Bob Rexault became a tour guide. He waited until a break in the conversation between Haegens and Hughes and began telling the Prime Minister facts about the land they were passing through.

"Mr. Prime Minister, from Fairbanks to Denali Park, this train will travel through the western borders of the Tanana Valley, an area of flat land and rolling hills leading to our majestic mountains. The Tanana Valley is larger than many of our US states. We'll soon be passing over the Nenana River into Nenana, at one time a major shipping port for the interior of Alaska. Afterward, we'll travel by the recently renamed Clear Space Force Station, one of the last sites known as a DEW Line Station, for Distant Early Warning. Military personnel and civilians at Clear maintain a huge radar array to watch the skies for incoming missiles and other anomalies. I've been informed they can pick out a pack of cigarettes at 100 miles in space. Before reaching the park, a distance of approximately 120 highway miles from Fairbanks, we'll pass by the massive Usibelli Coal mines at Healy which provide coal for Alaska and several countries such as South Korea. Coal is shipped by train car to the Port of Seward and loaded aboard massive ships for ports in the Far East."

Governor Hughes attempted to get Rexault's attention by tapping his shoe with his own, but Bob appeared to be on a roll. "You'll see our majestic Alaska Mountain Range in the distance. Even in June, most of our beautiful peaks remain draped in deep snow, and you may notice the bluish tint to our many glaciers."

Senator Sterns thought it a proper time to change the subject, "Mr. Rexault, I believe that if you ever decide to leave public service, you could find a position as a tour guide… a nice way to supplement your retirement pay."

Rexault jerked around to face the Senator and shot daggers at her. His hands clenched into fists, as he fought to keep from responding. Governor Hughes had accepted an iced coffee from Carlos and missed some of the exchange. But the animosity between the two didn't escape the Prime Minister. A seasoned politician, he saw how close the newspaper people were in the car and quickly broke into the conversation before an incident could occur. "Mr. Rexault, please tell me more about this Alaska Railroad. I've always been interested in trains," he lied.

"Sir, I believe I'll refer you to the Governor on that subject. He actually worked for the railroad while attending the University of Alaska in Fairbanks."

Governor Hughes sipped his cold drink and smiled. Sitting in the train car brought back a few memories of working on a late-night cleaning crew. In fact, he met his first real love there, a woman who would break his heart and go off with another man a short time later. He sometimes wondered if she had found happiness. After he suffered through the long months of heartbreak, he eventually met the woman who would bear him four children and become his life mate.

"Governor?" Bob sensed the Governor was off on one of his memory trips.

"Yes?" Governor Hughes sensed he might have dropped the ball but quickly recovered. "Well, let me see if I can remember. They began laying track in 1915 and it was finally completed in 1923. President Harding came north that year to drive the golden spike in Nenana to dedicate the railroad. Camps were set up so construction workers could have families nearby and some of those survived as communities we'll pass through. The track extends more than 500 miles across some of the world's most unforgiving terrain. Similar problems were faced when the Al-Can Highway was built in World War II and in the 1970s during the construction of the Alaska Pipeline. I've read several articles about the Canadian Railway's problems crossing your own great land. Many of the same issues our workers were challenged by deep, nearly impassible gorges, treacherous mountains, and of course, harsh winter weather.

"I believe nearly 70% of Alaskans live along the railroad's corridor. Over half a million people ride the train every year, mostly visitors during the summer months. The railroad currently employs more than 600 people. Our trains are like an ocean cruise for tourists, showing off a view they could not see from the highway. As Bob said earlier, we'll be crossing the Nenana River and its famous bridge soon. If I remember right, it's called the Mears Memorial Bridge. It's 700 feet long—one of the longest single-span bridges in existence." Governor Hughes shrugged, "I think that's about all I remember, Mr. Prime Minister."

"I'm impressed, Governor. If you'd asked me that same question about our railroads, I'd have to refer you to one of my assistants."

"To be truthful, sir, I learned most of those facts while cleaning these cars. It's true I worked for the railroad while attending college, but mostly on the late-night cleaning crew. I probably cleaned this same car we're riding in."

"Please don't be embarrassed, Governor. My father, although quite wealthy, insisted I learn the business from the ground up. At 13 years of age, I began sweeping the factory floor. I'd probably still be there if it hadn't been for my mother's strong will." A polite chuckle circulated the group as Carlos returned to refill drinks.

The 10-car passenger train rode the steel tracks set in place decades earlier by hardy men made of iron and sweat. Building dirt beds upon tundra was not an easy task to undertake back in the early 1900s. Hundreds of men labored daily, emptying dirt and rock-filled cars from stone quarries. Workers fought off hungry mosquitoes and swarm after swarm of black flies. They withstood bitter cold winds, subzero temperatures, layers of frost, and winter frostbite. Men armed with rifles stood guard against grizzly, brown, or black bears and the occasional wayward moose. These hardy men warred against nature through mountain passes, facing mudslides and mountainous avalanches of snow and ice. Men and the women who stood beside them battled fear of an untamed land covered in hundreds of waterways, vast tundra flats, and steep mountainsides. This was the Alaska wilderness. Only a few native Indian tribes dared to spread out from their coastal settlements and venture into the interior. America discovered this Alaska and like the Old West, the railroad and sailing ships brought civilization to the Far North. Many came in search of gold, furs, and other natural resources. They forged a hard-fought trail from the Seward to Fairbanks, 500 miles of steel track, and a million hand-cut wood ties.

The FLQ Prepares

Sweat ran down Munroe's neck and arms as he barked orders laced with crude remarks and profanity. Using the hillsides in the distance as a goal, Hugo physically pushed the team across broad streams and forded the great Nenana River at a narrow point until they reached the train tracks, where travel became more manageable. Crossing the river required they be roped together, and they promised themselves they would use a different route when this operation was over. A safety line kept two terrorists from drowning, though they took a thorough dunking.

The FLQ resembled an African safari with all the equipment they carried. At least the tracks made travel easier as they proceeded south to the mountain grade they had chosen for the ambush.

Hugo finally called a stop. "This is the spot." He knelt down and studied his map while the others admired the view. Far below, the Nenana River lay in a deep gorge, which they had crossed earlier. After a brief rest, the team readied the ambush site. Time was their worst enemy; Munroe and Hugo were hard taskmasters. Earlier, they had heard the train from Fairbanks travel by, but the thick forest growth prevented them from seeing it.

Gordi knew where the old cabin was and took Paul and Janene with him to get it ready for occupation and prepare the evening meal. A mosquito defogger powered by a five-pound propane bottle was placed just outside the cabin door. The propane tank had been lashed to a back frame, and by the time Paul reached the ambush site, his back was covered in friction burns from the straps. Several mosquito nets were brought to line the inside of the cabin. They may be terrorists, but these were terrorists who wanted to be as comfortable as possible, and mosquito netting was extremely light to carry and easily found in Alaska.

After the kidnapping, it would be cold meals. Hugo didn't want any campfires; smoke could give away their position. The authorities would search for them using satellites to detect heat sources. Later, he ordered a two-mile search of the surrounding area to ensure they were alone. He had read of Alaskan backpackers who traveled these woods and didn't want to discover any neighbors.

Standing alone, Hugo observed the track to the north. He needed to measure the distance from the top of the embankment, where the FLQ would be concealed above the train tracks. He also needed the distance from where they planned to cause a slide to stop the train to where they expected to set up the ambush. After taking measurements, Hugo set up explosives along the steep embankments. He didn't hook the wires; he wanted to ensure he had enough explosives to do the job first. The train going north from Anchorage would be allowed to pass; tomorrow the tracks would be blocked by tons of soil and rock causing the southbound train to stop as well, giving them the opportunity to attack the VIP car. Authorities would have a lot of unhappy tourists to deal with. In the meantime, the FLQ would escort their hostage over the next mountain to the cabin.

Hugo planned to set up a string of claymore mines across the hilltop, hoping the rescue parties would trigger them when they initiated their pursuit. More claymores would line the trails to dissuade any would-be rescuers from following the kidnapper's footsteps. The mines had been obtained from contacts in Whitehorse at a pretty penny. It had surprised Hugo to learn how wide open the Canadian/US border was, but it was an extremely lengthy border in the mostly undeveloped countryside. The munitions had crossed the Canadian border on horseback from North Dakota, purchased by a rogue militia with contacts in the National Guard.

The task of carrying the necessary equipment to the remote location had worn the FLQ members out, so Hugo gave them an hour of rest. He needed to view the trail to the cabin to decide where he wanted to place mines. Tripwires wired to fragmentation grenades strapped to trees would also be used. The cabin would be rigged to kill the hostage if the operation fell apart and that explosion would cover their escape into the wilderness. In an emergency, the exit plan was to make their way south to Talkeetna and separate into small groups. Then they would disappear into Anchorage and make their way back to Eastern Canada or other destinations. Though the Philippines had been suggested, most preferred Mexico and possibly South America.

The train ambush would involve a light anti-tank weapon, known as a LAW. Hugo brought along two rocket-propelled grenades, known as RPGs, that were purchased from the same militia outfit with Dr. Quison's money. By the time they entered Alaska, the FLQ had given the group a grand total of $100,000 in small bills of $50 or less. This came to quite a pile of greenbacks, but the militia contacts were satisfied with the sale.

Hugo's plan was a fast and hard strike, taking the lead engine out with the LAW, then filling the VIP train car with tear gas. Small arms fire would keep the tourists inside their train cars. During the confusion, they would enter the VIP car and kidnap the Prime Minister. Most likely, they would have to kill the security detail. This was very similar to the plan he had used in South America, and it had worked, even though he lost more than half of his group in the process.

RCMP Headquarters-Toronto Office Of Intelligence
June 10th, 6:45 p.m.

JP pushed himself back from his desk and rested his head between his clasped hands. With eyes clenched shut, he struggled to maintain some sense of composure. His thin hold on emotions was dueling with his inability to find his family's killers. It had been a long, tiring, and fruitless day. Not one source seemed to know anything about the FLQ's whereabouts or a link to their membership. They had leaned hard on their informants, first with repeat cash offers and then with threats of jail. However, no one could offer up a single shred of helpful information. JP felt as if he'd come up against a brick wall. Somehow the FLQ had simply vanished, gone into hiding, and to make matters worse, he had nothing to tell his Colonel. Unfortunately, the RCMP Colonel was under pressure from Parliament, who wanted answers to give to the people.

Sgt. Adler appeared in the doorway and walked into the office, carrying a single manila envelope marked "CONFIDENTIAL". He placed it on JP's desk.

"What's that?" JP straightened up, pulled forward on his wheeled chair, and took a minute to tighten his tie.

"I was visiting with an old buddy at TPD (Toronto Police Department), you know, see what their informants have brought in on the FLQ." He saw the look of hope appear in JP's eyes.

"No, don't get excited, Boss. Their people are coming up empty too, but something came across his desk while I was there, and he shared it with me.

"It seems US Customs and Immigration requested our assistance to ID some people who had crossed the border into Alaska. Two people were picked out from photographs taken at the US border station near Tok." Adler opened the envelope and removed two photographs, each having an attached typed biography of the person photographed.

"The first one is a known East German mercenary, a former officer in the East German Army and an expert with explosives. His name and some of his aliases are listed." Adler pointed to the biography. "He was last known to be working with a shadowy group of communists in South Africa, suspected of one car bombing and taking out a large bridge along with a small convoy of local militia unlucky enough to be crossing at the time. They stopped a train, a big shoot-out occurred, and this fellow rescued a political prisoner. The report says he was photographed with a woman while driving a large RV with Yukon license plates into Alaska." Adler walked over and sat down on the couch, "Isn't our Prime Minister going to be riding a train between Fairbanks and Anchorage? TPD is checking out the rental agency, which, according to the plates, owns that RV. They'll send me the info once they have it."

JP put Hugo's photograph aside and picked up the next one, a photo of a woman sitting in the passenger seat.

"That woman is quite a package. A former Canadian Naval officer who was kicked out for anti-government views involving the treatment of Canadian Indian tribes. She's a reported tree-hugger with extreme militant views. Supposedly, she has a connection with the Red Tide group, and that's some serious terrorists." Adler leaned over to open the door of a new refrigerator JP had purchased, claimed a can of cola, and popped it open. She was picked up by several activist groups over the last few years and finally landed a security position with that Red Tide bunch. Known to be good with automatic weapons. There's a slim chance she might be our shooter at the airport."

JP stared at Lesli's photograph for a long moment, trying to decide if she matched the vague description of the airport shooter which was only good enough to match about a third of the white women in Toronto. He looked over at Adler, "So, we have a known female terrorist riding in an RV rented in the Yukon and driven by a known East German mercenary who is an expert in explosives. They told the customs agent at the Alaska border station that they were on their honeymoon."

"So, what do you think?"

"Well, I had a hunch." Adler smiled at the eyebrow JP raised when he mentioned the word *hunch*.

"These two might be connected with the FLQ, and they might be planning to do a repeat of that East German's job in South America. This time, to either kill or kidnap the Prime Minister. If so, this means we have a serious leak. They had to know ahead of time about the Prime Minister's plan to visit Alaska to have the time to set this up. Having those two together is just too much of a coincidence."

"I like your hunch. We need to get copies of these photos with their information wired to our people traveling with the Prime Minister. If I remember right, they're spending the night at some hotel in Fairbanks, a hotel at Denali Park, and one in Anchorage. You'd better get communications on this right now, and I want to talk with whoever's in charge of the protective detail. Notify the Alaska authorities right away, and I'll brief the Colonel. Good work! We need more on this. Get that license plate and check this rental agency. See what names they used to rent this thing under and if it matches any they've used in the past. And find out if anyone else was in the RV with them who escaped being photographed."

"Right away, Captain," Adler replied.

"If this isn't the FLQ, and I can't see any reason why else they'd be traveling to Alaska, then it could be another terrorist group planning an attack on the US. Their FBI needs to have this information ASAP."

Later that night, Sgt Wilkens wandered into the office, complaining of sore feet and weary from listening to too many informants and hearing sorrowful woes on needing more cash for their services. Like most cops, Wilkens needed the information but had no respect for them. He often called informants and lawyers the worst sort of bottom feeders on this planet. Plain scum. Wilkens plopped down on the couch and slipped his shoes off to massage his feet. Only then did he give JP his full attention.

"Did you have a nice afternoon, Sgt. Wilkens?" JP asked.

"I talked with 14 people, but no one has anything to offer. Leaned on a couple pretty hard; you might get some backlash if they decide to file a complaint. Mostly attitude problems who think they need a pay increase—like I got enough money to toss around to this bunch. Too bad we don't get the funds our US counterparts receive to pay people."

"Well, while you were chatting with your so-called friends, Sgt. Adler stumbled into a possible lead." JP tossed the envelope with the photographs to Wilkens and allowed him a few moments to look them over.

"Okay. You've got two real outstanding citizens here; what's the catch?"

"They're traveling together in an RV rented from an agency in Whitehorse, Yukon. They rented two RVs simultaneously to two couples reportedly going on their honeymoons together. All phony names, of course, but they entered Alaska. I've requested the photos of that second couple but haven't received them yet. We're going through airport footage to see if they flew out of Toronto under assumed names. But that'll take time. The photographs were taken when those two entered Alaska. We only have the photographs because Adler had a coffee break with his TPD Intel buddy when the photographs happened to show up."

"So, you think this might be the FLQ or some other group of bad guys getting ready to hit a target in Alaska?"

"Right. It's still pretty thin but this East German took out a train in South America, and our Prime Minister is on a train in Alaska. We're trying to develop some leads on the second RV and who was driving it, and who else might have been aboard. If you think about it, taking an RV across is an excellent way to sneak a bunch of terrorists in, as long as they don't look Mexican or Middle Eastern. You can probably find a way to transport weapons and explosives in an RV, especially one the size they rented. We have the plate numbers from the rental agency, and we're running it through Canadian and US Customs to see what else might pop up. A couple of our men in Whitehorse interviewed the people at this rental agency and got some photos of the two RVs."

"Have you alerted US Customs to all of this?" Wilkens asked.

"They're the ones who requested Canadian assistance; weren't you listening?" JP took the manila envelope back from Wilkens and handed him a handful of photos of Hugo and Lesli. "I know it's a long shot but take a few uniforms with you and hit some key spots in North Toronto with copies of those photographs. See what turns up; maybe a bartender or store cashier might remember seeing them. Okay?"

"On the way." Wilkens slid his shoes back on, wincing as he felt the soles of his feet cry out.

"Wish they'd let us wear jogging shoes," Wilkens mumbled as he went out the door.

Alaska Railroad Office Building-Fairbanks
Office Of Special Agent

It was after 8:00 p.m. and Greg, who would have usually gone home two hours earlier, was still in his office. With both legs propped up on an open desk drawer, he glanced over the VIP itinerary. Greg felt something wasn't quite right in his gut, but he had nothing to base his feeling on. Tossing the papers aside, he thought again about going home and watching TV, maybe nursing his depression with a beer and a microwave pizza. The way he felt right now, perhaps even a night out with Mrs. Busy Body's middle-aged daughter could cheer him up. It sure couldn't hurt. "Yeah… right! A date with that woman, and I'd never be able to face my son again, much less Farber and Richards. I've got to get out of here." Greg stood up, slammed his desk drawer shut, and walked toward the door. His office phone rang, but he decided not to answer it, letting the recorder take the call and file it away for tomorrow.

Grabbing his windbreaker, he raised his fist and shouted, "Power over the machines; we will win the day yet!" He closed the office, locked the outer doors to the ARR Building, and headed to his car. Driving back to his apartment, with a stop at the store to pick up a frozen pizza, Greg decided one thing for sure. Tomorrow he'd clean this car, either that or move out of his apartment and take up residence in the back seat of his Ford Expedition. *I spend more time in this car than I do at home.*

Back at his place, Greg turned the TV on and caught a newsbreak. A flashy blonde with bright white teeth announced a breaking news story concerning Canadian Prime Minister Haegens and Governor Hughes's meeting.

"Hope he liked the train ride," Greg muttered to himself. "Donald would feel bad if the Prime Minister didn't enjoy his trip down the steel road."

After his third beer and bored with the cop drama, Greg turned off the TV and lights and tried to sleep. In the back of his mind was that ominous feeling of impending doom. Occasionally he had such feelings while working as a trooper, and it usually bore fruit. This time, Greg had no idea how well his sixth sense was working, and it was assuredly working overtime.

Denali National Park Hotel
June 10th, 10:55 P.M.


All the security positions were manned for the night, so Sir Jonathan Whiteburn and Agent Woods stopped at the hotel bar for a nightcap. Allowing themselves a single beer, they made small talk about the evening's dinner affair and how well everything went. Including the now laughable experience when one of the FBI agents, acting in an undercover role as a busboy, tripped over a chair and spilled a platter of dirty dinnerware across the floor including his undercover 9mm pistol. Much embarrassed, the agent quickly picked everything up and vanished into the kitchen. It would prove to be one of those experiences that the agent would be reminded of throughout his career.

"We train them to shoot, some martial arts, and how to look seriously pissed when talking with bad guys, but maybe a course in carrying dishes would seem appropriate for undercover assignments," Agent Woods said with a humorous sparkle to his eyes.

"Please deduct the broken dishes from my government's expense account," Sir Whiteburn replied.

Agent Woods added, "He's actually an outstanding agent, a might clumsy though, it seems. He'll probably end up with a call sign like 'Clumsy,' but I've heard of worse ones."

"Well, I think it's time I say good night, Agent Woods." Sir Whiteburn placed his empty bottle on the bar and turned to leave.

"One more item, Sir Whiteburn… please?" Agent Woods asked.

Sir Whiteburn turned to face Agent Woods with an inquiring look. "Yes?"

"It's about that lady, Ms. Wakefield. I've learned she's spending the night here and taking the train tomorrow. Will you have anyone watching her, or should I ask Trooper Richards to remain in her car?"

"Yes, the mysterious Ms. Wakefield." Sir Whiteburn thought for a moment, "Presently, she's in Room 118 on the far side of the hotel. I asked them to put her as far away from the Prime Minister and the Governor as possible. Agent Loury is watching her tonight, and I believe your offer of Trooper Richards is good. Maybe his presence might intimidate her into not acting. If she has a plan in mind and if, for a fact, she is someone we should be concerned with."

"Okay, then. I'll see you bright and early in the morning, and we can continue this wonderful train ride. Good night, sir." Agent Woods placed his partially full beer bottle on the bar and headed for his own room. He carried with him two radios in the event he was needed: one for his own agents and one for the Canadians.

Alaska State Troopers - Cantwell
June 10th, 11:45 P.M.

Captain Potter and his SERT Team were camped inside the Cantwell Post, a two-room building usually used by the single trooper assigned to this area. Responsible for patrolling the Parks Highway winter and summer, the Cantwell trooper was also responsible for half of the 120-mile-long Denali highway in summer when the road was clear of snow. The Denali Highway, a hard-packed dirt road, ran between Cantwell and Paxton at its junction with the Richardson Highway.

Most of Potter's men were laid out in sleeping bags, either asleep or trying to sleep. The space was cramped, but it beat trying to sleep outside with the fearsome bloodsucking mosquitoes flying about by the millions. Potter had heard that if you placed a naked man outside on the tundra, mosquitoes would have him sucked dry of blood within eight hours. *Now that's a grizzly fate!*

Potter was still awake, going over the next morning's flights for the next jump south to Talkeetna with Sgt. Olson. So far, this had been little more than a training exercise, and Captain Potter sincerely hoped it stayed that way.

RCMP Headquarters - Toronto Office Of Divisional Intelligence
June 11th, 0104 Hours

The nightmare was vivid; JP could hear their screams and see the flames rolling toward him. But before they could reach him, he felt someone shaking him. The nightmare faded as he opened his eyes, surprised to see Sgt. Adler's face looming over him.

"Wake up, Boss."

"It'd better be good, Adler! I was dreaming of dancing ladies, pots of gold, and a good cup of coffee." JP rose to a sitting position on the old couch; his gray blanket fell away and landed on the floor. He rubbed his eyes and waited for Adler to start talking.

Adler sat on the edge of JP's desk, "We got an ID on one of the passengers in the second RV. She matched the description of the missing daughter of one of our dignitaries, known to hang with various political activists in the past. And… get this, Boss, she's also a cokehead!" Adler waited for all the pieces to come together as JP's mind cleared.

"Okay. Write it all out for me, and let's head to communications. They have a four-hour time difference, and if I know Sir Jonathan Whiteburn, he's probably already up and showered." JP looked around the room, and his eyes fell on the family portrait on his desk. "I hope those people received those photos you wired to them."

9

—————

# A LITTLE CHANGE IN PLANS

Mt. McKinley National Park Hotel
June 11th, 06:12 hours

Aman used to waking up at 5:30 every morning, Sir Jonathan Whiteburn was already showered, shaved, and sitting at his room's corner table, glancing over the day's schedule. When the phone rang, Jonathan stood up and walked over to answer it, "Room 211."

"Jonathan, this is Jean-Paul Leon in Toronto."

"JP!" Jonathan recognized his old friend's voice. "Now, what's got you calling me so early in the morning?" Jonathan checked his wristwatch, "Oh, I forgot it's 10:12 a.m. back there."

"I needed to confirm whether or not you've received information on a couple of identified terrorists and two other suspects who entered Alaska in the last couple of days?"

"JP, this isn't a secure line... but to answer your question, no, I haven't. Call me back at this cell number." Sir Whiteburn hung up, sat on the bed, and waited for his cell phone to ring. When it did, he answered and listened as JP briefed him on what they had so far. Jonathan took notes but didn't interrupt until his friend finished.

"How long before you can fax me those photographs?" Jonathan asked.

"You should already have them, but give me the hotel's fax number, and

153

you'll have another copy immediately," JP replied. "We sent copies to your office yesterday; they must've got held up getting to you."

"JP, we do have a woman staying here that has us concerned. She matches the description of the woman traveling with this East German. We're keeping an eye on her; she's due to travel with us to Anchorage."

"I suspect the two in the other RV may fit the definition of terrorist. The second woman is a coke addict known to hang with political activists and a runaway from a political family. She could be one of two female suspects wanted for the murder of two Toronto Police Officers. A dope buy went bad, and the officers were gunned down by an automatic weapon. Possibly, this other woman you have under observation. The employee who witnessed the shooting couldn't give us a good description of the female shooter. We're planning on doing a photo line-up with him later today."

"You must pardon me, JP; with all that's been going on with this visit, I've forgotten my manners and failed to express my sympathy for your loss. I was very fond of your family, as you well know." Jonathan rose to his feet, picked up his radio, and called Tod Loury. "Respond immediately to my room; not an emergency but bring Agent Woods with you."

"Thank you, Jonathan. I know this information causes you several immediate problems. I sincerely hope this is the FLQ and not another faction. I'd like to end this before another bombing can take anyone else's family away."

"I fully understand," Jonathan whispered. "Now, you must let me return to my job. I'll have one of the agents call you, Agent Tod Loury, to give you the fax number for the hotel here. I must brief the Prime Minister and Governor Hughes and learn of their desires."

"Jonathan, I've seen the Anchorage train depot and the airport; each would be an easy location to take out the Prime Minister. Can you tell me what hotel you'll be staying at?"

"The Hilton in Anchorage, a rather large multi-level hotel in the middle of the city." Jonathan was walking over to his room door after hearing the knock. "I feel like I could use another set of hands here," Jonathan said to himself.

"The Hilton has an enclosed parking garage adjacent to it. Good location for a sniper. You might want to forgo the State dinner and fly on to Seattle."

"You know how it works, JP; we've talked about it enough over dinner. I am a servant to the Prime minister, and I must go where he directs." Jonathan glanced at his watch, "Please, my friend, I must leave you so I can get things arranged for this next leg of our journey and hopefully arrest this woman before she can do any harm. I'll have Agent Loury call you right away."

"Good luck, Jonathan. You must understand when I say that I sincerely hope these animals resist if and when you find them."

"So do I, JP, so do I." Jonathan hung up to look through the little peephole, and seeing Agent Loury and Agent Woods, he opened the door. Jonathan explained who JP was for Agent Woods's benefit and shared the information from the phone call. He sent Loury to the hotel office to obtain their office fax number and immediately called JP.

Moments later, Agent Loury had the photographs in hand. Seeing the photo of Ms. Wakefield, though a bit grainy, he smiled and congratulated himself for his inner sense that this Wakefield woman was indeed a bad one. Returning to Room 211, he handed the photos to Jonathan and watched as the old agent's right eyebrow shot up in recognition.

"So, one of the suspected terrorists is, in fact, riding along with us, but strangely without her former traveling partner." Jonathan handed the photographs to Agent Woods.

"Tod, do you remember seeing anyone like this on the train?" Jonathan pointed at Hugo's photograph.

"No, sir. I wouldn't have missed this guy, either. Looks like a scary dude—East German mercenary and most likely highly trained."

"From their bios, I'd suspect they're part of this FLQ, who may have come to Alaska with a desire to kill our Prime Minister. Or they've sold their services to another terrorist faction, such as al-Qaida or ISIS. Oh, for the days when there were only a few terrorist factions out there. In either event, we should consider them a risk and upgrade our security level immediately."

After Agent Woods finished reviewing the bios, Jonathan provided him with a brief description of the infamous FLQ. He highlighted their recent bombings and violent attacks on JP's home in an act of revenge. He advised the two men of the recent murder of the two Toronto Police officers and the suspicion this woman was involved.

"This East German Army officer sounds like a stone-cold killer and the item about the train in South America really concerns me." Agent Woods said. "I'd really like to know where he is now." Woods handed the photographs back to Jonathan. "With your permission, I'd like to have a few dozen copies made of these."

"Of course, but first, we must decide our next course of action regarding Ms. Wakefield. Since we're in Alaska, this must be your decision Agent Woods, should your men arrest her? Or do we allow her to continue with two of our men in the same car?" Jonathan waited for Agent Woods to respond.

"Well, she's plainly entered the US illegally, using an alias, and both your country and Interpol have several warrants out for her arrest for prior activity —all of which gives us cause to arrest her," Agent Woods said. "From what your friend in Toronto says, she is also a possible suspect in the murder of two Toronto Police Officers and most likely armed. Rather than endanger anyone else, I first suggest you notify those officers you have watching her to be extremely cautious. This attractive lady is to be considered armed and most probably a killer. If this Captain Leon of the Royal Canadian Mounted Police is right, she cannot be taken lightly."

"We must also consider that she is maintaining contact with her traveling partner, either by landline or cell phone," Jonathan said. "This means she is most likely carrying information about their purpose for entering Alaska. I'd dearly like to have a chance to talk with her."

"So would I," Agent Woods agreed.

Jonathan looked at his watch, "I must leave you in order to brief my Prime Minister. I'll let you know what he decides regarding future travel plans. I'll also advise Governor Hughes and Sgt. Niles of the situation. I leave this woman's arrest to you, gentlemen. Watch yourselves."

"You think there's a possibility these people might be supporting an al-Qaida network who plan to hit another target? Maybe the pipeline?" Agent Loury asked Agent Woods.

"Possibly, but doubtful. Too much of a coincidence with this woman on the train and staying here overnight."

Jonathan, put his coat on, "I suspect this woman and her associates have diabolical plans for our Prime Minister, which may include Governor Hughes. We must know where and when they plan to strike." Jonathan walked out the door with Loury at his heels, leaving Agent Woods standing in the middle of the room alone with a 500-pound gorilla riding on his shoulders.

Agent Woods decided this was a decision to be made by his boss, Special Agent in Charge Harold Wright, a 63-year-old paper pusher who hadn't been in the field since Jimmy Carter was President. Passing the buck up the chain of command was an old game too often played in government circles and many civilian companies. In a harsh world of competition, making a decision that could turn sour can quickly lead the decision maker to a position on the bread line. Using his government-issued cell phone, Agent Woods called the Anchorage office and learned SAC Wright had arrived for work.

Agent Loury left Jonathan's shadow and went to brief Lesli's shadow on precisely who he was watching and how dangerous this petite woman was. "Think of her as a pit viper, small, sleek, and deadly."

Alaska State Trooper Post - Healy

His back sore from a rough night sleeping on the floor with his team, Captain Potter was in a foul mood when his cell phone chimed the first notes of the 1812 Overture. "This is Captain Potter." By the time he hung up, the AST SERT Commander was fully awake and had grabbed his uniform. Potter shouted orders to his men, his enthusiasm apparent, and started looking around the room for his pilot. They'd been given the green light to take down a suspected terrorist. Potter quickly envisioned the newspaper's bold headline, AST NABS TERRORIST, naming him the on-scene commanding officer. "I'll brief you further in...," Potter looked at his watch, "...in eight minutes."

It fell on Sgt. Olson's shoulders to get the team geared up and out to the helipad while a frantic Potter went in search of the pilot. A red-faced Captain Potter was about to blow a fuse when he found Trooper "Bud" Watson, making an early morning visit to the post's old outhouse. Pounding on the door, Potter ordered him in a loud surly voice to get his bird ready to go. "This is a code-three response, Trooper!"

Watson opened the door and shook his head. "Keep your shirt on, Captain." Watson didn't like this man, and because he was one of the few helicopter pilots in the Troopers, he wasn't about to cow down to him.

Ignoring the pilot's rudeness, Potter asked, "We'll be flying to the Ranger Station rescue helipad inside the park; how long will it take to get there?"

"About 12 minutes flying time, but it's gonna take me at least 10 minutes to get her pre-flighted, warmed up, and ready to fly."

"Then you'd better hurry; I need my whole team inside the park ASAP! We're assisting the feds in taking down a suspected terrorist."

"Any coffee made?" Bud asked. The man wasn't the excitable type, having flown over 100 combat sorties during Desert Storm in '91, followed by two years as an instructor pilot with addlebrained cadets, who tried their best to kill him.

"No! And there isn't any room service either! So, get your butt in gear, Trooper, and get that helicopter ready to lift off!" Potter bellowed. He dashed off to join Sgt. Olson, who was hurriedly packing up his gear.

"No time for that; just leave it here. We're only taking our full-breach gear. Make sure you have your gas masks, double-check all weapons, and ensure we have the proper equipment to take down a barricaded suspect."

"Sir, all equipment is in readiness, the men are champing at the bit, and we're ready to rock and roll," Sgt Olson replied.

"Good." Potter hated that rock and roll term, but this wasn't the time to correct Olson. "Officially, this is an agency assist. The FBI cannot get their own people here in time, so they've requested us to back their people. I imagine it's gonna be all our show once the 'GO' order is given."

"Are they evacuating the hotel? We've got a lot of tourists in that place." Sgt Olson asked, but his CO didn't seem to care about civilian liabilities by the sour-faced expression on Potter's face.

Captain Potter briefed his team on the FBI's request while Watson finished his pre-flight at the helipad. Just as they had come down from Fairbanks, getting the whole team on site would take three hops. The last group had nearly an hour to wait before they'd be in the air. But with Captain Potter, they had to look ready to make the hop. After Potter lifted away with the first group of three, Sgt Olson returned to the AST house to scrounge up some coffee and chew on a breakfast energy bar. The helicopter wouldn't be back for at least 30 minutes, long enough to brew a pot in the post's Mr. Coffee. The others followed, appreciating their sergeant's low-key approach to life.

Mt. McKinley Park Hotel
June 11th, 0758 Hours

Agents Woods advised Sir Jonathan of his orders to take Ms. Wakefield down immediately and how he'd already requested Captain Potter's SERT team to back them up.

Jonathan informed Agent Woods that Prime Minister Haegens, Governor Hughes, and Senator Sterns had agreed to continue by train to Anchorage and their plans for a State Dinner in the hotel. As a precaution, the Anchorage Police SWAT team would split duties between the Anchorage ARR terminal and the Hilton Hotel. By the time the train arrived at the ARR Depot, sniper teams would be in place, along with extensive crowd control. Bomb dogs would conduct searches of the ARR Depot, the hotel, and the parking garage.

They all believed that if the terrorists were planning an attack on the Prime Minister, it would be at one of those locations or possibly between the sites. Extra police officers would be brought in from regularly scheduled days off to provide added security at the depot and the hotel, initiating Code Red Security procedures for the downtown vicinity and the airport.

This resulted in Special Agent (SAC) Wright informing the military forces at Elmendorf Air Force Base and Fort Richardson of the increased security level, prompting the commanders to heighten their own security levels. *Terrorist* was a word that heightened everyone's awareness and required actions to be taken. Nothing was ever the same after 9-11. Not only had the terrorists destroyed the

Two Towers and killed thousands of people, but they affected the day-to-day way of life for all of America. Standard everyday freedom was no longer assured as security levels were upgraded.

With heavy morning work traffic already arriving for jobs downtown and at the bases, local military police found themselves dealing with bumper-to-bumper traffic. Vehicles were backed up for over a half-mile down the main arteries outside the Elmendorf and Fort Richardson vehicle gates. Mandatory ID checks were initiated at all military checkpoints. Some people were forbidden entry and turned away for various reasons, which only added to the confusion. Tourists were kept away from the ARR depot; unless they had tickets or confirmed reservations to travel north on the train. A valid ID and passports were required for all foreigners.

Authorities upset the Hilton Hotel's daily business. Federal officers and local police nearly took over the ground floor, keeping all but hotel guests from entering the building. The same happened at the hotel's parking garage across the street.

Photographs of Hugo, Lesli, Munroe, and Janene were faxed to law enforcement agencies, and copies handed out to officers. Every cop on patrol and every military gate guard was looking for the suspects. Except for only a few senior officers, no one else was informed that Lesli was currently in the hotel at Denali National Park.

Bomb dogs that could be spared from Elmendorf and Fort Richardson were brought in to assist APD K-9 units in searching the ARR depot and the Hilton Hotel. Eventually, the enclosed parking garage near the hotel was closed for the day, requiring private security officers to direct unhappy drivers to other parking locations in an already crowded downtown area. Only the hotel's guests and employees could park inside the multi-level garage. Citizens weren't told the reason this was occurring. Irritated Anchorage citizens complained on the local talk radio shows. Not that it mattered much to law enforcement authorities. Most listeners assumed it was due to the Prime Minister's arrival in Anchorage and the planned state dinner.

For those in Alaska Law Enforcement, it appeared Alaska had become involved in the world of International Terrorism. Only a few people between Denali National Park and Anchorage were aware of the circumstances. That changed quickly as news services bribed, borrowed, and stole to get the nitty-gritty in hopes of getting one up on their competition. What had begun as classified information blossomed into the day's major news story, "Terrorists in Alaska".

It left local police officers in Anchorage and on the military installations to issue the same line to civilian complaints; "We're following orders issued by Federal authority. Please, Sir, just move your car… and have a nice day."

Room # 118, Mt. McKinley Park Hotel

Restless and unable to sleep, Lesli tossed pillows to the floor in frustration, climbed out of bed, and began pacing the room. With daylight from outside streaming in, she didn't bother turning on the room light. Wearing only light blue panties and a bra, she walked the length of her room with her Glock pistol loosely held in one hand. Occasionally, she swung the gun up to her face and leaned the barrel against her forehead as she thought over her options. She suspected the authorities had somehow recognized her on the train, having spotted the one man watching her in the hotel. She couldn't figure out how they identified her and why they hadn't tried to arrest her.

Picking up the satellite phone from the nightstand, she called Munroe and told him what was happening. Lesli heard the familiar *whump-whump-whump* of a helicopter flying overhead and told Munroe to hold on. She walked to the window; her instincts were ringing true; flying over the tops of the trees was an Alaska State Trooper helicopter, easily identifiable by the white and blue coloring and the AST shield on the bird's body. Too far away to see who was inside, she felt a sudden chill run down her backside, and her palms became clammy. "Steve, they've got the state police flying in—I don't like it!"

"Go to your door, open it slowly, and peer outside. Look down the hallway, and tell me what you see," Munroe told her. Signaling Hugo to come over from where he was wiring grenades to the bottoms of trees, he told Hugo about what was happening with Lesli.

Laying the phone on the bathroom's white countertop, Lesli squeezed the handgrip on her pistol as she quietly unlocked the door's deadbolt. Holding her breath, she eased the door open a couple of inches to peak out. Expecting to see the barrel end of an M-16 in the experienced hands of a SWAT Team member, she was surprised to see the hallways in front of her door empty. She breathed a sigh of relief and opened the door wider. As Lesli looked to her left, down the adjacent hallway, she knew she was in serious trouble. Two uniformed armed US Park Rangers, wearing burley-looking bulletproof vests, were escorting a family out of a room three doors down the hall.

That was enough. Lesli knew her time had run out. She picked up the satellite phone and whispered, "Steve, they're getting ready for me. Cops are evacuating people down the hall, and they're wearing heavy Kevlar." She fought to control the trembling, but the phone shook in her hand more from the adrenaline surge than fear. "Listen, Steve… my time's run out; looks like you'll have to go to an alternate plan for that train engineer."

"Lesli…" Munroe hesitated, which was very unlike him. Lesli waited impatiently. "Lesli, you don't want to be taken alive. Take as many cops as you can. Goodbye." During the road trip to Alaska, Munroe appreciated Lesli's sarcastic wit and political savvy. Not that it mattered now.

Lesli threw the phone onto the floor and looked at her reflection in the room's large wall mirror. She nodded as she realized this was indeed the end. "I couldn't stand prison anyway." Lesli smashed the satellite phone with her pistol. She thought about her life for a brief moment and then surprised herself by wondering what hell might be like. From her past violent actions and poor decisions, she would never be welcomed through the pearly gates some of her family members had believed in. Not even bothering to get dressed, Lesli put a clammy hand on the doorknob. Getting her courage up, she let out a lung full of air, took a deep breath, exhaled again, and then quietly opened the door.

Corporal Richards, in the process of escorting a honeymoon couple from Colorado out of their room, heard two shots fired from down the hall. Violently, he shoved the startled young couple back into their room. Staying glued to the wall, Richards spotted a uniformed Park Ranger spread out on the hallway carpet in an unnatural position. The female suspect was positioned in a shooter's two-handed crouch over the dead park Ranger.

Richards dropped to one knee to bring his pistol up when Lesli shot him in the left shoulder. He bounced off the wall and landed on his right side.

Like most police officers or military trainees, Lesli was taught to fire two bullets quickly to ensure an effective hit. Her second bullet, a hollow point round, exploded against Richards' left hip and put him flat on his back.

Moaning and fighting to stifle a scream, Richards rolled across the hallway in agony and onto his good hip. He brought his pistol up with his right hand. Lesli, thinking Richards was down for good, jerked around to fire off two more shots up the other end of the hallway striking a second uniformed park Ranger. In his attempt to protect two hotel guests, the Ranger was hit in the back, where his Kevlar vest absorbed the bullets. But the force of the shots sent him sprawling forward to land on top of one of the guests.

Agent Woods shouted, "Shots fired! Shots fired! Officer's down—I repeat—officers down! Suspect outside her room armed with a semi-automatic pistol. I need assistance, and I need it now!"

Richards fought to ignore the fiery pain and sighted in on Lesli's back. He pulled the trigger twice, and his rounds struck Lesli in the back, right between her shoulders. At the same time, Agent Tod Loury fired his own weapon and shot Lesli in the head. She was thrown forward, landed on the carpet face down, no longer breathing. One of the bullets had struck the center of her heart, killing her instantly. Loury's bullet penetrated her brain.

Agent Loury rushed forward from farther down an adjoining hallway to Richard's unconscious form. Seeing he was still alive, he grabbed his radio and shouted, "Officers down, suspect down! Code four (all clear), I need EMTs right now!

Unsure the suspect was alone, Loury led three arriving uniformed Rangers through her room's doorway. They found it empty, except for an overnight bag of clothes and a smashed phone lying on the floor by the bathroom.

"Don't touch that phone! We might get some useable evidence from it," Agent Loury ordered.

Outside The Hotel

When Captain Potter arrived, he learned that shots had been fired inside the hotel. He and his first team of men double-timed to the hotel lobby only to find they were no longer needed. The suspect was dead, killed by a Canadian Secret Service agent. One Park Ranger was killed, apparently taken by surprise, and another wounded. Potter was informed that Agent Woods and Corporal Richards were wounded in the shooting. Saddened by the Ranger's death, Captain Potter fought disappointment for having not participated in the terrorist's violent takedown. He wanted the credit for this operation in hopes it would eventually lead to another promotion. It seemed other officers, including an AST corporal, would share the prestige of their involvement in this action.

Captain Potter was even more surprised to find out the suspect, a woman, had killed one man and wounded three other trained professionals before she was killed. Asked for assistance, Captain Potter provided his team to help with crowd control and a search of the hotel for other possible shooters. Nothing turned up. The AST SERT Team was assigned to guard the VIPS as they boarded the train to travel to Anchorage.

Briefed on the recent intelligence concerning suspected FLQ involvement, Potter expressed his belief that Anchorage would be the location for the group's assassination attempt. He began preparing for his unit's operation in Alaska's largest city. The APD SWAT Team would be the primary team inside the city, and Potter's crew would handle the outlying areas. The SERT Teams members could tell this fact did not sit well with Captain Potter.

Mt. McKinley Hotel Lobby- 09:14 Hours

"Captain Potter, with this recent change of events, I am inclined to ask that your team assist the State Airport Police at the Anchorage Airport," Jonathan said as the two men conferred in the lobby. Anchorage Police and their SWAT unit will assist us at the railroad depot and the Hilton Hotel. We'll need your men for added security tomorrow morning." Jonathan stopped as a man, and his small son walked by. "Although inside the city, the airport is considered state property, and we may need both teams to cover. There are a lot of buildings and hangers there, far more than can be safely covered by the existing force of airport police and private security. Can I count on you, Captain?"

"Of course, Sir Whiteburn," Captain Potter agreed with pleasure. "As soon as the train pulls into Anchorage, I'll turn the duties over to APD and shift our concern to the airport. We've run several training exercises out there, boarding aircraft with hostages aboard and various other scenarios." Potter took a notebook from his left back pocket and made some notations. "I'll move my team south once the train departs the park, and we'll be in Anchorage by late afternoon."

"Thank you, Captain." Jonathan shook hands with Potter and walked off to check with Agent Loury. He knew Loury was feeling a bit low over the shooting.

In standard cases when a suspect was killed, a lengthy investigation was involved. Diagrams of the shooting scene would be done, accounting for every bullet fired with detailed drawings and measurements and dozens of photographs taken before the body could be moved. However, the on-scene investigation would be handled very quickly with multiple agencies involved. Typically, Agent Loury would be relieved of duty pending the review by the shooting board. However, Jonathan was waving that rule because Agent Loury was still needed to protect the Prime Minister.

Agent Woods, who was treated at the scene, dictated a statement. Richards was airlifted to Fairbanks Memorial Hospital, where he was interviewed following surgery. The National Park Ranger, who took two hits to his vest, was treated at the scene and back in the office filling out one of many required forms. Mourning his buddy's death, the Ranger was congratulated for his excellent job in shielding the civilians from harm.

News of the event and all the details were passed on to the U.S. Secretary of the Interior and the US President within an hour. It was all over the radio and television by noon. Most of the details and names of those involved were withheld for the moment.

Loury dictated his report into a tape recorder for the National Park Service. Prime Minister Haegens, Governor Hughes, and Senator Sterns were confined to their rooms under heavy guard until the Fairbanks train arrived and was ready to depart. That train was searched thoroughly, and every passenger identified. Passengers continuing to Anchorage were confined to their train cars for the remainder of the trip. The train car ahead of the VIP car was cleared of passengers for added security. There was talk of flying the two VIPS to Anchorage, but that option was turned down by both the Prime Minister and the Alaska Governor.

Volunteer Rescue Services from Healy and Cantwell arrived on the scene to treat the wounded. Afterward, they provided emergency care to civilians who had observed the traumatic episode and needed a soft shoulder to cry on.

Denali ARR Depot-10:35 A.M.

After breakfast in their rooms, the VIP party prepared to walk to the park's ARR depot with an escort of 12 armed officers. Some were in uniform and carrying shotguns, and others wore long trench coats that concealed automatic weapons. Inside the VIP train car, nearly everyone was discussing the lady terrorist and the why and how of her being in Alaska aboard their train. Sir Jonathan was concerned about the two RVs that crossed into Alaska and what those people may have smuggled across the border.

During a meeting with Prime Minister Haegens, Jonathan shared his suspicion of the terrorists. "Sir, if indeed that woman and her confederates are members of this FLQ, they could be planning an attack to hit our vehicle convoy en route to the airport, or they may make an attempt at the hotel. The airport is too well protected by established security procedures. Our protection detail must consider options with so many factors involved. We feel that the deceased female was probably on the train to keep an eye on you and observe your security detail. She was apparently reporting information by satellite phone, which is why she destroyed that phone before her demise. In any event, we have a strong presence of law enforcement watching over you and our other VIPs. We must acknowledge that these terrorists could be in Alaska for another reason. Alaskan authorities have raised their alert status due to this shooting."

Agent Woods, cradling his injured arm, brought up that the Anchorage depot and hotel would be heavily guarded, "I'm sure by now, these people know we're on to them and our security level has been upgraded. They would be foolhardy to take on a target now."

Jonathan shook his head, "Agent Woods, these people are not kidnappers or bank robbers. We're talking about the filth of the earth—terrorists! They're people who enjoy killing for their cause. They often use suicide bombers to blow up hospitals or buses full of families. Alaska is fairly new to terrorism, but we've been experiencing it in Canada since before your 9-11 tragedy. The old FLQ carried out its reign of terror back in the 1960s and '70s. The word 'terrorists' wasn't even used much back then. The news people called them gangs or political extremist groups." Jonathan gave his people a stern look, "These people feel they're true patriots to whatever cause they're fighting for. They're as fanatical as those who rode the planes into the Twin Towers or set off bombs worldwide. They carry out assassinations blowing up trains, buses, schools, and hospitals. Extra police won't stop them from attempting to strike at us. Hopefully, we can stop the attempt once it's in progress before we lose any of our people."

"How about moving the prime targets to other vehicles, maybe police cars, and keep the limos empty," Sgt Niles suggested. The train began to jar from side to side and then back and forth as it pulled out from the depot.

"Not a bad idea. Let's discuss several different options and then select a final plan." Jonathan gave Niles a friendly nod before he pulled out his cell phone to call headquarters in Ottawa. Seeing Loury's rough shape, he wanted to arrange a short leave of absence for him once this detail was over. Unfortunately, no one ever broached the subject of a possible attack on the train itself. Taking on a moving train had never been done in Alaska. The rough ground between the park and Anchorage made it quite improbable. It was one of the main reasons it was chosen. The surprise would be on the terrorist's side.

Newspaper reporters had their hands full, jumping from notepads to laptop computers and cell phones to get their stories turned in. Out of the kindness of their ink-filled hearts, publishers shared the accounts with TV and radio news services, but only after they got the first stories ready for the next day's editions. Everyone knew that TV and radio services could broadcast on-the-spot news. The newspapers brought out complete details of the events taking place.

By noon the shooting was international news. At approximately the same time, the FLQ began its ambush on the Alaska Railroad train. As unlikely and improbable as it seemed law enforcement would again find themselves unprepared for the terrorists.

10

———

# AMBUSH!

Four Miles South Of Cantwell, Along The ARR Tracks
June 11th, 10:54 A.M.

Tony Rogers gritted his teeth as a painful spasm burned through his lower back. He laid his chainsaw on the ground and pulled a near-empty bottle of pain pills from his pocket. Tony checked the number of pills remaining and twisted the lid off and dropped three of the white tablets into his palm. Counting the larger vial of painkillers in the cabin, Tony realized he was getting dangerously low and needed to contact the Veterans Hospital in Anchorage to see why his medication hadn't arrived. As summer chores increased with the season, he used more of the pills due to the extra work. Tylenol Three Codeine tablets barely dented the fiery pain he dealt with, but anything stronger left him confused and groggy. Living as he did in the wilderness required a clear mind and a lot of physical labor. Living anywhere else was out of the question.

Tony used a recently rebuilt chainsaw to drop the beetle-killed spruce trees near his cabin. He estimated the trees he was cutting would provide more than two cords of good dry wood. His red ATV four-wheeler was parked nearby.

His legs burned, as pain shot up through his hips into his lower back. He washed the pills down with a gulp of distilled spring water he carried in a two-quart canteen.

When Tony heard the train off to the north, he looked toward the tracks and waited for the recognizable yellow and deep blue locomotive to appear around

166

the bend. The distinct colors of the ARR train made it stand out beautifully in the natural greens of the Alaskan wilderness. As the southbound train drew near, Tony moved behind a stand of tall spruce, not wanting to be seen. Because of his disfigurement from the Huey crash, he disliked passengers pointing at him.

Tony shied away from tourists, believing the passengers would try to capture him on camera. Though he knew they couldn't see his many scars, Tony felt self-conscious about his looks and took to hiding.

He was surprised to see two locomotives pulling the train. Usually, there was only one, but he figured one might be on the way to the shop in Anchorage for routine work.

He tried to imagine what the passengers might think as they stared out the train's large windows and admired the Alaska scenery. It was probably the first trip to Alaska for most of them. In Cantwell, Tony had listened to many express their love for Alaska's great outdoors. He had heard many promise to return someday. *Who wouldn't want to return with so much openness and a soothing feeling of complete freedom?*

Comparable to the Pacific southwest's great deserts, Alaska's untouched wilderness held a mysterious aura that drew people back again and again. Tony never grew tired of looking across the massive tundra plains, the low blue mountains, and the state's majestic towering giants draped in a constant white blanket. There were no moose or bears in the immediate vicinity, his chainsaw had seen to that with its loud grinding sound, but there were always the untouched and eye-appealing mountains to snap photographs of.

As he watched the train go by, Tony wondered about the tourists visiting here. He remembered how green he was when he first arrived in Alaska. In time, he learned that many of these citified tourists rarely left their hotels unless they traveled with tour groups operating on tight schedules. There were young adventurous ones who carried a pack and sleeping bag and vanished for a week or two in the wilderness for an authentic Alaska experience. His least favorite were those who carried expensive video cameras, rarely seeing anything until they returned home to watch the tapes on television. "Sign people" tended to drive Tony crazy as they posed for photographs in front of manmade signs to show where they were. *See, that's us standing in front of the sign at Denali National Park... This is us standing in front of the sign showing where the camp restrooms are located... And this is us...."*

Tony smiled, his disfigured face resembling a grizzly bear snarl. He hoped the people got their money's worth coming to Alaska, he knew how expensive such trips could be. When the last passenger car went by, he noticed it was oddly placed behind the baggage car. He spotted a man who was either Governor Hughes or someone who closely resembled him which surprised Tony as very few governors traveled by train between Fairbanks and Anchorage. *Sure looked like Governor Hughes or his twin brother!*

After the train passed from view, Tony fired up the chainsaw and went back to work. He estimated this job would likely be an all-day affair. He loaded six-foot sections onto his single-axle trailer and took them back to the cabin to be cut into 12 to 14-inch rounds to be split again into stove-size chunks. It was a tiresome backbreaking job that he did not enjoy but he appreciated the warmth the wood provided. It usually took him 10-12 hours to split half a cord because he had to take frequent breaks to rest his back and legs. Afterward, he had to stack the wood in one of his two woodsheds to protect it from the weather.

Mosquitoes and black flies were extremely bothersome as the pesty things dive-bombed seemingly unaffected by his heavy dousing of mosquito repellant. At times, it got so bad that Tony smeared thick mud over his exposed skin, a lesson he had learned from his former mentor. When flights of black flies went for his eyes, he donned a mosquito net hat. Unfortunately, he didn't have it with him and could kick himself for forgetting it.

Although he loved the summers, he looked forward to winter and the absence of pestering bugs and busybody tourists who frequented the Reindeer Lodge. When Tony went in for a meal, rude tourists often stared at his disfigured face. Curious and insensitive ones approached, to talk, "How'd it happen, mister? Does it hurt much?" or, "You get that in the war, buddy?" He found them insulting and ignored them. Tony wanted only to sit at the bar, read his books, and occasionally listen to Old Man Taylor's television. He found it bothersome that he still needed some human contact. He rarely participated in conversation unless it was with someone he knew well enough to be comfortable with. Such talks were primarily one-sided, with Tony nodding or saying an occasional yes or no.

Tony didn't think much about the train or the people riding it after it disappeared.

On Board The Southbound Train

As he accepted a cup of hot Earl Grey tea from the hostess, Sir Jonathan Whiteburn noticed the man's blue plastic nametag, 'Richard.' Sir Jonathan thanked him and waited as Richard presented Bob Rexault with a can of Dr. Pepper and a glass of ice. The two men were discussing security issues with Sgt. Niles and Agent Tensley. The main topic of discussion concerned the vehicle convoy and whether or not the Governor should be in the same limo as Prime Minister Haegens. There would be two convoys: one to the hotel and the next day's ride to the airport. Dozens of cell phone calls were made, breaking in and out as the train traveled through dead zones. Sgt. Niles called AST Headquarters in Anchorage and Juneau to keep the Commissioner of Public Safety and his AST Colonel up to date. There were phone calls to Captain Potter and the Assistant Police Chief for APD. Sir Jonathan wished he had brought a satellite phone.

Extra police officers and field agents were called in to provide protection for the formal dinner that night. A press conference was to be held in the Hilton Hotel lobby following dinner. Afterward, Governor Hughes would fly back to Juneau on the late-night red-eye flight. The Prime Minister would fly out of Anchorage just before noon the following day for his trip to Seattle.

Senator Sterns was quite unhappy pestering nearly every law enforcement entity on the train, demanding to know how a suspected terrorist could enter Alaska or travel with them to the park. "How could she just board the train and spend the night in the same hotel?" She wanted answers and was overly persistent in her demands. Her screechy voice was getting on everyone's nerves, especially Bob Rexault. He imagined himself throttling the woman to shut her up. Luckily, seeing the stern expression on Rexault's face, Governor Hughes sent him to the other end of the car to keep the newspaper people happy.

Sitting by himself, Agent Tod Loury looked out the large picture window with a blank stare. He was still coming to terms with shooting the female suspect in the hotel. Loury knew the possibility of taking someone's life came with the job but never suspected it would involve shooting a woman in the back of the head. After the shooting and seeing Lesli's body, he leaned over a toilet and vomited. His bullet entered her head and splattered blood and brain matter all over the hallway floor and walls—a sight he would never forget. He had fired more from instinct to save lives as he had been trained regardless of others doing the same. If any one of them had missed, she could very likely have killed someone else. He might not have felt so bad had it been a male suspect. Shooting a woman was too tough for him to deal with.

Sir Jonathan ambled back and sat with Loury, hoping to let him talk it out. Seeing him, however, Sir Jonathan realized the man needed time alone. He asked another agent to keep an eye on him, then patted Tod's shoulder with fatherly affection. "Give it time, Tod. Don't rush it. With any wound, healing takes time, both mental and physical."

Tod nodded and returned to watching the landscape race by. He felt the train begin to slow as the two locomotives started the challenging task of pulling a steep grade. It was these steep mountains that required two engines for this passenger train.

ARR Mile Post 259.4

Janene and Michael were the spotter team, north of the ambush site ready to signal the train's arrival with a call over the satellite phone. If the phone failed to connect, they would fire a single shot with the handgun. Hugo told them that with the train pulling the steep grade, it was doubtful anyone on board would hear the shot.

Hugo prepared a series of explosive devices to take the hillside section down to block the tracks. His plan was to wait until the engineer was close enough to see the landslide occur. The engineer would be too busy to send an alarm to the security people on board. An earlier explosion was discussed, but Hugo and Munroe decided that having the slide come down right in front of the engine would cause the engineers to brake hard. The sudden stop would jar the cars and put the security teams off-balance for a moment.

Concealed behind a rock embankment, Gordi, Paul, and Shawn were ready with two LAW rocket tubes, and Munroe and Thomas were armed with 40mm RPGs. Each man was assigned a different target. The rest of the team would use automatic weapons to keep the passengers inside the train cars. They were not to shoot at the windows but to aim for the gravel bed below the tracks.

Hugo was responsible for detonating the explosives and setting plastique charges in select locations for the best possible effect. There were enough deadfalls and old rockslides to conceal most of the team. Once the train came to a sudden stop, Gordi would hit the lead engine with a LAW rocket to prevent the train crew from attempting to back the train up or call for help. Shawn would launch his weapon against the second locomotive to be followed by sporadic automatic weapons fire into the track bed in front of the passenger cars.

When the lead engine rounded the bend, Janene jumped to her feet with delight. In her excitement, she wrestled Munroe's satellite phone out of Michael's grasp and called Hugo. "They're here! The train's here!"

Hugo stood behind a stand of spruce trees at the top of the hill and looked out over the team. He waved his right arm and yelled to Munroe, "NOW!" Hugo detonated the first series of explosives when the locomotive passed Gordi's position. That was the signal to detonate twelve charges of 10-ounce blocks of C-4 with blasting caps wired into four electronic detonation boxes secured to trees or behind rocks. All the explosives would detonate when Hugo pushed the button sending an electronic signal that would bring the side of the hill down to cover the tracks.

Hugo spent most of the previous night and that morning wiring his devices and setting up individual anti-personnel booby-traps on the three pathways leading to the cabin. Knowing professionals would deviate from the paths, Hugo scattered assorted explosives for overzealous rescuers. He didn't consider there might be hunters and hikers going through those same woods in the future. It didn't concern him, and he didn't care.

High above the tracks, most of the upper hillsides were bare of growth from years of mudslides or snow. The ground was dry, covered in loose rocks, dead-fall, and thick brush springing up from the long summer days. Hugo estimated it was approximately 70 feet from the tracks to the top of the hill he stood on. At his feet was one of three long coils of rope secured to trees that would unravel as he threw the weighted ropes down the hillside allowing the team safe fast access down the hill past his hidden minefield. When the prisoners were pulled up, the ropes would be recovered to hide the route up. The last man up would use a branch to wipe away footprints.

Janene and Michael stayed concealed while the train moved past their position. Michael was weary of Janene's almost maniacal laughter over what was about to happen. As the train cars went by, Michael looked into the happy faces of people on board and saw children. For the first time, he realized how many women and children were aboard. A knot formed in his stomach, and he wrestled with his ideals and beliefs. He wondered if these ideals were worth the cost of even one child. Unable to deal with Janene's strange behavior, Michael reached across and rapped the top of her head, "Knock it off!"

Janene recoiled for a startled moment then suddenly spit out a loud string of profanity and threats at him. "Steve's gonna hurt you for that! He's the only one who can do that to me—you're gonna pay for that, dude!"

"I ain't your dude," Michael said harshly, "Let's get movin'! We've got to get to the cabin and cover the retreat if things turn sour."

"I know mah job... Dude." Janene picked up a loaded black MP5 machine gun, and for a brief moment, thought of threatening Michael. She hesitated a moment, shrugged, and followed him back through the trees.

Michael continued to struggle with concern for the kids; he knew they needed to get clear or risk injury of getting shot by police on board the train. "Make sure you follow me exactly, or you're liable to set off one of Hugo's toys and neither of us will have to worry about your boyfriend." He stepped behind a tree and slid his eight-shot Remington 12-gauge from his shoulder, then made his way up the hillside listening for the explosions. Michael carried a holstered

Glock 9mm and three fragmentation grenades hung on his black Kevlar combat vest and hoped he wouldn't have to use any of them. After seeing the children, Michael's hardline idealism began to give way to a religious upbringing where compassion and belief in one true God actually meant something. A weak link in Munroe's control over the members of the FLQ was beginning to show, if not in action, at least in thought, which was a beginning.

Hugo watched the first engine approach, his eyes hard with the maniacal look of a rabid dog as he relished the sheer thrill of the disaster he was about to cause. Like nearly all explosives experts, he loved the act of blowing things up, and being close enough to watch added to his excitement. He glanced at his wiring layout one last time and pressed a single red button on his battery-operated detonator and watched as the first charge exploded followed by the others in perfect sequence. Like a small child, his face broke into a joyful smile as he watched the hillside give way, bringing down an avalanche of dirt, rock, and wood. Hugo expected to bury the track under a 10 to 12-foot-deep layer of rubble that would reach out to block a good 30 yards of track. Looking at the pile he had just caused, it would take track crews several days to clear up the mess. So many passengers on board would add to the confusion and hopefully delay rescue parties and in turn, pursuit by the authorities.

The series of explosions, followed by the screeching of the locomotives' brakes had broken the relative quiet of the wilderness. Then came the brutal jolt and a loud smashing noise when the locomotive piled into the slide and was knocked off the rails. The train cars rocked forward and jarred right back in a microsecond; car couplings snapped back and forth with loud metallic clanging. Passengers were jolted from their seats to land on the floor. Those who were standing were hurled about as screams and cries came from one car after another.

The security detail in the VIP car was knocked off their feet and slammed to the floor. Two men standing on the rear platform were sent flying over the platform's handrails and landed hard on the dirt embankment, one on each side of the tracks. Both sustained numerous contusions and one sprained an ankle. The two men on the forward platform were discussing the upcoming night in Anchorage when they were both smacked into the car's handrail. Unable to grasp the rail in time, they were propelled off the platform. Knocked unconscious, one lay in the dirt near the car's metal steps, his left leg broken. The other lay on his face with a broken collarbone and a sprained left shoulder joint.

Gordi appeared behind a stack of three dead trees and fired the LAW. The rocket shot through the engineer's wide-open window. A fiery explosion of red and yellow flames blasted outward and upward, accompanied by black plumes of smoke. The explosion killed both crew members and destroyed the engine, which set off a secondary explosion as the diesel fuel exploded transforming the locomotive into an exploding wall of shrapnel.

Hearing the second explosion, Sir Jonathan Whiteburn pulled himself up from the floor. He drew his pistol and moved down the length of the car to protect his Prime Minister. Agent Tod Loury arrived first, shaken out of his gloomy mood. Loury ignored his physical pains from the previous night, grabbed the shaken Prime Minister by the shoulders, and jerked him to the floor. He covered the stunned man with his own body, drew his pistol, and looked the entire length of the car. Jonathan appeared at his side, touching him lightly to reassure him he was not alone.

Black and gray smoke plumes rose upward from the lead engine just as the next rocket impacted the second locomotive. People screamed as panic erupted through the passenger cars. With over 400 people aboard, it was utter pandemonium. Children, some of them injured, cried out in pain and fear. Mothers and fathers cradled infants and pulled children close. A few wide-eyed teenagers pressed their noses against the window glass in an attempt to see what was happening. Several men and women ran over each other as they dashed for exits but were abruptly turned back when automatic weapons fire opened up and impacted the rail bed.

Enjoying the moment, Hugo detonated the second set of plastique explosives, destroying the tracks and rail bed approximately 200 yards behind the train. Another embankment crashed down on the tracks, leaving the passenger train isolated. Thirty yards of railbed was damaged by the second track explosion. The bombs frightened the passengers and more screams and cries erupted.

Munroe was pleased with the results; he knew the authorities would have their hands full getting a train out here to transport the passengers to safety. And with the large debris pile to the south, a relief train would most likely have to come from Fairbanks which meant additional time for their escape. His only real fear was helicopters, but Hugo had a defense for them.

Gripping two tear gas grenades in one hand, and his pistol in the other, Jean-Luc jumped from behind a large spruce tree, slid down the embankment for ten yards, and dashed to the side of the train. Louis covered him firing short bursts into the air to force everyone in the VIP car to keep their heads down. The back door of the VIP car was open, but Jean-Luc saw no one other than the two men lying unconscious on the ground, and he shot both in the head. Hugo had told him these men would likely be security. He climbed up the metal stairs onto the rear platform, stood to one side of the entrance, and lobbed the first gas grenade in, followed quickly by a second one.

When Sgt Niles saw the smoking grenades bounce off the carpeted floor and roll under the seats, he rose up and ran to the door. He fired at the fleeing Jean-Luc hitting him in the back, killing him. One bullet penetrated Jean-Luc's heart and another his lung, His body sprawled across the gravel track bed.

When Louis saw his best friend gunned down, he forgot all about the operation. He rose up from behind cover and raked the side of the VIP car with automatic fire breaking most of the windows and killing Secret Service Agent Tensley and young Walter Brown, Senator Sterns' assistant, and favorite nephew. Senator Sterns screamed and crawled to her nephew's side. The broken windows allowed most of the tear gas to escape and two more Canadian Secret Service agents were seriously wounded when they attempted to leave the front of the VIP car.

Munroe fired an RPG into the baggage car. The fiery explosion set that car ablaze and sent out a blossoming wave of burning shrapnel that peppered the VIP car. Several passengers were wounded in the nearest passenger car. Munroe wanted this to be a violent attack, and he was getting his money's worth. Two engines and the baggage car were on fire, and the casualty count was growing fast.

"Cease fire! Cease fire!" Hugo yelled.

An eerie silence fell over the scene as pillars of black smoke filled the sky. Terrified passengers clung to the floor; parents draped over children, all waited in fear for the next move. Friends, family, and strangers huddled together expecting the worst. When a head popped up to glance out a window, a burst of automatic gunfire into the rail bed drove it back down. Trying to show some semblance of strength, the train conductor crawled through the second car and ordered everyone to stay down and remain quiet. "There are police on the train. They'll handle this! Just please remain quiet and stay down—do not try to leave this car!"

In the VIP car, Agent Woods shouted into his cell phone calling for help. Sgt. Niles was on his cell phone trying to reach Captain Potter, however, there was no cell phone service. Thankfully, a newspaper reporter in the VIP car had a satellite phone, and Sgt Niles used it to call for help.

Bob Rexault panicked shouting at Sgt. Niles, "Do something, you idiot! That's what you get paid for. Can't you do anything? Shoot someone, for God's sake!"

"Bob shut up!" Governor Hughes ordered; his voice strained. He knew Niles was trying to get a message out by phone. "Sgt. Niles is doing his job. Go check on the others, and crawl—stay below the windows."

Niles had the governor against the opposite wall to protect him from a stray bullet through the car's side. He was, in fact, doing his job, but Rexault was too scared to notice.

Sir Jonathan was glued to the Prime Minister's side, his mind racing as he tried to estimate the number of attackers. The tear gas was rapidly leaving the car, but several of them had breathed in the initial burst of the painful gas. Those affected coughed and hacked as they clenched their weeping eyes shut or wiped tears away with their hands.

"Don't use your hands!" Niles hollered, "They're covered in the gas, too. Use a damp handkerchief or pull the bottom of your t-shirt out and use that! Use cola cans or water bottles; they'll work!" He raised his pistol and waited for a bad guy to show up.

Jonathan knew time was running out fast. They had to get out of the VIP car before someone started lobbing in real grenades. But an inner voice told him that since they had used tear gas right off, these people wanted hostages. They had to be members of the dead woman's group, and with her deceased, they would probably also be out for revenge. *Everyone but the PM and possibly the governor is going to die!* As Jonathan took stock of the situation, his mind raced; any chance of rescue was too far away to help. There were other passengers to consider; they had become hostages as well. He saw no choice but to rise up on one knee and shout out, "This is Agent Whiteburn of the Canadian Government; please hold your fire—we surrender!"

"What?" Agent Woods asked in alarm, seconded by a blubbering Bob Rexault, who recoiled in horror when he stared down at the bleeding bodies of Tensley and Brown.

"We have no choice, Gentlemen," Whiteburn said. He stopped coughing and wiped his eyes with a handkerchief, then lifted a water bottle to rinse them, which helped. "Listen, all of you, they'll use the passengers up front as hostages, shooting them until we give up our VIPs. Personally, I don't want to be responsible for the death of any civilians, especially women or children." His eyes still watering, he looked to his Prime Minister, who nodded in agreement, washing his eyes from a water bottle. "If they had wanted us dead, they could've blown up this car from the sounds up ahead. They want our VIPs alive to use as bargaining tools or to hold for ransom." Jonathan didn't mention that it was probably only the two politicians who would survive—he could already see how shaken Rexault was. Jonathan cautiously rose to his feet and stood before an empty window frame. His movement wasn't greeted with a hail of fire, so he reached down and helped Prime Minister Haegens to his feet. The governor's protector didn't budge; he wasn't too sure of Jonathan's decision. But Governor Hughes gently moved his Trooper bodyguard aside and slowly rose to his feet, coughing again from the effects of the tear gas.

Using a small battery-powered P.A. system hanging from a black shoulder strap, Munroe addressed the train, "This is the Front de Liberation du Quebec, freedom fighters for the liberation of our beloved Quebec from Canadian tyranny. We have taken this train hostage as a display of our resolve to show the world that we can strike anywhere to further our great cause for freedom. Our battle is not against America or other foreign nationals. We have attacked this train because you carry the Canadian Prime Minister. If everyone remains quiet and makes no attempt to leave your cars, no one else will be harmed. This is your only warning! All passengers will remain in their seats or on the floor. Any movement to leave your cars will be dealt with harshly." Munroe smiled as he surveyed the blue and yellow passenger cars lined with large observation windows. One of the cars was a double-decker with a large grizzly bear painted on the side; no one was visible in the windows. He loved this utter feeling of power, a high that no simple street drug could ever touch, and only personal failure could bring down. "Attention!" Munroe shouted into his hand-held microphone. "You in the last car… step outside. Leave all firearms, knives, and any other weapons in the train car. You will be shot dead if you are found in possession of even a pocketknife. Understand, this is not a threat, but my promise!

Exit the rear of the car with your hands above your heads and fingers interlocked. If you are injured and unable to comply, remain where you are. Select one who will advise the nearest member of my group of wounded people left inside. If any of you attempt to flee or disobey any command, dead civilians will be the price you pay—as well as your own. A Light Anti-Tank Weapon is aimed at a passenger car to ensure your cooperation. I will not hesitate to use it. For those who do not recognize our name, the FLQ blew up the Canadian Parliament Building in Toronto. We have nothing to lose by adding to those numbers. Now—VIPS and party; move outside!"

Fighting to breathe normally, Jonathan helped Prime Minister Haegens to his feet and moved toward the back door. Sgt. Niles, with a look of utter contempt on his face for the terrorists, helped Governor Hughes. As the governor reached the doorway, Niles returned to drag a weeping Rexault to his feet. Niles didn't believe the tear gas caused the tears; the man was terrified.

Unhurt, except for some minor bruising, Senator Sterns sat on the floor beside her dead nephew and cradled his bloody head in her lap as tears ran down her face. She had trouble believing Walter was dead, but his chest and upper body were bloody, and he wasn't breathing. Unable to speak, her hands and dress soiled in his blood, Senator Sterns used her right hand to close his lifeless eyes. She was helped to her feet by Agent Loury, who was also a bit unsteady on his feet.

One by one, they shuffled out the rear door and onto the back platform. Under the close supervision of Gordi and Louis, they were quickly patted down and allowed to lower one hand only long enough to use the guardrails to step down to the rocky ground. Struggling to ignore the three dead bodies near the tracks, the survivors lined up against the train car while Steve Munroe walked over to inspect his prizes.

Shawn and Paul searched the prisoners more thoroughly, removing cell phones and tossing them aside, along with pocket computers, wallets, and purses. Munroe wanted to know exactly who he had as guests; several of the people he did not recognize.

Newspaper reporters, unhurt except for bruises, were shoved off to the side and eventually escorted back to the next train car and ordered inside. Still upset over his friend's death, Louis roughly shoved Prime Minister Haegens and Governor Hughes toward Munroe. Bob Rexault, foolishly took that moment to show some sand; he stepped forward and shouted, "Hey, take it easy! You can't treat them like that, he's the Governor of Alaska, and he's the—"

"Bob shut up!" Governor Hughes shouted, knowing his old friend was drawing too much attention to himself.

"Who would you be?" Munroe asked of Rexault.

"Rexault, his Chief of Staff," Bob said harshly and gestured to Governor Hughes. Suddenly he realized his mouth had gotten him into trouble again.

"Well, Mr. Chief of Staff, I sincerely hope you have a good medical plan." Munroe pulled the trigger of the MP5 in his hands, firing off a short burst into Rexault's legs from extremely close range. Bob was thrown backward, bounced off the side of the train car, and landed hard on the ground. Screaming in pain, Bob clutched his broken bleeding legs and struggled to stem the flow of blood that flowed onto the rocks.

"BOB!" Governor Hughes attempted to reach his friend, but Louis clubbed him to the ground with the butt of his weapon. Sgt. Niles rushed forward to the Governor's defense and received a similar blow to the back of his head from Gordi. Niles fell unconscious.

Sharon Marbles, gambling the men wouldn't shoot her, went to assist Rexault. She tore the sleeves off her blouse to put pressure on his wounds.

"My, a real Florence Nightingale," Munroe said glaring at the rest of them. "Listen, heroes, we can do this all day, or you can stand there and listen to my demands." Munroe sensed Hugo approaching and turned around to smile at his associate.

Sir Jonathan gave his remaining two men a look, advising them not to try anything foolish. He addressed Munroe, "Okay, you've got our attention now. What are your demands?"

"And who might you be? Oh, I recognize you now. Sir Jonathan Whiteburn, a Canadian hero! Wow, a real celebrity in our midst. Now, shut up!" Munroe asked everyone to give their name and profession. When they were done, Munroe addressed them again. "Prime Minister, Governor, welcome to the Alaska wilderness." Munroe looked at Sir Jonathan, "You're a brave man, Sir Jonathan, and oddly enough, a smart one, as well. I failed to recognize your name earlier when I was told you would be accompanying our esteemed Prime Minister. I imagine it was your idea to surrender rather than risk the lives of so many civilians. I might kill most of them anyway—after all, we are barbaric terrorists and have nothing to lose. Our bombing of the Parliament Building went well above our intentions, getting a bigger bang than we had thought possible. It must have something to do with the building's age or someone saved some money with inferior building materials. Whatever. It sure got everyone's attention, didn't it?"

"You have us, so why would you want to kill a lot of innocent tourists who come from all over the world to experience Alaska? You might make enemies of some people that you would rather have on your side. You're in the United States, where a good-sized bunch of cowboy heroes would love to hunt you down and leave your bones for the ravens to pick. It's not like Canada. Almost everyone here carries a firearm."

"You're probably right, Sir Jonathan. No need to tarnish our image further while vacationing in this beautiful land."

Hugo stepped forward, "Take too much time. The first helicopter be here 10 minutes."

Sir Jonathan and Agent Woods picked up on the harsh German accent. They recognized Hugo as the man driving the RV across the Alaskan border.

"Okay." Munroe glared at Sir Jonathan, "Here it is, so listen up. I will not repeat myself. I want $25 million US dollars deposited in a bank account within four days from now. That's a total of 96 hours from this very moment. I'll give you a slip of paper with the bank's name and the account number. If the money is received, I will release your precious politicians. If not, I'll serve their livers and other vital organs to the bears in these woods." Munroe pulled out a slip of paper with an imprinted Cayman Island bank account and handed it to Sir Jonathan. "There'll be no further talks, discussions, or any deal-making. 96

hours from now, I will call the bank. If the money isn't there, you'll need to have their second-in-command take over because these two men will be victims of a tragic circumstance."

Gordi walked over, showing Stern's U.S. Senator ID card, "Check this out."

"Well, lookee here, we now have three special VIP hostages to take with us. And being that I'm such a nice guy, I won't even raise the ransom."

Louis grabbed Sterns by the back of her hair, lifted her up from helping Rexault, and roughly pushed her over to stand beside Haegens and Hughes.

"A word of warning," Munroe said as he glanced down the line of people standing before him. "If you come for us, one of these three will die. Their carcass will be left staked to a tree for you to find. I'm feeling friendly, so I'll warn you… we've booby-trapped the hillside. I'm sure you've noticed we'll be climbing up paths using ropes which will also be pulled up. I can't make it too easy for you." He chuckled at his own humor. Hugo's face remained deadpan. Why would Munroe warn of the traps he had worked so hard to conceal? "The forest is mined with claymores, grenades, and other surprises. So, please inform any would-be heroes what they can expect if they choose to come after us." Munroe noticed Agent Woods, who had his wounded arm in a sling, "Did you get that in the shootout at the hotel?"

"Yes." Agent Woods wanted so much to shoot this arrogant ass.

"Was Lesli killed?"

"Was that her name? We only knew her as Ms. Wakefield. But yes, she was killed." Woods didn't want the terrorists to know all of the intelligence they had gathered so far.

"How many did she get before you killed her?" Munroe asked with a noticeable sparkle in his eyes.

"Just me. The poor girl couldn't shoot straight and was so frightened, she—"

Agent Woods wasn't allowed to finish. Munroe lifted his MP5 and fired a short burst into Woods' chest, instantly killing the courageous FBI agent. The brutality of his attack on the unarmed agent stunned the others, who had already witnessed the clubbing and wounding of other members of their party.

"Does anyone else has something to say about one of our fallen comrades?" Munroe waved the MP5, his eyes radiated flashes of insanity.

Sir Jonathan spoke up, "Your comrade killed a Park Ranger and wounded three others before she was killed." He didn't want to see anyone else killed by the maniac.

"Thank you, Sir Jonathan. I'm glad to hear she represented herself well."

Munroe looked down at the body of Agent Woods. "Stupid fellow, brave but stupid." He made sure all the weapons were collected and ordered Gordi, Paul, and Shawn to start the VIPs up the first rope. "Remember, we have plastique explosives wired into the train bed. My friend will trigger the devices if we hear a helicopter following us through the woods or sense a rescue party behind us. Then you'll have to explain why a couple hundred passengers were sacrificed because of your stupidity." He grasped the next rope and turned. "96 hours, no pleading, and no excuses. $25 million in the account or else." He slung the MP5 back over his shoulder and scaled the embankment. Reaching the top, he waited for the others. Before disappearing into the trees, he looked down the embankment, waved to the train passengers, and shouted, "Don't forget the landmines!"

Agent Woods was dead, so Johnathan immediately checked on Bob Rexault. "Ms. Marbles, please get me the first aid kit out of the train car. It should be by the back door."

"I'll get it," General Ridley replied and ran back inside the VIP car.

Sgt. Niles, returning to the land of the living, slowly rose to one knee as his head began to clear. "They're gone?"

"Yes. They took Senator Sterns, Governor Hughes, and the Prime Minister. They're demanding $25 million for their safe return," Sharon Marbles said. She knelt beside the trooper and used his handkerchief to wipe the wound on the back of his head. "Does it hurt much?"

"Yeah, it does. But thanks." Niles rose to his feet unsteadily with Marbles' help. "Anything else I should know?" He shook his head when he saw Rexault wounded and the dead FBI agent.

Turning first aid over to Lloyd Bruce and General Ridley, Jonathan filled Niles in on what happened after he was knocked out and about the booby traps in the train bed and up the hillsides.

"Offhand, I'd say they told us that to slow us down, but we can't take chances with so many civilians. Especially after you told me about this bunch, explosives seem to be their thing." Niles looked down the track embankment, hoping to see fresh digging marks to indicate where mines might be, but saw nothing. "From my experience and training, I doubt there are any land mines on the tracks. The heavy vibration of the train would've set them off as we crossed over. But that depends on what sort of explosive devices they're using. Sort of a no-win situation until we get some help out here." He turned back to Sir Whiteburn, "Where's the satellite phone?"

"In the VIP car, where you left it. Which works for us. If you'd had it, they would've destroyed it." Sir Jonathan sent one of his men back into the train car to retrieve the phone.

Sgt. Niles looked around the group, "I suggest we send a team through the cars to brief the passengers, and let them know it's okay to move around but not to leave the cars until further notice. Warn them of the explosives. It would be good to know if we have any EMTs or, with luck, any doctors onboard." He looked down at the severely wounded Rexault, and for the first time, felt compassion for the man.

"As a trooper, I think you'd better do that, Sgt. Niles," Sir Whiteburn said. "I'll send one of my men with you. You'd probably better go forward and check on the engineers and see if one of the locomotive radios might still be working. From the explosions and the smoke, I doubt it. Probably one of the reasons they used shoulder-mounted rockets was to take the engines out and keep them from radioing their dispatch center."

General Ridley turned to Whiteburn, "In the event the rail bed is mined, or possibly the hillside, I think we should move around as little as possible until we can get some explosive ordinance people out here. Check passengers for cell phones or satellite phones, we seem to be in a dead zone. Possibly why the terrorists picked this spot." More of an advisor to the Prime Minister, Ridley had last seen combat as a young major in Iraq. By the pale look on his face and slight trembling, Sgt. Niles could tell he was visibly shaken by the attack on the train and the brutal slaying of Agent Woods.

Niles went back into the VIP car, and after retrieving the phone, returned with a rolled-up cloth napkin and inserted it between Rexault's teeth so he had something to bite down on. Grinding teeth into pulp while struggling with a high degree of pain added to the man's discomfort. Niles was surprised the man hadn't passed out yet, knowing his wounds had to be quite painful. "It's not much, Bob, but it'll help a little. We have a first aid kit, and a couple of these guys are EMTs."

Rexault nodded while they worked on his legs to stop the blood flow and make him as comfortable as possible. Two men carefully lifted Agent Woods' body and carried him back into the train car and covered him with a thin blanket. They knew they were violating crime scene integrity. But with the chance of mines in the vicinity and so little room to walk around, it was good to get his body out of the way.

Niles walked over to Sir Jonathan Whiteburn and handed him the satellite phone. "It's not working; maybe some techno wiz can fix it. I'm all thumbs with this sort of thing. I'll go see if any passengers have a working phone. If I can get through, I'll get ahold of Captain Potter and have them start working on this. Potter's team should hopefully be en route."

Jonathan looked around. "They can probably set the helicopter down on the tracks north of us, but we must make them aware of the danger of mines. And the weaponry they possess."

Sgt. Niles and one of the Canadian agents moved toward the passenger cars. The FLQ had put a lot of shots into the track bed, so Niles didn't believe there were any mines along this stretch of track. The bullets would have set off at least one or two charges, which hadn't happened. Still, when they reached the next passenger car, the two men climbed aboard. They moved from car to car until they reached the engines.

"Well, what now?" General Ridley asked as he tied off a tourniquet on Rexault's leg.

Jonathan turned to Ridley, "General, I think you should follow Sgt. Niles and Agent Loury through the train cars. While they search for phones and medical aid, check the passengers and give me some idea of their condition. We might have to walk out of here, and I want to know how many stretchers we'll need to make up." He pulled out his notebook and ripped out a page containing emergency numbers. "This top number is the Anchorage Alaska State Troopers. They'll have radio contact with Potter's helicopter. Advise them of the threat of mines and the projectiles used on the engines; one of us will be able to direct the helicopter down when they get close. We'll have them land north of the destroyed tracks. That explosion would have set off any mines in the immediate area. Our rescue party can check the tracks for wires. Recommend they bring bomb dogs or at least some mine detectors."

Jonathan turned to the other security officer on his team "Work your way north. Don't try to balance on the rails, but do not leave the track bed; the outlying areas could be booby-trapped. I agree with Sgt. Niles, the vibration should have set off any mines passed over. But don't take any chances. We've already seen what these people can do with explosives from the Toronto attacks. I don't wish to lose anyone else out here because someone is foolhardy."

General Ridley quickly caught up with Niles. The three men entered the passenger car and cautiously made their way forward. The fire in the baggage car had burned out but was still smoking. Both engines were still smoking, but there were no visible flames.

The two Canadian agents who had fallen from the front platform regained consciousness in no shape to do anything but rest. Bob Rexault had mercifully passed out from the pain. It would be a very long time before he would walk normally, if ever. One of the bullets had torn his left knee apart, another had broken his right leg only inches below the knee. A third bullet smashed his right ankle bone, but they left his shoe on and wrapped the whole foot.

In the distance, Jonathan heard the sound of a helicopter coming down the valley. Unarmed and with terrorists in the area, Jonathan would feel more comfortable with heavily armed police nearby. When he looked at his two injured agents from the front platform, he was surprised to find them still armed. The terrorists hadn't searched them. Jonathan removed the agent's firearms and extra ammo clips, kept one pistol for himself, and gave the other to Sgt. Niles.

Tromping through the woods as tail-end Charlie, Hugo also heard the helicopter and took off at a run for the cabin, "Pull down safety guide ropes as we go through woods!" He raced past the others along the path and hurried to one of the green metal boxes. He needed one of the Stinger missiles right away in the event the helicopter tried to follow them and possibly locate the cabin. With Janene's help, he got one box open and carefully removed the contents. The elongated green tube with the sci-fi-looking device on it sent chills down Michael's back. He'd seen these before and knew they were called Stinger Missiles; a device first created by the US to take down Russian helicopters. The American CIA had later provided them to the Taliban when the Russians occupied Afghanistan. Those same Taliban would later use them to take down American and British helicopters during the Afghan War.

11

# BIRD DOWN-A CAPTAIN'S FOLLY

Denali National Park Ranger Headquarters
June 11TH, 12:08 p.m.

Captain Potter's men, bored with the wait time and anxious for action, milled around the helipad awaiting the helicopter's return. They had learned the FLQ bunch were real hardline killers before word of the train attack reached Captain Potter. A frenzy erupted as Federal and State law enforcement personnel rushed out of the hotel and headed south, code three, news crews and volunteer emergency services following closely in their wake. The fact that the governor and one of their senators had been kidnapped, along with the visiting Prime Minister, stirred the blood in the SERT Team members. The helicopter could only carry four and the pilot, so by the time Captain Potter and his three men boarded with all their equipment, they were practically in each other's pockets. The Feds turned to the Army for additional helicopters to be brought to the park from Fort Wainwright or Fort Richardson to carry personnel to the stranded train and evacuate wounded passengers.

Additional troopers were called in, and a Command Post was set up in Cantwell. The Army National Guard was alerted to standby status. Law enforcement officers including Troopers, FBI, and Secret Service moved into action mode. Troopers quickly established a roadblock at Sheep Creek on the Parks Highway, nearly 12 miles south of the accident scene. A second roadblock was set up just south of Cantwell. The Parks Highway was officially closed to through traffic, pending the apprehension of the terrorists. State personnel didn't wish to endanger any citizens as long as heavily armed terrorists were in the hills east of the Parks Highway, Concern was raised for the safety of campers and hikers already in the danger area.

As the helicopter lifted off from the Park Ranger's helipad, Potter glanced down and saw the madness below as ground units raced south on the highway and smiled. He had the only AST helicopter for the moment and would be on the scene long before ground units could make it south and travel in on foot. *This time I'll be the first one on the scene and can claim all the glory.* Glory wasn't uppermost in the minds of the three troopers in the back seat. They were more concerned with being mentally prepared to drop into unknown conditions.

ARR Dispatch was alerted, and a convoy of high rail vehicles headed south to rendezvous with law enforcement personnel using the highway until they reached Cantwell. There they would lower the rail wheels onto the train tracks and transport AST and Federal Agents to the disaster scene. Canadian Secret Service was flying additional agents to Fairbanks from Whitehorse, Yukon, to assist in the manhunt and reclaim their Prime Minister.

Flying 200 feet above the ground as they traveled towards the train, Potter held an ARR track map in front of him and traced the route. He showed it to Bud Watson, who estimated their remaining flying time to be approximately 25 minutes at most. Potter estimated it would take close to four hours to get his entire team on location, but there was little he could do about that. He wasn't even really thinking about eight train cars with 400 passengers, several of whom were injured. In his thoughts, gold major's leaves were being placed on his uniform and he was receiving an award for heroism for saving Governor Hughes and a foreign dignitary. He smiled imagining the ceremony, and, maybe, the possibility of entering politics.

Bud Watson followed the river, scanning the thick wilderness below, and grew concerned. Those onboard agreed this would not be a leisurely pursuit through dense wilderness. With that silly grin on his face, Potter thought he could probably have this whole affair wrapped up within the next ten to twelve hours. He considered splitting his team into two factions, sending half south to the Sheep Creek area to proceed north in a high rail. The other team would be dropped off at the train and proceed south on foot. Potter hoped he could use the high rail in his pursuit. He felt sure the terrorists would stick to the tracks to keep from becoming lost in the mountains. He hoped sending part of his team north would cut them off.

Unfortunately, only a few high rail vehicles were dispatched immediately, most of them were still being organized in Fairbanks. Those to the south hadn't been organized yet, but Captain Potter was not aware of this. The vehicles traveling from Fairbanks would be unable to get past the wrecked train and the massive debris field caused by the slides. Potter would have to rely on the ARR high rail vehicles from Wasilla or Anchorage.

As they flew south from the park, Potter instructed Bud Watson to radio AST Command in Anchorage. "Tell them we'll need at least four high rail vehicles with qualified drivers. I'll know more about where to send them after we reach the train. Just get those vehicles moving toward Sheep Creek. I'm going to split our team, sending half to Sheep Creek. You can do that with your last two flights; drop team members near the tracks at Sheep Creek. They can wait there to flag down vehicles coming north, then proceed about 10 miles and stand by for further orders. I'll know more after seeing the train and what those people have to tell us."

Bud nodded that he understood and passed the request on to AST Command in Anchorage.

ARR Depot - Fairbanks

Alaska Railroad personnel raced to put another passenger train together to send south to transport the 400 passengers from the damaged train back to Fairbanks. Those in need of medical assistance would go to Fairbanks Memorial Hospital which had already been notified to expect an unknown number of casualties. Passengers would be interviewed by a joint task force of investigators for any possible information they could provide concerning the terrorists. ARR legal officers would be on hand to handle any claims against the railroad and the State of Alaska. Those able to travel would be transported by bus to Anchorage. The ARR had not had time to provide information concerning the number of foreigners onboard the damaged train, the Fairbanks Train Dispatcher expected the number to be high as the train was a well-known tourist attraction.

Two work trains were being put together, one in Fairbanks and one in Anchorage, ready to move out once the terrorists had been apprehended. Track crews from the south would not be moved north until that occurred, but at this point, no one seemed to know where the terrorists were. The ARR sent notifications to news services and travel agencies, advising that Alaska Railroad service between Anchorage and Fairbanks was temporarily suspended. For the next few days, the ARR predicted they would be chartering tour buses to transport passengers.

Aboard The AST Helicopter

As the helicopter proceeded south, Potter struggled with the reality of how FLQ people could have carried off the hijacking of a moving train. He figured the grander the crime, the more prominent the awards would be once these bad guys were locked up, wounded, or dead.

Members of the SERT Team readily agreed that Captain Potter's capabilities and intelligence ran hand in hand with his strong arrogance and wild stunts. More than half of this SERT Team were concerned that Potter would get some of them killed sooner or later with his failure to adhere to safety guidelines. Two of the Troopers sitting in the back of the helicopter were part of the group who didn't like the way Potter had been leading the team. One was a history buff who saw a relationship between Potter and General Custer. Custer was infamous for leading the 7th Cavalry into a massacre at the Little Big Horn. They hoped this train incident would slow the good captain down before he went charging off into the wilderness to the sound of bugles and glory.

With The FLQ

The two green oblong metal boxes had cost the FLQ a tidy sum, but in Hugo's opinion, they were well worth it. He had used these weapons before in South America, with positive effects. He prepared one Stinger for the expected police helicopter. Before leaving Canada, Hugo studied the Alaska State Troopers, their helicopters, and SERT Team, and the Alaska National Guard and their helicopters and knew that his Stinger surface-to-air missiles would easily handle them. The AST still used Bell Rangers which meant he wouldn't be facing any military attack helicopters. He had downed an army helicopter and an observation plane during his South American venture.

He inspected the Stingers and two extra missiles and took a moment to admire the technology. Hugo had learned the United States had given such weapons to the Afghanistan rebels. The irony didn't escape him. Hugo recalled his briefing on the weapons by one of his American colleagues before the South American venture, "This is a shoulder-mounted, FIM-92 Stinger which will deliver a 70mm missile through an infra-red homing system, flying at a maximum speed of Mach 2.2. It was manufactured by an American firm, General Dynamics one of our better American suppliers of fine weaponry."

Hugo was unusually jovial, like a small child on Christmas morning, as he held one of the Stingers and inspected its aiming device. When Munroe entered the old cabin, he was surprised to see a smile on the big German's face, which was scary. "This will slow them down!" Hugo said excitedly.

Munroe nodded and checked on their VIPs. "Think about the books you can write later, folks. 'I was a Prisoner of the FLQ', probably get you re-elected, Governor!" Unable to respond with gags over their mouths, the three prisoners only looked at him.

Back Inside The AST Helicopter

"Bud" Watson conversed on the radio with AST Command in Anchorage, receiving orders to land on the tracks 200 yards north of the train. He was reminded again of the possibility of explosive devices and that the terrorists had threatened passengers if anyone attempted to follow them. AST Command advised him not to pursue the terrorists until an explosive ordnance disposal unit arrived on scene. "EOD personnel are en route from Fort Wainwright with a K-9 explosive dog.

"Copy," Watson replied and flipped a switch so he could talk to Captain Potter over the onboard intercom. "Command wants us to land directly north of the train, at least 200 yards away. They have a couple of spotters to help bring us in. There is concern of explosive devices in the track bed. Command has ordered that you not pursue the terrorists until Army EOD is on scene with a K-9 team. The terrorists have threatened to harm passengers if we attempt to follow them."

Captain Potter didn't respond right away. He scanned the terrain below and wondered how best to use his team as an effective strike force.

"Captain, did you hear me?" Watson asked.

"Right… I hear you just fine, trooper, but Anchorage doesn't know the situation as we do." Potter glanced over his shoulder and gave his men in the back seat a thumbs-up sign, to which they merely nodded. "We're less than four hours behind them, Watson. Maybe less. Possibly, we can get the jump on them. By splitting into two teams, we can set up a blocking position to drive them back to the tracks where our main force should be on scene to handle the situation." Captain Potter was running the plan through his mind, making Watson and the Troopers in the back seat nervous.

*Why would any sane commander want to drive the terrorist back to where 400 train passengers are waiting,* Bud wondered. "Sir, I've got orders to land this bird near the train. I don't plan to endanger passengers or hostages."

"Listen, trooper…" Captain Potter glared at Watson, "I'm in command here, and you'll fly where I tell you and land where I tell you to land. Got it?"

Watson didn't like it. He'd seen that *for the glory* look in Potter's eyes before, back in Vietnam, where glory-hunting officers endangered their men and usually ended up getting almost everyone killed. He knew the Army lost a lot of second lieutenants in Vietnam within their first 90 minutes of combat, taking many young American kids with them.

"No, Sir!" Watson exclaimed. "I'm responsible for this bird and my passengers. I am the aircraft commander and I'll land this helicopter where I've been ordered to land and by someone with more rank than you!"

The troopers in the back seat heard the conversation and hoped Watson could talk their not-so-well-loved leader into following Anchorage's orders. They'd seen that pit bull expression on Captain Potter's face before. Anything could happen, and they knew they were simply along for the ride with no say in the situation. The only thing that concerned them was landing safely, preferably not in a hot landing zone.

Sgt. Niles had reported the weapons used against the engines, but somehow the information didn't reach Potter or Bud Watson.

Potter glared at Watson and pointed his finger at him, "I am giving you a direct order, Trooper. You will fly this team and the next four men to that long knoll up ahead. You will then fly the other two groups to Sheep Creek. If you fail to do so, you'll never fly for AST again, and I will ensure that no one in this state will ever employ you! Do you understand me?"

Watson struggled with whether to obey AST Command or oblige this ass sitting beside him. He knew that for a man to reach the rank of Captain in AST, he had to be in the inner sanctum of the state hierarchy and suspected Potter could probably back up his threat. "Okay, Captain, but I hold you responsible if anything happens to those train passengers because of this. If it does, you'll be the one concerned with finding another job."

"You let me worry about the passengers. You just concentrate on flying and get us to that knoll."

After leaving the park, Watson followed the train tracks and the river. As he aimed for the knoll, he could see the disabled train below. Instead of making his recommended landing approach, he banked the bird to the right and proceeded to the location Potter was pointing out up ahead. Ironically, Potter's orders took them right over the top of the terrorist's encampment, which surprised both Hugo and Munroe. Hugo heard the helicopter before he saw it, aimed, and pushed the button that launched the missile. He only needed to aim and fire, and the Stinger missile would do the rest.


At The Train


Sgt Niles had returned from the passenger cars with half a dozen volunteer EMTs from several fire departments and ambulance corps. He discovered an emergency room nurse from Galveston, Texas. They found a doctor, but there were several injured seniors in need of his services. After leaving the wounded in their care, Niles turned and looked up as the helicopter flew overhead. Men were on hand to act as spotters to show the pilot the safest place to land. To be safe, Niles walked the track bed north to the point where they believed it safe to land the bird. Sir Jonathan Whiteburn joined him, and they made their way cautiously, walking on the rails. They expected to see the bird circle and then land, but instead of changing direction, the helicopter headed for the hills to the south.

"What's he doing? Don't they know the terrorists may still be in those hills?" Sgt. Niles waved his arms, hoping to get the pilot's attention. "AST Command ordered them not to pursue those people until Army EOD was on the scene!"

Jonathan stood speechless, watching the helicopter fly well past the planned landing point. He wondered if the pilot hadn't received Anchorage's instructions. Jonathan knew how often communications could break down or be misinterpreted in such emergency situations. Several people from the train watched as the helicopter flew overhead; many saw the missile shooting up from the trees and head straight for the helicopter. Within seconds the missile merged with the helicopter, producing a thunderous and fiery explosion.

The FLQ

As the helicopter exploded, the three hostages remained safely inside the cabin, their mouths gagged, and their hands and ankles tied in front of them with heavy plastic ties. In this rough terrain, it was safer to have their arms bound in front of them if they were to stumble and fall. Hugo knew injured hostages would hamper their escape to the south. Once inside the cabin, extra ankle ties were added to ensure they could not escape.

The burning helicopter fell to the earth, producing a secondary explosion when it hit. Instantly, trees and brush burst into flames. Hugo was very proud of himself and grinned at Munroe even though they now had a brush fire to be concerned about.

"We've got to move! That fire may jump the tracks and come right toward us," Munroe ordered. He wanted to get everyone moving south and across the river below. "If that fire spreads, it'll keep the cops busy, but we need to get off this hill and down to the river!"

Seconds Before; Inside The AST Helicopter

Bud Watson had a bad feeling about this. Especially when his mental combat antenna began to send out warning signals. "Captain, I really think we should—" Watson saw the bright flare of a launch off to the right, which immediately brought frightening memories of bad times back in Vietnam. Bud was shot down by a Russian missile, fired by a North Vietnamese soldier, and lost two crew members. He had received his first Purple Heart and a Bronze Star for Valor in that incident for carrying his one surviving crew member to safety.

"Incoming! Incoming!" Watson shouted over the intercom, an automatic response to old memories. He banked the bird hard to the left and dove for the trees, hoping to confuse the missile's tracking ability.

Having never been in a war, Captain Potter was ignorant to Watson's warning and immediately demanded to know why he turned the helicopter over on its side and dived toward the ground. "What the Hell are you doing? Get us back in the air!"

The troopers in back, combat veterans from Desert Storm, grabbed hold of their shoulder straps as Watson fought to avoid the oncoming missile. He attempted to make the helicopter do things this bird was not designed to do.

"Watson!" Captain Potter shouted, but Watson was too busy to respond.

Launched, the 1524 millimeter-long missile deployed its two spring-loaded control surfaces milliseconds before the second stage ignited. With the target so close, Hugo expected detonation within seconds. The pilot, obviously a combat veteran, had spotted the ground launch and tried to escape the missile with a great aerobatics display. However, Hugo knew the weapon's capabilities; the pilot's attempts would be fruitless.

Captain Potter finally spotted the oncoming missile over his right shoulder, and his eyes grew wide with horror. Only a second or two later, the weapon struck the right side of the helicopter's engine cowling. The explosion transformed the AST helicopter into a fiery ball of flame and a billowing black cloud. All five occupants were killed instantly, ending Captain Potter's quest for fame, glory, and promotion.

The Train

The helicopter's burning wreckage ignited a small forest fire on the east side of the tracks. Sgt. Niles did not believe the fire would spread very far with the river below and the track bed uphill to the west. There was no wind, and the rocky terrain would help to contain the burn area. Niles contacted AST Command on the satellite phone and advised them of the crash. "The fire will make it impossible to check the crash site for some time. No one could have survived that explosion. Some sort of rocket or missile was used to bring it down. I believe the terrorists are less than a mile from our location based on its launch point. Request emergency backup out here ASAP!"

AST Command notified the ARR Dispatch Center, which advised the US Forestry Department of the fire. ARR personnel would assist the Forrest Service in extinguishing the remaining hot spots to prevent a major fire from developing. Airdrops would be made to extinguish the fire, and ground teams would be sent to knock out any remaining hot spots.

Startled by the air explosion, Sgt. Niles let out a cry of anguish for his dead comrades. He had known everyone on board and had gone fishing with Bud Watson several times. They had scheduled a moose hunt this coming September along the Denali Highway. With tears cascading down his cheeks, Sgt. Niles vowed to hunt down the people and kill each and every one.


A Very Satisfied Customer


Hugo placed the Stinger back into the box. He knew the authorities would send additional aircraft into the region, especially with the VIPs at risk.

"The forest is burning… I can see the smoke," Gordi said.

"He's right," Shawn said, with a look of alarm.

Munroe tried to reassure them, "When we get across that river, it won't be a problem. Get everyone moving. Shawn, you and Gordi get those prisoners ready to move. They need to walk; cut the ankle restraints and get 'em moving down the trail!" They followed an old well-used moose trail across the mountainside. Many Alaska hunters and guides used them while hunting or trapping. Munroe glanced around. He hadn't planned on leaving so soon. A thorough planner, he had laid out another route that would eventually lead them to a ghost town labeled on his map as Curry about 18 miles south of their current position.

"When we leave, I'll take point!" Munroe exclaimed. "Keep the hostages in the middle. Hugo, bring up the rear. Do we need both of those missile boxes?"

"They'll send more helicopters. We keep them!" Hugo replied, and Munroe agreed.

"Janene, I want you to stay close to that woman. She doesn't look too well; you may need to prod her along," Munroe said.

"Where we goin'?" Janene glanced over at Senator Sterns with childish amusement.

"Just stay in line! We need to be out of here before that fire can reach us.

Everyone, stay behind me. Let's move! We have to hurry and get across that river if the breeze picks up."

"Yes, General," Janene whispered. She had grown weary of Munroe's abusive treatment, both physical and vocal. Janene suspected she had taken a back seat in Munroe's life. Unlike the others, she had finally learned the truth; the so-called love of her life cared little for Quebec's freedom or this group. His drive was all about money. He enjoyed the killing; she saw the sheer thrill on his face when he killed or shot someone. Janene still recalled his maniacal eyes when he killed Claudia and feared her boyfriend might be planning her death when this job ended. *Why did he give me another chance? It's not the sex; he hardly enjoys it anymore.* She was confused by her boyfriend's topsy-turvy thinking and to herself referred to it as his Dr. Jekyll and Mr. Hyde routine. If anything, his recent actions had driven a wooden stake through the heart of their relationship.

At The Disabled Train - After Midnight

The forest fire caused by the helicopter crash burned toward the southwest, away from the tracks, and the 400 stranded passengers. Firefighters were making their way south by high rail vehicle with hopes the fire would burn itself out as long as the wind didn't spring up.

Nearly every high-rail vehicle in the ARR inventory was in use. Sgt. Olson and the rest of the SERT team traveled to the train in high rail cars. EOD personnel from Fort Wainwright and Eielson flew in by military helicopters to Cantwell and were transported to the train by high rail. A National Guard Blackhawk Helicopter took medical staff and emergency supplies to Cantwell. Helicopters stayed clear of the train in order to prevent spreading the flames with their spinning rotor blades. A passenger train and a work train were en route from Fairbanks. The work train from the south was held up pending the capture of the terrorists. State Troopers at the wreck site kept passengers aboard the train out of concern for possible FLQ snipers. Thankfully the ARR brought enough water and food to the site to care for the people.

The passengers were still frightened and worried about further attacks, and while most of them remained calm and subdued some had become angry and agitated. A couple of men got into a fistfight because someone took too long to use the restroom. Another tense moment erupted when two-vacationing honeymooners began shouting at one another over whose idea it was to take this "damn train!"

Sir Jonathan and Sgt. Niles went through the cars to explain what was happening. Niles quickly broke up the fight and addressed people in the car, "Another train is due to arrive shortly from Fairbanks. It will stop in Cantwell where buses are waiting to take you to Anchorage. For those of you who do not wish to continue, the train will go on to Fairbanks where the airlines are prepared to get you back to Seattle as quickly as possible."

The Alaska Railroad Legal Office worked hard to defuse the situation with the passengers, offering free train rides and paying medical costs for injuries, including care for those who suffered mental trauma. There would be funds for the loss of baggage, hotel, taxi, and food costs. Before this was over, the ARR legal staff knew it would be an expensive disaster.

A work train was sent south from Fairbanks to begin work on the tracks after the site was cleared by ordinance. A platoon of National Guardsmen arrived to watch over railroad personnel until the terrorists were caught. The slide that took out the lead engine would have to wait until the Feds finished their part of the investigation. A special heavy crane from Fairbanks was with the work train to move the damaged engines and destroyed baggage car to a hastily built sidetrack. Heavy machinery arrived on flat cars to work on the slide area after it was declared safe. Track crews set to work tearing up damaged rails and wood ties north of the train.

It was precisely 3:56 a.m. when Corporal Larry Krejci of the AST SERT Team set off one of Hugo's surprises. Cleared by EOD personnel, Krejci began climbing up the hillside on Sgt. Olson's orders and stepped on a pressure plate hidden under a half-inch of dirt. The metal plate was wired into a buried detonation box, setting off simultaneous explosions from three separately spaced claymore mines. Krejci was killed instantly. The explosion peppered the first three passenger cars behind the locomotives with hundreds of lethal metal balls. Fortunately, the cars were evacuated during the demining operation, so no passengers were injured. At the time of that explosion, passengers were boarding the new train that had arrived. Sgt. Olson pushed himself off the ground after the blast and immediately ordered everyone to freeze in place and demanded to know how the EOD team missed the hillside trap.

"Our gear didn't pick it up. A pressure plate was used to detonate the explosives based on where your trooper was and where the mines were. Whoever did this, knows a lot about explosives. Except for wire and a low-voltage battery, there was nothing for our dog to alert on. Those mines were placed where we hadn't searched yet. So, keep everyone off that hillside until we clear all of it!" MSgt Brady Williams gave Olson the only form of apology he was going to get. He sent his slightly less-confident EOD teams back up the hillside to reexamine it for additional traps. The trooper's death rattled everyone. "No one enters that tree line!" Williams ordered loud enough for everyone to hear.

Another 40 minutes passed before they could remove Corporal Krejci's mangled body from the scene. EOD personnel discovered five additional anti-personal booby traps on the hillside. It was decided that the teams would hike over the debris field caused by the slide and down the tracks for a couple of hundred yards before climbing the hillside to enter the woods. They followed single file with the EOD K-9 unit leading the way.

MSgt Williams warned Sgt. Olson, "I can't guarantee there isn't something else up there. By the time you hit the tree line, you'll probably run smack into a whole mess of stuff. Look for tripwires. Keep looking ahead. Some clowns will put a fake trip wire out and then hang a live wire at eye level. Go slow and look everything over twice before moving ahead. It looks like they've had enough time to lay a series of deadly traps for anyone daring to follow them. Either trip wires or pressure plates. Like I said, they know their business."

"Thanks." Olson was not happy to hear that. He had lost a good man, one who had a family waiting for him at home, and Olson would have to explain what went wrong. He'd been around long enough to know that mistakes happen in this kind of work, and people died because of it. It came with the job, and the bomber was the only one to blame.

Meanwhile, Federal, State, and Canadian authorities burned up phone lines and satellite communications with calls and faxes. The FBI Hostage team, one of the best-trained SWAT teams in the US, was ordered north from the Lower 48, but wouldn't arrive for 20 hours at best.

Lt. Governor Troy Sanders was called off a Juneau fishing charter and notified of the hijacking. After checking with the state's Attorney General, he activated the Army National Guard Scouts and Air-Rescue Detachment out of Fort Wainwright for the extent of the emergency. The air unit used six specially equipped Black Hawk MH-60Ks capable of reaching higher altitudes needed for rescue work on the perilous mountainsides of Denali mountain. The National Guard would only support on-scene law enforcement. FBI Senior Agent Harold Wright, directed by FBI Headquarters in Washington DC, supervised the operation, keeping the Lt. Governor, the Canadians, and FBI Headquarters in Washington DC fully advised.

Sir Jonathan Whiteburn, Agent Tod Loury, and Sgt. Niles were the only members of the VIP party to remain with the wrecked train; the others were returned to Fairbanks. The FBI and AST conducted lengthy interviews with them in hopes of learning something more about the terrorists. Investigators interviewed park personnel, train passengers, ARR employees, and others who might have information regarding the terrorists and their activities. Photos of Munroe, Janene, Hugo, and Lesli appeared on the front page of countless newspapers; and TV news services added them to their broadcast. Anyone with information concerning the four people was asked to contact AST or the FBI. Descriptions of other FLQ terrorists observed at the train wreck were provided though most were found to be unreliable.

Stretchers bearing dead and wounded filed past the second train to high rail vehicles hooked to special flat cars for transport to Cantwell and then Fairbanks. Army medics and EMTs were aboard the special transports to attend wounded during the journey. Severely injured were moved to Army Chinook helicopters waiting near the highway for immediate transport to Fairbanks Memorial Hospital. National Guardsmen escorted Bob Rexault and the Canadian Secret Service Agent aboard one of the Chinooks. The Forest Service estimated at least 24 hours before the helicopter crash site could be reached and those bodies recovered.

Additional Guardsmen were transported to Talkeetna, Sheep Creek, and Cantwell. An operations center was set up inside a 30-man canvas tent across the road from Old Man Taylor's Lodge in Cantwell. Law enforcement and the military were the only vehicles moving on the Parks Highway between the two roadblocks. The FAA established a no-fly zone over the area, except for Forest Service, AST, and military aircraft. Satellite imagery was established, but there were a lot of summer campers, backpackers, and hikers. The ARR VIP car was transformed into an on-scene command post, with high-rail units bringing in extra radios, food, water, and most importantly, heavy weapons and communication equipment.

Almost everyone in the country had heard news reports about the incident. People listened to interviews with frightened train passengers or heard the story second-hand. Cantwell and Trapper Creek quickly became hubs for news people. As passengers from the wreck arrived, news people became pests; harsh words were exchanged and even a few fights developed. The FLQ had effectively created a significant event involving tens of thousands of people in Alaska and Canada. Roadblocks backed traffic up for miles, with travelers complaining about the delay or wanting information. Troopers ordered numerous people back to their vehicles or risk arrest. Finally, the north roadblock at Cantwell was moved to the intersection of the Parks Highway and the Denali Highway. Drivers were told they could wait at the closure or turn east and travel the Denali Highway, a 120-mile-long two-lane road east to Paxton.

Sir Jonathan provided the terrorist's demands to all governing bodies, leaving it to the bigwigs to either come up with the money or refuse to deal with terrorists. Not dealing with terrorism was the standard response in America and Canada.

Army experts estimated the missile's trajectory and determined that the FLQ was just over four miles from the train when they fired the missile. The forest fire likely caused the FLQ to move southeast toward the river to escape, however, their destination was still unknown and there was a lot of wilderness to conceal them. Law Enforcement didn't believe the FLQ was headed for the Park's Highway, where they could easily be taken. A range of steep mountains lay ahead of them. The western edge of the Tanana Valley was about the size of Oregon. Looking at a large map of the area, Sir Jonathan noted the FLQ had an area of roughly 100 square miles to move around in. Not being able to use aircraft was a serious problem since the 96-hour time limit was rapidly dwindling.

Morning newspapers ran large-print banner headlines - "TERRORISM STRIKES ALASKA", "FLQ KIDNAPS CANADIAN PRIME MINISTER-ALASKA GOVERNOR AND KILLS FEDERAL AGENT", "BIG SHOOTOUT IN NATIONAL PARK HOTEL-US PARK RANGER AND ONE TERRORIST DEAD", and "CANADIAN PM, AK GOVERNOR, AND US SENATOR KIDNAPPED". Reporters from primary cable news services flew to Fairbanks, setting up base stations in rented RVs as there were no hotel rooms available and some of those drove to Cantwell.

AST personnel flew in from outlying areas to assist in the manhunt. All unoccupied parked cars found between Cantwell and Sheep Creek were checked, license plates run, and owners identified. Two stolen vehicles from Anchorage were discovered in the sweep but were unrelated to the FLQ incident. Campgrounds were checked, and hundreds of people were questioned. An overdue camper and hiker were looked into. Nothing was left to chance, not with so many lives lost, and dignitaries kidnapped.

Extra rail workers were brought in from Whittier and Seward to clean up and repair. When the two destroyed locomotives and baggage car were on the new side track, crime scene specialists from the FBI and AST were brought in to inspect them. A lot of overtime pay would be paid out by the time this job was completed.

Many out-of-state television reporters and crews were surprised with the long summer days, vast open wilderness, and higher prices; not to mention the unofficial state bird, the mosquito. The first news crew to drive a rented RV south nearly suffered a collision with a rather massive bull moose. Startled by the sight of the 1500-lb critter, the driver took a beeline for the ditch which caused some harm to the RV and slightly disfigured the pretty face of the on-air female personality who wasn't wearing a seat belt. Apparently, someone forgot to advise her of Alaska's mandatory seat belt law. The State Trooper didn't forget and cited the driver for it.

Authorities didn't want to deal with news services, so they established a communications center in Cantwell to keep them from interfering with law enforcement. Hourly briefings were conducted by department civil affairs officers. Cantwell was about two miles from the highway, however, several roadside businesses on the Parks Highway were considered part of Cantwell. Taylor's Reindeer Lodge was located in the central part of the little hamlet, and the owner wasn't too friendly with pesky news people even though they did bring a lot of money to the small community.

Reindeer Lodge
June 12th, 10:35 A.M.


Old Man Taylor tuned the giant television to CNN. He took a short break to watch the news while he finished a breakfast of shredded wheat swimming in Pepsi, a strange concoction he started eating while working in the Prudhoe Bay oil fields when a mistake was made in the ordering of milk and suddenly there wasn't enough to meet the needs of the kitchen. "The gall of those thugs, coming here to our neighborhood to carry out their terrorist crap," Taylor proclaimed loudly as he was partially deaf.

"I knew it was going to happen sooner or later," Berry Thompson, a local self-employed mechanic, replied. Thompson was a small man who almost always had oil and grease on his face and hands. He wore faded blue mechanic coveralls and often came to the lodge for the latest news. Thompson, originally from northeast Oregon had lived in Cantwell for 13 years and ran his own one-man garage and tire service, which allowed him to work when he wanted, a matter he frequently boasted of. He was finally accepted as a local two years previously when Taylor allowed him the privilege of participating in the lodge's morning rituals: watching the news, sharing local gossip, and cooking his own breakfast of scrambled eggs and a slice of ham on the antique wood cooking stove. In return, Thompson kept Taylor's old Suburban and ATVs running. Taylor started renting ATVs to hunters several years back and paid for all three by the end of the second hunting season.

Old Man Taylor cussed up a storm as he labored to get one of his two-beer coolers back up and running with a two-lb. hammer, a battle he appeared to be losing. Hearing the front door swing open, Taylor looked surprised to see Tony Rogers walk in. Tony didn't often come to Cantwell this early in the day. He was also surprised at the crowd of strangers in Cantwell. "Hey, Tony, not used to seeing you in here so early! Want a root beer—maybe some eggs?" Taylor laid his hammer down, wiped his hands on a soiled rag, and walked to where Tony leaned against the bar.

"Couldn't sleep las' night… thought a mornin' ride… might help. Right rear tire… my ATV… needs… air." Heavy scars around his mouth, cheeks, and jawline made speech difficult for Tony.

"Sure, let me get the air compressor going. I shut it down at night. Otherwise, it keeps me awake." Taylor walked toward the door. "Grab a stool; I'll take care of your wheels; you know where the root beer is."

"Thanks." Tony sat down and tossed a casual wave in Thompson's direction.

Though they'd known each other for over 10 years, Thompson was still uncomfortable around Tony. He attempted to act cordial, "Have you been following the news about the train heist?"

"No." Tony reached over the bar and pulled a bottle of root beer out of the soft drink cooler. He made sure to leave two single dollar bills on the bar in payment.

"Yeah, some terrorists from Quebec, Canada hijacked the train yesterday, just south of here. Over 400 passengers onboard and they took hostages; Senator Sterns, Governor Hughes, and the Canadian Prime Minister. A reporter fella said they hauled 'em off into the bush near Mile Post 259, the railroad milepost, not the highway." ARR mileposts begin in Anchorage. Thompson slid his eggs out of the skillet onto a paper plate. Putting his breakfast on the bar, he glanced over at Tony, "Don't you know that area? I heard you trapped down that away."

"Couple seasons ago… I move… mah areas aroun'… Time for… critters to… re-populate." Tony slurred the last words often having trouble with letters such as p, b, and m.

"So, whcrc'd you think those terrorists took 'em—any place down there to go?"

"Couple cabins… old… falling a-part… lots of b-ears." Tony sipped his root beer and looked over at the television as another high-jacking update came on.

Hearing of the downed helicopter and the killing of state and federal officers disturbed him. He was glad to hear that most of the train passengers were okay. Listening to the news brief, Tony remembered the area mentioned and the long winter nights he spent running trap lines through there. He had spent many bitterly cold nights in a small cabin right close to where the train was stopped and wondered if this was where the terrorists had taken their hostages. With all the new technology, he'd be surprised if the authorities didn't have a fix on the terrorist's position at this very moment. Yet, with a gun leveled at the Governor's head and that Prime Minister, he knew law enforcement wouldn't be charging in like the US Cavalry.

Taylor came in, gave Tony the "OK" hand gesture, and returned to working on his beer cooler. If he couldn't get it working, he'd have to drive to Fairbanks to purchase a new one or have his wholesaler deliver one. Either way, it was going to cost him a bit.

"Can I… use… the phone? It's a… 800 call?" Tony asked.

"Sure, just don't be making any of those 900 calls. Caught some clown doing that a couple of years back, ended up costing me over $90.00, and I thought he was talking to his parents."

The bar phone was an old black 1960s-era office type with a 50-foot extension cord. Tony carried the phone to his favorite table, as far away from the bar and TV as possible. He pulled out a white slip of paper, dialed the phone number written on it, and was connected with his Veterans Hospital contact within moments. After several minutes of conversation, the woman at the other end promised to check on his overdue pills and, if need be, order another shipment.

Tony hung up and coiled the cord as he carried the phone back to the bar. He finished his root beer in two gulps, said goodbye to Old Man Taylor, and walked outside. He started his ATV and headed off into the back trails where he hoped to clear his head. These last few nights, he'd had strange dreams in which the faces of total strangers appeared. After seeing the news report, he suddenly recalled sensing something to do with the train in his recent dreams, *or was it a nightmare?* He'd seen bullet-ridden bodies but couldn't differentiate between the nightmare and old war memories that had haunted him for years. Tony shrugged it off for the moment and turned his right wrist a bit to accelerate, leaving a cloud of dust behind. Mounted on his ATV was a hard plastic rifle case, which held his shotgun. He kept it handy in case he crossed paths with an angry critter. Over the years, he'd had many such run-ins with bear and moose, usually giving them the trail. The rutting season would start soon and bull moose tended to act a bit crazy as they fought over cows, so kept his eight-shot police-style riot gun loaded and ready.

RCMP Headquarters - Toronto
Intel Division - Captain Leon's Office - June 12th, 10:07 A.M.

JP looked a bit haggard after spending another rough night behind his desk and a couple of hours on the office couch. He was awakened by the sounds of the day shift coming to work and wasn't much in the mood for sparkling conversation when Adler walked in and immediately headed for the coffee pot only to find it empty. Rather than complain, Adler found the makings in a file drawer and left to refill the pot with water from the men's restroom sink. When he returned, JP was still sitting with his unshaven chin resting in the palm of his right hand.

"If you plan to see the Colonel this morning, you might want to spiff up some," Adler said.

"The Colonel?"

"Yeah, the Colonel." Adler poured clear water into the coffee machine, made sure it was plugged in, changed the filter, and poured the grounds in, then turned it on.

"You're a class act, Sergeant. Still hard to believe they trust you with a loaded firearm." JP stood up, walked over to his desk, and pulled out his electric razor. "Okay, you got me." He looked at his friend. "Why am I supposed to see the Colonel today?"

Adler reached over to the desk and picked up the morning paper dropped off earlier by a uniformed officer who was very quiet so as to not wake the captain. Adler placed the newspaper in front of JP and stood back as he knew what was about to happen.

JP grabbed the paper. The bold headline print said it all, "FLQ IN ALASKA - KIDNAP PRIME MINISTER!"

"I thought that might wake you up." Not waiting for the pot to fill, Adler picked up his coffee mug, pulled out the coffee pot, and placed his cup underneath to fill. After he topped his off, he did the same with JP's mug.

"The FLQ actually pulled off a train hijacking; I can't believe it," JP said in astonishment.

"Well, we suspected they were there. The woman we identified was as dangerous as we thought, she killed one federal officer and wounded three others. Her name is being withheld. Typical until a relation can be notified."

"Pest control." JP set his coffee mug down and went about zipping up his pants. "I want to kiss the man who took her down."

"Yeah, too bad she took out one of the good guys," Adler said as he waited for JP's reaction.

"Listen, I'm as sorry about losing a cop as you, but she's dead, and that's what counts to me right now. So don't give me a hard time about it, okay? You just don't understand."

"Understand? What's to understand? I see you eating yourself up; not with mourning, which I could understand, but with hate. You sleep in the office, catch an hour here and one there, your clothes are a mess, you're not eating right, and then you're out on the streets pushing and shoving everyone around to find these people."

"Back off, Sergeant." JP glared at him, but Adler wasn't backing down. They had been friends too long, and he wanted to save JP from ruining his career.

"She wouldn't like it, JP. As much as she loved you, she wouldn't like what you've become."

"I'm giving you a direct order, Sergeant Adler. Stay out of my personal business!"

Adler presented a mocking gesture of a salute and walked out of the office, just as Sgt. Wilkens stepped in.

"Hey, good morning to you too," Wilkens saw the look on his friend's face and stood out of the way as Adler walked by and disappeared down the hall.

"Did I come in on something?"

"Forget it!" JP stood behind his desk reviewing the story of the train hijacking.

"I heard about that this morning on the news. Those FLQ clowns have really buffaloed those Alaska boys. Imagine, a train hijacking in these times?"

JP set the paper down, picked up the phone, and called the Colonel's office. His secretary answered, and they made arrangements for an appointment in 45 minutes. "Thanks." JP hung up and ran his hand over his chin. "Got just enough time for a shower and a shave."

"Are you going to tell me what's up?" Wilkens asked.

"Yeah, I'm going to Alaska. Officially, or on leave. Set me up with an afternoon flight for today. I want to be in Fairbanks, Alaska, by late tonight."

"Yes, sir." Wilkens wrote the info down, "Adler or I going or is this a solo trip?"

"You guys mind the store and keep working on the properties they hit. Find out who really owns them. I have a hunch, but I don't have much to go on." JP pulled out the four-inch-thick file on the Parliament Building. "I can understand terrorists hitting this; that's what a terrorist does—maximum damage for maximum exposure." He pulled out the smaller file on the parking garage. "But this one doesn't make sense. Why hit it when no one is supposed to be there? No body count except for an unfortunate cocktail waitress. Something smells here, and I want you two to find out what it is." JP walked to the door, "I'll check in twice a day so you can keep me up to date on everything here. But this FLQ thing has top billing."

"Yes, sir." Wilkens watched as JP headed down the hall to the locker room for a quick shower.

Forty-four minutes later, JP, in a clean shirt and tie and freshly shaven, walked into Colonel Augustus's office to make his presentation about why he should be sent to Alaska. Thirty-five minutes later, an extremely frustrated RCMP captain stepped out of the Colonel's office with leave papers in hand and a strong warning burning in his ears, "You will not become involved in this investigation. Sir Jonathan Whiteburn and his agents have the situation well in hand. You may have your 10-day leave, but I do not—I repeat—do not want to hear about you showing up in Alaska gumming up the works. You have no authority there, JP. You have no police powers and cannot carry a weapon there. So, with all that in mind, if you decide to spend your leave in Alaska, it had better be for tourism, or don't bother coming back here except to pick up your separation papers."

At 4:12 p.m., JP was on board a puddle jumper to New York City. From there, he flew United Airlines to Salt Lake City and grabbed an Alaska Airlines flight to Fairbanks, Alaska. He landed in Fairbanks just over 12 hours later, in need of another shower and a good breakfast.

12

# NATURAL ENEMIES CAN POP UP ANYWHERE

Susitna Mountain Range
22-Miles South Of Broad Pass, West Of The Susitna River
June 13th, 5:12 A.M.

The FLQ members struggled all night to make their way through thick brush forging a trail through unforgivable mountainous terrain. The terrain forced them to free the hostages from their bonds with a warning they would be shot if any of the three attempted to escape. The crazed look in Munroe's eyes was enough to convince the three politicians. By then, they were all frustrated, sweating, and short-tempered and no one wanted to push the man to action. Their clothes were soaked in sweat from lugging heavy packs and equipment up one hillside and down another; steep inclines and sudden drop-offs had worn them out. Many sustained scratches and minor lacerations struggling with the heavy brush. Several were bruised from stumbling and falling. Senator Sterns had the most trouble due to her age and dealing with the death of her nephew. Six hours in, she fell to the ground unconscious which forced a frustrated Munroe to call a halt near a small flowing creek.

Michael and Paul took guard duty while the others rested and ate a cold meal of beef jerky and dried fruit washed down with gulps of ice-cold stream water coming down from massive glaciers in the mountains high above them. They were enclosed on three sides by the majestic Alaska Mountain Range, a natural fortress separating coastal south-central Alaska from the state's massive interior. Most of the mountains that make up the Alaska Range maintain a snow cover throughout the year with freezing temperatures when the sun goes down, even in midsummer.

Munroe felt they were safe for the moment. Their reputation for ruthlessness would give the authorities pause before pursuing them into these mountains and it helped having three hostages along. Hugo warned Munroe of possible satellite coverage sensing body heat, but Munroe wasn't concerned. He pointed to the hostages, "As long as we have these three, they won't take any chances. Having the governor and lady senator is just icing on the cake. Those two will help keep the Alaskan Cowboys from causing any problems. We're safe right now, and this GPS system works fine. We'll know where we're at all the time."

Hugo knelt by the stream, filled his canteens, and shook his head in frustration. He knew the authorities would be stationing forces at several locations to prevent them from leaving these woods with the hostages. He wasn't sure whether they could hold on to the Prime Minister for the five days Dr. Quison had requested. The politicians were in no shape for this strenuous hike. Senator Sterns would have to be carried in a handmade stretcher if they continued at Munroe's pace. He preferred leaving her and the Alaska Governor behind to wander freely through the woods hopefully diverting rescuers. But Munroe refused; he wanted to keep all three of his prizes together for now. Alone, Hugo believed disappearing into the woods wouldn't be that much of a problem. He had Munroe's GPS system to navigate with and knew he could live off the land through the rest of the summer if need be. He had done it before, and Alaska was much friendlier than some stretches of Eastern Europe. Hugo's $600.00 GPS was damaged in the initial river crossing, so he'd tossed it aside back at the cabin with other supplies to save weight.

Gordi who was helping lug one end of a Stinger box, wished they'd left the Stingers behind. He'd already stumbled several times and nearly dropped off a steep embankment; his shoulder muscles ached from carrying the metal box. If it wasn't for his fear of Munroe and Hugo, he would've gladly tossed both missile boxes over that last ridge. Gordi took a brief nap and was snoozing when Hugo walked away from the creek.

Hugo rested in low brush between Michael and Governor Hughes realizing he was not as spry as he used to be. The hike had left him winded, not that he let it show; he was too disciplined for that, but he sure felt it. He checked his pulse and realized his heart was racing at more than 120 beats a minute. He hadn't expected to live this long with his dangerous life and was looking forward to retiring with millions in his bank account.

Between sweat and bug dope, a soft breeze carried the party's odor down the hillside, alerting every critter downwind of their presence. Unfortunately, animals upwind were still unaware of the human presence.

Paul walked slowly in a loose circle around the camp maintaining a weary alertness as he waited to be relieved. A confirmed city dweller, Paul was uncomfortable with all this wilderness. He kept his eyes moving, fearing whatever large creatures could lurk behind the trees. Flies hovered around his eyes and ears, even with the mosquito spray lacquered on. He spent more time waiving pests away than watching the surrounding area. Hugo told them that Alaska had no snakes, but Paul didn't believe him. He had seen photos of the Canadian Timber Rattler where a bite made an arm look as if it had exploded. Paul figured if Canada had venomous serpents, Alaska probably did too. As he checked the ground for snakes, he stopped to dampen his handkerchief with water from one of his canteens and wiped his eyes with it while he waved a swarm of bugs away. He heard a noise in the nearby brush and quickly brought his MP5 up.

When Michael saw Paul take the defensive stance, he stood up with his own weapon at the ready and surveyed the woods. Michael couldn't hear or see what had spooked Paul from the opposite side of their temporary camp. Strange sounds continued from the brush as Paul approached with his weapon at the ready.

Unable to sleep, Governor Hughes sat up and watched Paul's movements. He wondered what could be out there to cause the man's reaction. Once an avid sportsman, Hughes knew these woods were full of wildlife and suspected it was probably an arctic hare, squirrels, or a ptarmigan. He thought it extremely doubtful any had ever seen a man before. If it was a squirrel, they'd be hearing the critter's threatening sounds. An enraged squirrel often reacted vocally if anything dared to enter his area of the woods and then threw small spruce cones at the intruder.

Paul's MP5, with its 30-round magazine, was pointed into the brush, with its selector set on full-automatic. Cautiously, he reached out his left hand, pulled the taller brush aside, and stared down with a strange, dumbfounded expression. Not knowing what to expect, he was unprepared for what he found on the other side of the brush. With their own look of surprise, two brown bear cubs stared back at him with large black eyes. They tilted their heads as if to question Paul's intent, making themselves even more adorable. Being a true city boy and not one to frequent a zoo, he grinned at the cubs, swung his weapon behind him, and reached down to pick up one of the grizzly bear cubs. They were spring newborns and far more dangerous than Paul ever suspected.

"Hey, look what I found!" Paul held up one of the cubs for everyone to see.

Not even bothering to warn the idiot, Governor Hughes grabbed Senator Sterns by the shoulder and shoved her away from where Paul stood with his prize, then grabbed the snoring Prime Minister by the shoulder and shook him awake. "Wake-up! Move—now!"

Hugo knew the hostages weren't attempting to escape; he helped hustle them toward Michael. "Guard them!" Hugo ordered and turned around to shout at Paul. Several people warned Paul to put the bear cub down and move away quickly.

"What's the matter with you people?" Paul saw the horrified expression on Janene's face. Her mouth was wide open, she was too frightened to speak as she pointed over Paul's shoulder. Not sure what all the concern was about but uneasy at Janene's look of utter terror, he slowly started to turn around. He froze at the sound of the loud threatening roar of an angry grizzly sow charging at him. His trembling hands released the noisy cub, and his mind went numb as the cub cried out when it hit the ground, and the bear increased the speed of her charge. Not more than twenty feet away from Paul, one really ticked-off momma bear made her attack. Governor Hughes estimated her at close to 700 pounds. Seeing their mother, both cubs moved in her direction. She didn't stop; she zeroed in on Paul.

Unable to budge, Paul's eyes grew wide, and everything seemed to slow way down. He forgot he was armed and turned to flee but tripped on an exposed tree root and tumbled to the ground. Not knowing what else to do, Paul rolled himself into a ball and covered his head with his arms. Had he stood his ground, the MP5 might have saved his life, but he was too frightened to think. Unfortunately, Paul blocked the others from shooting the enraged bear.

Like an oncoming locomotive, the sow plowed into Paul. Huge powerful paws lashed out and four and five-inch razor-sharp claws tore into his flesh. Her fangs ripped into his body, and a single long scream escaped him. He tried to break away, but the enraged bear was much too strong. She continued to mangle Paul and clamped her jaws around his head.

Shawn knew he had no choice; he opened fire and 9mm bullets struck the grizzly and Paul. Wounded but in a killing frenzy, the bear's heart rate was slower than a human's. She discarded Paul's lifeless remains and charged the next nearest target which, unfortunately, happened to be a petrified Janene. A mighty swipe of the she-bear's paw sent the little woman flying, her neck broken, her head nearly severed from her body. Janene landed near Steve Munroe's feet. He stared down at her, his frozen face ash white. He couldn't even shoot the bear that just killed his girlfriend.

Hugo brought his MP5 up and fired into the bear with a long burst, but not before the dying bear got her front claws into Thomas's leg. Screaming like a wild man, he beat the dying bear's skull with his weapon and died instantly when one of Hugo's bullets entered the side of his head. Thomas's body lay partly covered by the dying sow's massive body; its heart finally stopped.

Munroe, still stunned by the attack, hadn't fired a shot. He glanced back and forth between Janene's lifeless form and the dead sow, unable to speak. His mind struggled to unravel the sheer savagery of the attack and Janene's sudden death. He looked over at Paul's bloody remains and Thomas's body. In less than a minute, three members of his little band were dead and not at the hands of the authorities. They were killed by a grizzly bear, and he was overwhelmed by it. "How could this happen? How? Why?" Suddenly he remembered the two bear cubs. Now he had something to focus his anger on, to direct his inner torment against. He stomped through the brush with his weapon in hand until he found the cubs and emptied his weapon into them without saying a word. The act of such coldhearted butchery even revolted Hugo. The whole event caused Senator Sterns to vomit all over herself. The other two politicians weren't doing too well, either.

During the attack, Sterns found herself rooting for the bear. After what these people had done to her nephew, she didn't feel any loss for the three terrorists. The killing of the cubs made her heartsick. Sterns leaned against the Governor and wept.

Michael, revolted by the whole scene approached Senator Sterns with a canteen and a clean handkerchief to wipe her mouth. She refused but would later remember his strangely polite gesture. Seeing it, Governor Hughes decided to keep an eye on the quiet young man.

Fairbanks Police Department
June 13th, 7:25 a.m.

The attack on the train and the shootout at Denali Park put the Fairbanks Police Department on full alert status. Officers were called in on their days off, and everyone worked back-to-back 12-hour shifts. The increased alert was partially due to the hundreds of travelers stranded in Fairbanks. Every few hours, another flight landed at Fairbanks International Airport with tourists and news media filling motels and hotels. The possibility existed that other FLQ members might arrive, so extra security was added to the airport. Until the train and highway were reopened, Fairbanks would remain in readiness posture.

Working 12-hour shifts, Lt. Farber supervised the 8:00 p.m. to 8:00 a.m. shift and stood in the dispatch area when Captain JP Leon of Toronto RCMP walked into the foyer. Though JP was in civilian clothes, wearing a dark brown sports coat, a white button-down shirt, and tan slacks, Farber recognized him from a previous encounter. Both men had attended the 1992 Alaska Peace Officers Association's first International Police Conference. JP hoped someone at Fairbanks PD would be able to help him. He recognized Lt. Farber. They had competed against one another in the pistol shoot, both losing in the final round to an expert shooter, Police Chief Mark Habib of the Craig Police Department in Southeast Alaska.

Though it had been a number of years, Lt. Farber walked out to welcome him. Farber recalled hearing of JP losing his family to the FLQ bombing and jumped to the conclusion for JP's presence in Fairbanks. "Are you here officially, Captain?" Farber asked as he offered JP a Styrofoam cup of hot coffee.

"Unfortunately, sir, I am not." JP sipped his coffee and sat in the chair across from Farber.

"Vacation then?"

"Yes, of sorts."

The way he said it and the haunted look in his eyes, Lt. Farber understood why JP was here and why he wasn't sent officially. "We've all heard of your loss, Captain. I wish to add my sympathy and the sympathy of my department for the loss of your family." Lt. Farber stopped talking when the shift sergeant appeared and handed a clipboard to him.

"Pardon me, Captain; this will only take a moment."

Hearing the title of captain, the FPD sergeant became curious as to the identity of the man talking with his lieutenant. It was clear Farber wasn't planning to introduce the captain. Farber signed the paper and handed the clipboard back to the sergeant, who disappeared into the dispatch room leaving the two men alone.

"If I may ask, why don't you tell me why you're in Fairbanks, and I'll see if I can help."

"I truly miss working with Alaskan officers. You're usually to the point with no tiptoeing around issues."

"Oh, we tiptoe a lot around here, but we try to keep the doors open to fellow law enforcement officers."

JP smiled. "I need some help. I want to be at a certain spot, to meet particular people at a place my superiors have ordered me not to go or become involved with."

"What you're saying is, someone in your chain of command is afraid you might try to involve yourself in this country's current affairs. I imagine, in doing so, you might save our two countries from some outlandish court costs. Possibly even further incidents from continuing in your home area. With the worldwide publicity, these… particular people have generated, it is possible they may generate sympathy from the far left and create further problems if taken into custody. They could be looked upon as poor misunderstood liberals—even freedom fighters—am I close?"

"Someone could say you think like a police officer," JP smiled. "So, my friend, where do we go from here?"

"Well, as much as I would like to help, I can't do much for you here. Everything is happening about 150 miles south of us." Lt. Farber tapped a #2 yellow pencil on his notepad. "But I may have an idea. Do you have any plans for lunch?"

"No, I have no plans."

"You do now." Farber inched closer to his desk and wrote down the directions to a local hamburger joint and handed it to JP. "Meet me here at 1:00 p.m. I need to get some sleep; a couple hours at least—I've been going steady for the last 34 hours."

"Thank you, Lieutenant." JP started to rise.

"I'm asking as a friend, not a fellow officer, are you armed?"

"No. I was hoping someone here might be able to furnish me some of the tools I might need for my… ah… vacation." JP had a sheepish grin on his face, but his eyes remained hard.

"Well, like a true Alaskan, I can say that one should be well-equipped to vacation in this state. I'll see what I can do."

JP knew that Alaska citizens could carry concealed and walked freely with weapons handy unless they were convicted felons. They couldn't enter bars, liquor stores, or banks, be on school grounds, or enter any location with a legal sign posted at the entrance that the business did not allow concealed weapons to be carried on-premises. A Canadian citizen, JP couldn't legally purchase a firearm or ammo in Alaska, nor did he have a right to carry; by law, he must obtain a special license to hunt in Alaska and hire a licensed guide. The hunting he planned had nothing to do with Alaska wildlife. He was violating numerous US and Alaska laws on this trip, and it could cost him his life or his career in law enforcement. But none of that mattered; he was focused on revenge. He hoped one of his law enforcement friends might help him gain access to a firearm. If officers at FPD couldn't help, he would have to take a chance on buying an illegal firearm off the street. However, it appeared a weapon would be provided by a fellow police officer.

Fairbanks ARR Building - Office Of The Special Agent
June 13th, 8:55 A.M.

Through his boss, Donald Osborn, Special Agent Greg Hansen was kept up to date with the ongoing manhunt for the Canadian terrorists. Though their services had been offered more than once, law enforcement asked ARR special agents to assist only with logistics and supplies. The coordinators felt it unwise to bring in another law enforcement agency with the FBI (assisted by U.S. Deputy Marshals), Canadian Secret Service, Alaska State Troopers, and the Alaska National Guard already involved. Especially one whose jurisdiction was restricted to railroad properties.

Greg was troubled by Potter's death. He grieved for the other men whom he knew quite well and was concerned for their families. While the manhunt was going on, families of the dead would be all but forgotten after the initial notification. He thought Potter's death would have him jumping up and down, but he felt a wave of remorse thinking of how Debbie would take the news. It wasn't something he wanted to wish on her even though he thought about carrying out the act himself several times. The bottom line was that Potter was still a cop who had lost his life in the line of duty. That alone stood for something that weighed heavily upon Greg's heart. When he had his courage up, he called Debby to offer his condolences, half expecting to have the phone slammed down in his ear. He learned that no one had bothered to contact her since they were not legally married, which surprised him.

Realizing he had just become the notifying officer, Greg girded up his loins and forged ahead. She didn't slam the phone down but did drop it, collapsed to her knees, and began to weep. John ran up to pick up the phone. Breaking the news to his son was even more challenging, not for how the boy felt about Potter but for his son's concern for his mother's well-being. They talked for a while until Debbie came back on the line. She asked questions, but Greg had little information on the incident; she hung up without saying goodbye.

Debbie called the next morning before Greg left his apartment, "I wanted to thank you for your consideration last night. I know how hard it was for you to call and not rub my nose in it."

"A stupid question, but are you going to be all right?" Greg asked.

"I… I… really don't know, Greg. As the saying goes, I've made my bed, and now I have to sleep in it. At least, I think that's how it goes, doesn't it?"

"You want me to take John for a while? Give you some time alone."

"I considered that. But if John wasn't around, I might just vanish in the night and become one of those statistics you liked to bring up all the time."

"Wow. Was I that much of a bore?"

"No, you weren't." There was silence on the line for a moment. "Greg, I can't talk about this now, okay? We can talk later... and... thanks again." Debbie hung up.

When Greg reached the office, he set his coffee and donuts on his desk and answered the ringing phone. He was surprised to hear Lt. Farber's voice on the other end. Knowing his friend had been working a lot of overtime, he thought to open with a joke, "No rematches in the middle of the week, buddy. Be a man and take your loss." Greg was referring to their last pool game.

"Hey, as I remember, you lost and owe me a pitcher of beer, you skinflint," Farber remarked.

"So why aren't you home in bed snoring?" Greg propped his feet up, pulled the lid off his coffee, and spread out the morning newspaper. He'd already heard the latest on the terrorists; what he wanted to know was in the comics. He'd had enough real news for one day.

"Listen, are you clear for lunch? I've got someone I want you to meet. Then again, you might already know him. Didn't you attend the 1992 APOA Crime Conference—the one we had the Russians come over for?"

"Sure, but only the first day. Had something going on and had to leave."

"Did you meet an RCMP Officer by the name of Jean-Paul Leon?"

"No, but I know the name from the FLQ bombings. It was all over the news."

"He's in Fairbanks. Needs some help, and I thought of you."

"Me? Why me?"

"I'm not sure; your face flashed in my mind when he asked for help. Anyway, I'm meeting him for lunch at Jay Bird's on College Road. One o'clock, can you be there?"

"Okay. It's not like the feds have us doing anything else. My boss is fit to be tied, they won't let him near the crash, and it's our train."

"I'm sure it'll still be there when they've caught all the bad guys. Anyhow, I need to catch a few Z's before I collapse. We'll talk more at lunch." Farber hung up and was snoring moments after setting his alarm for 12:15 p.m. He hoped to appear somewhat awake with a cold shower when he brought the two men together.

The meeting between Greg and JP went well, and Lt. Farber took off. Greg and JP continued talking, taking a corner table in the rear of the room. Greg nailed JP down on what the trip was really all about and JP realized that Greg was precisely the right man to assist him. He could see it in Greg's eyes, the desire for vengeance for the loss of old comrades.

"We've got a lot to do and getting our equipment is first. I want to hit the road tomorrow morning. Our first stop will be Cantwell, where the roadblock is set up. I know the tracks, but we'll need a guide, someone who knows those woods. I've flown over the area but never hunted those mountains before. Can you afford a guide, JP?"

"No problem. Where do we get our supplies?"

"This is Fairbanks; we've got a dozen or more outfitters in town. Hope you brought a credit card; we'll probably be maxing it out. I have much of what I need, but you'll need everything from boots to rain gear, a sleeping bag, and whatever else I can think of. One thing I learned about Alaska—when you go into the wilderness, you go prepared or die."

13

———

# THE GAME IS AFOOT

Reindeer Lodge - Cantwell, Alaska
June 14th, 10:07 a.m.

His back shirttail hanging out, and a soiled white apron covering his paunch, Old Man Taylor hummed music from an old show as he cooked. Gracefully, he scooped up a spatula full of scrambled eggs with bits of tomato and Swiss cheese sprinkles and slapped the food down on a white stoneware plate, "Your breakfast is served, Mr. Anthony Rogers... Sir!" He walked to the end of the bar and slid the plate of eggs, hash browns, four strips of bacon, and buttered toast in front of Tony. "You really want another root beer to go with this? I mean, I got milk, you know?"

Tony shook his head and pointed to his nearly empty bottle of root beer then proceeded to enjoy his breakfast. Usually, milk would've been sufficient, but riding to the lodge on his four-wheeler, Tony got a real hankering for root beer. Taylor made sure to keep a good supply of soda on hand to keep his friend happy. It was one of the few joys the former chaplain had; that and his books.

"You know what they'll say, don't you? You're addicted to this fuzzy stuff." Taylor walked away, shaking his head, but remembered the root beer. He stopped to open the beer cooler nearest Tony's traditional seat. "I'd better stock up again the way you're going through this stuff."

It was unusual for Tony to four-wheel to the lodge for one of Old Man Taylor's breakfasts during the summer months. He usually made his own morning meal, which often consisted of pan-fried toast covered in peanut butter. However, the night before, he'd spent more time pacing the cabin floor than lying in bed, and he needed to get out. It didn't help that it was the time of year when the sun vanished over the horizon for less than thirty minutes before rising again. The summer solstice was only a week away, and then very gradually, nightfall would initiate its return.

When he finished the last chapter of a *W.E.B. Griffin* novel, Tony found it easy to lay back and drift off to sleep. He kept dark curtains over the cabin's two windows, but daylight still got in like he had left a lamp on. The nightmares attacked, waking him up, and Tony knew he wouldn't be sleeping much. According to his watch, he'd only been asleep just over two hours when he awakened with a start and found his body covered in night sweats.

For the fourth night in a row, his nightmare wasn't filled with the familiar Vietnam horror scenes. Instead, he was hiking through trees in an area he knew well from trapping. In the dream, he led two men in pursuit of some unknown trouble. He awakened as gunfire sounded off in the distance and remembered one thing clearly: that was the distinct sound a weapon made when fired on full-automatic. Each time he awoke, he massaged old wounds, where an AK-47 came very close to ending his life in that faraway jungle.

A renounced Christian and former pastor, Tony remembered earlier days walking in faith and his ability to occasionally see glimpses of a future event. Some said he had spiritual insight through pictures instead of words. It was seldom when such dreams had come, even back then. However, some of those dreams did become reality. Tony didn't speak to God anymore or acknowledge his past as an ordained pastor or Army Chaplain. Since abandoning his faith, he couldn't recall another occurrence of seeing into future events. These latest dreams reminded him of the old days; he was curious about what it meant. Were the scenes some future event? There was something strange about the dreams and the two strangers in them. It troubled him that he couldn't see their faces. Individual mannerisms stuck out, and something about their personal histories seemed to have a bearing on why they were in the woods, but he didn't understand it.

Grumbling all the way to the Lodge, he asked God to leave him alone. *Haven't I suffered enough in your service? Do I really need to kill someone else—I'm done with that! Why can't you leave me alone and move on to the next guy?*

As Tony sat at the bar eating breakfast, he looked around the bar. A people watcher, Tony studied the customers sitting at the tables. Most were complete strangers. Cantwell had swelled to the bursting point with RVs of all types and sizes parked bumper to bumper throughout the community. There were private tour buses equipped with tents and kitchens and a couple hundred cars and pick-ups driven by agitated tourists who stood around complaining about their woes and attractions they were missing because of the roadblocks.

The ARR had rented tour buses to transport passengers, and several were parked and waiting on nearby rail property. Passengers were shuttled from the wrecked train to Cantwell on a three-car passenger train brought down from Fairbanks and loaded aboard buses. The ARR offered to take people north to Fairbanks and then fly them to Anchorage on a charter flight as Fairbanks was crowded with new arrivals, and hotel rooms were hard to find. Some intrepid tourists chose to travel by bus to Fairbanks, then south through Delta Junction to Glenallen on the Richardson Highway, and then west to Anchorage on the Glenn Highway. These didn't want to miss out on Alaska's landscape and wildlife. Many in Anchorage chose that route to Fairbanks.

In Cantwell, businesses informed anyone who asked about the roundabout way to Fairbanks. For those wanting to visit Denali National Park from Anchorage, it was the only way until the road re-opened. Most people continued hanging around Cantwell, hoping the roadblock would end soon. Troopers who manned the roadblocks were constantly questioned by travelers. "What's the latest?" "How much longer will the road be closed?" and "Why the hell is this highway closed, I pay my taxes!" Though many people were parked around the lodge, most travelers remained in the dirt parking lots of the two service stations on the highway and the one campground.

It hadn't taken long before travelers learned where the rest of Cantwell was located, and the Reindeer Lodge became a hot spot. Old Man Taylor's joint was reported to be a decent watering hole. "That place is run by a colorful Alaskan character." The locals warned them that Taylor's bite was far worse than his bark. Old man Taylor was colorful, to be sure. His vulgarity had already sent several people on the run. His steamy temper had driven out a group of Frenchmen; Taylor disliked the French or anyone who dared to complain about his limited menu. He had promptly launched his anti-French tirade running from international events after World War II through Vietnam with this last group of French travelers. His cantankerous moods and off-color jokes nearly caused a few fights in the bar. He was always ready with a Louisville Slugger to stifle the more aggressive ones.

In all the activity, Old Man Taylor remained protective of Tony and ensured everyone stayed clear of his favorite spot at the end of the bar. Taylor valued Tony, sensing the turmoil he suffered from his Vietnam experience, leaving his faith and profession behind to become a near hermit. He had offered to take Tony to Fairbanks on a supply run numerous times, but Tony always declined.

Tony had ridden his ATV into Cantwell and was surprised by all the vehicles parked outside the lodge. At first, he thought Taylor was having a going-out-of-business sale, or, to shock the locals, had finally offered to buy a round of drinks for everyone. Tony believed all of Cantwell would show up to witness that occurrence. He had liked Old Man Taylor right away, though he often found him a contentious old bear. One of the local ladies had once voiced her hopes that some sight-challenged she-bear would wander into the Reindeer one day and carry Taylor off. Tony knew that would never happen, as no bear would be so blind as to confuse Taylor with some handsome bruin. Besides, on his best day, Taylor smelled worse than any grizzly. Tony suspected bathing was not one of the old man's favorite things to do nor did he use aftershave or underarm deodorant. He simply considered himself a natural man. Thankfully, heat from the stove prevented most of his odor from reaching the food he prepared for customers. For all that, Taylor constantly washed his hands, all the way up to his elbows because he didn't want any problems with the state health inspector. Tony had noticed the state's health certification was dated five years ago and wondered how Taylor got away with that. *Threats or bribes? Maybe he told the state office he was closed, and by the looks of this place, he could get away with that.*

Usually, with such a crowd, Tony wouldn't go inside but he was hungry and thirsty for an ice-cold root beer. The thought of crispy bacon and Taylor's special scrambled eggs, which were legendary, made his stomach growl. Taylor told Tony the secret was in the seasoning for he seldom cleaned his grill. When the grill was covered with hamburger patties or other meats, he switched to an old model gas burner stove. Then his collection of ancient cast iron pans came in handy, layered with years of curing. He used bear grease on his stovetop; he didn't like to waste anything, including yesterday's grease. Old grease was stored in the pantry in five-gallon buckets. It was said that you could order a steak or a cheeseburger, and both might end up tasting like last night's fried rainbow trout. Even when Taylor offered some weird pasta dish, there was a definite taste of French fries. But he had the only game in town, the cafés on the highway only served pre-made sandwiches and sold packaged snacks.

As Tony entered, he kept his dark blue sweatshirt hood up to hide his face. Taking his seat at the bar, he listened to the TV and learned of the situation along the railroad tracks south of Cantwell. When voices got too loud to hear the TV, Old Man Taylor roared them into silence, yelling, "Either shut up or get out!" He sounded like a grizzly on the prowl, much to the entertainment of a group of Japanese tourists. When they left Cantwell, it would be with several photographs of this red-faced old geezer behaving like some wild man from the

Alaska wilderness. Of course, Old Man Taylor was not about to let such times go by without adding a bit of street acting for the cameras.

Most visitors would buy a beer and spend the next hour chomping down on free popcorn or pretzels Taylor always had out for the locals. Someone would often buy a glass of hard stuff, which Taylor sold at a premium. He figured out early on, the hard stuff was where the money was for a bar. A $17 bottle of gin from his Fairbanks wholesaler could bring him over $100, as long as he measured his shots, and used a one-ounce stainless steel measuring cup, to be exact.

The previous night, the big spenders were in, and he'd made over a thousand dollars in just over 13 hours. Adding the kitchen receipts, he put $1,322.75 in cash and credit card receipts into his floor safe behind the large beer cooler by the back door. Besides receipts, the safe held the latest version of his will, life insurance policy, and a loaded .357 magnum two-shot derringer with ivory grips. He wanted to be ready in the event some whacko tried to hold him up some night and wanted more than what was in the cash register. Taylor didn't think his life was worth more than the few bills plus change he kept in the register, but the safe was another matter.

As news people swarmed over the community, Cantwell moved into the international spotlight for the first time anyone could remember. Reporters wandered about hoping to find a true down-to-earth story that might lead them to a Pulitzer Prize or a headline. One such reporter worked on a colorful piece on how the folks of this small town came to terms with international terrorism at their door. To their surprise, out-of-state news people realized down-to-earth Alaskans didn't want their privacy invaded by nosey reporters. Old Man Taylor posted a sign on the Reindeer's front door, "NO REPORTERS-NO JEHOVAH WITNESSES-NO MORMONS–NO DRUGS & NO TERRORISTS" A photo of the sign later made the front page of the Fairbanks News Miner.

One man asked Old Man Taylor what he had against Mormons. Taylor spat out the side of his mouth and as it landed on the floor behind the bar replied, "Nothin', I just didn't want those dang JW's thinkin' I was pickin' on just them. Got too many customers who are Baptists or Catholics—can't afford to offend them either." He turned slightly, "You want any more bacon, Tony?" Tony shook his head but offered a quick OK sign with his finger and thumb, bringing a smile to the old man's face. "Thanks. A man likes to have his cookin' appreciated."

A sudden hush fell over the room when another news bulletin broke in during a daytime talk show. An Anchorage reporter from Channel 13 News filled the screen. Wearing a brown suit and a dark blue tie, the handsome newscaster with large white teeth and dark brown hair addressed the television audience:

"We've been informed that US Army Explosive Ordnance Disposal teams have cleared the pathway leading from the Alaska Railroad tracks to a small cabin in the hills above the train. Investigators arriving on the scene have verified the terrorists had used the cabin for a short time. They apparently abandoned it as the forest fire, ignited by the crash of the Alaska State Trooper helicopter spread to within 25 yards of the dilapidated structure. The fire in the immediate area is now 80 percent contained. We have been told to expect further news concerning the downed helicopter and recovery of bodies any time now. Other news involving the FLQ could also be forthcoming. Please stay tuned."

"They broke into our talk show for that bit of nothing," Sam Watterson complained. A TV fan, Sam thought Taylor's new TV made his favorite shows more entertaining than his 19-inch at home. "We already knew all that." He looked over at Taylor, "Funny, they didn't mention what's happening here in Cantwell. Those damn terrorists have sure messed up that area for hunting and fishing. No one's going to enter those woods knowing they might trigger some damn landmine."

Trooper Bosley closed the lodge's door behind him," Cantwell is a speck on the map, Sam. People outside want to know about Anchorage and Fairbanks."

Old Man Taylor waved to Bosley and addressed Watterson, "No one wants to give any more credit to those lowlifes out there in the woods." He looked over at Tony and, in a lower voice, said, "From what I hear, the ARR is goin' to take an absolute shellacking with what this train wreck is costing them. Probably be a significant rise in train fares and shipping costs. Even if insurance covers all the expenses, the railroad people will say the price rise is based on this incident. Those damn Canuks should've kept their terrorists in their own country— Alaska sure didn't need 'em!"

Immaculate in uniform, Bosley wandered over to the bar and ordered a Coke. "Lots of ice; I need something to wash the dust down with."

"What dust?" Taylor wiped the bar, looked down at the other end, and gave an evil leer to a 30-something female tourist leaning over the bar to reach a pile of napkins. Her stretch exposed most of her female charm.

"I call it touri-dust," Sam Watterson ambled over to say hello to Trooper Bosley and shake his hand. "These people are worse than my little brother's cooties. I know I'm gonna get a rash from bumping into all these foreigners."

"Only reason you'd ever get a rash is your need to take a bath, Sam. Most of these people ain't foreigners; they're just not Alaskans. Look outside; you'll see Lower 48 license plates from all over." Taylor poured Bosley a Coke over a tall glass of ice cubes.

"Same thing! I consider anyone south of Talkeetna a foreigner. If you ask me, Anchorage is like another planet. We should call it North Seattle."

"Sam, here—" Taylor pushed a can of Budweiser across the bar at Sam. "Take your beer an' find a corner to take your weird ideas to. Trooper Bosley is too busy to listen to your lame complaints"

"I like the sign on the door," Bosley said. Lifting the glass, he took a gulp of his drink. "You'll probably get an ACLU complaint out of it."

"My place, my sign, and my rules. If ACLU folks come around, I'll show them what this former Marine thinks of their politics. Besides, I didn't say anything about Black, Brown, Red, and little yellow people. I ain't no racist; I'll sell my booze to just about anybody, but those JWs drove me crazy last time they stopped in. Tried to tell me my version of the Holy Bible was wrong."

Bosley nodded, "Oh, they're not all bad. Most of those ACLU people really believe in what they're doing. They'll represent a Christian preacher who's been wronged for his beliefs just as well as a convicted serial rapist. They believe in the Constitution, completely—word for word— and think everyone should. I'd prefer they didn't object so much or get violent, or infringe on someone else's rights. Which makes their belonging to the ACLU a lie in my opinion."

"I've heard them compared to communists, atheists, and a lot of other dirty names. But you're right; our Constitution allows for such freedoms," Taylor said.

"Mr. Taylor, I'm only saying you can find good people out there doing things we disagree with, which is what makes this country great. You can still hang all the lawyers as far as I'm concerned."

Old Man Taylor chuckled, sharing Trooper Bosley's sentiments about lawyers. In fact, he thought about making up a new sign and adding lawyers to the list. "I'll take the Mormons off and replace them with lawyers. How 'bout that?"

"Freedom of speech, that's what it's all about," Bosley replied.

"You want anything to eat?" Taylor asked.

"Naw, I only stopped by for a bar check and a coke. Consider yourself checked." Bosley offered a casual wave in Taylor's direction and started for the door. Then he stopped, turned around, and walked over to where Tony was sitting.

"You doing all right, Tony?"

Tony nodded, and because he liked Bosley, mumbled a greeting. He saw Bosley as a man of integrity who understood the people in this area.

"Everything okay out your way?"

Tony garbled his words, but Trooper Bosley had no trouble understanding him. He'd known Tony quite a while and had learned to understand his garbled speech.

"If you have any problems, you let me know. Now that summer's here, we can expect about anything, so keep your place locked up when you're not around. I don't just mean bears either; I'm talking about the two-legged varmints. We've already had several cabins broken into this last spring; I'd hate to see it happen at your place." Bosley patted Tony's arm, smiled, and walked out.

"That Trooper Bosley is a good man; I hope we never lose him. The last trooper we had here thought everyone should behave like city folks. Glad he got transferred out," Old Man Taylor said. Then with a damp rag in hand, he wiped the bar surface again. He looked up when a few strangers walked in looking for a table. "You'll have to sit at the bar; my place is full."

"Only wanted to use your bathroom," One of the men stated.

"Chevron Station up the highway." Taylor pointed them toward the door. "You want to use my septic system, my well water, and my electricity and not buy something. No way! Move on!"

The lunch rush was arriving and there were no fast-food joints in Cantwell, Tony waved his goodbyes to Taylor and walked outside his four-wheeler. A 40-foot RV with Florida plates nearly backed into him, and he only escaped injury through rapid acceleration and a sharp right turn. He didn't bother to look back and blame the driver, knowing how hard it would've been to see him from one of those big beasts.

His relaxing ride back to the cabin was interrupted by the sound of helicopters flying overhead. He stopped, turned his engine off, and watched as two Sikorsky UH-60 Black Hawk Helicopters zoomed overhead and proceeded south. He knew where they were going and wondered if they were dropping troops off or picking someone up. He hoped it wasn't anyone hurt and caught himself considering a prayer for those who might be injured or the safety of the crewmen inside the Black Hawks. But he thought, *You may be up there, God, but I sure won't bend a knee or bow down before you. Not now, not ever again!* Then leaving a cloud of dust in his wake, Tony roared off toward his cabin and a long day of chores.

Greg's Apartment - 11:14 AM

Piled up on Greg's bed were boxes of new hiking boots and outdoor wear for JP and black backpacks and sleeping bags for both men. There were two foam sleeping pads, four belt canteens, small hatchets, expensive Buck sheath knives, and several boxes of foil-wrapped freeze-dried foods; *Just add water and ignore the taste,* he thought. On Greg's desk sat two top-of-the-line miniature radios with a working radius of four miles, with extra batteries. They wouldn't need flashlights with all the daylight, but they'd need wooden matches and a good first aid kit. They each had new cotton socks and dark-colored T-shirts to wear under the latest in camouflage clothing. Greg, who was ever so glad to use JP's money, had purchased a Winchester 7mm rifle with 4x Leopold Scope to top off the equipment. JP had once owned a rifle precisely like this, and it felt comfortable with the rubber butt plate snug up against his right shoulder.

From his closet, Greg removed a well-used Mossberg 12-gauge shotgun that he'd had the barrel length cut to the legal minimum of 18 inches. Some of the bluing was rubbed away, so he plopped down on the floor with his cleaning kit and started breaking the weapon down and cleaning each piece with a lightly oiled cloth. He carried the shotgun inside a leather sheath attached to his backpack frame whenever he went hiking. It made for an easy grab in case he encountered a bear in the woods. Besides his Glock, he took a Colt AR-15, the civilian semi-automatic version of the military M-16A2. He had owned it since joining SERT, but usually kept it safely tucked away in a hard plastic case in the back of his bedroom closet.

"I think I may have maxed out my Visa Gold Card, Greg," JP said as he admired his new 9-inch Buck sheath knife with a black ebony handle.

"My dad always taught me it was better to have too much than not enough. No stores where we're going," Greg responded.

"We have a lot of weight here for two middle-aged men to carry through the bush."

Greg ignored the middle-aged crack, "Not really. Once we have everything loaded into the packs and distributed equally between us, it won't be too bad. But you lug your own ammo."

"The next question is… when do we leave?"

"Early morning. The sun will be high by 5:00 a.m. We'll drive south and try to find my buddy. He's a trooper, and he'll either be standing the roadblock or getting some shuteye back at the post. My railroad I.D. should get us past the roadblock."

"Do you think he'll help us?" JP pulled the new brown leather boots out and tried them on. He knew before long he'd be using up band-aids on the blisters he expected.

"That's what I hope to find out. All I need from him is the name of a good guide, someone to take us into the backcountry. Someone who won't ask a lot of questions."

"How much is this guide going to cost?" JP stood to his feet and walked around the room. He'd tried the boots on at the store, but he was wearing heavier socks now.

"Look, Captain, I've got about $1,500 in my checking account, a little bit more in savings. Anything over that, and you'll have to chip in."

"I've $2,000 in American Express Travelers Checks, so I think I should cover the guide fee. And please, call me JP." He sat down, removed his right boot, and tried to stretch it with his hands.

"Make sure you waterproof those with that salve we picked up and Scotch-Guard your outer garments, backpack, and new sleeping bags. It may be summer, but where we're going, the morning dew can soak everything."

"How are we going to find the FLQ?" JP Asked.

Greg reached underneath his bed and pulled out a box. He removed the lid and lifted out a black leather case about the size of a portable cassette player. "This will help some." He opened the case to remove a handheld GPS, last year's model. "Thought I might take my son moose hunting last fall, but it didn't work out. Wanted to make sure we wouldn't get lost in those rolling hills behind Fairbanks; they can get mighty confusing at times. Had a buddy who got turned around and after two days of hard hiking, found his way out. Things can get a mite off-kilter in summer daylight."

"I understand how a GPS works, and I know we've got a portable radio to listen to the newscasts, but how will we locate them?"

"They're heading south, but they're new to these woods. So, I imagine they'll have to stay parallel to or in sight of either the train tracks or the highway, possibly a river. Or they risk getting lost. They'll probably want to give the highway a wide berth because they know the feds are watching on satellite. Unfortunately, this time of year, there are a lot of hikers and campers out there making it difficult to detect a certain group of heat sources."

"And?"

"They've got to be going somewhere, someplace they can hold up. They're betting on the good guys not wanting to risk the lives of those hostages, especially after the blood bath they left in Toronto. So, they'll hole up and wait the 96 hours they gave the authorities, which is running down fast." Greg put the shotgun back together as he spoke. "They'll either stumble onto a hunter's cabin or maybe they'll hike all the way to Curry."

"Curry. What's curry? Besides an Indian food dish."

"Ghost town, more or less, a railroad stop in the old days. A few people live around there still, mostly survivalists or old veterans wanting to get away from civilization, plus a few die-hard prospectors. Nothing but a few run-down buildings."

"How far from where they ambushed the train?"

"Quite a ways, so they may not go that far. Take 'em 30, maybe 40 hours of hard going to get there. They have Senator Sterns with them. She's not a spring chicken anymore. I'm sure the Feds have the place surrounded by now, closing off all points south, and then they'll start closing in on them."

"Why wouldn't they try to go north?" JP took his backpack into the bathroom, laid it in the tub, and sprayed it with a heavy dose of Scotch Guard.

"They'd never make it over the mountains. Besides, when you leave the mountains, you hit the flats where it's too easy to be seen from the air. Unless they left the tracks and went into the backcountry." Greg shook his head. "Too easy to lose themselves until a rescue party stepped on top of 'em. I don't know much about the Canadian wilderness, but Alaska never gives anything away freely. It's not a very friendly land unless you learn how to respect and survive in it. People have starved to death or died from exposure within 100 feet of the highway. If they head into the mountains, they'll either freeze to death when they hit a snowline, get eaten by a bear, or fall into some river gorge. Possibly slide off some glacier."

"You don't sound like you like it here."

"No, I love it here. But I've learned to respect Alaska's serious side. You could live off the land in the backcountry, raise healthy children, home-school them, and never see another soul unless you wanted to. But most people prefer civilization, and gradually, Alaska is losing its wild side. It won't happen in my lifetime or my son's. But eventually, Alaska will become one big stinkin' metropolis filled with a billion people, all in some hurry to get here or there. From what I've read, we're overpopulating our little planet. Thankfully, Alaska still sits at around 750,000 people, and I hope we don't get much bigger while I'm still living."

Greg stood up, slid the shotgun into its sheath, and strapped it to his pack. He pulled out his AR-15, cleaned it, and ensured he had at least eight loaded magazines ready. It wouldn't be light, but he needed his AR-15 to combat the terrorist's automatic weapons. "You'd better grab some shut-eye, JP. I'll wake you for dinner."

"Okay, but I've been running hard since—since I got out of the hospital, I'm not sure I can sleep." JP slid some of the boxes off the bed and laid down. A moment later, Greg heard him snoring.

Pike's Landing - Fairbanks - 7:22 PM

Lt. Steve Farber couldn't meet them for dinner; too much was happening in town. Fairbanks police had responded to a murder scene earlier in the day. A couple of young GIs from Fort Wainwright apparently stumbled into a drug buy off South Cushman. One soldier was dead, shot twice through the chest with a large caliber weapon, another man was wounded.

News of the shooting had reached the Army barracks, prompting some 100 soldiers to rush downtown on a quest for revenge. Fights had broken out at the Airport Way McDonalds and in two-strip clubs. A knifing occurred in a beer joint that sent one soldier to the hospital and another citizen to jail for attempted murder. Police were struggling to curtail angry grunts all over town. The night was still young, and the Chief of Police called Lt. Farber in early. Farber quickly got too busy to think about Greg and JP; he knew that if things didn't calm down, another shooting war could break out downtown.

Holding themselves to one beer each, Greg and JP consumed a shared plate of curly fries with cheese and a couple of hamburgers decked out with bacon, cheese, and mushrooms. "Enjoy it; for the next few days, we'll be on freeze-dried cardboard," Greg licked the burger's juice from his fingers with a slurping sound.

"I'm anxious to get going," JP dipped a fry into a dab of ketchup. He munched down and looked forward to having one of the terrorists in the sights of his new rifle. The ketchup had made him think of blood, which caused his memory to flashback to his beautiful LeAnn. The pain was still too fresh, and he fought tears welling in his eyes.

Greg saw it and understood or tried to understand. He lost his wife to another man; this man had a loving partner murdered, along with his two young sons. "Look, just relax for a while. It's only a four-hour drive to Cantwell. We won't be able to find a guide until morning anyway, and that's if we're lucky. Spring black bear season is almost over. Most guides are probably sunbathing in Hawaii until fall moose season."

"If that's the case, we may not be able to find anyone to help us," JP said with a noticeable look of concern on his face.

"There's always a few who hang around. Don't worry; I'm sure we'll locate someone." Greg took a sip of beer and thought about his boy, wondering for a moment if this was really the right decision. Looking at JP, he knew he couldn't let the man go out there alone. *And those people just killed five troopers who were my friends. I owe 'em for that.*

"How many hours do you think it'll take us to catch up with them?"

"Depends. On foot, maybe 40 hours or less, if they've stopped. But I'm hoping for transportation."

"What kind of transportation?"

"Most guides have access to four-wheelers to take their clients out. With an ATV, we could locate them in say… 10 hours or less from Cantwell. It could or probably will take longer. Remember, Alaska is a big place, and we're going to be scouting a pretty large area."

"So, in a couple days, we could be live heroes or dead fools, correct?" JP asked.

"That pretty well sums it up, but there's a lot to consider; the guide and finding these…" Greg looked around the room, "friends of ours."

"You sure about this, Greg? You're risking so much." JP picked up his beer and took a sip, but his eyes remained locked on Greg's.

Greg smiled, "This makes me think about that movie—'The Magnificent Seven'. Ever see it?"

"Yul Brynner hires six other glory seekers to go up against two hundred Mexican bandits, right?"

"That's the sequel. In the first one, they only go up against 40 bandits. But they're not glory seekers, simply gun hands with nothing better to do and tired of their lives. And they hate to see the little guy get kicked around. It's one of my favorite movies. My son and I watch it about once a year. I have it on DVD now."

"So, you think you're Yul Brynner, and I'm?"

"You're Steve McQueen, second in command."

"They're both dead now, you know that?" JP asked with a sly smirk on his face.

"Not in the Magnificent Seven, they rode off into the sunset, and old Yul went on to dance in the "King and I" for some 15 years or more on Broadway."

"From what you say, I've gotten involved with a Western hero wanna-be?

"You'd better say that with a smile, buckaroo, or meet me outside at sunset." Greg pointed his right index finger with his thumb and fired a make-believe shot at JP.

"I'll share a dark secret with you. Because of my looks, I was often, behind my back, you understand, referred to as a Sgt Preston look-a-like."

"Hey, I remember that show. Picked up a collection of episodes on DVD last year. My kid got a kick out of it. Loved the dog."

JP nodded, "Well, hopefully, our lives last much longer than his television contract did."

"As my kid would say, it's not worth sweating out the test until it's time to take it."

"Smart kid, hope I get to meet him."

"So do I," Greg said.

Truth be told, Greg struggled with the whole idea of the two of them hunting down the FLQ. He was still angry about the way the other agencies had shoved him aside, and there was the loss of his fellow troopers. Men Greg had trained with, shared meals at their homes, led three of them in do-or-die operations, and now they, along with Captain Potter, were burned up in a helicopter crash. He may not have lost a wife and two sons, but Greg desperately wanted some payback. He needed to know he had done all he could. *And maybe, just maybe, a real big maybe, we'll locate these bad guys before the 96 hours are up.* Greg agreed with JP and Lt. Farber; if the authorities didn't take the terrorists down by the deadline, the gunmen would murder the hostages and leave their bodies for the good guys to find. He needed to be in on this. Greg almost felt he was going on some quest and wondered if he would survive to return to his son. *These next 68 hours will possibly be the worst three days of my life. I sure hope this Mountie is up to it; he's taken a bad beating.*

On The Trail - 12.6 Miles North Of Curry - 8:40 P.M.

Munroe, his eyes radiating a maniacal glare, called a break when Sterns collapsed for the umpteenth time and rolled several feet down the hill. This time, they couldn't revive her with cold water from a canteen or repeated kicks in her back from Munroe's boot.

"We carry her," Hugo said.

Senator Sterns' hair was a mess, and her arms were scratched and bloody as she lay unconscious on the ground. Munroe paced nervously behind her. Her breathing was dangerously shallow, her body was twitching. Hugo ordered Governor Hughes and Michael to cut two-alder poles for a stretcher. They would use one of the shelter halves to create the sling.

At first, Munroe thought to just leave her then agreed after a few minutes of consideration. He assigned Hughes and Michael the chore of carrying her. Prime Minister Haegens was barely able to walk and much too important to lose. Though winded, the governor was still able to keep going.

They'd been taking 10-minute breaks after every 20 minutes but never stopped to make camp. Twice they'd come across bears but had been able to scare them off with a couple of rounds fired into the ground in front of them.

Hugo tried to get them to use something other than firearms, for fear the authorities would hear the shots, but throwing rocks and shouts hadn't worked.

They expected to see moose or other wildlife, but, during their last break, Governor Hughes informed them that they were too high, and the canyon walls too impassible for moose. "Over the top, you'd find moose and probably some wolves on the other side. Bears are mostly after shrews, early berries, and coming down for creek water. Salmon won't run this far north until August, so bears have to forage for what they can get."

"I don't need no wildlife lesson!" Munroe exclaimed. "Just keep your mouth shut."

Besides soreness from the strenuous hike and the backpack straps cutting into his shoulders, Michael was concerned about Munroe's recent behavior. Twice, Michael feared Munroe would shoot either Hughes or Sterns, maybe both. Since the bear killed Janene, he'd been acting very strange, and when he walked by Hugo, the German tensed up and put his hand on his weapon.

Michael could see Hugo no longer trusted Munroe if he ever had. He wondered how long before a showdown and who he would have to side with but hoped there might be a third choice.

14

---

# A WHISTLE-STOP CALLED CURRY

Cantwell Trooper Post
June 15th- 08:10 a.m.

Greg Hansen's back ached from spending over four hours behind the wheel. JP had a kink in his neck that wouldn't release. They arrived at the small Cantwell Trooper Post, a single-story-gray painted structure with a metal roof. Not much larger than a two-car garage but it housed Trooper Bosley and served as his office. Greg's railroad I.D. and JP's RCMP I.D. had gotten them past the north roadblock.

In place of a holding cell, Trooper Bosley handcuffed prisoners to either a standpipe or an office chair. He transferred prisoner(s) to Fairbanks Correctional Center when necessary. The Trooper in Trapper Creek handled calls in Bosley's area when this occurred.

In Cantwell, most arrests came from driving intoxicated, disorderly conduct, domestic assaults, and an occasional drug bust. Now and then, a driver or passenger might be picked up on a warrant. Cantwell Trooper duties usually involved writing speeding tickets on the Parks Highway or investigating motor vehicle accidents. With the nearest trooper in Nenana or Trapper Creek, Troopers assigned to Cantwell usually worked alone. As a result, this post was traditionally given to seasoned veterans.

When Greg and JP arrived, an AST white Ford Expedition was parked out front. A blue stripe and a large gold badge were displayed on the front doors of the car. The head of an Alaska Brown Bear was at the top of the shield and "Alaska State Trooper" was printed across the rear door and rear quarter panels with the emergency number "911". A light bar was attached to the roof, along with a police radio antenna. Trooper Bosley, who had just returned to the office from a call to complete paperwork, heard Greg drive up and stepped outside.

Greg stretched his arms to get his circulation going when he saw Bosley's smiling face. "Howdy, Bos!"

"Hey, Greg!" Bosley held out his hand. He had known Greg since they were young Troopers working in Anchorage. Because the ARR tracks ran through the valley, Greg was often down in the area and usually stopped to visit his old friend. Ten miles south of Cantwell, the Anchorage ARR office took over ARR property and handled investigations south into Anchorage, Whittier, and further south in Seward.

"Trooper Bosley, this is JP—Captain Jean-Paul Leon of the Toronto RCMP. He heads up their Intelligence Division, so, watch your language."

JP and Bosley shook hands, "I'm very pleased to meet you, Trooper Bosley."

"You're a friend of Greg's, so you can call me Bos. Greg and I go way back, so watch your wallet and your women around him." Bos' hoped to get a smile, but the look in JP's eyes told him he had somehow committed a serious social blunder.

"JP, as he likes to be called since we Alaskans have trouble pronouncing Jean-Paul correctly, recently lost his wife and children to terrorists. The same ones you have on the loose here."

"Oh, God, I am so sorry! I don't watch a lot of news down here. I know all about the terrorists in our mountains and the train wreck but not much about what happened in Canada. Sorry about what happened to your family."

"It's OK, you didn't know." JP's voice reflected the grief that made him look tired and old.

"Again, my condolences, Captain."

"Thank you, Bos—"

"We need to talk, Bos." Greg interrupted the exchange, "Were you going somewhere in particular or just out? Can you spare us a few moments?"

"I just handled a minor disturbance, a lot of heated tempers with the road closure. Before that, I worked traffic control at the roadblock south of here. I was just headed over to the lodge for some chow. I've grown a might weary of my own cooking."

"I thought the Reindeer couldn't open—oh, yeah, it's after eight, isn't it?" Greg looked at JP, "In Alaska, licensed premises close at 5:00 a.m. and cannot reopen until 8:00 a.m.—state law. Never did understand the reason for the three-hour closure. Probably to force drunks to go home for a nap."

"Old Man Taylor swings a mean spatula, and his eggs are famous. He uses a lot of spices I've come to appreciate... if you don't mind his...Taylor has a really... colorful personality if you know what I mean? The road closure has increased his business, but the people are driving him crazy. Wait 'til you see his new door sign!"

"Can we join you?" Greg asked as Bosley closed the door and locked it with a deadbolt.

"I'd appreciate the company. What's with all the camping gear in the back of your rig? I've never known you to be a woodsman, and with JP here, I'm curious as to where you're headed."

"I always said you should have taken that transfer to Major Crimes; you're a natural investigator," Greg replied.

"Didn't like the people I'd be working for. I like it out here where I can stretch out my arms and not hit someone with my backswing. I've found it to be a bit too crowded in the cities. Can't even imagine how it is for all those cops who work in the Lower 48."

"We'll follow you over." Greg headed for his car with JP in tow.


Reindeer Lodge, Cantwell


Heavy vehicle traffic in Cantwell surprised Greg. Congestion around the lodge made him wonder if they could find a parking place within walking distance. He'd never seen it this crowded before; they'd have to find a place in the trees down the road. "The roadblock must be irritating a lot of people. Can't remember the last time the highway was closed down this long," Greg said.

"Your friend, Trooper Bosley, seems to be an amiable person. Do you think he can assist us?"

"Bos is a good man, but we'll limit the info on why we're here. I don't want him to find himself chest high in shark-infested waters. We get caught out there, and it's liable to create a problem. I don't want to cause any trouble for Bos or anyone else, except for those clowns out there who caused this problem."

"Clowns?"

"A word we often use for the bad guys," Greg replied.

"I'll have to remember that one. You mean you believe Bosley would probably lose his job for helping us if his superiors could verify he knew about what we have planned?"

"That's what I mean."

"I thought so. Surprising how different our use of English and your English differ so."

"You're a bit more formal in your word usage. Up here in Alaska, we tend to use the more casual form and toss in a lot of slang. Why waste words when you can get by on less."

"I've heard the Russians want this country back, upset with the trade they made with that Seward chap. After seeing these mountains and these massive valleys, I can understand why. This land is quite beautiful. Photos don't do it justice."

"They'd have to bring in a whole lot of tanks and bombers to get this land back. You'll find Alaskans dislike anyone treading on our land without permission; we're a real independent lot. Nearly every home has at least one firearm, and most have more. Even those people living in Anchorage still retain some attitude for dealing with trespassers."

"What if politicians in Washington D.C. opt to give Alaska back to prevent war?"

"I believe Alaska would quickly secede from the Union and take on the Russian bear ourselves. I don't think that'll happen. Russia has too many ongoing problems to mess with us right now. From what I read some time ago when the Russians sold Alaska, they only owned about seven acres on the Island of Sitka. Native tribes in Alaska had no idea Russia had laid claim to the whole territory. I'm more concerned about China getting a bit close. Some people believe China may one day attack us even though we have a strong military presence and a good-sized militia."

A black Dodge pick-up backed out of a spot in the trees close by the lodge, and Greg pulled into the vacant spot. "Let's go see what Old Man Taylor's cooking up."

"You know this Taylor well?"

Greg hesitated and then turned his engine off. "You might say he's one of Alaska's few remaining true-to-life characters. You'll understand when you meet him. Most everyone around here would warn you his bite is worse than his growl."

"Growl?"

"Normally, people would say bark, but Old Man Taylor is like an old grizzly bear. He tends to growl a lot. When he bites, heads roll because he favors a baseball bat to get his point across to troublemakers."

JP looked at Greg with a raised eyebrow.

"He's just a crusty old fart who owns this place and runs it pretty well for a guy who's been here long enough to be a true sourdough."

"Sourdough?"

"That's a name we use for old-timers who've been here a very long time. When the old prospectors came up for the Klondike gold rush, they carried bags of sourdough—a flour and yeast mixture to make bread and flapjacks. They tucked it inside their shirts so their body heat would keep the yeast active. They always smelled like sour dough. The name sort of stuck to stand for old-timers. Alaska has a lot of respect for our seniors. The state provides a financial perk for them when they hit those golden years."

The door to the lodge stood open, held by an old green five-gallon military gasoline can filled with murky water. A large four-foot-tall fan aimed out the door kept mosquitoes and black flies out. Trooper Bosley elected to park his AST vehicle in an area clearly marked, *No Parking*, space Taylor reserved for three red Honda ATVs, which, when not leased out, were parked and secured to the building by a heavy logging chain and high-security padlocks. There was still room for the AST vehicle. Had any other person parked there, Taylor would've warned them once, and then start throwing rocks until the culprit got it moved.

Bosley met Greg and JP at the door, "This place is busy from 8:00 a.m. 'til Taylor kicks everyone out. He won't hire anyone to help—says it cuts into his profits. I can tell by his recent display of sunny disposition that the work is tiring the old guy out."

"Sounds like him," Greg said. They noticed the inflammatory door sign right off, which caused them to smile. The lodge was packed with early morning risers when they walked inside. Because it was a bar, no one under 21 years of age was allowed inside. Both cafés on the highway were also overcrowded. Bosley learned that one of them had problems with its septic system from heavy use. The owner had already hung a "CUSTOMERS ONLY" sign on the restroom door.

Four men sat at the bar. Three nursed early morning beer, and the fourth man, Sam Watterson, was arguing with Old Man Taylor about something Greg couldn't hear. The heavy smell of a morning grease fire apparently kept most civilized people away, which made Sam Watterson quite happy. He liked a lot of elbow room for his daily argument with Taylor. The two old men held different views on politics, movies, and everything else. Bosley had decided these two old cantankerous duffers just liked to argue about life in general.

The television was on quite loud, and several people in the booths and at the few tables watched the Fox News channel while they ate or waited for their orders.

Behind the bar, Taylor, who clearly liked making signs, had posted a large sign that read, "DON'T LIKE YOUR ORDER- LEAVE! DON'T LIKE THE PRICE—LEAVE!—WAITING TIME FOR ORDERS BASED ON COOK'S DISCRETION—LARGE TIPS HELPFUL IN SPEEDING UP ORDERS—NO SPECIALS!"

JP read the sign and grinned. Seeing the grossly overweight, sloppily dressed cook with huge hands and a Santa Claus beard, he guessed him to be Old Man Taylor. And understood Greg's admiration for the man. *A truly independent thinker.*

"Morning, Trooper Bosley. Where'd you pick that reprobate up from?" Taylor came from behind the bar to shake Greg's hand. "Ain't seen you for a month of Sundays, Greg. Thought you'd be involved in that mess south of here, and here you are."

"It's a Fed operation; they chased me off." Greg looked at JP, "Mr. Taylor, this is a friend of mine, Jean-Paul Leon of Toronto."

"You French?" Taylor asked in a challenging tone before he offered his hand.

"Be nice. JP is an RCMP Captain, Mr. Taylor," Greg explained. He was relieved when Taylor stepped up with his sweaty hand held out and JP shook it.

"Pardon my rudeness. I actually like Mounties. A tough job that requires tough men. Just not all that partial to those Frenchmen from across the big water. I've got a lot of respect for you Mounties. Welcome to the Reindeer Lodge, Captain. Coffee's on me, but the eggs you gotta pay for."

"Thank you, Mr. Taylor," JP couldn't believe the old man's strength when they shook hands, a knuckle crusher to be sure. He could only imagine what Taylor was like in his younger days.

"Let me clear the table for you. I do breakfast until 11:00 A.M. and then start making hamburgers and a few sandwiches. If you're 'round tonight, I serve up a mean side of barbecued beef. Or straight cow or caribou. Even have salmon when it's in season, but not right now—too early."

"Trooper Bosley mentioned your scrambled eggs. I believe I'll have that." JP glanced around, saw stacks of bacon and sausages, and added, "With all the trimmings." He stepped back to allow Bosley and Greg to nod agreement; they'd have the same.

Once he was told how they wanted their eggs, Taylor replied, "Take me 'bout 10 minutes. Got some orders backed up. Not used to makin' breakfast, or lunch for that matter, for so many people. Gone through most of my summer supplies, I'll have to make a run to Fairbanks damn soon."

Pulling out three mismatched wood chairs, the three men sat down around an uneven wooden table with a scratched tabletop and looked around the room.

It was standard police procedure to check the place out before getting comfortable. If anyone were to notice, they'd see that none of the three were sitting with their backs to the door.

"I've got to get some sleep before relieving Trooper Bedloe at the roadblock. He's pulling days from 7:30 a.m. until 7:30 p.m. with guard troops. Then I come on with another group of guardsmen. 12 hours makes for a long shift, turning people around and listening to all the gripes about how the government infringes on their right to free travel."

"Yeah, I can imagine what would happen if you allowed some tourist from Maine or Utah to drive through, and they got kidnapped or, worse, shot. You'd have hell to pay," Greg said.

Sliding his chair back, Bosley stood up and walked to the bar to get some cold water. Old Man Taylor was busy, so Sam, who knew Trooper Bosley, went behind the bar to hand him three cold water bottles and three large plastic cups filled with ice.

"Thanks," Bosley said. He carefully lifted all three up between his two hands.

"Don't mention it; the Old Fart's got himself so far extended he's liable to collapse any minute from overwork. Probably hasn't slept in three days," Sam complained and dashed back around the bar as Taylor lashed out at him with a string of profanity for not minding his own business.

"So, now that we're here, what's up?" Bosley asked as he sat back down.

"We need a guide, Bos. Someone you can personally recommend to take us into the backcountry south of here." Greg moved closer to Bosley and lowered his voice, "Someone who won't ask any questions, and I hope that goes for you too."

Bosley looked back and forth between Greg and JP, "You're a couple of crazy bastards if you're planning on doing what I seriously hope you're not planning on doing."

"We've been friends for a long time, Bos. I'm calling in a big favor here. I hope you forget this conversation and our visit once we leave."

Bosley scooted his chair closer to Greg. "Are you out of your mind? Do you know what you're going up against, even if you can bypass the feds and the National Guard? Do you know anything about these, *people*, how they're armed, how many shooters— anything?"

"Bos', I helped you out a long time ago; I'm calling in a marker on this." Greg studied his friend's eyes. "I already know my job is toast, but I feel I've gotta do this. We lost five troopers that I know of. They were your friends, too. I will not let these clowns get handed off by one of our liberal federal judges in Anchorage or Canada. They have no death penalty and along the way, some other bad guy, maybe one of their friends, will do something to force their release. Like holding a couple hundred people hostage in some mall or movie theater. We've all seen how the game is played. These clowns need to be stopped right here. Send a message that Alaska won't tolerate terrorism." Greg looked to JP, "Sorry, no reflection on your legal system, but I've read how your courts have handled some of your significant cases. They've killed a lot of people and need to go down hard. I'm not out to murder anyone but if they resist—JP knows this bunch; his unit was investigating them when they dashed to Alaska. We know they've got one German mercenary with them, maybe others. We might not even find them, but with a knowledgeable guide, we have a slim chance."

JP nodded, "I'm in complete agreement about our courts. I'm concerned that if these people are handed over to our government—" He shook his head, "I won't let that happen. They've killed too many people, as well as my family. No!"

Bosley looked over at JP, who openly glared back at him because he thought Greg might be wrong about this man. A guy who might stand in the way of his blood quest or, even worse, decide they should be arrested to protect his old friend from harm. If he did arrest him, it would assuredly end his job with the ARR. Bosley knew Greg was right; he did owe him big time, saving his life in a shootout in Anchorage.

"Your breakfast is ready!" Taylor shouted loud enough to be heard by the three men.

"I'll grab it," Greg said, leaving the table.

Bosley sat back in his chair and looked into JP's bloodshot eyes. "Look, I can say I understand what you're going through but that would be a bald-ass lie. That man over there at the bar saved my life once, and I owe him dearly. I won't go into details, but I wouldn't be sitting here if he hadn't taken a chance at the risk of his own life. What concerns me is that there is an excellent chance that you'll get him killed, and I helped."

Before JP could reply, Greg returned to the table and set three overly full plates down. "That man knows how to pile it on the plate; must be six eggs apiece." Not only eggs, but six strips of bacon, six sausages, and a good-sized mound of fried potatoes on each. "He said the toast would be up soon, bumped us ahead of a few customers 'cause he knew you needed to sack out."

"Hard to get mad at a guy who can care like that," Bosley said. Picking up a piece of bacon, he bit into it and sighed.

While the others dug in, Bosley continued, "That old bear's been warned several times that he's not a package store; it's illegal for him to sell cases of beer or liquor to people to take hunting. He could lose his license, or at least have it suspended for a time."

"I'm surprised Gary hasn't already," Greg said as a dribble of grease ran down his chin from two sausage links. "Gary's usually on top of things."

"Gary Wing is gone, Greg. Thought you knew that." Bosley wiped grease off the side of his mouth with a paper napkin. "ABC Board lost their best investigator a couple of weeks ago. Gary got fed up with the bad politics and handed in his walking papers. The new guy is still getting his sea legs, but he'll be down this way soon enough."

"Gary was a good cop. Any word on where he might be going?"

"Rumor has it he may take over as North Pole's Chief of Police; he's sure got my vote. If I remember right, he spent 12 years with the Tucson P.D. and ended up running their police academy before coming to Alaska."

"He'd make a good chief. North Pole would be lucky to get him." North Pole was 13 miles east of Fairbanks and a major Santa Claus/tourist stop.

Greg laid his fork down and repeated his question, "Can you give me the name of a good guide or at least point me in the right direction?"

"First off, I do owe you, and you can keep your markers, but you've come at a bad time, and that's the truth. You know the spring bear hunt is over, and fall hunting is a ways off. I don't know any guides still in the valley; at least anyone I would trust with what you have planned. Many have already headed for Hawaii and elsewhere. The few I do know who are still around, I wouldn't recommend to lead you across the highway; mostly young dopers taking over their father's business, and don't have the good sense to know you don't mix dope with guns."

As if on cue, a shadowy figure blocked the doorway and caused the three men to look up and observe a hooded man enter. He walked directly to his favorite spot at the end of the bar, and his presence surprised Old Man Taylor, "What got you up this early two days in a row?"

Tony shook his head, making sure the hood of his sweatshirt stayed in place to hide his facial scars. Someone once told him he looked like he had squabbled with a tiger and lost. The VA had offered him plastic surgery, but Tony declined when the doctor warned him it could require as many as five procedures.

"Breakfast?" Taylor asked ignoring Watterson's request for another beer.

Tony nodded and put up two fingers, meaning he wanted two bottles of ice-cold root beer. He had weathered another sleepless night, maybe getting three hours of shut-eye before feeling a strong urge to get out of his cabin. His first thought was to cut wood but felt the air thickening around him and knew it was time for a ride. He never could explain it to the doctors, but sometimes the air became heavy reminding him of the heavy humidity in Vietnam. It was often a prelude to a flashback or a bout of temper. Doctors blamed it on Post Traumatic Stress Disorder.

Tony planned to make a left and head out onto the flats at a Y-intersection in the trail. Before he realized it, he suddenly turned right and drove toward Cantwell. He decided one of Old Man Taylor's root beers might just help shake off that old feeling of doom and gloom. Ice-cold root beer was a blessing since he didn't have ice at the cabin.

Bosley studied Tony as he walked across the room, a hint of an idea gnawing in the back of his mind. Greg figured the guy was just another patron, one of the many Alaskan characters you could find in any small town. JP's attention returned to finishing his plate of eggs, knowing all he had to look forward to was freeze-dried junk over the next few days; if Bosley allowed them to even leave town.

"Gimme a moment," Bosley said and scooted back his chair. Greg and JP watched as Bosley walked over to the hooded figure at the bar.

Giving him a good once over, Greg looked down at the man's feet and saw that he had leg braces strapped to his boots. Greg wondered if the guy might know of a guide or if Bosley was discussing an entirely different issue.

"Hey, Tony, are things staying quiet out your way?" Bosley asked.

Tony nodded and held his hand out as Taylor slid an open bottle of A&W root beer across the bar. Taylor stuck around, wondering what Bosley had on his mind since he left his two friends sitting at their table.

Bosley moved in closer, but not enough to cause Tony alarm. "Tony, I need a huge favor. See those two gentlemen sitting over there," Bosley turned around to gesture at Greg and JP, "Those two men are my friends, and they could use your help."

Old Man Taylor started to say something, but a quick look from Bosley told him to back off and give Tony some room. "It's all right, Mr. Taylor. Tony's okay. No trouble."

Tony glanced back at Greg and JP once more and then nodded to Taylor, who understood. Taylor returned to the grill and poured blueberry pancake batter into saucer-sized mounds.

"I'm kind of in a bind, Tony. Would you be willing to come to my table and meet my friends? I promise they'll not cause you discomfort in any form. They're good people."

Tony turned to look directly into Bosley's tired eyes, showing his horribly scarred face.

Glancing over at Greg, his one eye widened as recognition dawned on him. He knew these two men, and after some reflection, he realized they were the two men in his dream. He'd never seen them, so he didn't recognize their faces. Yet, deep down inside, something said these were the two men who haunted his nights as he led them through darkened woods. Tony picked up his root beer without a word and slowly moved to Greg's table. Bosley followed and slid an empty chair out from another table and put it into place for Tony to sit down.

Old Man Taylor stared at Tony in disbelief from behind the bar. Something was happening here, but he didn't know what. He'd never seen Tony act so calm with total strangers. Trooper Bosley, he knew, but the other two men were unknown, or at least Taylor had thought so. Tony never sat down at the tables when other people were around in the summer. Only in winter did Tony make himself comfortable at a table, usually sharing it with Taylor or another local.

Greg watched as Tony walked over, noticing the facial scars and the limp.

JP looked into Tony's face and saw the pain and stress the man was in from some unforgettable experience. He rose from his chair to offer his hand in greeting. Seeing the scars and torn skin about the mouth, he wasn't expecting an audible reply.

Greg rose and waited until the two men shook hands. He sensed something exceptional in this hooded man. He began to catch a faint hint in the air, a feeling that there was a link between this man and the plan they were still formatting. *How is that possible?*

"Tony, I'd like you to meet a dear friend of mine, Greg Hansen, Alaska Railroad Special Investigator, and a former Alaska State Trooper. This other gentleman is JP Leon, Royal Canadian Mounted Police out of Toronto." He waited as the men shook hands, "Please, let's all sit down. Tony, I know you've hunted and trapped nearly every stretch of ground between here and Talkeetna. I've been told you've built several temporary cabins along the canyons south of here. You can even get across the lower snowfields if you need to. Am I right?" Tony nodded. "My friends need to go south, and I wonder if you could guide them. It's imperative."

"I'd be willing to pay the going rate for summer guides," Greg added.

The table was silent as Tony studied the two men for a moment. Uncomfortable with the silence, Trooper Bosley signaled Taylor for three coffees and another root beer for Tony.

Less than two hours later, Greg and JP, with their equipment, followed Tony to his cabin mounted on two ATVs rented from Old Man Taylor. During the ride, Tony wondered why he had decided to lead these two complete strangers on the trail of international terrorists. He had looked into JP's eyes as the men attempted to bypass the truth with a tale about a desire to observe Alaska moose in their natural habitat and how the one called Greg had waved JP into silence.

That's when the truth came out, and Trooper Bosley excused himself from the table. "I gotta go, I need some sleep." Bosley shook hands with JP, wrapped Greg in a bear hug, and clasped Tony by the shoulder. "Thank you, Tony. Be safe; we'll talk when you get back."

"I can't lie to this man, JP. He needs to know the truth; this could lead to a perilous situation, and, I've got to go with my hunch. Tony needs to know all of it, and then he can decide whether or not to lead us."

Tony had known JP was lying to him; there was too much pain in the man's eyes to be some nature lover. Not that he had anything against animal lovers. He watched Greg's eyes and mannerisms and recognized the man's body language from his dreams. After hearing their real story, Tony knew he had little choice but to join them on this absolutely idiotic venture. Refusing to give God credit, he recognized that a line of tragic events had brought them together. He had seen his nightmares that they were headed for a violent confrontation. *Why me?* He thought.

They spent an hour at Tony's cabin while he got his gear together for the trek ahead. He secured three plastic five-gallon gas containers to a small ATV trailer he would pull. He knew the trail quite well and wrote several notes to Greg and JP on how far they could ride before having to continue on foot. He knew the cabin the terrorists had used. He hadn't built it but had added to it eight years ago while trapping the area. Ten miles further south was another cabin. Even further along the old trail was another much older cabin built long ago by his mentor—Jake Baker.

"Can we bypass the trail? I don't want to run into the feds," Greg said.

Not wanting to mumble, Tony continued using a writing pad, *I know a route along the snow line, but dangerous.*

"What about the authorities spotting us by air?" JP asked.

Greg answered, "Once we're on the trail, they won't be able to stop us without dropping guys from a helicopter ahead of us. They must account for others out there; many people use this backcountry. They don't all come in off the highway near the roadblocks. I imagine several groups, from Boy Scouts and rock climbers to extreme hikers running around these woods. There's bound to be a lot of people who made their way out there before the train attack. We may get a shouted warning to leave the area from a National Guard helicopter. But as long as we keep moving, they shouldn't be able to block our path. The trees are too thick for the authorities to see us for long stretches." Greg glanced over to Tony, who was packing foodstuffs. "With Tony here guiding us and his knowledge of the ground, well, this means we'll have a great advantage over that group."

After securing his cabin and making sure all the trash was picked up to keep bears from getting too nosey, Tony started his ATV and turned south with his trailer in tow. His 7mm rifle was secured across the handlebars and he wore a Ruger .44-Magnum Revolver with an eight-inch barrel on his right hip for dealing with bears. He wouldn't shoot unless he absolutely had to, though, as this was not grizzly season, and they would have no time to deal with a dead bear. The less dangerous black bear would usually scamper off at the sound of the ATV. What he really had to watch out for was the wayward moose that might suddenly shoot out in front of them. Moose were prone to use the trail he planned to use. *Nightmares have shown this to happen, but the conclusion has eluded me. Which of us will fall or return? God, why me, and why now? I made my peace with you; stay out of my life, and I'll stay clear of you. But no, you have to meddle in my life again. WHY?*

On The Trail With The Feds

Sir Jonathan, Sgt. Niles and Agent Loury stood outside an old, dilapidated cabin, discussing their next course of action. Agent Jackson Stewart of the FBI Hostage Team and Corporal Jim Williams, AST SERT had earlier assumed they were in charge of the operation and spent very little time confiding with the Canadian Secret Service regarding any plans. Sir Jonathan contacted his home office in Ottawa with his satellite phone and voiced his concern. In Washington DC, the Canadian Ambassador paid a visit to the US Secretary of State, who made a phone call to the FBI Director. From then on, Sir Jonathan shared equal status as on-scene commander with Agent Stewart.

The most challenging obstacle to overcome was Hugo's booby traps; three more men had been wounded by his devices. EOD personnel worked harder to clear the trail ahead. Another unit of National Guard was dropped by helicopter just south of Curry and proceeded into the woods. The plan was to use the guard unit as a blocking force.

Yellow and orange tape was used to mark EOD-cleared trail from the ARR tracks to the first cabin. EOD personnel were extremely cautious as additional mines and tripwires connected to fragmentation grenades were discovered. Two other EOD K-9 teams flown north from Elmendorf were busily inspecting the trail for explosives.

Overhead, two Black Hawk helicopters operated above 3,000 feet, attempting to locate the FLQ through thermal imagery. They had already located others including a large group proceeding north along the river's edge three miles south of the Curry townsite. That group was a Boy Scout troop from Wasilla on a three-day 30-mile hike. Authorities attempted to drop messages on them but failed. There wasn't a clearing nearby for a Black Hawk to land or even safely hover to drop personnel by rope. Search coordinators thought of dropping teams in Curry but were discouraged as the possibility existed the terrorists had already reached the townsite, and any aggressive movement might cause the death of the three hostages. That plan was put on hold.

A small team of soldiers, assisted by State Troopers were dropped off well south of the townsite to work north with orders to keep Curry under observation. If the Boy Scouts were in danger, the soldiers and troopers were to get them out of the line of fire. The Blackhawks that had dropped off the teams flew south to stand by in Sheep Creek.

Authorities attempted to locate knowledgeable guides in Talkeetna but failed. Most of the guides were on vacation between hunting seasons and coordinators couldn't find anyone willing to work with the Feds against the terrorists. Thanks to news services, everyone knew the risks involved in leading a rescue party into such a highly wooded area. Guides weren't afraid; they just weren't foolish. Going up against a grizzly was one thing but going up against terrorists armed with Stingers and automatic weapons was another thing altogether. One highly intoxicated former guide offered his services for a very high bounty, but it was decided they didn't have enough time to sober the old man up.

As the deadline drew closer, people across Canada and the United States asked each other if the ransom would or should be paid. The issue was hotly debated in Juneau on whether or not the government should step in. It was suggested they use part of the state's permanent fund to get the three hostages back, but that was shouted down. Though the Governor and Senator were both popular, no one wanted to reward terrorists and set a standard of paying off these kinds of people.

After receiving the go-ahead from Sir Jonathan, ARR high rail cars from Anchorage and Wasilla moved in from the south to transport FBI agents, State Troopers, and additional National Guardsmen to the position set up south of the Curry townsite. They took to the woods west of the tracks while the first unit of guardsmen stayed on the east side and met in Curry to establish a defensive perimeter.

When authorities approached the old townsite, they discovered several small groups camping there. Having no idea what was happening, the arrival of armed troops surprised them. They were evacuated to Talkeetna by ARR high rail vehicles. The Boy Scout Troop couldn't be located, and for a while, it was believed they had headed back to their cars. However, when parents were contacted, they reported having no word from their sons. Satellite imagery had some unexplainable difficulties; they couldn't find the FLQ or the scouts, which worried the authorities. Tech experts advised that Alaska's uniqueness and abundant wildlife can cause imagery problems. It was difficult to tell a group of people from a gathering of pack horses, wolves, coyotes, moose, or bears as all life produced heat signatures.

Expecting the FLQ to head for Curry, defense positions were set up in the tree line at the north side of the old town. Snipers were assigned to well-camouflaged positions in case the FLQ made it that far. Additional Guard troops were flown north from Fort Richardson to find the Boy Scouts, which meant at least a 10-mile hike through rugged terrain. According to their home post in Wasilla, the boys were expected to camp overnight at the Curry townsite and head back the following day. Once contact was made, they would be turned around, escorted back by Guardsmen, and eventually removed from the area by either helicopters or high rail vehicles.

Greg, JP, And Tony

The three ATVs made time on Tony's trail through heavy brush and up and down steep hillsides. More than once, JP or Greg found themselves in trouble handling the wild terrain. The old trapper's trail had become overgrown with alder, spruce, cottonwood, and birch trees. They had to stop a few times to enable Tony to get his bearings, as nature trails often intersected trapper trails. Tony hadn't trapped in this area for a couple of years, having moved his trapline twice since then. This was routine for trappers, allowing young animals in the area to grow.

Greg had ridden ATVs numerous times but had trouble keeping up with Tony, who seemed to sail over the landscape like a low-flying bird. JP was used to motorcycles, but this was his first ATV ride, and the so-called trail was nearly impassable. It wasn't long before they came up against the backside of some low mountains and happened on the ghastly scene where the terrorists had the misfortune of tangling with the grizzly sow. They stopped to look the area over; Greg was stunned to find that the FLQ hadn't even bothered to sprinkle dirt over the bodies of their dead friends. Since the bear attack, dozens of small creatures had moved in to feed on the fresh kill. The three men moved on, not wanting to lose any time. The authorities would come upon the bodies and transport them back to the Alaska Crime Lab or the Army morgue at Fort Richardson.

Tony grew angry when he came upon the murdered cubs, troubled by the people's vileness. He could understand the need to slay the momma bear to save one's life, but not the cubs. A sow without cubs might have come by and adopted them; a male would kill and eat them. Tony was surprised coyotes and wolves hadn't moved in to ravish the bodies. When he mentioned it to Greg, he was reminded of the forest fire and the number of men and women moving through the woods to pursue the terrorists. "Coyotes and wolves are long gone by now."

"Let 'em rot! They're all murderers who have killed dozens of people and injured dozens more!" JP said.

The three men were relieved that none of the hostages were among the deceased.

JP knelt beside Janene's mangled body and felt a lock of her hair. "You won't kill any more children now. I pray you and your friends are in the fiery pits of Hell for what you've done!" He whispered. He moved to the grizzly sow, laid a hand on her brow, and mumbled a quiet "Thank you." He smiled, a response that at first surprised Greg until he realized this was what JP had planned for every member of the terrorist group, a painful death if possible. He tried to understand how the man might feel but couldn't. Having not experienced such violence in his family, Greg had no idea what JP was going through. He hated the terrorists for killing and injuring victims but tried hard to leave judgment to God. On the other hand, he wanted revenge for his friends' deaths and justice to be served. As a law enforcement officer, he felt they should be taken alive if possible.

"We don't have time to bury them, but I've got the coordinates marked down on my GPS," Greg said. "We need to keep moving."

"Why? Leave them here to rot—let the bugs have 'em!" JP turned abruptly and walked back to his ATV. As soon as they had discovered the bodies, their rifles came out in case a terrorist was in the area. After a quick search, JP sat on his ATV and secured his rifle waiting for the other two men.

Tony watched the two men and noticed the distinct differences and reactions. He thought he understood. One had lost good friends; the other, his entire family. One could behave with civilized justice; the other was dead inside and wanted vengeance. Tony felt only anger for the bear that was slaughtered protecting her young, and the barbaric murder of two newborn cubs. For now, he tended to agree with JP—*Let the bugs have 'em.* Tony walked over and stood beside what had once been a human male; he looked to the heavens and mumbled, "You… you judge… You always do!" *You give, and you take away. You sit on that golden throne, looking down on us imperfect pitiful humans, and play your games.* Tony looked at Greg and then over to JP. *Once again, I've become one of your game pieces—a pawn. Once again, I find death and destruction all around me. You put me here—you filled my mind with those nightmare images, knowing full well I couldn't turn these men away after seeing what lay ahead. A game! That's all it is for you—a game!* There was no response, and the sun continued to shine; Tony shook his head and remounted his ATV.

15

# THE DEADLINE HOUR DRAWS NEAR

With The FLQ

Hounded by swarms of flying insects, his exhausted body near the point of collapse, Governor Hughes relied on the sheer strength of will to keep going. Their hands and backs sore, Hughes and Michael carried a homemade stretcher with the unconscious Senator Sterns. Hughes focused his bitterness and contempt on the sour-faced terrorist named Munroe, who remained in the lead.

Michael wished they had dropped the unconscious woman off along the trail. But his voice didn't carry any weight; Hugo told him to keep his mouth shut. Walking five yards behind the stretcher-bearers, Hugo prodded them along. Behind Hugo walked the Canadian Prime Minister, who was helped along by Gordi.

Hughes couldn't wipe the sweat from his eyes or swat at pestering insects. He shook his head from side to side to drive bugs away and failed to notice a large rock on the trail; the toe of his dress shoe caught it, and he stumbled forward and nearly lost his hold on the stretcher poles. His startled cry alarmed a weary Michael, who thought another bear was nearby and struggled to maintain control of the stretcher.

The Prime Minister was in no shape to help with the stretcher, much less keep walking. His face was sweaty and flush, his breathing labored; he needed another break.

Hughes dropped to one knee and tried to steady the stretcher. Michael turned his head, "You okay?"

"Tripped on a rock, sorry."

"No sweat, I should've warned you," Michael said. "You ready to go on?"

"Yeah, go ahead."

"Keep moving!" Hugo ordered gesturing with his rifle.

"Hugo, the PM needs another break. If we don't take a break, we'll need another stretcher for him," Gordi said.

Hugo yelled to Munroe, "Stop now!"

"Not yet," Munroe yelled back. "There's another clearing up ahead; we'll stop there."

Governor Hughes knew this forced march was draining everyone's strength; they needed a long rest. Even the German was showing signs of weariness and leaned against a tree for a brief respite. Hughes had also noticed that whenever they stopped for a break, Munroe walked to the rear of the line and stood studying the trail behind them. He began to suspect Monroe was searching for someone.

In fact, Munroe was. He was looking for Janene. In his escalating state of madness, he believed she had somehow survived the bear's brutal attack and would catch up with them. His strange behavior was not unnoticed and caused a degree of apprehension in the terrorist ranks.

When they reached the small clearing, Munroe ordered a short break. Hughes and Michael laid the stretcher down as Gordi helped the Prime Minister sit on a large flat rock and offered him a drink from his canteen. Hugo glanced about the clearing and plopped beside a large boulder to catch his breath and take a drink. Unscrewing his canteen cap, he spotted Munroe wandering back down the trail again to reappear in a few moments with an almost mournful look in his dark-ringed eyes.

Hugo wished he had some tripwire left to set up down the trail for Munroe to run into. While some of the others might object to Hugo gunning Munroe down, they might understand how Munroe, in his current mental state, could stumble into a booby trap. But Hugo was out of supplies. He had used his last explosive device a couple of miles back. In his weary state, he fanaticized about coming upon a tall cliff and finding a way to accidentally bump Munroe off. He shrugged the idea off with a sigh and set his rifle down at his side. After another drink from his canteen, he swatted at a mosquito buzzing his face. He missed the bug and wondered how many hours before the Prime Minister could be released to escape. He considered releasing the Governor to give the Prime Minister a hand in reaching safety. He'd leave the sickly US Senator behind with the bodies of the FLQ, a thought that cheered him up. Hugo disliked politicians, especially ancient female ones; he disliked the German Prime Minister, another middle-aged female. Hugo was an old-school Marxist, believing females did not belong in politics or big business.

Hugo smiled as he thought of the money going into the bank and finally the pleasures of retirement. This was definitely his last job. Hugo glared at the PM; the man was unconscious and in sorry shape. He doubted the frail man would survive this ordeal, even with the Governor's help. Hugo could imagine the two men getting lost and falling prey to large Alaskan predators. He studied the Governor for a moment, watching him bathe the unconscious Senator's brow with a damp handkerchief. At least he displayed some inner strength. To some degree, he respected the middle-aged politician and briefly wondered if the man had prior military training. Hugo thought to ask but then decided against it. The less he learned about a person, the easier it was to kill him.

The plan was to reach a point where he felt the PM could make his way to safety and be found by one of the search teams. Hugo knew there were teams out there because the PM and the Alaska politicians were too important for there not to be. He would kill the FLQ members during a break and vanish into the trees giving the PM and the Governor a chance to escape. Hugo would follow to ensure they weren't attacked by predators. When he knew a search team was nearby, he would head to the west and make his way to the highway. Hugo believed he could find another deserted cabin and live off the land while he waited for search teams to give up and leave. Over time, Hugo had used several aliases and forged identification for each one. As soon as he had his money, he would disappear forever. He wanted to ensure that Dr. Quison and his group would never find him. He had dealt with such people before and knew they felt Hugo was a liability that needed to be dealt with. *They will never find me; no one will.*

When Hugo glanced at his watch again, he was struck with a painful cramp in his left thigh. The Alaska climate, hiking and the icy river crossing were taking a physical toll on this old mercenary. He believed he could execute the escape plan in 20 hours. Until then, and from the pains in his legs, he decided they should look for another cabin and wait. It allowed the PM and the Governor time to gain strength for their escape. Hugo decided that if Munroe disagreed with him maybe it was time to remove Munroe. With his recent actions, Hugo didn't believe the others would put up many objections to a change in leadership.

The sounds of someone stomping through the woods down the trail they had just covered ended up being Munroe, who had that sorrowful expression on his face. *Maybe he's just checking our back trail, looking to see how close the authorities are. But that strange look on his face, those mournful eyes. I wonder how close this man is to blowing his own head off? Maybe I should take his gun away before he gets stupid again and shoots the hostages.* Hugo stood up and walked to where Munroe had stopped to lean against a tree and catch his breath. Pulling a soiled handkerchief from his back pocket, Munroe wiped the sweat from his brow then moistened the cloth with a dribble of water from his canteen and continued to wipe his face.

Munroe looked up as Hugo approached. He was worn out from the long climb and wished they could've stayed at the last cabin. When the money was deposited, or the deadline was reached, he would gladly execute the three hostages before making a dash for freedom. But the helicopter crash and the resulting fire changed everything. He pointed his right thumb over his shoulder, "I spotted another old caved-in cabin just up ahead. It's off the trail about 50 yards from here with thick brush all around it." Wiping the back of his neck with his handkerchief, Munroe looked up into Hugo's cold eyes. In an unnaturally soft childlike voice, he asked, "She's really gone, isn't she?"

"Yes, Janene is dead." *You wanted to kill her a couple of days ago, and you do not remember this? Do not worry, soon you will join her.*

After a moment of silence, Munroe looked around at the others and shouldered his rifle, "We'll move to the cabin and hold up there for a while." He turned back to Hugo, "I wanted to reach that Curry place, but I don't see how right now. We're too beat up and need a good 12-hour rest. Soon, we'll be done with this, they'll have the money, and you and I will be rich."

*Sure...* "Okay, we go!" Hugo got everyone moving again. Governor Hughes felt pain shoot up through his arms like lightning bolts when he picked up the stretcher. He thought, just for a brief moment, of leaving Sterns on the ground. *Only a little way more, she can rest quietly then. Damn, I should've cut off a piece of rope back there and used it as a strap to wrap over my shoulders to help handle the load. Too late unless I can find something that'll work in place of rope. It'll make carrying this accursed stretcher a whole lot easier.*

Sharing in the physical agony, Michael dropped to one knee and grunted as he picked up his end of the stretcher. Seeing Hughes glance back at him, Michael grinned at him briefly, "I'll take the front since we're going that way."

"Watch out for those rocks; they seem to reach up and grab you." It surprised Hughes that he could converse with this terrorist, but he started to see something different in the young man. Hughes had watched Michael and didn't find him as hard-shelled as the others. He was looking for any advantage that might present itself and wondered if Michael was the organization's weak spot. He had to remember how many people this group had killed, and Michael was still a member of the FLQ. *He had to know what he was getting into when he joined this little group.* Again, Hughes looked down on Sterns' prone form and saw her terrible condition. Her skin was pasty white; her breathing shallow and irregular. He wondered whether or not she would survive. It seemed that even the mosquitoes were ignoring her. *Not enough blood to bother. I'm no doctor, but it looks like the Angel of Death is hovering over her.* He watched her chest inflate ever so slightly. *It must be her heart giving out; too much for her to endure, and the tragic loss of her nephew only made it worse.*

Not able to see Michael's face, Hughes wasn't aware that Michael was beginning to whisper prayers for Senator Sterns. Prayers he recalled from his Sunday school days. Michael realized that she would die if something didn't happen soon, and he would be partly responsible. Only recently had he realized the killer he had become. With his renewed thoughts about the Lord, Michael knew the Father would judge him harshly for his past actions.

When they reached the old cabin, they found only three log walls standing, and half of the roof collapsed. Another trapper's cabin and it wasn't very large. Michael and Hughes lowered the stretcher to the ground near what was left of the door. The decaying structure was mostly a pile of crumbling logs. With Michael's help, Governor Hughes moved debris out and reset the roof to provide some degree of protection from the rain. The Senator was moved into the cabin and placed on the dirt floor. They tried to get the semi-conscious woman to drink some water, but she refused. Hughes poured some water on his filthy handkerchief and wiped her face, arms, and the back of her neck. He moistened her lips, but she was again unconscious. Worn out himself, Hughes collapsed beside her.

Greg, Michael, and Louis went to work, clearing out some of the brush, and stacked supplies outside the cabin. Packs were unloaded, bedding unrolled, and a cold meal was served. Smoke would give away their location, so there was no fire. A guard shift was set up, placing Greg and Louis on the first watch while the rest of the group fell into a restless sleep.

Except for Hugo, who didn't trust Munroe. Hugo sat on the hard ground with his back resting against the cabin's north wall and used the GPS to find their exact location with the railroad tracks. Munroe paced back and forth in front of the cabin his rifle slung over his shoulder with the barrel pointed down. A light rain started falling, and squirrels objected to the presence of intruders. "You need rest," Hugo told Munroe after putting the GPS away.

"This is going bad; we've taken on too much," Munroe said in a strained voice.

"Look bad, but we be okay."

"No! This isn't what I wanted." Munroe glared at Hugo, "You're the professional; you should have warned me about this whole kidnapping scheme. Blowing up buildings, and frightening authorities, that's what we did. This was too big, too soon. We should've had more time—they pushed us too fast!"

"Too late now," Hugo replied. "We did it; now we be rich. Dr. Quison had to take advantage of this man's trip. We made it work!"

"No, we're all going to jail—or worse!" Munroe exclaimed.

"You worry too much! They won't catch us. Cops know we shoot Prime Minister, maybe Governor too. They won't move on us, not yet. They'll come after the hostages are safe."

Munroe looked around at the sleeping members of his band. "I doubt if our little army could shoot its way out of a kid's garden party. We've lost Lesli, Claudia, Thomas, and Paul, our main muscle—and my Janene." Munroe's bloodshot eyes began to well up with tears. "A bear, can you believe it?" Munroe pointed in the direction they had come, "Killed by some stupid bear in this God-forsaken wilderness. If it was someone else, Janene would be laughing her head off."

"You need sleep," Hugo suggested.

"I'll sleep when this is done." Munroe shook his head and walked to where Senator Sterns lay in the cabin. Governor Hughes had fallen asleep beside her, but not before he used one of the dead terrorist's sleeping bags to protect them from the bugs.

For a long moment, Munroe stood in the doorway and stared at the two lumps under the open sleeping bag. Without warning, he suddenly brought his weapon up and fired a short burst into Senator Sterns' body. Her body bounced as the bullets struck, and she died instantly. The sleeping bag was drenched in her blood, and the Governor, who had rolled clear when the shots awakened him, shouted, "WHY? Why did you have to kill her?"

Hugo jumped to his feet, his weapon at the ready. All the others were on their feet. In utter shock, Governor Hughes glared at Munroe. Hughes would have attacked him if not for the weapon in Munroe's hands. Without offering any explanation, Munroe sighed deeply, slung his weapon's strap over his shoulder, and ambled away.

"Why?" Governor Hughes asked mournfully. "Why'd you have to kill her? She hadn't hurt any of you." He jumped to his feet and chased Munroe; his hands clenched into fists.

Hearing him, Munroe turned and leveled his weapon at Hughes's stomach, about to fire. Seeing Munroe's crazed look, Michael quickly tackled Governor Hughes to the ground and wrestled him into submission.

"Another word, and he will kill you," Michael warned. Unable to fight off the younger man, Governor Hughes glared at Michael. After a show of defiance, he could read the plea in Michael's eyes. "He will kill you, Governor." He whispered. "He's insane. Back off!"

When Munroe saw that the Governor was no longer a threat, he shouldered his MP5 and walked to where the food was stored, ripped open a small package of beef jerky, and began chewing on a length. Observing the expressions of those around him, he shook his head, sighed, and ignored them all. Finally, after finishing his jerky, Munroe explained, "She was an extra weight we didn't need. The old sow was already dying. I just saved her some time, and it was fast. She's done suffering. No longer a burden."

Concerned that Munroe might decide to kill the Governor, Hugo wandered over to where Munroe stood for a quiet word, "We need Hughes."

"Why?"

"Haegens is too soft, too weak. Won't make it. If Hughes escapes with him, Haegens will make it."

"Okay, I can accept that." Munroe washed the jerky down with a gulp from his canteen. "How are we going to make that happen?"

"You or I will take the two hostages down to tracks. We say we look for stream to refill canteens. We let them wander off, maybe fire a warning shot to scare them and get their blood flowing. Run faster. We follow from trees. Make sure they stay safe."

"Okay, Hugo, you carry it off, and I'll keep an eye on the others. When you return, we'll decide on the best way to finish this. I'm tired of these trees, Alaska, and especially this plan. I want this over!"

"Yes, soon over. You and I rich…we go our separate ways." Hugo smiled a look that could freeze the blood of a grown man. *Soon you'll be dead, and I'll be even wealthier.*


With The Search Teams


The sound of Munroe's MP5's automatic fire echoed off the mountainsides as it traveled north and south through the canyon walls. It was heard by the pursuing search teams and by Tony Rogers, Greg Hansen, and JP Leon. The National Guard and SERT members in Curry, and the Boy Scouts on the trail heard it echoing through the mountains. Everyone asked themselves the same question: *Had someone been shot, who was it, and why now? The time limit isn't up.*

While normal rifle fire wasn't unusual in the mountains, automatic weapons fire was. Scout Master Ed Anderson, a Gulf War vet, recognized the distinct sound and stopped his boys. He was pretty sure the weapons fire came from the north, the direction they were traveling, and wondered if he should turn his troop around and move further east. *There is no sense risking these boys out here if some poacher is wandering the canyon with a machine gun.* He decided to turn on the cell phone he had turned off to save battery power and called his wife. *Maybe the National Guard is running some maneuvers up near the Curry townsite?* If so, his wife Linda could check on it for him before he turned the boys around. They would be disappointed. The scouts had looked forward to this venture, which would earn them their wilderness survival badge. Unfortunately, his phone couldn't pick up a signal in the canyon. He wasn't aware of the terrorist situation or that his wife and other parents were glued to the television news channel and calling Ed every five minutes. Seven mothers were in her living room while the husbands, armed to the teeth, were en route to the area the scouts were hiking. When they made it to the southern roadblock on the Parks Highway, they were stopped by the National Guard. Tempers flew, and offensive language was exchanged, but the soldiers on the roadblock were able to keep order.

The fathers didn't like it, but they joined the rest of the people camped out along the roadside waiting for the roadblock to be lifted. The Guard and Troopers radioed ahead to the Command Post to report Boy Scouts in the area. Several worried mothers had already called in and the scouts were being looked for.

No more shots were fired and thinking that was the end, Ed Anderson decided to push on. He knew of two friends with Class III gun licenses, allowing them to purchase and possess automatic weapons. Ed had even gone to the rifle range to fire a World War II .30 Caliber water-cooled tripod-mounted machine gun, which was quite a thrill. He slowed their pace through the thick woods.

Ed had planned this hike to fall between the hunting seasons to lessen the danger. Getting a sense of direction, he decided to head toward the ARR tracks. He didn't want to have one of his kids accidentally shot by a poacher or some survivalist hiking through the woods. They would be in plain view once they were on the tracks headed for Curry. Ed had chosen these trails through the woods to heighten the experience for the boys, though he soon realized the bugs were pretty bad this year. He picked up the smell of smoke, which worried him.

Not part of the usual Boy Scout equipment, Ed carried a 12-gauge pump shotgun for bear protection, loaded with two one-ounce slugs and two of .00 buckshot. With all the noise the boys were making, he hoped the bears would have plenty of notice to move along. If not, he wanted to be prepared.

Office Of Intelligence, RCMP Headquarters
Toronto, Canada - June 16th, 09:20 a.m.

After a long night researching insurance and financial records, Sgt. Steve Adler was ready for a well-deserved cup of hot coffee. While Adler worked the files, Sgt. Brady Wilkens was on the streets, pumping every known snitch the department had for information that might lead to the financial backers supporting this FLQ. Both Mounties knew the FLQ had deep pockets to support bombings and the trip to Alaska, plus the purchase of heavy weapons like that Stinger missile that knocked down the helicopter. Before leaving Toronto, JP had spent an hour with his two right-hand men and issued a parting order—"Find the money trail."

The old FLQ received financial support from members of the Parti Quebecois, so this new group had to have financial supporters somewhere in French-Canadian society. Wilkens and Adler agreed with JP; they knew blowing up the Parliament Building was one thing, but a simple empty parking garage smelled of insurance fraud. Both sergeants had worked such details before, and their experience would lead them toward a target. The only thing that concerned them was how long it would take them to get a break in the case.

"Dig deep, and you'll find the people financing these fanatics, and if it's all about the cash, they're using this terrorism as a cover for a grand scheme. Such news could have a negative effect on people in Quebec who desire sovereignty," JP had told them before leaving for Alaska. Sgt. Wilkens had driven JP to the airport, where he had added, "Go beyond the dummy corporations and find out who has the most to gain blowing up that garage. Check the long-term lease papers for the Parliament Building; someone owns that land and might have a tie-in with those who own the garage. There's a link; I can just about smell it."

Wilkens made sure JP had plenty of money with him and made one more attempt to talk JP into taking him along.

"I'm leaving you and Adler behind to locate the money people. If we can cut off the funds, the FLQ will lose its ability to act outside its sphere of influence. We'll cut them off at the knees. Then, we'll liquidate the financer's assets and bring them before a federal magistrate for murder, and a thousand more criminal charges."

Wilkens stood at the terminal window and watched as his friend's plane took off. Knowing how JP felt and his sole desire for revenge at any cost, he wondered if he would ever see his captain again. As he came through the office doorway, Wilkens' first question was, "Have you found anything, anything at all?" Adler sat with a steaming mug of hot coffee and a glazed donut in front of him.

"I may have, but if I'm right, we have to see the Colonel. We'll be taking on a lot of political weight, and I wish JP was around to cover our backs."

"What have you got?" Wilkens sat down on the couch and waited to hear, but Adler wanted to wash his face first. When he returned from the restroom, he walked Wilkens through his discoveries and line of thought for connecting the dots. He'd constructed a line chart, shooting off in a dozen directions from one company to another. The end result gave Wilkens a start.

"You're right! We need the Colonel in on this, or you and I could be writing parking tickets before the week is out," Wilkens agreed.

"It's all here," Adler said. "I only hope he'll believe it."

"You awake enough to present your findings? We could put it off until tomorrow." Wilkens could feel the excitement growing. He only wished it had been him who found the answer. But they both had their own expertise; white-collar crime was Adler's baby while working snitches and street vermin was his.

"No. I'll call the Colonel's office and get us an appointment as soon as possible. While we're waiting, I'm going to grab a shower. How about picking up some breakfast for us?"

"Sure thing," Wilkens said. "I'll be back in a half-an-hour, so don't pass out in the shower."

"Not donuts; I need protein."

"Bacon and eggs, heavy on the bacon. I got it."

ARR Railroad - On Scene Command Post
June 16th- 10:45 a.m.


Working around the clock, ARR emergency track crews finally cleared the track of all debris which involved moving more than a hundred tons of dirt, rock, brush, and trees. A new gravel bed had to be put in, new wooden ties set in place, and lengths of new steel track secured on the ties. Railroad cranes fitted atop railroad flat cars raised twisted metal and debris and placed it into yellow rock cars brought down from the Fairbanks rail yard. The Anchorage work train was still on hold until the terrorists were caught or rendered harmless. On site, the work train from Fairbanks unloaded two Caterpillar D-8 bulldozers with massive steel blades and three large Caterpillar Backhoes.

With the aid of heavy equipment, the 35 men from the Fairbanks yard put their shoulders into it and cleared the tracks in record time. The hardest part was getting the damaged locomotives and burned baggage car off the track and onto a temporary sidetrack the crews had installed for that purpose. It took both dozers, the crane, and a loader pulling together to move the damaged locomotives. Three steel tow lines snapped in the process, severely injuring two men who hadn't been fast enough to get out of the way. The ARR's bleary-eyed safety officer ran around with a bullhorn and was a complete nuisance. After the injuries, people began to heed his warnings.

When the new locomotives were hooked up and ready, the on-site rail supervisor allowed the train cars to be taken back to Fairbanks. The engine crews and repairmen were prepared to roll north when the tracks were cleared. Dozers cleared the debris field that had trapped the lead engine when Hugo blew the hillside.

The VIP car would remain on a section of the sidetrack as the Forward Command Post. There wouldn't be any passenger or freight trains running through until the terrorists were caught, so there was no need to move the VIP car any farther for the present time. Workers dismantled the baggage car down to the frame and wheels. Eventually, the damaged cars and locomotives would be moved to Anchorage. A photographer for the ARR's insurance company took photographs of everything. Federal and State officers photographed crime scene evidence including each of the locations a trip-wire grenade had exploded.

Chief FBI Special Agent Donald Osborn arrived with the work train and took photographs. Two video cameras took footage to be provided to the news services, and later for court trials. Because of the danger of the terrorists, no news people were allowed at the train wreck which angered them, but they had no choice but to accept the orders of the government.

News helicopters weren't allowed to fly through restricted air space. Authorities only allowed them access to the area below Sheep Creek or Cantwell. A no-fly zone began at the Parks Highway Command Post set up at Mile Post 148.6 and continued to Cantwell then south to Sheep Creek. Many highway travelers unable to pass Sheep Creek went to Talkeetna. The lodge at Sheep Creek was doing some of its best business due to the disaster.

The FBI had seized all of the train passenger's cameras and cell phones. They were later returned after searching photos for possible evidence. The film from the older cameras was seized as evidence by the authorities. However, the AST and National Guard security detail didn't find all the cell phones. Somehow, photographs of the incident had found their way into the press's hands, showing some of the dead and wounded, fire-damaged cars, and the escape route taken by the terrorists. Selected shots were broadcast by news services.

A teenager from Oakland, California, an amateur photographer with dreams of better things, received $5,000 for his photos and wished he'd held out for more after finding out his pictures were the best to be had. When the shooting started, he was sitting in the upper level of the observation car, grabbed his cell phone, and began taking footage of the action. When he saw they were seizing cameras and phones, he hid his phone in his underwear.

Supervisors from the disaster site returned to Anchorage ARR Headquarters by small aircraft. Taking off from a dirt runway near Cantwell, they flew wide of the no-fly zone, adding 20 minutes to their flight time. They met company officers to update them on the extent of physical damage. Insurance representatives were there, grinding numbers from the tally sheets of required repairs. Though the damaged locomotives were still on scene on the temporary side-track, they had Osborn's photographs to give them some idea regarding the extent of the damage. Osborn hoped the locomotives' massive diesel engines could be repaired, but he knew it would be costly. As for the baggage car, he suspected only the bottom frame and wheels could be re-used. It would be days before they saw how much of the passenger's property was destroyed in the baggage car fire and its replacement value.

Everything possible was being done for the families of those killed or wounded. The ARR Company's President saw to that task himself, as he felt it should be. When the ARR President radioed Osborn and asked for Special Agent Greg Hansen's current location, Osborn replied, "Greg is taking some sick time off, sir."

"Now? With all that's going on here! Is he okay?"

"I agreed with him, sir," Donald said. "The last couple of days have been emotionally draining for him. Those troopers killed in the helicopter were good friends; one was about to become a stepfather to Greg's son. He and his family needed the time; besides, federal authorities weren't letting us near the train anyway."

"I understand," The president said. "When this is over, we'll take those same authorities to task. This is our train, our tracks, and most importantly, our state!"

"Yes, sir." Osborn was glad to have his boss behind him. A former Alaska Governor, he would make some big waves when all this was finished. Osborn was concerned for his friend, Greg. He'd known him for some time and didn't buy into the sick leave excuse. He called Lt. Farber on his cell phone. Finally, after promising he wouldn't take any action against Greg for whatever he was involved in, he got the whole story. Fighting to control his temper, Osborn's face turned red, and he unleashed a loud burst of profanity that shocked his secretary. In response to Osborn's reaction, Lt. Farber hung up and returned to his job. If everything remained quiet for another eight hours, the Fairbanks PD would return to regular shifts. Farber planned on taking a two-day trip to Chena Hot Springs for a well-deserved soaking and a good drunk. Steaming over what his good friend might be doing didn't settle well with him. He'd keep it between him and Greg. After he got control of his temper, Don Osborn made a call to Toronto. He left a recorded message for the acting commander of RCMP Intel. "This is Chief Investigator Osborn of the Alaska Railroad. Tell whoever that we need to talk—now! It concerns Captain Jean Leon; he might be in danger." Osborn left his phone number and hung up.

Donald looked out the window of his office and stared at the Chugach Mountains in the distance, "You haven't heard the last of this, Agent Hansen. If they don't kill you first, I will make you wish they had," Osborn promised. "Such juvenile behavior! Who do you think you are… John Wayne?"

Reindeer Lodge, Cantwell, Alaska

Cantwell Volunteer Fire and EMS teams arrived at the lodge eight minutes after receiving the 911 call. When Old Man Taylor collapsed behind the bar, Sam Watterson made the call. A Swedish female tourist started CPR and teamed up with a Navajo teenager from Holbrook, Arizona, who'd recently received his First Aid Card from the Red Cross. He did the compressions, struggling with the old man's girth and greasy apron, while she performed mouth-to-mouth. By the time the ambulance crew arrived, Old Man Taylor was breathing on his own. The fire truck rolled in right behind them.

Trooper Bosley heard the call, and though he wasn't on duty yet, rolled out of bed. Hearing that an 85-year-old man had collapsed at the Reindeer with possible heart problems, he knew it had to be Taylor. The old man had pushed too hard, refused to hire help, and his heart must have given out. Bosley rolled code-two, with red and blue lights flashing but no siren, and arrived at the scene in time to find the EMTs kneeling around Taylor in the limited space behind the bar. Sam kicked everyone out, so about 40 to 50 people stood outside the Reindeer. Bosley locked his patrol car and shouted, "Make way! Comin' through!"

When Bosley walked into the lodge, he was relieved to see Taylor alive. The old fart was already complaining about losing money and trying to kick the EMS squad out, "I ain't sick, now get out 'a here!" He could tell by Taylor's skin color that he was having problems.

The EMS squad briefed him, "Taylor's blood pressure is 260 over 180; he's about to blow. Pulse 150, and his breathing remains shallow, at least when he's not cussing us out. I cannot believe he's still alive; must be because he's just too tough to give in and die."

Bosley refused to honor Taylor's demand for refusing medical treatment. He turned to the head EMT, "I'm putting him under a 72-psychiatric hold, ignore his mouth and transport him to Fairbanks Memorial. Restrain him if you have to; I'll call ahead and give 'em a heads up."

"Bosley, I can't—" Taylor was out of breath and couldn't talk further.

"Yeah, you're in great shape. Go with them, or I'll Taser your butt."

"You want me to close things up, Trooper Bosley?" Sam asked, his face a mask of concern for the old man.

"No, I'll lock it down. If I leave it to you, he'd probably shut you off permanently for conspiring with me."

"Well, okay. Call me if you need me." Watterson hung around, knowing they'd need all hands to lift Old Man Taylor into the ambulance.

Bosley made sure everything that needed turning off was, except the fridge and freezers. The windows and coolers were secured. Then he cleared the building and locked the outside door. He knew he'd never hear the end of it from Old Man Taylor, but at least this way, the old fart might live another day or two.

With the Reindeer Lodge shut down until further notice, most people moved to the Chevron station on the highway. A small café inside the station suddenly found itself overwhelmed with moody customers, most upset to learn the café didn't serve alcohol.

Trooper Bosley returned to the post and called the Fairbanks Detachment. He wanted to make sure Fairbanks Memorial understood his 72-hour hold. One of the Fairbanks troopers would have to sign the paperwork for the hold, but at least this way, Taylor could have 72 hours of bed rest, and hopefully, some doctor could look at his ticker and run some tests. Within the hour, Bosley was back in bed, snoring loud enough to drive the moose away. A skittish critter, they could only handle so much audible abuse.

16

---

# BOLD MOVES & SCARY TIMES

3.7 Miles North and .4 Miles West Of The FLQ Campsite
June 17th – 4:35 a.m.

Greg admired another beautiful Alaska morning with his arms outstretched wide as he took in a lungful of clear mountain air. There wasn't a cloud in the baby blue sky, and though it was only half-past four in the morning, the sun was above the mountaintops. Greg estimated the current temperature around 60 degrees with little to no breeze. He preferred a breeze, which often drove flying insects back into the trees.

After riding the Honda four-wheeler all day, his backside was sore from having ridden over some of the most extraordinary gut-wrenching terrain. When they finally made camp, Greg wasn't sure he'd be able to walk in the morning. There were moments of utter terror when they seemed to defy gravity. He fishtailed down a hillside on one wheel and bounced about like some out-of-sync blender to the tune of bruising a kidney and unraveled nerves. Then, without warning, he dropped over a five-foot cliff that rattled his brainpan. He thought he might have chipped a tooth and he'd nearly bit his tongue off once or twice. The adrenaline rush didn't stop until they reached the summit and took a breather. So, the act of stretching wasn't so much to loosen things up as to make sure everything still worked. His aging body was one large mass of pain.

Not wanting to be outdone by a one-eyed disabled trapper, Greg tried to keep up with Tony, but Tony was in his natural element. All those years of riding through this challenging territory to check trap lines and gather wood paid off. Greg had told him that there were lives at stake.

For JP, the ride had been like running through a challenging gauntlet, from a white-knuckle adrenaline pumper to absolute hell. Sure, he'd been on a four-wheeler before, a couple of times at least if memory served, and he'd hunted in the Northwest Territories of Canada. But not at the speeds, Tony was doing. Numerous times they exceeded 30 miles per hour over trails that JP was sure were last used by some gangly-legged near-sighted moose. He collided with a tree on three occasions. His ATV's massive tires bounced off as low-hanging branches swatted his helmet and shoulders. He was thankful to be wearing a helmet, which had already saved his life several times. JP sideswiped one large deadfall, lost his balance, and came close to being knocked off the ATV. At one point, he was a hair breath away from taking a dive off a rocky cliff into a deep gorge. He ended up tearing a chunk of leather off one of his new boots and bruising his ankle, but he was alive to complain about it. The thought that lives were at risk, and terrorists needed killing kept him following Tony's insane journey into the wilderness.

Tony had to stop numerous times to let the other two men catch up. He had expected this, and without saying anything when they met up, accelerated and kept going. They plowed into heavy brush and forded a dozen or more creeks or streams, with only Tony's instinct and memory to guide them. Tony was out front breaking trail, his small trailer bouncing behind. Thankfully, the tow hook-up was reinforced by heavy chains to keep him from losing it altogether.

Before nodding off for a few hours of sleep, Tony shared that he was nearly sure he knew where the terrorists were going with their hostages. He kept their three-man group west of that destination, using the hills to silence their ATVs' engine sounds. If they did hear them, Tony counted on the bad guys believing the sounds were coming from the southwest. Alaska was big in all-terrain vehicles. Many people hit the trails during the summer months, some for fun and others to scout out future trapping or hunting areas for moose and bear seasons.

Greg suspected the terrorists would know there were search teams out and hopefully believe the echoing engine sounds could be coming from a valley in some other direction. Greg blamed himself for the fierce pace Tony kept, telling him what little time they had before the deadline. He wondered if that was smart. Greg would prefer slowing down a bit before his lower body went from pain to complete numbness. He wasn't sure he'd be able to walk normally for a few days, much less take on a group of armed terrorists.

They consumed a few gulps of water, a handful of trail mix, and some beef jerky before hitting the trail. Tony decided to drop his trailer after they topped off all three of the ATVs' fuel tanks. They checked equipment loads roped to the racks on the back of the ATVs and continued on.

Though he knew how dangerous it was, Tony chose to risk riding near the snow line to bypass other rescue parties. He knew how easy it would be to start a landslide or cause a rollover at this time of year, but time was also the enemy. He had warned both Greg and JP to stay in his tracks. He knew where the more dangerous spots were and often pointed out rocky outcroppings that looked firm but were ready to go with the slightest movement. They traveled much slower through these dangerous areas.

After another hour of travel, Tony stopped and turned his engine off. He climbed off his ATV to stretch his legs and reset his braces on a wooded bluff. The heavy vibration of the ATV often loosened them. Tony signaled the other two men to recheck their ATVs.

Though he was in a lot of pain, Tony didn't want to dull his thinking with drugs. He pulled out a small handmade map from a black canvas pack attached to the handlebars of his four-wheeler. He spread the map over his gas tank, glancing back and forth from the map to the valley around him. He checked the snow line above. From many years in the area, Tony could point out their position to the two men.

Four years ago, Tony had bagged a wolverine not far from here in one of his traps, which brought him $170.00 from an Anchorage furrier. Those critters were intelligent and seldom walked into a trap. When baiting traps, he used animal urine to cover the human smell, one of the things his mentor had taught him. Tony admired the wolverine's courage and downright stubbornness to give ground until satisfied it had proven its point. This area of the woods had belonged to that wolverine. From reading and tales he'd heard, Tony knew that even a grizzly would back down from an aggressive wolverine.

When Greg and JP climbed off their four-wheelers and appeared at his side, Tony noticed that both struggled with the effort of walking upright. He shook his head to show his humorous side and pointed to a spot on the map. "Here," he mumbled.

Greg removed his helmet and cringed as he snapped back his shoulder blades and rolled his head around to loosen his neck muscles. "Had I known it was going to be this rough, I would have scrounged up a couple of back braces for JP and me."

"Sure, now you think of it," JP complained.

Greg asked Tony, "Do you think we've passed the other search teams?"

Not wanting to garble his words, Tony pulled a small writing pad out of his vest pocket and wrote. Greg read it aloud for JP. "I saw someone moving below us earlier. On foot. Trees too thick to see who they were. Some distance below us, moving along a trail our ATVs cannot use. If we get any closer, and that's the bad guys, they will hear our motors. We must trail them by foot and leave the ATVs here."

"You mentioned earlier another cabin up ahead; how far?" Greg asked.

After removing his helmet and listening in, JP took advantage of the stop for a drink of water. He poured a couple of handfuls of water over the back of his neck and wet his face. Wearing the full-face helmet caused his face to sweat but he felt safer with it on. Riding in the number three position, he could see where Greg ducked and swerved which allowed time to take less abuse on the treacherous trail.

Tony wrote on the pad again and handed it to Greg. "Tony says, 'The next cabin, the one built by my friend Jake, is maybe two hours ahead by foot. Maybe less.'" Greg looked at JP and added, "I agree with him, but first, let's take a break. My back is really killing me."

Tony nodded and reached for his canteen.

"Sounds good to me," JP replied. "I feel like I've been trampled by a herd of buffalo. Hard to believe people do this for fun."

"We'll move the four-wheelers over there," Greg pointed to a shallow drop between two rock embankments. "Cover them with brush and come back for them later. I'd hate to face Old Man Taylor and tell him we lost them, nor would I enjoy having to pay for new ones."

Tony nodded. He took a small drink of water to rinse out his mouth and spit it out then took a sip. After securing his canteen, he put his pad and pen away, placed the map back in his pack, and pushed his ATV toward the spot selected by Greg. It took 15 minutes to get their gear off-loaded and the four-wheelers covered over with deadfall. They weren't too worried about theft. They were concerned about another search team finding them and knowing others were in the area. Greg didn't want to be stopped by the authorities and figured the three of them on foot could probably get closer to the terrorists than a larger group.

"I've marked this spot on the GPS. We'll have no problem finding it again," Greg carried his pack and weapons to a bare hillside of loose gravel and plopped himself down for a well-needed rest break.

"How long are we going to stay here?" JP asked as he hoisted his pack over his right shoulder and grunted from the weight. He moved to where Greg had set up accommodations, "Is this spot reserved, sir?"

"No, but I warn you, this is low-class accommodations with no room service." Greg laughed.

"What, no television?" JP exclaimed in mock annoyance.

"Lions and Bears, oh, but what a view!"

"Lions?" JP set up his backpack to use as a pillow.

"So, I goofed. Just be happy we don't have flying monkeys out here, but we do have bears. Big bruins with sharp teeth and long claws. We're in an area where grizzlies, brown bears, and black bears move about. We also have wolf-packs, not to mention the FLQ terrorists running loose with automatic weapons. You've already seen what a bear attack looks like, and I'd rather not experience that firsthand. Those she-devils are a terror if they're protecting cubs. That's what happened back there. Someone may have got too close, and that sow took matters into hand. Even moose can get aggressive if they have a calf or a bull when it's in rut, which comes in late September."

JP's response was thoughtful, "I notice our definition of being in a rut is far different than a moose's definition. When we're in a rut, we're all depressed. When the word is used with a bull moose, the animal is excited and not thinking too straight. Bulls are ready to do battle over a cow moose. I find nature fascinating and sometimes a bit crazy."

"And boy, do they battle. I once heard two bulls going at it, smashing their racks against one another. I had to walk over a mile before finding where they waged war. Blood was everywhere, velvet off their antlers, and hair from their hides, but both survived. My moose hunt was a bust that year, but it felt good getting out in the woods away from everyone."

JP grinned, "How long do we stay here?"

"Couple hours," Tony mumbled.

Greg out a pouch of food, "Good! That'll give us time to eat, get some more water down us, and an hour of shuteye with alternating bear watch. I'll take the first hour, and JP can take the second shift. Tony, you're the leader here, so you don't have to pull the afternoon watch. That gives us time for some chow and a latrine break."

Tony sat his pack down beside Greg's and lay down against it. Mosquitoes had found them, and bug dope was quickly applied. Tony, displaying the fore-thought of a true outdoorsman, pulled a strange-looking hat out of his pack and put it on. The green floppy-brimmed Boonie hat came with its own mosquito netting that could be pulled down to cover his face and neck. Seeing this, both JP and Greg were highly envious.

"Didn't see any of those at the store," Greg said.

Tony opened a package of homemade trail mix. He offered some to the others and reviewed his map once more before closing his eyes. Like the other two men, Tony felt that his age was catching up with him, and the beating they took on the trail had left him worn out. He doubted if he would sleep, but the hour of rest would prepare him for the hike they had ahead of them.

Because of his leg braces, Tony was not looking forward to climbing down the hill; he knew it would be slow going through the steeper parts. On level ground, he'd do all right. Without the braces, he'd be in a wheelchair and not living out here in the wilderness.

More concerned about bears than meeting the terrorists for the moment, Greg finished off his handful of trail mix and pulled his shotgun out of his backpack's rifle sheath. He'd sling his rifle and carry the shotgun. He knew slugs effectively stopped a big bruin if it didn't want to share the trail. He found a reasonably flat rock to sit on above the others and watched for wayward bruins. After such a ride, his butt hurt, and he struggled with drowsiness. He splashed his face with water and washed down an aspirin with water from his canteen.

JP had trouble going to sleep. He was too close to the enemy. Whenever he closed his eyes, he saw his wife and children lounging in their living room. His mind replayed the night that ended his family life. Over and over again, he stood, unable to move, frozen, as the flames came toward him. Sometimes, he could almost hear LeAnn's screams from inside the burning house. No, this wasn't the time to sleep. He'd stay awake and contemplate these final hours and the revenge about to play out. When he checked out of the hospital, the doctors had warned him of the effects of Post-Traumatic Stress Disorder. They had recommended for him to see a psychologist, but JP wasn't interested.

Thankfully, he never had to look at his family's remains. By the time he was released from the hospital, their closed caskets were already in the grave. His wife's family handled the burials. Before going to the airport, JP stopped by the graveyard for a few moments with his family.

He didn't think of himself as an RCMP captain anymore, only a man out to bring justice for the wrongs against him by sociopath fanatics. JP wondered how Adler and Wilkens were doing running down the money trail. He'd have liked to confront the vile people who had financed this group, to go nose to nose with them and ask each one how they felt about causing the deaths of so many innocent people. He'd let Adler and Wilkens handle their end; this part of the hunt was all his. No defense counsels, no left-wing liberal judges looking for a technicality to let someone off. Just three armed and determined men to make a stand against terrorism and cause great pain to those who had taken JP's family and killed Greg's AST friends.

While Greg kept watch, he took a moment to study his two new friends; Tony was dozing, and JP was gazing out over the canyon below lost in thought. *I imagine he's thinking about his family—I would be. Too many memories to escape. So much joy was lost in that brief moment because he's a cop.* Greg tightened his grip on the shotgun. *We're out here dealing with life and death. Life for three hostages and the probable end of the terrorists. Makes me wonder how God feels about all this and the actions we're about to take. Am I committing murder if I kill to free a hostage, or is it like killing in a war, defeating the enemy to save one's country and family?* In his rush to assist JP and find the killers of his close friends, he'd chosen to put himself between the FBI's Hostage Negotiating Team and the killers. Cops against lowlifes, who had already reached infamous standards by killing so many people with their bombs.

*How small this world is. I didn't know these two men or the terrorists over the next hill a few days ago. Some weird quirk of destiny has brought us together; a crippled veteran, an RCMP captain bent on revenge, and me. Who am I? What leads me on, drives me into this bizarre quest. Maybe I've watched way too many John Wayne and Randolph Scott movies. I can almost imagine us as the three Musketeers coming to the rescue of the French king. Except it's the Canadian Prime Minister, my Governor, and a US Senator I never voted for. I really never liked that woman; too liberal. It's not quite movie material. I hope we're the heroes who survive, not poor dudes who get a "You are a certifiable idiot" medal awarded posthumously. I wonder what they'll say about this whole mess afterward, especially if we blow it. My kid will never hear the end of it, how his dad got everyone killed trying to play the hero.* A noise to his right brought his thoughts to an abrupt end. He came alert, pointing his shotgun at a tree squirrel, making a mad dash up a tree.

"Sorry, little fella... I'm a bit on edge."

9.2 Miles North Of Curry, FLQ Campsite
June 17th, 05:15 A.M.

With Michael's help, Governor Hughes buried Senator Sterns' body in a shallow grave close to the cabin's north wall. They covered the mound of loose dirt with gravel and rocks, hoping to keep varmints from reaching her body. Hughes was confident he could locate the grave later to have the senator's body removed and transported to Juneau for a proper burial and honors. He whispered a quiet prayer which Michael finished with a somber, "Amen."

When he saw that Munroe had fallen into a restless sleep and Hugo was busy with Louis, Hughes asked Michael about his faith, "Are you a believer, Michael? Christian, Jewish?"

Michael didn't reply immediately and raised an eyebrow at the Governor. "Yeah, I was once a Christian. No, that's not correct. Not anymore. I am a believer, but I've been so angry—so bitter towards God most of my life for what He's allowed to happen in my world."

"Your world? Care to explain? We've got time."

"Why should you care? You're a rich politician with hardly a care in the world." Michael smiled, "Well, except whether or not some crazy dude with a rifle is going to shoot you in the next few minutes. Other than that, why care about me? I'm a terrorist responsible for killing more than a hundred and fifty people. Don't even know exactly how many. Or is this some psychological ploy to reach my better half? If so, good luck; I killed my better half off a long time ago."

Governor Hughes wiped sweat off his forehead with the cuff of his right sleeve. "I could say one country's terrorist is another country's hero or patriot, but neither of us would believe it. Not in this situation, at least, and I'm not here to grant you absolution. I'm no priest, but I do study people, and I've had time to look into your eyes. You're not a killer, Michael. You joined this group out of concern for your country, and a desire for independence from a government that doesn't understand you. Am I right? You joined, then found yourself in way over your head. You know there's no need for taking innocent lives. You know when violence has gone too far." Hughes looked about to ensure he and Michael were still alone.

"You're talkin' sense. And sure, this wasn't what I expected or what I signed on for," Michael glared defensively at Hughes. "Don't paint me as some wishy-washy idealist, someone who doesn't want to get his hands dirty to bring change about. I could've pulled my weight and offered my flesh and blood freely if we'd gone into a real war. I'd be in line to sign up, but women and children—people that have nothing to do with our issues—it's tearing me up inside. Seeing all those little body bags in the news, photographs of dead women, and when we killed that RCMP's family. It's all crap!" Michael looked down at his hands, wringing them together to wipe the blood off that wasn't there except in his mind. "It's just too much!"

"How long have you believed in God, Michael?"

"Longer than I can remember. But I don't see him as a nice, charitable God like most people do. I see him as one in great power who neglects the little people, plays the power curve, and lets the marbles fall. Maybe he's the one true politician."

"That hurt," Hughes said.

"Yeah, I can see the pain in your eyes," Michael said mockingly.

Hughes looked down at Stern's grave, "No, that's real, and your leader did it."

"Trying to split us up, aren't you? Use the silk politician's tongue to sway this city boy? I've learned that politicians and sanctimonious lawyers were spawned from the same two-faced snake. You're both good in the acting department when it suits you."

"Wow! Your mom or dad was a lawyer or a politician? I can see the hate on your face."

"You got me, Governor," Michael said. "Dear ole' dad was a lawyer. He taught me how to lie when I was eight years old. Missed my birthday party—unfortunately, delayed by a court proceeding."

"And that was a lie?"

"Dear ole' pop was out playing patty-cake with his secretary, and not for the first time. I overheard him talking to her on the phone later while Mom was out buying pizza. It seems dear old Mom knew about it, though. Dad wasn't a very convincing liar, but she stayed by him through one affair after another. I guess she was afraid to be on her own, find a job at some two-bit store for minimum wage, and struggle to pay rent for some fleabag shove-over."

"What brought you into this… organization?"

"Anger… no, revenge mainly. I was mad and needed something to direct my frustrations at. My best friend lost his job with the federal government because of his connections with the Parti Quebecois. They told him it was due to cutbacks, but his position was filled with a loyal Canadian within a week. So, my buddy ended up on the streets, had to send his family to live with his wife's parents, and she ended up leaving him for another man—*a* guy who had a job."

"Was he… was he a militant like yourself?"

"Hardly; he attended a meeting maybe once a year. Closest he came to wanting armed rebellion was helping me paint a banner for an anti-Canada march, or perhaps it was an anti-British rally. Too long ago to remember. I never joined the Parti Quebecois. Didn't want anyone to know my political connections. I supported almost any cause against whoever my father funded with his money or free legal services. I wanted to be involved with anything that would get back at him. Not so much for me, but for what he did to my mom; he turned her into a robot, like the ladies in that old movie *Stepford Wives*. Later, she became an alcoholic, a drug addict hooked on anti-depressants, and a whore. She slept with anyone who'd offer her a kind word, a tender touch, or a sweet lie. They never got divorced, but my parents quit living together after I left for college. In my sophomore year, she killed herself with sleeping pills."

Michael casually gestured toward Munroe with his right index finger. He whispered, "Steve lost his mother much the same way, but with booze. We're not supposed to, but I know the details."

"You're not anything like our Mr. Munroe, Michael. Do you still believe in the Lord Jesus Christ?"

"Yeah, I guess I still believe in Jesus. You have to believe in someone to hate them."

"I'm sorry, Michael," Hughes offered sincerely. "Did your mother take you to church while you were growing up?"

"Oh yeah, Mom took me to Sunday school and Wednesday night prayer services. She really liked all the singing. She had a good voice until she took to boozing."

"But you got saved? You accepted the Lord as your Savior at some point?"

"Sure did," Michael raised both hands, and in a loud whisper, blurted out, "Halleluiah, brother, and Amen!"

Governor Hughes ignored the slam, and in a soft voice, asked, "But you walked away?"

"Sure did, and never looked back. No more church services for this kid."

Governor Hughes decided he'd spent too much time on the belief aspect and switched to politics. "I notice you're not really French-Canadian, so why the FLQ?"

"Like I said, Governor, anything to counter my father is my cause. My dad works for the Parti-Quebecois, part of their legal team. So, I joined this group…" Michael pointed to the others around him, "…for revenge. I know the Parti Quebecois got credit for supporting the first FLQ. This is a way to get back at dear old Dad."

"I thought the FLQ and the Parti Quebecois were working for the same outcome; the sovereignty of Quebec?"

"You know as well as I do that when this is over, news people will crucify the FLQ and embarrass the French-Canadian movement for wanting its independence. In this way, I've hurt my father," Michael glanced at Munroe and Hugo, "Those two are in it for the money, but for me, it's all about revenge, Governor. That's my cause. I doubt the Canadian government will ever allow Quebec to have its sovereignty. That'd be like Alaska separating from the United States—ain't never going to happen. Alaska is too rich in natural resources and makes a nice buffer with Russia."

"But you're not happy anymore, Michael. Munroe has pushed you nearly over the edge, and this revenge you so dearly crave is no longer the answer you thought it would be. You believed so once, but you don't anymore. You tried to act like the others; raised your fist in defiance, but your old belief in God is dragging you back to a place of conscious thought. Am I right?"

Michael hesitated, studying Governor Hughes' eyes and glancing over his shoulder to check on Munroe. "Okay, let's say you're right. What can I do without getting my head blown off? Munroe's growing more insane by the hour, and Hugo—that guy's a stone-cold killer. Munroe has him around to keep us in line. That Nazi would cut your throat without blinking an eye. He's pure evil."

"There'll come a time—" Governor Hughes didn't finish. Munroe was suddenly staring directly at him with that cold maniacal glare. He reminded Governor Hughes of the news file photographs of Charles Manson, a murderer and self-proclaimed prophet of the late 1960s.

Curry Townsite – June 17th, 6:30 A.M.

Corporal Williams, a SERT Team member was wide-awake sipping hot coffee from a blue plastic insulated cup. He was standing by a small fire, concealed by a thick stand of alder and a large deadfall of spruce. He looked up to see Sgt. Jeremy Miller of the National Guard approaching with a long line of tired-looking Boy Scouts.

"The lost boys have been found," Williams said to Trooper Sheldon, kneeling by the fire and refilling his coffee cup from a charred metal pot.

Sgt. Miller, a third-generation Irish American, was dressed in dark camouflage leaf pattern fatigues, a dark green and black combat bulletproof vest, and armed with an M4 automatic rifle. He introduced Corporal Williams to the Boy Scout leader, "Corporal Williams, this is Ed Anderson and his scout troop. We picked 'em up 'bout 500 yards down the trail; they looked a bit peaked. They had no idea what's going on out here."

"Well, Mr. Anderson, welcome to Curry," Williams said. The two men shook hands. Sgt. Miller moved the scouts into the trees to keep them safe.

Sgt. Miller set up a two-man listening post 150 yards to the north, manned by National Guard Scouts, and briefed them on proper radio call signs. The men were excited to be in the field for something other than a training exercise and armed with real ammo instead of blanks. Several older guardsmen were veterans of combat tours in Iraq or Afghanistan and heroes of the younger inexperienced troops. Corporal Williams was glad to have experienced guardsmen assigned to him, especially Sgt. Miller. Secretly, he hoped when the shooting started, it would be his own men taking the terrorists down. Trooper blood was spilled, and Williams and his SERT Team members wanted blood in return.

Williams offered Anderson a cup of coffee and learned the entire troop was from the Mormon Church and Anderson, who politely refused the coffee, was a church bishop.

"We've learned about the train attack and the hostages. What can you tell me about getting my kids out of here? This place could easily turn into a war zone. I experienced that during Desert Storm. My boys don't need to go through that, not at this age."

"Since you're a vet, you know weapons," Williams said. "We believe these guys carry MP5s, and maybe a couple M-16s. They took out a helicopter with what looked like a Stinger Missile. A LAWS rocket and RPGs were used against the train engines." Williams sipped his coffee and waited for Anderson to respond.

"What you're saying is it could be really unsafe for these boys to walk back through the woods? We risk getting hit by a wayward bullet. Well, I agree with you. We'll stay right here until you decide to move us. My wife is letting all the parents know we're safe. The boys are having the time of their lives. It's all one big adventure, and I hope to keep it that way. Thank you for pulling us out before we stumbled across those people. Kids make good bargaining tools."

After hearing about what had transpired and who was kidnapped, Anderson shook his head and muttered, "Leave town for a few days and—" He looked at Williams. "Where do you want us?"

"Some of my Guardsmen will escort you and your Scouts, back down the hill. I'll get the Alaska Railroad to send some high rail vehicles up this way to pick you up. Until then, find someplace close that's well-protected by large rocks. I'll assign four Guardsmen to watch over you."

"The boys will be disappointed when we leave, but I'm sure we've got some pretty worried parents waiting down at the trailhead."

"The parents are at the roadblock on the highway, and they're none too happy about it, not that I don't sympathize with them." Trooper Sheldon grinned; he was a father too. "We've had a few dozen complaints called in over the last eight hours. One parent felt he had some political pull and threatened to call the Governor if we couldn't locate you and get you out of there. He must not be following the news closely, or he'd know where the Governor is at the moment."

Anderson smiled. "That would probably be Archie Goodings. Very big in the Republican Party and likes people to know it. He owns two car dealerships and has a lot of money but apparently, not much common sense, if you know what I mean."

"Know a few of those people, myself. Always like to drop names to add weight to a complaint or a threat," Williams acknowledged.

"I'm his Bishop; his son is one of my Eagle Scouts. A really great kid. We have hopes he'll attend West Point next year." Anderson looked over where his kids were sitting. Sgt Miller was showing them how his M4 worked.

"Don't worry, I'll calm Mr. Dad down when I get back and express my sincere goodwill to all for how the Troopers and National Guard took outstanding care of us."

Williams and Sheldon shook hands with Anderson, who gathered his troop. The Boy Scouts disappeared down the hill after a short rest break escorted by four-armed guardsmen. Williams used a satellite phone to contact the CP and advise them of the current situation. He requested information about the scouts be forwarded to their parents, then walked to where Sgt. Miller was filling his coffee cup from a near-empty coffee pot. "One more thing to mark off, at least we won't have those kids running around up here when the shooting starts."

William sighed, "They're still in the area—no one's safe until we know exactly where those scumbags are."

"From the last satellite report, they believe the bad guys are stationery about nine miles above us trying to stay below the radar. No fires." Sgt. Miller took a sip of hot coffee, tossed the rest onto the ground, and shook his head in dismay. Apparently, the troopers got their coffee from the same place the National Guard did. "Next time, I'll bring my own coffee grounds. This stuff tastes like the coffee you get at some homeless shelter.

"There should be another satellite flyover within the hour," Sgt. Miller said.

Corporal Williams nodded, and, with Miller accompanying him, walked around to inspect the defense positions. Williams struggled between hoping this situation would end without any shooting and wanting a chance to nail the people who had killed his friends, but his primary concern was ensuring the safety of his people and the hostages.

The FBI Hostage and Rescue Team was pressing in from the north facing a nearly unclimbable steep, snow-covered mountain. Above them was an impassable canyon gorge blocking the terrorists from the east. It appeared the only way the FLQ could escape was through Corporal Williams' blocking position in Curry. Williams' current force was comprised of six Trooper SERT Team members and nine Guardsmen. Sending four troops to guard the Boy Scouts had put a severe dent in his force, but Williams knew it was the thing to do.

RCMP Headquarters-Toronto
June 17th, 9:10 A.M.

Colonel Augustus, dressed in fresh military greens and wearing only the mandatory RCMP uniform brass, and gold buffalo head Mountie shield, arrived to find Sgt Adler and Sgt. Wilkens waiting for him in his outer office. He stopped before them, "All right, what has the two of you up here so early in the morning? Or is it late in the shift for both of you?"

"Colonel, we've found a money trail of sorts, a possible connection between some extremely wealthy people and the FLQ," Sgt. Adler said.

"My office," Colonel Augustus ordered and turned to his receptionist, Jean Wrightly, "I am not to be disturbed, Mrs. Wrightly."

"Yes, sir," Jean said. After several years of working for the Colonel, she knew this meant that he would accept interruption from only the people on his "A" List. The list included two people from the Prime Minister's office, the four general officers representing the Canadian armed forces, the Cabinet Secretaries of the Immigration and Customs Department, and the Toronto Chief of Police.

As soon as JP left, Colonel Augustus had directed Mrs. Wrightly to place JP on the "A" list. He'd known all along where JP was headed and unofficially wished he could have accompanied him. As an RCMP Colonel, he must maintain his official stand concerning the FLQ. As a friend of the family who'd bounced JP's boys on his knees more than a time or two, he'd like nothing better than to execute those thugs. He prayed JP survived to do just that. Colonel Augustus gestured for both sergeants to take a seat and sat behind his massive mahogany desk. "Tell me what you have," he said, with a distinct tone of authority.

Sgt. Adler rose to his feet, cleared his throat, and began his presentation. Colonel Augustus reviewed documents as Adler handed them to him. Sitting in a comfortable chair covered in crushed red velvet, Sgt Wilkens fidgeted, glancing back and forth between Adler and the Colonel. When Adler finished, he sat back down and waited. Either the Colonel agreed with them, or the two stood a good chance of becoming parking meter attendants before the end of the day.

Colonel Augustus reviewed Adler's chart and the documentation obtained from the Ontario provincial property records. Documents followed organizations that eventually led to the owners of the properties destroyed by the FLQ. In the paperwork for the parking garage, five different corporations were used as dummy fronts before they found the legitimate owner. Adler had to trace through eight dummy corporations for the property leased to the Parliament Building before he struck pay dirt. A lot of names had to be checked and rechecked.

Nine names listed as current company officers for the parking garage came up as persons who had died prior to 1960. Parliament property documents were very similar. When the lease was investigated, someone in the government real estate office didn't do their job or was paid off. One of the officers listed for the primary ownership company had a vice president who died as a two-year-old in 1953. Adler had a photocopy of both the birth and death certificates.

"I want search warrants for these people's bank and credit union accounts and company records. Serve them at the addresses shown on the documents. If these are, in fact, dump addresses, I want photographs taken of those locations to show a jury later," Colonel Augustus ordered. "Then find the actual offices and leave no stone unturned. Make no arrests yet. I want to see political donations, amounts, and recipients. I want the names of government employees paid from these bank accounts or other money accounts you find. I want surveillance initiated immediately on key figures you've identified. If you find any government involvement, notify me right away. If you find any dirt on any Mounties, bring in our Internal Affairs immediately and take those people into custody immediately. Borrow manpower from Major Crimes, but you two will lead this investigation until I say otherwise. You'll work directly under me for the time being. To protect both of you, I may assign a senior officer until JP returns."

"Sir, should we try to contact Captain Leon?"

Colonel Augustus considered Adler's question for a moment, "No. We all know where he is and what his intentions are. Officially, he's on vacation and well overdue for one. Unofficially—" Colonel Augustus didn't continue; he shook his head and hoped JP survived to lead the Intel Section.

"Colonel, I have one more item to show you. I found it in the old FLQ file." Adler handed a yellowed piece of paper to the Colonel. It was an old RCMP form used for file work and labeled under the RCMP Intel Section. "An investigator by the name of Sgt. D. Simmons, retired, worked on a link between the former FLQ and a Richard Quison. From a snitch inside the Parti Quebecois, Simmons learned Quison was a liaison between both factions. He was developing further investigation when the FLQ fled the country. The case was placed on hold and eventually sent to the archives. This may have been done because there were too many other groups causing problems, so they simply moved on." Adler pulled a piece of paper out of his pocket, "I followed up using Quison's birth date and last known address, and found he is the same Dr. Richard Quison, a prominent and extremely wealthy industrialist living in Montreal. He has a vast hunting estate. Neighbors have filed noise complaints concerning excessive helicopter traffic and weapons fire. I checked, and he does have several helipads and a licensed shooting range. And he is the current legal owner of the Parliament property. Our records show Quison was killed in a shooting accident in 1994. As of yet, we're unable to find who the current Quison really is. During the 1960s and '70s, he must've paid serious money to keep his real identity secret from the RCMP and local police. We may not be able to get positive ID without fingerprints. Takes big money to do this, Colonel, and this Quison may not even be the same fellow associated with the original FLQ."

"Seems you two have your work cut out for you, gentleman," Colonel Augustus said. "Use whatever resources you need. I want a briefing once a day at, say 1700 hours here in my office. If I'm called away, use this phone number." He reached over, pulled one of his business cards out of a desk holder, and wrote his personal phone number on the back. "Use that number only for this case; it's a secure line. I recommend you use a secure line, if possible. If not, advise me to activate my scrambler from the start. We can arrange to meet somewhere to discuss what you have."

"Yes, sir," Sgt Adler said.

"Who do we use for legal counsel, Colonel?" Sgt. Wilkens asked.

Colonel Augustus unlocked his left-hand desk drawer and pulled out a black metal index card file holder. He went through the cards and selected one, "Write this name down—Jeffery Townsend." He gave Adler the address and phone number. "Call him and use my name to initiate the case. We've used him before on special cases. He's safe, has no political ties, and I've known him most of his life. His father and grandfather are retired RCMP. A sports injury kept him from joining our ranks, so he became a government prosecutor and a damn good one."

"Thank you, Colonel." Not in uniform, they didn't salute before leaving but did come to attention.

"This will probably be the biggest case of your careers if you two can pull it off." He thought about offering an atta-boy for what they'd done so far but knew they didn't need a pat on the back to push them along. "Watch your backs," Augustus warned. "Anyone tries to pressure you, give you any grief, or stonewall you, call me, and I'll look into it from my end. We're about to tip over the proverbial apple cart, and it's liable to become very messy. Those people you identified have a lot of clout, probably right into the Prime Minister's Office. So, be careful and stay tight-lipped."

Adler and Wilkens left the office, nodded to Mrs. Wrightly, and disappeared down the hallway. They had a long day ahead with little or no sleep between them. Before 5:00 p.m., a lot of complicated paperwork would have to be initiated, mainly manning charts and affidavits for search warrants. Manpower would have to be obtained, and all personnel briefed for surveillance details.

Toes were going to be stepped on, egos hurt, and tempers would flare, but right now, neither Sgt. Adler nor Sgt. Wilkens cared. Their main concern was an absent supervisor, officially on vacation and unofficially running through the Alaska hills searching for the FLQ.

1 7

# DODGE CITY ALASKA STYLE

3.7 Miles North and .4 Miles West of The FLQ Campsite
June 17TH, 10:05 a.m.

Refreshed from his brief nap, Greg checked his backpack and pulled out a length of dried hickory smoke-flavored beef jerky. Beside him, Tony sat on the ground with his legs outstretched as he adjusted his leg braces. He would need a bit more freedom to handle the hike ahead, so he loosened one of the retraining nuts with a special tool. JP was on his feet smearing another heavy dose of bug dope over his cheeks, neck, and the backs of his wrists. Tight leather gloves protected his hands from bugs, branches, and sharp rocks.

"There's a tall tale in Texas that mosquitoes grow so big that if you killed one inside your house, you had to kick it outside before it bled all over the floor," JP said. "I'm beginning to think that story is true here in Alaska."

"Yup, been known to carry a small child off," Greg replied. "But when it comes to pester-some insects, Alaska has these little things with big teeth—their bite can feel like a bee sting. We call 'em *no-see-ums;* they don't usually appear until the latter part of the summer." Greg spread bug dope on his hands and forearms because he had his sleeves rolled up. "You have much of a mosquito problem in Toronto?"

"Probably a long time ago, but we're much too civilized now. Our government fills the air with poisonous toxins to kill them off. No telling how many people die every year of cancer from anti-mosquito fogging operations. I imagine the government keeps those figures hidden. The only blood-sucking insects we have now are the ones we foolishly elect to Parliament."

Tony shook his head and grinned at JP's remark. Over the years, Tony had heard all the jokes and lies about Alaska mosquitoes, seen the miniature bear traps sold to tourists, and postcards identifying the mosquito as the Alaska state bird. The one thing he did know, you could take it for granted that these little bloodsuckers would always be here, and they'd always be hungry. Tony had seen giant swarms buzzing wild game. He'd even watched them nearly smother a moose calf. From his experience, very few commercial repellants worked very long. *Deet may have been bad for the environment, but it worked on these pesky insects. Most of this new stuff dries up, then works as an appetizer, gets 'em all in a frenzy, and ready to party down.* Tony pulled out the notepad from his vest pocket and wrote a message and handed it to Greg, "Tony says, 'The people we're after will probably hole up at my old friend's cabin, two, maybe three miles below us. The only place after that is Curry, and he thinks the troopers will already be there." Greg returned the pad to Tony. "The feds probably have all of us on satellite imagery and wondering who we are," Greg added.

"Why can't the FLQ just climb up into these mountains or drop down into the canyon to escape?" JP asked.

Tony shook his head, wrote something, and handed the pad back to Greg, "Snowline is too dangerous; a lot of chasms up there; easy to start an avalanche if you don't know where to walk." Greg looked up at the snow-covered mountainsides above and continued. "Tony says, 'Down below, the canyon walls become sheer drops, nothing but a deep gorge for several miles and near imposable to make it through. They'll either hold up at the old cabin or try for Curry on the tracks."

"If we start now, when do you think we'll reach this cabin?" Greg asked. Tony considered his answer before writing it down. "He says we'll follow the upper ridgeline to make up time, but we'll be visible to any aircraft flying over. Will this be a problem?"

"No, they can't stop us now," JP replied. "We're much too close for them to drop anyone in on us. And, it's too dangerous to bring a helicopter in and risk alerting the terrorists. The noise would carry down the canyons, plus they may have another missile or two."

"So, how long if we push it?" JP asked again.

Tony wrote and Greg read, "Three hours. Should arrive above the cabin by 1:00 p.m., we'll need rest before engaging the bad guys.' I agree. I want to be sharp when we take those people on."

"Then we'd better get going," JP hoisted his backpack over his shoulders and flinched from the back pain. He took a moment to adjust the weight into the most comfortable position.

"By the pained look on your face, JP, you haven't reduced your load down to essentials yet. Right?" Greg asked.

"Wasn't thinking, sorry. Give me a moment." JP took his pack off and began removing the items he wouldn't need for the operation ahead. With plans to engage the terrorists later, he pulled most of the food and extra clothes out, along with his sleeping bag and ground pad. He would need extra ammo for his rifle and handgun, drinking water, and a day's worth of rations. He kept five emergency energy bars, rain gear, and a trauma first aid kit. Items not needed were piled beside the other's stuff. When he shouldered his pack again, it was half the weight. He glanced at Greg with a guilty smirk. "I'm not much into backpacking these days," He recalled the last time he took the family out camping and became starry-eyed for a moment.

Tony, who carried only a green canvas daypack, shoved another handful of homemade trail mix into his mouth and began walking south across a steep ridgeline. He carried two canteens on his canvas canteen belt, which also held his sidearm, hunting knife, and two ammo pouches.

"How much longer do we have until the deadline?" JP asked.

Greg considered his answer for a moment looking at his watch. "Not sure exactly, but approximately two hours based on the last newscast we saw before heading into these woods."

For the first mile or so, Tony followed a well-traveled moose trail. From his experience, moose primarily used the route in late fall and early spring, passing through the canyon to reach better feeding grounds. This time of year, he didn't think they'd be running into any moose, knowing most of the cows had their young to worry about. Bears primarily stayed on higher ground to dig for shrews and voles until fish began running in the rivers below and thrived on the late summer blueberry crop. Tony was a little concerned about the Bruins, especially grizzly's, so, he kept a round chambered in his weapon with the safety on.

Taking the tail-end Charlie position, Greg kept a close eye on Tony, walking where he did to avoid stepping into holes or on loose gravel that might send him sliding down the hillside. *It's a wonder this man with crippled legs can be so agile. I wonder how much pain he's in. He's got a lot of guts to be out here with us. The money we're paying him isn't bad, but it can't be enough compared to the discomfort we're putting him through. Not to mention the risk of getting shot, yet, he seems determined to lead us. Something else besides money is driving him, maybe a death wish or a chance to relive lost days of the war. Taking one last hike in the Valley of Death—a feeling—an act, to bring back to life some long memory of being more than half of a man. I'm way too harsh on a guy who wants to help us. But it bugs me!*

Jake Baker's Old Cabin - FLQ
June 17th, 11 A.M.

Michael knew he was taking a significant risk. The way Munroe was behaving, Governor Hughes' life was on the line. Standing up, he positioned himself between the two men as Munroe approached. With his MP5 at the ready position, Munroe's weapon was aimed right at Michael's stomach. Frightened, Michael looked into Munroe's wild eyes and glimpsed the man's growing insanity. "Hey, we've got the old lady buried, Steve. Got anything else you'd like us to do?" Michael asked nervously, hoping the man would lower his weapon. Munroe didn't answer. He stood glaring over Michael's shoulder at Governor Hughes. Michael tried to reason with him, "Ah Steve, we still need the Governor. He's worth a lot of money to us alive."

"Not that much." Munroe moved closer and tried to sidestep Michael. He thought a nice belly shot would give Hughes a long excruciating death. "I hate Alaska. I hate their politicians." He shoved the end of his rifle into Michael's midsection. "Killing a politician from Alaska would make it doubly nice. Don't you think? Now, get out of my way!"

Michael changed his tact, "The cops are probably nearby. They'll hear any shooting, and think we killed the hostages. They'll be all over us in no time and from the air with gunships. They may even have drones over us right now photographing us."

Munroe stopped pushing against Michael with his rifle and considered that possibility for a moment. Hugo, who had been checking on the Prime Minister, saw what was happening and moved in to prevent things from turning sour.

"Michael's right. We shoot Governor, they come fast." Hugo didn't place himself in front of Munroe. He knew Munroe was crazy, and it would be too risky. "We need the governor—part of the plan," Hugo reminded him. Hugo kept a sheath knife concealed behind his back in the event he needed a weapon right away. The cops would interpret any shooting as the FLQ executing hostages, and they'd come in like avenging angels to equal the score.

Munroe shifted his cold glare from Hughes to Hugo, almost making the mistake of pointing his rifle at the big German. Instead, he slowly lowered the weapon, shouldered it, and started walking away. Before Michael could breathe a sigh of relief, Munroe abruptly turned around and pulled his sheath knife from his belt. "This is silent. I can do it quietly, just like I did Claudia." He moved towards Hughes, who was backing up startled.

Michael didn't budge; he held his hands up in defense and was about to try talking to Munroe when Hugo shouted, "No!" and moved in quickly to intercept Munroe. "No, we need him!"

"No… no, we don't." Munroe moved even closer, and Hugo had no other choice but to disarm him. He stepped in and brought his left hand down hard in a chopping motion knocking the knife out of Munroe's hand. Michael moved in when the knife hit the ground and quickly scooped it up.

Enraged, Munroe stepped back and began to bring his rifle up. But before he could level it and take a shot at Hugo, the big German quickly wrestled the weapon out of Munroe's grasp. He kicked Munroe's feet out from under him in the same fluid motion. The leader of the FLQ hit the ground hard. Hugo tossed the MP5 to Michael and dropped down hard with a knee in Munroe's chest. Bringing his knife around with his right hand, he placed it under Munroe's chin and, in a calm voice, warned Munroe, "Move, you die." His eyes ablaze with lunacy and hate, Munroe fought to raise up. Hugo applied a small amount of pressure with the knife and a small trickle of blood ran off Munroe's neck. Hugo reached over and grabbed a handful of Munroe's hair and used it to slam Munroe's head against the ground several times until Munroe was unconscious. "You no longer lead! I take over." Hugo looked around the campsite, "Anyone say no?"

No one said anything. In fact, the remaining members of the FLQ were relieved to have Hugo take charge. Since Janene was killed, Munroe's grasp on reality had steadily slipped away. His attempt to kill Governor Hughes, a prize to be ransomed, had lost him their loyalty. Munroe had forgotten or no longer cared that the governor could be vital to Prime Minister Haegens surviving his escape off the mountain.

Hugo looked to Michael and gestured to Greg Landis, "Tie him up, but search for weapons."

Munroe groaned as he regained consciousness and thrashed about, trying to fight free as Greg wrapped him up with the rope. With his arms pinned to his side and both legs lashed together, Landis and Michael carried Munroe into the cabin. Michael covered his mouth with a piece of silver duct tape to stop his obscene rantings.

Hugo nodded at Governor Hughes. The latter offered a hesitant smile of thanks. Hughes realized how close to death he had just come and found it ironic that a terrorist had saved him.

4-Miles North Of The FLQ Encampment - FBI Hostage Team
June 17th, 11:05 A.M.

Wearing borrowed FBI black utilities, Sgt. Niles, Sir Whiteburn, and Agent Loury kept pace behind FBI Agent (SAC) Jackson Stewart. In single file, rifles held at the ready, they followed an FBI point element of two highly trained agents. Both had seen combat in Iraq with Army Special Forces; in front of them was a three-man EOD detail led by MSgt. Joe Brady.

EOD personnel searched the pathway for hidden booby traps, which made for slow travel. They checked each tree and bush for an explosive device or trip-wire. The two-point agents kept watch for any sign of ambush. After finding Hugo's booby traps along the way and seeing his use of dummy tripwires to slow a rescue party, MSgt. Brady had come to respect the talents of the FLQ explosive expert. Too many men had already been killed or hurt to think otherwise.

During a brief rest period, Brady came back to chat with SAC Stewart, "This man certainly knows what he's doing. When you think he might be out of explosives, he trips you up with a live tripwire. He uses C-4, grenades, and even a nasty punji stick leg trap the enemy used in Vietnam."

MSgt Brady examined the booby traps, "This guy has East German training, possibly Russian, and I'm betting he's been in the jungle before."

"You're right on, Sergeant, the man is a former East German soldier, now a mercenary who hires out for high fees," Stewart said.

Brady smiled, "Hey, that's an idea. Get my twenty in, go out as an independent contractor, and make big money, The wife would sure enough kill me for even thinking about such a job. She already has a tough time with what I do."

SAC Stewart laughed. "Yeah, the responsibilities of a married man can often outweigh one's adventurous spirit. But don't worry, some contractor firm will come looking for you as soon as you've wrapped up your Army time or possibly even the CIA. Somehow, they always know when the good ones are getting out of the service."

"Sure hope so; got college expenses for the kids, and retirement, although well appreciated, just doesn't stretch that far."

"When we get this operation wrapped up, I'll put some feelers out for you," Stewart said.

"Thanks. I'd appreciate that."

SAC Stewart walked over to where Niles, Loury, and Sir Whiteburn rested.

"You know, if the Chinese or Russians ever attack Alaska, I hope it's in the wintertime. I'd hate having to spend months fighting them and Alaska's wildlife —including these insects." Sgt. Niles said.

"From what I've heard, unless they nuke us, the only way for them to attack us is to come across the Bering Strait, which would have to be in the dead of winter. So, you may get your wish."

"Let's get back to our current operation and leave World War III for another time," Sir Whiteburn interjected.

"Right. Sorry about that," Niles replied.

"According to the National Guard, the terrorists haven't moved from their encampment about four miles south of here. We've got someone else on the move, staying parallel with us and slightly ahead. CP counts three warm bodies on thermal imagery that appear to be closing on our targets. They were moving pretty fast earlier, probably on four-wheelers." Stewart informed them.

"Any idea who they might be?" Sir Whiteburn looked at the others, who shook their heads. "More terrorists coming in to join the others? Odd we didn't hear their vehicles pass by."

"A lot of hunters have them set up special so they won't make a lot of noise in the woods and chase off game. My friend has one like that. You can be 100 yards away and never hear it." Niles looked up the mountainside, "They could have come up from the other side, or dropped down from a higher elevation. It could be hunters scouting for this season's moose hunt, even prospectors, It's rumored there's still a lot of gold in these mountains. Why they dropped off their ATVs has me wondering. But it does get pretty steep, and they may have gone as far as they could. Some prospectors believe there's a lot of gold up under those glaciers and they're withdrawing faster than usual. Still, that's mighty dangerous work."

SAC Stewart nodded, "I think we'll have to assume they could be terrorists. It might even be their rear guard. It's impossible to drop a team in on them, they're too close to our targets, and I don't want to lose another helicopter. We'll just have to let 'em join up. If they're bad guys, that'll make them about a 20 percent larger fighting force. We should be able to handle them if we can surprise them."

"I'm sorry those bears were killed, but that she bear did us a big favor by reducing the enemy's strength by three," Agent Loury said.

"Ghastly scene," Sir Whiteburn added. "Shooting those two cubs was cruel; it takes an evil man to do such a thing."

"After what this bunch has done, I can safely say they are very evil by any sane man's standard," Stewart said and walked back to where his radioman was sitting by a tree. "I want to know if and when those three question marks join up or encounter the terrorists. *Maybe they're glory boys, hoping to claim some sort of reward for rescuing the hostages, but I doubt it. It could still be hunters, prospectors, or people out exploring nature. Poor timing, though!*

RCMP Headquarters-Toronto - Major Crimes Section
June 17th, 11:25 A.M.

"Let me get this straight, sergeant. Colonel Augustus has authorized this special op, and you're here to draw 12 of my people for surveillance work. Am I right?" Captain Frederick Fowler, Commander of Major Crimes-Ontario Province, asked in a disgruntled voice.

"That's correct, Captain," Sgt Adler said. "And we need them as soon as possible. The Colonel wants our surveillance teams to shadow these people by late afternoon. I'm also taking personnel from White Collar Crime and the new Prevention and Anti-Crime Unit. This is top priority and has the Colonel's blessing."

"Look, I don't care about those other units, especially that new anti-crime unit the voters are so pleased with. I'm up to my eyeballs with three murder investigations, two rapes, and a bank robbery, much less the bombings and JP's tragic affair. Now, this has top priority?" Fowler slammed the top drawer of his desk closed and kicked his trashcan. Adler knew it wasn't the first time by far, from the number of dents on it. "How am I supposed to do my job if I've got my people doing yours?" Fowler growled. "Where's JP? Why isn't he here?"

Adler was reluctant to answer, but by the look on Fowler's face, he couldn't make matters worse by telling the truth, "On vacation. Colonel Augustus thought he needed time off before burning himself out."

"Great. Oh, I know JP lost his family, and he's got my sympathy. I've got probably three investigators ready to burn out, and one's about to toss his badge in the trash. He'll walk out on me before his wife gets fed up and leaves him. You know how this place works; Major Crimes is 24/7, and matrimony comes in a close second around here—maybe third or fourth."

"Captain, I'm only delivering orders. Don't shoot the messenger." Adler didn't want to mention this was all due to his investigation; he figured Fowler would probably want to shoot him. He showed Fowler the memo Augustus had Mrs. Wrightly type up for them. Sgt. Wilkens had made copies, gave them to Adler and took one copy, and searched for the hotshot prosecutor the Colonel told them about. This left Adler with the task of handling the manning problems. He sure hoped Wilkens had an easier time than he. By the angry look on

Fowler's face, puffy red complexion, and cold icy glare, he figured the man was about to explode.

Federal Court Building - 3rd Floor-Toronto - 11:25 A.M.

"Sgt. Wilkens, I appreciate the fact that this investigation has gained such a high profile, and there is cause for urgency, but I'm smack in the middle of trial prep for a murder. I'm talking about two months of work here," Jeffrey Townsend said as he sat behind his large ornate desk.

"Sir, Colonel Augustus said you're the best. He has a lot of confidence in you, and this investigation needs someone we can trust," Sgt. Wilkens said.

Townsend glanced over the letter from the Colonel, "By the look of things and these manpower requirements, there are going to be a lot of angry supervisors over at RCMP headquarters. You're pulling a lot of investigators for this one case, and I know everyone is feeling undermanned right now. We've got organized crime on the rise, with the Russian Mafia pushing hard. Violence is picking up throughout the eastern provinces. As the summer goes along, our caseload doubles and triples before the first snow sends all the rats back underground. I might also point out that the FLQ is not the only domestic terrorist group operating in Canada. We have Muslim fanatics moving in to stir up trouble and even a new Chinese influence that's got everyone curious. The list of violent nut bars is growing longer every month. I Wish we could put a bounty out on them, make things easier all around."

"Sir, you're preaching to the choir. I've worked the streets for years, and I know how bad it is out there. But I can't do all these search warrants affidavits by myself and then lose a case on some legal technicality I might have missed. We've got to have someone with us right from the starting point. Double checking our affidavits, preparing the search warrants and wire warrants, and covering our butts so these people don't get off on some technicality when the trial eventually comes. They helped kill over one hundred and fifty people, and I'm sure some of those Parliament office workers were your friends."

Townsend felt the blow to his gut, knowing Wilkens had sunk the three-point shot with that last remark. In fact, he had lost several friends in that bombing, including a first cousin who worked in the records department. Townsend looked up at the ceiling and exhaled. He could feel his blood pressure rising as he clutched the side of his desk. He knew it wasn't Sgt. Wilkens fault; the man was only a street cop, but an exceptional street cop. It finally boiled down to the fact that Townsend owed Colonel Augustus a lot. Not only had he saved his father's life years ago when a stakeout had gone badly, the

Colonel also helped Townsend land this prosecutor's job with the federal government. The man knew he'd never be able to look into his aunt's face again if he failed to act. She lost her oldest son the day the Parliament Building went up, and she would never forgive him for turning the assignment down. Especially if these criminals got off on some kind of legal technicality. Townsend pushed himself back from his desk, planted his feet, and stood up. He nodded with a mournful hangdog expression on his face. The same expression he often used in court to mess with an uncooperative witness.

Wilkens suspected Townsend had been in his office all night from the stubble on his chin, most likely preparing for the upcoming trial. A couple dozen file folders were piled high on his desk, and his yellow legal pad was covered in scribbled notes. A white ceramic coffee mug was half full of cold coffee, and a partially eaten deli sandwich was beside his phone.

Townsend shared a near-exhausted 44-year-old married paralegal with two other government prosecutors. He occasionally had the services of a Chinese Canadian law student in her second year of law school. Outside his office was a small lobby, which Townsend shared with two other lawyers. The 57-year-old receptionist sat behind her government-issued desk typing at 65 words per minute with very few mistakes when plied with chocolate-covered raspberry jelly doughnuts and the occasional kind word. At times like this, Townsend wondered if working in the civilian market would be easier on his nerves.

"Okay, I'll talk to my boss, who'll probably call Colonel Augustus to verify the urgent need. If my boss gives the okay, I'll pass my cases on to another over-worked prosecutor, who will hate my guts and utter foul words about me during the next Christmas party." Townsend looked at his watch. "I'll be at your office as soon as possible to review your documents. Please, have it in some form of order." He gave Wilkens a guarded look and sighed, "I sincerely hope this is all worth it, Sgt. Wilkens."

"As you said, the FLQ has killed many innocent people here in Toronto and Alaska. We've discovered that these are not card-carrying Quebec freedom fighters. They're your basic lowlifes; murder for hire using fear of terrorism to cover a major scheme to defraud both the provincial and federal governments. We're talking about millions of dollars and some very influential people. In my book, the people who support this—who hope to benefit from these actions, are worse than the criminals they hired. They're gutter slime of the lowest order. We need to find all of them and identify any government employees who might have helped them."

"I only hope we can, Sergeant."

1-Mile North And .2 Miles West Of The FLQ Encampment
June 17th, 12:50 P.M.


Tony knelt behind a large deadfall of dried graying spruce and used a small pair of 10x50 binoculars to do a 360-degree search. Unable to hear the terrorists or the good guys in the distance, he could almost feel the FBI rescue party closing in from behind. Tony knew the FBI was still a mile or two back moving cautiously. He imagined they feared spooking the terrorists and getting the hostages killed. They were well within an easy 45-minute hike to one of Jake's old trapper cabins. He had last been there two winters ago and found the cabin in need of repair. Part of the roof had collapsed from a heavy snow load. He spent two days doing what repairs he could, not wanting to see a structure his old friend had labored so hard on be destroyed. Besides, there was always the chance that Tony might need to use it if he returned to this area to trap. The cabin brought back memories of all the time he and Jake had spent here as the old man taught Tony the fine art of trapping and surviving Alaskan winters.

Greg took his pack off and knelt down beside Tony. JP did the same, more than happy to be rid of the painful pack straps and the load off his back. Even with the lighter load, the straps cut into his bruised shoulders. JP admitted that he was paying for all those months of sitting behind a desk with no exercise.

Tony took out his writing pad and filled them in on what he knew, and Greg read it aloud, "Take us 45 minutes, it'll be rough going to come in from the west. We leave everything here but weapons, water, first aid, and GPS."

"Can't we climb down to the trail they used?" JP Asked.

Tony shook his head and wrote; Greg read aloud, "You told me they were good with explosives. Too easy to leave traps for police. You follow me. We stop 100 yards from the cabin to look and make our final plan."

"Well, it sounds good to me," JP replied.

Greg decided to eat something quick and make a last nature call while JP rechecked his weapons.

Tony started to put the binoculars back into their case but decided to take them with him and left them hanging around his neck by a leather string. He was in need of some pain medication, so he removed two Codeine #3 tablets from a plastic baggie he kept in an outer vest pocket and washed them down with a sip of water. He hated using pain meds at a time like this but knew he wouldn't be in any shape to help Greg and JP without something to take the edge off. The others were ready, so again, taking the lead, Tony headed down the ridgeline, with the other two men following close behind. Greg, shotgun gripped in one hand, and rifle slung over his shoulder, brought up the rear.

All three men knew they could be alive or wounded or cold stone dead before the day was over. Greg and JP felt a sense of exhilaration as they drew closer to their prey. Tony felt neither anxiety nor a rush but did wonder how God was planning to deal the cards. For reasons he couldn't understand, God had placed these two men in his hands and given him dreams to show him he was part of the events that involved them.

As he moved closer to the unfolding scene, Tony recalled the moments on that fateful day in Vietnam. He felt the Huey shudder as enemy rounds struck deep into the bird's soul, he heard the cry of alarm from the men with him. Up front, the co-pilot screamed, "Mayday-Mayday! We're goin' down!" The helicopter dropped, and for several seconds terror caused him to stop breathing as he gripped the seat belt and the shoulder of the man sitting beside him. He nearly bit his tongue off from the terrifying series of jolts when the helicopter started smashing sideways through the treetops. At first, he thought they would be stuck in the trees, but the weight and motion of the helicopter carried the dying bird through the thick canopy of growth. One pilot screamed then stopped abruptly when he was impaled by a large broken branch. Tony lost consciousness when the helicopter impacted the ground. When he awakened, he was in intense pain. His legs were broken, something was wrong with his vision; his head felt like it was in a tight vice, and his face burned. Then he heard Vietnamese voices in the distance drawing closer. He prayed so hard for God to save him and the others with him but realized that all around him lay dead and mangled bodies.

Tony heard a quiet whimper and spotted one live person nearby. The man was semi-conscious and bleeding profusely from his many injuries. Through somewhat blurred vision, he saw someone coming out of the trees and as the man came closer, Tony knew from his clothes he was the enemy. The soldier carried an AK-47. Tony knew the man would kill him and the wounded man beside him. He had seen captured NVAs before and was shown what an AK-47 looked like and what it could do to the human body. A second and a third man came out of the trees and cautiously approached the wreck. Tony, an Army Chaplain, realized he was smack in the middle of an enemy patrol. He clutched the small silver cross attached to his dog tag chain and whispered a prayer. The enemy came closer, one careful step at a time, until Tony saw eight of them in a loose line. His depth perception was screwed up a bit, he figured due to his headache which had grown quite painful. The shock was wearing off, and the leg pain reached a point where he wanted to scream, but something was wrong with his jaw; he could barely open his mouth. Gradually, he pulled himself closer to the wounded man. But there was nothing he could do for him other than pray and with the enemy so close, prayers were silent for fear they might hear.

At first, the nightmare terrorized him a couple of times a day, later an occasional once a week. Gradually it was only when something reminded him of Vietnam that he would see the faces of his enemy again. Many years later, they were still clear—sweaty oriental faces, mostly kids in their mid-twenties or younger. An older officer issued orders in a stern, commanding tone, pointing at the helicopter. They must have thought it might explode from their reluctance to obey. It was a troubling thought that had also raced through Tony's mind. Not that he could go anywhere in his condition. He expected teeth-grinding pain would probably render him unconscious soon enough. He fought it off, not wanting to give up with the enemy so close and especially not with the wounded man he felt responsible for at his side. He reached out and felt around for something to defend himself with. He'd heard how the enemy treated wounded American soldiers, often torturing them in devious ways and finally killing them.

His fingers located the crew chief's M-16, loaded with a 30-round magazine called a banana clip. Tony pulled the rifle to him. He had only fired an M-16 once, shooting a dozen rounds through it to see how the weapon worked. Chaplains didn't carry weapons, even in war zones. An officer took him and a couple other chaplains to the range to fire a few rounds for the experience. "Look, Gentlemen, out in the jungle, you're just another American. The Viet Cong rarely takes prisoners, nor does the NVA. You need to know how to use this rifle, and I'm here to teach you."

Tony slowly pulled the rifle to his chest and pushed the small selector lever from semi-fire to full auto, and waited. He would have only one chance to catch the enemy by surprise. If he remained motionless and make them think everyone was dead, they would come closer to search the bodies. Only a ridge of dirt in the jungle floor, caused by the wreck, protected him from view. He hoped they didn't see him before he was ready to make his move. Every muscle and bone in his body wanted to cry out as he shifted position for better concealment. He kept his body between the wounded man and the enemy. He knew they wouldn't last very long once the bullets began flying.

His moral sense was not giving him any beefs; he knew it was either them or him and the wounded soldier. Tony was pretty sure it was the patrol that had shot down their helicopter, killing his traveling partners and the helicopter's crew.

His face burned as if it was on fire, and not crying out was nearly impossible. If not for the wounded man, Tony was sure he would've announced himself to the enemy with screams of pain. He remained silent, enduring the fiery pain that ravaged his body. When he knew he didn't have any more time, Tony rolled to his right side, cringed as he fought against the pain, and brought his rifle up to shoot from a prone position. He tried to make himself as small a target as possible. The butt was snug against his right shoulder; trembling from pain or fear, he pulled the trigger. Everything flashed brightly in front of him as the M-16 seemed to dance in his hands. He swept the barrel from left to right and back again as he continued to fire. He knew he was screaming, but he only heard the rifle discharging. He saw the men fall before him and the shock on their faces. The enemy reacted like a small wave of fans from a football game. Many threw their arms up before toppling backward with frightful looks of surprise on their faces. One man, whom he thought was the sergeant or an officer, dropped to his knees and fired his rifle.

Tony couldn't hear the AK-47s or the bullets impacting all around him, but he felt the pain when his right shoulder was hit. Thrown back from the impact, he dropped his rifle. He had been shot. A hot spike was driven through his body, and his whole right side burned. Something in him gave him supernatural strength to control the pain enough to sit up slightly, pick up the rifle again, and continue shooting using his left hand. His shots began to climb without the other hand to steady the barrel. He couldn't prevent it from happening, though he tried to stop it by slowing his rate of fire with shorter bursts. A bullet zinged by his ear, and a third missed his left foot by inches. His body screamed out in burning pain, but he couldn't stop shooting. He knew that to stop was to welcome death, and he couldn't abandon the other soldier to horrific torture. That one thought kept him going, driving him on. He needed to find some form of cover. However, before Tony could drag himself in any direction, a bright flash filled his vision, and he felt a piercing bolt of fire surge through his face and head. In microseconds and before the blackness carried him away, he saw the last enemy soldier fall only a few yards away. Later Tony learned he had emptied his rifle with that final round.

Tony couldn't remember what happened between the firefight and waking up inside Danang's 95th Field Evac Hospital. He was in an open ward filled with busy nurses going between beds filled with casualties. He wasn't in severe pain, but with all the IV lines running into his body, he knew it was due to the drugs they were pumping into him. His vision remained blurry, he couldn't move his arms and hands. A nurse checked on him and told him of his many wounds. "You were shot twice, Captain, both bullets were removed, and you have two broken legs. You were in surgery for nearly 11 hours. You have a large bandage on the side of your face, so your vision will be slightly off for a while. The doctors believe you'll be fine, but additional surgeries may be needed in Hawaii or back in the States. A major battle is underway, and we're getting many wounded. But you're going home, Sir. I'll check on you again in a few minutes; now, try to sleep." She checked his IV and moved on to the next patient.

Tony strained to look down, and though he was covered in a white sheet, he knew his legs were in casts all the way up to his hips. He passed out. When he regained consciousness, an older nurse with a major's gold leaves on her uniform came over. "Good morning, Chaplain," she said. "You had us pretty worried there for a while. Another two days here and you'll be on your way to Hawaii."

"What about the man with me?"

"He survived and from what I've been told, he's alive because of you and what you did out there. It would seem the Good Lord was watching over both of you."

"Lord… God… No, He abandoned me, and I had to kill all—" Tony's mind began to fog, and the nurse injected something into his IV line.

"You rest now, Chaplain."

*Rest? After what I did!* Tony glanced up at the Alaskan sky and then at the men he had led out here. He was glad to be with men such as these two; he felt their courage and desire to do what was right, but he also felt their desire for revenge. He looked ahead and wondered, m*aybe this is the day I die. I can almost sense their eyes on me, those eight men I killed—I can feel their hatred. Those men are up there waiting, wanting to welcome me to Hell and pay for what I did so many years ago.* He turned around and looked at Greg and JP. *Why you two? What God, why have you brought these two men into my life? What have they done to deserve my fate?* He looked upward between the branches of the taller trees in his search for God. *Yeah, I ask the questions, and you ignore me as usual. Did I really think this would be any different from before? Okay, God, bring it on! Bring it ON!*

18

CONFRONTATION

1.3 Miles North of The FLQ Encampment
June 17th, 1:43 p.m.

Special Agent (SAC) Stewart's radio officer, Agent Tom Sharp, contacted the command post in Cantwell for an update. The drones had been withdrawn so as not to alarm the terrorists. A Black Hawk flying at approximately 3,000 feet to the north kept an overview of the rescue parties. Stewart walked over to where a fatigued Sgt. Niles, Sir Whiteburn, and Agent Loury sat on the ground beside a tree. They shared a bag of store-bought trail mix, and Loury watched as Niles threw away the raisins.

Asked about it, Niles complained, "I really hate raisins. They always put them in these prepared trail mixes. Don't people realize they're just dead grapes that dropped off some vine? They're nipped at by some bird, crapped on by nasty lookin' bugs, and then left to rot until some underpaid illegal alien working below minimum wage from Central America rakes them up for some rich farmer in California."

"I don't think they do it that way anymore. Not too sanitary. But it sounds like you have a raisin issue, Sgt. Niles," Agent Stewart said. "I hate to interrupt your lunch, Gentlemen, but I've got the latest update from our eyes in the sky and thought you might be interested."

"Yes, we would be," Sir Whiteburn said.

"The FLQ hasn't budged, but what's interesting is that the second group of three people has failed to join them. They remain stationary about 100 yards west of the FLQ, at a higher elevation. One of the illuminated FLQ targets suddenly went cold and vanished from the scope. We think one of them has died. Could've been a victim of the bear attack. Command believes the other three people might be observing the terrorists, but why remains a mystery. It could be they're wondering who they are, and after hearing all the shots, are afraid to approach. Again, a lot of questions and no answers, yet."

"They might be terrorists, positioned as a blocking force from the west," Agent Loury offered, then shook his head. "That doesn't make a whole lot of sense. If they wanted to position a blocking force, they'd place them on the trail to keep us from reaching them and give enough advance notice so they could kill our VIPS and make a run for it. If they split up, we'd have difficulty scooping them up."

"Well, those three could still be hikers—locals. Our mountains are full of summer hikers. They may have spotted the FLQ, seen their weapons, and are staying back," Sgt. Niles said.

"This news makes me feel really uncomfortable," Stewart shook his head in frustration. "We can't engage the FLQ with innocent citizens in the way. We've got to reach them, identify them, and if they're non-combatants, get them out before the shooting starts. If they're with the FLQ, we could set off a hornet's nest that gets our VIPS killed."

"I can send Agent Loury forward. He has some experience tromping through the woods unseen," Sir Whiteburn offered.

With a strained look of acceptance on his face that said, *Thanks, Boss, I love being volunteered without asking,* Agent Loury nodded.

"No, not yet," Stewart replied. "I'll send my two agents up for a look-see. They love this kind of work; eat snakes, sleep in mud, and pound their chests like a couple of silver-backed gorillas. My only problem is keeping them from taking scalps."

"Well, if they need company… " Agent Loury offered. Sgt. Niles could tell he wasn't serious by his tone, and Sir Whiteburn also noticed it.

"I'll keep you advised. We'll be moving out again in five minutes." Stewart walked off to talk with one of his teammates.

Sir Whiteburn stood up and addressed Agent Loury, "I must say that your lack of enthusiasm concerns me. Our Prime Minister is out there in the hands of dangerous people. Our sworn duty is to risk our lives to protect him from any harm at all costs." Sir Whiteburn gave Loury a stern look and walked off for a nature call.

Loury put his right hand over his eyes, leaned back against the tree, and sighed. At times like these, he wished he'd taken his mother's advice and become a dentist.

"What was that all about?" Sgt. Niles asked. He closed the baggie of trail mix and placed it in his daypack. A significant number of raisins lay scattered about him, and he knew the squirrels would love it.

"I left the army because I acquired an extreme dislike for slithering across the ground like a snake and sneaking up on people who were usually armed with superior firepower. The days of pounding my chest are long over—it's a young man's game, and those two kids can have it."

"You were Special Forces, right?"

"Yeah, our version of your Green Beret and British SAS," Loury said. "I spent time in your John F. Kennedy Special Forces Training Camp and made many good friends, far too many of whom are dead. After several years of doing that, I just got fed up and left the military." Agent Loury pulled at his borrowed uniform. "I *liked* coming to work wearing a suit and tie. I enjoyed staying in nice hotels and flying around the world in very nice airplanes. Now, look at me! I'm back in the woods, wearing combat gear—it's as if I never left, and Sir White-burn wants to volunteer me for recon duty."

"So, this isn't a fear thing?" Sgt. Niles asked, with a bit of a grimace, remembering Agent Loury was armed. "I mean, you haven't gotten so relaxed in that three-piece suit that you don't want to get down and dirty again?"

Loury laughed. "That's just it, I hate getting dirty again. I'm tired of getting my mouth full of whatever I'm slithering through, or my eyes gouged with twigs. Whoever goes to check on that other group will be doing it on his belly, and I don't want it to be me! If Sir Whiteburn orders it, I'll go, but I hate volunteering for anything that makes me filthy. I guess you Americans call it PTSD. I've had my belly full of that crap. When the shooting does start, I'll be right there in the thick of it. Too many good people have died because of this bunch, and I hope to help take them down."

"You have a weird way of looking at things, Tod."

"Look, I once spent five days crawling through Iraqi sewers, and if you ever tell anyone, I'll have to kill you. Do you have any idea how bad their sewers are? I mean, really! Or how long it took to get that stink out of my nose."

"Hey, I don't even like to pick up dog poop," Niles replied.

Loury shook his head in disgust, recalling those five days of utter misery. "When we get out of here, I'm going to spend several hours in a hot shower. After which, I will douse my magnificent body with a pint of cologne." Loury looked up as Sir Whiteburn returned. "But first, I've got to get back in the good graces of my boss again."

"Tell him the truth."

"You don't understand it; how would he?"

"Yeah, you're right. You'll probably have to take a bullet before Sir Jonathan smiles your way again. He's one tough dude."

"Tell me about it." Agent Loury shrugged, pulled out his canteen, and took a sip. "The man took a bullet for the Queen; how do you stand up to that kind of thing?"

100-Yards West Of The FLQ Encampment

Too close to chance a whisper, the three men used Tony's notepad and pen to converse with each other. For the last 50 yards, they low-crawled to a position above the FLQ's encampment. Heavy brush concealed their approach, but they were within range to launch their attack. Jake's old cabin was set in a small clearing of mostly flat rock, hardened dirt, and loose gravel. The open area was between 20 and 30 feet in a 360-degree circle. A bluff overlooking a creek was southeast of the cabin. Tony had always thought it was a choice piece of real estate for a cabin; it was probably the only flat spot of this size in the whole canyon.

Jake's old trapping trail was south of the cabin, gradually following down through a clump of bushes between a stand of aged spruce trees. Spruce beetles had killed many of the trees but there was still a large stand of flourishing alder. There was another sheer drop-off of nearly 100 feet or more behind the cabin. Below this drop-off were piles of granite, which extended down to the bottom of a gorge, where a rushing river could be seen from the cliff's edge. North of the cabin was the moose trail the FLQ had come down on; more pronounced now after being used; branches were broken, and brush stamped down. One of them had dropped a Baby Ruth candy wrapper.

Greg was the first to write what he wanted to say to Tony, "You've done your part. Sit back and cover our retreat if we need it."

Concealed behind a grouping of large man-sized boulders several yards or more above the FLQ position, Tony replied with a determined shake of his head. He grabbed the writing pad and pen from Greg's hand. "I'm in this all the way! Tell me where you want me."

Greg hesitated and looked at JP, who nodded and placed his hand on Tony's in a display of acceptance. Greg reached over and put his right hand on top of JP's, signifying the three of them were in this together, come what may. Smiling briefly, Greg pulled his hand away and took the pad and pen back from Tony, but instead of writing, he whispered, "Wait, I wanna take a look."

He borrowed the binoculars from Tony and used natural cover to conceal his approach. He moved to the right a few feet and studied the hillside below. Greg wanted to see what was happening around the cabin. From this viewpoint, he couldn't see inside the old cabin, but he did spot what appeared to be a new grave beside the structure. He wondered, *who was dead, Hostage or terrorist.* Greg counted five armed men standing or sitting outside the cabin and two older, unarmed men. He recognized one as Governor Hughes, but he wasn't so sure about the Prime Minister. Greg had only seen him once before, but it was a good bet by the man's bedraggled condition that he was the second man. One terrorist sat beside the Prime Minister; another was conversing with Governor Hughes.

Greg couldn't be sure who might be inside and wondered if that was where Senator Sterns was. He examined the terrain and saw they would have pretty good natural cover as they made their way down the hillside. As long as they didn't make any noise or start any small avalanches, Greg felt they could get close enough to make their attack and catch the people by surprise. He pulled back in behind the boulder, wrote down what he saw, and made a small diagram to pinpoint where the terrorists were. When he returned, Greg gave Tony his binoculars and handed the pad to JP, asking for his view on what they should do next.

JP gestured for the binoculars and belly-crawled down beside the boulder, so he could make his own observations. He first checked to see where the sun was; he didn't want any reflection coming off the binocular lens. When he returned, JP checked his weapons one last time. Greg and Tony did the same. They had already chambered a round and ensured they had put extra ammo into shirt pockets. Loose rifle ammo went into Greg's left pocket while a handgun magazine was slid into the right pocket. JP had two extra magazines for the AR-15 and his pistol.

Tony wiped sweat from his brow on his arm sleeve. He wished this whole thing was over so he could return to everyday life. He had established a routine; a safe, regular pattern that lacked outside interference and almost no danger of getting his head blown off. Bears weren't a problem as long as he was careful. Terrorists with automatic weapons were another matter. This would definitely be his last venture as a bounty hunter/rescuer.

JP took the pad and pen to write and showed the pad to both men. "We need a three-point semi-circle above their position, so we don't shoot one another. I'll go to the right, using that stand of spruce as cover, missing you with my crossing fire." JP pointed to where he meant, making sure they understood.

Tony looked at the pad to see where JP wanted him. *I'm to stay on this side of the cabin to ensure no one escapes up the hill or back up the trail.*

JP pointed to the next part of his suggested instructions for Greg; *I'll come down from the north end, coming out from behind the cabin. I'll make sure the cabin is empty. If someone is in it, I'll hold off firing until someone opens the show."*

Greg looked over JP's plan again and nodded to say he agreed with it. He took the pad back and wrote, "We can't give them any chance! They're killers! Only shoot the younger men. Governor Hughes and Prime Minister Haegens are the two older men in filthy dress clothes. Unsure where Senator Sterns is—probably inside the cabin. If I open fire first, and the cabin is empty, I'll shoot the man beside the Prime Minister. Soon as he's down, I'll yell out for the hostages to lie down and not move. If I cannot fire, it's because someone is in the cabin," Greg pointed to JP. "As soon as I'm in position, give me a slow count of 10 seconds to ensure I'm unable to shoot first, then fire and take out the man by the Prime Minister."

Greg pointed at Tony and wrote, "You shoot the guy closest to you by the cliff. He's a long-haired blonde with an AK-47. Shoot him more than once, three times, to make sure he's down. Don't need a wounded man shooting the hostages."

JP studied the terrain below and saw the best way for him to low crawl down the hillside to avoid detection. He looked back at Greg, smiled, and offered his hand. After shaking Tony's hand, he was on the move.

Greg nodded a couple times and patted Tony on the shoulder then moved in close to whisper, "Thanks!" He crawled down the hill to a large dead spruce tree lying across a small ridge adjacent to the encampment only a few yards from the cabin. It offered him maximum protection and a good field of fire.

***

Hugo rubbed his broad forehead with his left hand to fight off a growing headache. He decided it was time to arrange for the Prime Minister's escape. Hugo held his MP5 machine gun with a thirty-round magazine in his hands as he walked over to Governor Hughes and Michael. He gestured with his weapon for Governor Hughes to get on his feet. "Need water. You and him," Hugo said in blunt English and pointed to where Prime Minister Haegens sat against the trunk of a large spruce tree. "You two, grab empty canteens… get water!"

Governor Hughes looked from Hugo to the semi-conscious Prime Minister and hesitantly replied, "All right, but the Prime Minister is in no shape to be hiking down the hill and back up again. Can't I take Michael with me? I'll carry the water, and he can guard me."

Hugo looked at Michael for a long moment, "Michael, you go with them too.

Keep watch. But he goes too." Hugo gestured again with his MP5, pointing it at the Prime Minister.

"Sure," Michael replied, "Whatever you want, Hugo."

Michael was tired. The stream was a couple-hundred-yard hike to the south, and he'd have to help the Governor and the Prime Minister up and down the hill, which meant he'd be carrying the water too. "Can't I take Greg or Louis with me?"

"No," Hugo said abruptly and walked over to pull the weakened Prime Minister to his feet with a sudden yank of the arm. The man fell at Hugo's feet, and Governor Hughes rushed over to help him. It was dangerous to provoke the German, however, he gave Hugo one of his better scowls for the Prime Minister's violent treatment.

"He's in bad shape. You don't have to be so rough with him."

The Prime Minister was unsteady on his feet; his complexion, pale white. From the man's looks, Hugo didn't think he could survive another night out here and still make it out. If this was going to work, Hugo needed the Prime Minister in the hands of a rescue party before the man keeled over and died. Using the Governor was the only way his plan could succeed, but he was running short of time. Sooner and not later, the authorities would make their move, and he needed to be gone when that happened. Hugo figured that with only Michael escorting the two men down the trail, he could sneak up behind Michael, slice his throat, and disappear back into the brush before Hughes or Haegens spotted him. Without a guard, the Governor would help Haegens to the tracks, and within a few miles, they would most likely stumble upon someone to help them.

Hugo assumed the cops and military had people staked out in Curry and were probably moving north. He knew another group was coming down from the north and not too far off. Several explosions alerted him to that fact, echoing off the canyon walls. The last of his booby traps had caught someone unaware, reducing the number of good guys who might pursue him into the bush country during his own escape.

Once the Prime Minister was on his way, Hugo planned to vanish into the wilderness. He had his GPS, and his pockets were full of beef jerky, vitamins, and several granola bars. Water wouldn't be a problem with so many creeks and rivers. He also carried two extra-large magazines for his MP5. By midnight Hugo felt he could be ten miles from here, and hopefully, the cops would have killed or taken prisoner the remaining members of the FLQ. If no one talked, he could be free and clear to live off the land for a week or so and then make his way to the highway. In his outer shirt's upper breast pocket, was a forged

Argentina passport and an international driver's license issued from the same country to a new alias. Both pieces of identification had cost him $2,000. Back on the highway, Hugo would be no more, replaced by Herr Hansel Dorschman on his way to Whitehorse, Yukon Territory. He planned to catch a flight from there to Vancouver, British Columbia, and disappear entirely. Hugo picked up the canteens and was handing them to Michael when the first shot was fired.

Shawn, who'd been pouting about pulling guard duty instead of catching some sleep, was leaning back against a tree gazing down into the canyon below when Greg's first round hit him between the shoulder blades. He was killed instantly and dropped to the ground.

Greg yelled out twice, "Hostages on the ground! Don't move! Hostages on the ground! Don't move!" He shot Shawn a second time to ensure the man stayed down. The second AR-15 bullet entered Shawn's chin and exited through the back of his head. Greg acted because he saw that one of the terrorists was moving the hostages. After he fired the first shot, Tony, who already had his crosshairs in the middle of Greg Landis' chest, pulled the trigger. His bullet struck a startled Greg Landis and sent him over a 20-foot drop. Tony wouldn't have to worry about a second shot. Landis landed hard on top of a deadfall and broke both his back and pelvis. His lifeless eyes stared off into the distance while the shooting continued above.

JP didn't have a shot yet, but he, too, had seen Hugo addressing the hostages and jerking the Prime Minister around. The going was slow, and JP was just making his way down behind the cabin when the shooting started. He was surprised to see a figure lying prone under a blanket with feet exposed and saw whoever it was had been tied up. He thought it was probably Senator Sterns, but it was dark inside the cabin, and the prone figure lay in the shadows.

Hugo dropped to the ground when the first shot was fired relying on training and instinct. He rolled down the hill several feet and dove under a rock abutment protected from shots from above and waited for a target.

Louis fired a long burst toward movement he'd seen and ran for the cabin and the Stinger. He didn't make it. Tony's next shot caught him in the side, piercing his chest cavity, and Louis dropped without a sound. Tony thought of a second shot but saw no need. Louis wasn't breathing.

Prime Minister Haegens curled up in a fetal position on the ground, trembling and pleading like a lost child for someone to come save him. Governor Hughes started to rise but seeing him, Michael dropped his weapon and dove on top of him. "Don't move! Not until this is over!"

Seeing the man lying on top of Governor Hughes, Greg knew he couldn't chance a shot, and saw that the terrorist was unarmed. *It looks like the guy is trying to protect the Governor. What's going on here? Do we have an undercover officer working with this bunch? Can't shoot him until I know for sure.*

Gordi, who'd been asleep on his sleeping bag in front of the cabin, opened his eyes and sat up when the first shot was fired. He shook his head to clear the cobwebs and reached for his M-16 just as JP came around the corner of the cabin's north wall. When the stranger appeared with a gun pointed at him, Gordi's eyes grow wide with fright. JP shot him in the middle of the chest. Gordi was dead.

JP kept moving, surprised when Hugo, his MP5 on full auto, rose above the embankment and swept the face of the cabin with auto fire. Two 9mm bullets struck JP in the side and left shoulder driving him to the ground. He released an animal-like growl of rage and pain and dropped his rifle as he fell.

Believing JP was down, Hugo raked the downed trees after seeing one of the other shooters use it for cover. Greg ducked down as wood splintered above him. He wasn't hit but took a handful of wood splinters in his hand.

Seeing JP down and Greg unable to shoot, Tony hobbled over to the next tree to get a shot off at Hugo. His right leg froze from too much physical abuse, and he barely made it behind the tree before Hugo splintered the front of it with a short burst.

Half-A-Mile North Of The FLQ Encampment - Same Time

Hearing the firefight erupt down the trail, SAC Stewart had no time to send out his planned scouting party. He ordered the EOD personnel back, disappointing MSgt Brady, and sent his first two agents ahead. The rest of the party followed at a quick pace. Had there been any booby traps, SAC Stewart would have been responsible for killing most of his team. His primary concern was saving three dignitaries from what sounded like a war zone. Thankfully, Hugo had run out of explosives and quit setting out fake traps; only Stewart didn't know that when he sent his men ahead. The rest of the team followed.

Curry Townsite - Same Time

Corporal Williams feared the worst when he heard the shots echoing down through the canyon and quickly conferred with Sgt. Miller. After instructing Trooper Sheldon to hold the fort he proceeded across the tracks at a fast jog. Sgt. Miller and two Guardsmen with him.

FLQ Encampment

Blood ran down Greg's arm from the splinters in his shooting hand. He couldn't see anything from where he lay. As far as he knew, all the bad guys were down except for the one shooter on the embankment rim. Greg knew that JP was either wounded or killed, and he didn't know where Tony was or if he was still alive. Taking his Glock out of his shoulder holster, Greg pulled the receiver back to make sure a round was chambered and switched it over to his left hand. He wasn't as good a shot with his left hand, but he had little choice. He began inching toward the end of the log.

An eerie silence lay over the encampment; even the dreaded mosquitoes and flies had disappeared for the moment. But they'd be back. Too much blood had spilled for the little pests to stay gone long.

Haegens remained curled up whimpering like a small child; he was emotionally and physically drained. Michael stayed on top of Governor Hughes; an act of self-sacrifice that made Hugo snicker. He'd seen the discussions between the two men and knew Michael was too weak-minded to hold up his end as a militant. That's why he'd chosen him for the water detail. Hugo figured if Michael were taken prisoner, he'd be the one to talk. He wanted the extreme pleasure of cutting his throat before leaving this company of losers. Hugo wasn't sure what to do about Munroe and it didn't really matter at the moment. Munroe had lost it, anything he said would probably be taken as the ravings of a crazy man.

With his back against the rock, Hugo decided to take a chance and yelled, "You surrender; I don't kill Prime Minister. I give you one minute. If he move, he dies. You try a rescue, and he dies!" No one answered which angered him. He rose a few inches up over the rock abutment and fired a short burst that sent five bullets into the ground beside the cowering Prime Minister then quickly dropped down, "Next time, I kill… Do we have deal? You surrender; I leave you these men. Only two of you left—better talk now!"

Greg was glad Tony was still alive, figuring the terrorist had killed JP. He couldn't let the Prime Minister or the Governor die but surrendering to a person like this would mean almost certain death for all of them. His only hope lay in the chance that the rescue parties were closing in at this very moment.

"Time up!" Hugo yelled.

"Okay! Okay! Hold your horses!" Greg hollered and slowly stood up with his hands held high, his weapon in his left hand. He expected to be shot and was surprised he wasn't. "I'm putting my pistol down." Cautiously, he bent down and laid his pistol beside the butt of his rifle. "I'm unarmed now!"

"Other guy, too," Hugo said. He rose up and kept his weapon trained on Greg, most of his body hidden behind the rocky embankment.

"You heard him, go ahead and leave your rifle and revolver behind the tree and step out. It's a no-win situation." Greg hoped Tony would do it but was ready to dive for cover if Hugo began shooting.

With a lot of reluctance and in pain, Tony stepped out from behind the tree. His appearance surprised Hugo, seeing he was a one-eyed man. "Good, now walk to Governor."

Greg stepped around the end of the log he had used as a barrier and slowly moved down the hillside. As he approached, Michael stood to his feet and helped Governor Hughes stand. Hughes was astonished to see that his rescue party consisted of only three men; one believed dead, and another disabled from a long-ago injury.

"You," Hugo said to Michael, "Make sure no one has guns, knives, phones, or radios."

Without saying anything, Michael approached Greg with an almost mournful expression on his face. Greg was confused by Michael's actions; he figured the man would be smiling from ear to ear to have the upper hand. As he patted Greg down, Michael whispered, "I'm sorry, officer, I couldn't do anything to stop him." He pulled Greg's knife out of the sheath and dropped it to the ground then walked to where Tony stood, about 30 feet away, and patted him down. He was amazed that the man was wearing leg braces but didn't say anything to Hugo about it. He removed Tony's knife. "They're both unarmed, Hugo. No radios or cell phones, and I took their knives. Now what? Do we take off or what?"

"First, I kill one-eyed man, then I kill that one!" Hugo cautiously walked up the rise and began to point his black MP5 at Tony. Just as Greg started to shout, "No-o-o!" Michael suddenly jumped in front of Tony and was hit by three bullets in the chest.

Hugo laughed. He watched as Michael dropped to the ground and muttered, "Dummkopf!" in harsh German.

Governor Hughes saw Michael go down and began to move toward him, ignoring Hugo. but Hugo didn't care. In a moment, both of the cops, as he supposed they were, would be dead and Hugo would be on his way before other rescuers could arrive. If everything worked out right and he had the time, he would stop by the cabin and put two bullets in the back of Munroe's head.

Hugo began to apply pressure to the trigger again, aiming for a definite kill shot. Tony stood frozen awaiting his fate and felt a sense of relief pass over him.

Greg leaped back over the log to reclaim his weapon as he heard a gut-wrenching scream from above. Knife in hand, fueled by animal-like wrath, JP plowed into the startled Hugo. The German mercenary was just beginning to turn toward Greg when JP came from behind a tree and drove his knife blade deep into the top of the German's chest with all his remaining strength. Both men were propelled backward off the cliff. Joined together by the knife, they fell to the rocks below. When they came to rest, JP still had one hand on the knife handle, and his lifeless eyes glared into the dead German's surprised eyes. It would be several hours before the rescue party could reach them to recover their bodies.

Shocked by what he had seen, Greg slowly for his pistol and turned to ensure Tony was all right. Shaken by what had occurred, Tony waved a hand to signal he was okay and slowly made his way to the VIPs. After making sure all the terrorists were dead, Greg ventured over to stand by Tony. Seeing the two VIPs alive, Greg and Tony walked over to the bluff to look down on JP and Hugo. "He saved everyone in the end and had his revenge," Greg whispered.

The world would eventually know that Captain Jean-Paul Leon killed the man responsible for the Toronto bombings, the death of his family, and the destruction and death caused at the train. JP would be recognized in Canada and the United States as a hero.

Governor Hughes sat on the ground at Michael's side, holding the young man's head in his lap trying to stem the blood flow from Michael's wounds. He ripped his dress shirt off and applied direct pressure, b——ut there was too much blood; Michael was dying.

Stunned by why this man, a terrorist, had saved his life, Tony limped over and knelt down beside Michael. He looked into Michael's eyes and mumbled, "Why? Why'd you do that?"

Struggling to breathe, Michael opened his eyes and whispered, "God loves you, Anthony. He wants you to know that... always been with you." Michael's eyes closed; his chest became still.

The words startled Tony, he laid his hand on Michael's shoulder and whispered, "Thank you—" *He knew my name, he knew my difficulty with the Father. Oh, Lord, forgive me! You've used this man to let me know the truth.*

Governor Hughes wept over his fallen friend while Tony sat back, looked up to the heavens, and began to weep. A hardened shell cracked as he wept over the body of the man who had given the ultimate sacrifice. For the first time in a very long time, Tony began to feel a longing growing in his heart for the Father.

Greg glanced at Prime Minister Haegens and saw that except for being a quivering mass and totally worn out from exhaustion, the man appeared to be unhurt. Greg heard a noise from inside the cabin and walked toward it, expecting to find the Senator. He was surprised to find another man on the ground glaring at him with a wild look in his eyes. The man was chewing the silver tape over his mouth and struggling against his bonds. Until Greg knew otherwise, he would leave him that way. Greg looked at the Governor, who held the other terrorist in a caring embrace much the way someone would cradle a small child. Something had apparently happened between the two men; a relationship had formed between a terrorist and his hostage. Unlike the famous Stockholm Syndrome, where a hostage sympathizes with their captors, the terrorist had befriended his hostage. Close enough to sacrifice his life. Something had happened to Tony as well; he knelt in the dirt and appeared to be praying. "Are you hurt, Tony?"

Tony looked up and shook his head. He was okay, at least physically, but somehow, through God's mysterious ways, the Father had sent a message through the dying terrorist. The man had given his life for him only moments earlier. Greg sensed something powerful had transpired, but he'd have to give it more thought. He needed to ensure his VIPs were safe and find out what happened to the missing Senator.

SAC Stewart and his two lead agents broke into the small clearing, their weapons pointed first at Greg and then at everyone. Sgt Miller and his two men stepped into the clearing from the opposite side. Their rifles pointed directly at Greg. "Drop your weapon now! On your stomach, hands held out wide, and your fingers open," Stewart shouted.

Greg didn't hesitate; he knew who these people were and didn't want to be shot by mistake. He dropped his Glock to the ground and followed, going spread-eagled on the dirt as ordered.

Tony wasn't armed, but he was an unknown and too close to the governor. Stewart rushed over, put his weapon in Tony's ear, and ordered him flat on his belly. By this time, Sgt. Niles, Agent Loury, and Sir Whiteburn arrived with the rest of the team close behind. A moment later, out of shape, huffing and puffing to keep up, MSgt Brady joined the group, trailed by his two officers.

Sir Whiteburn rushed past Stewart and went to Prime Minister Haegens' side. Seeing his poor shape, Whiteburn comforted him with words of reassurance that it was all over. Agent Loury handed a canteen to Sir Whiteburn who began washing the dirt from Haegens' face and hands.

Seeing that the Governor was uninjured, Sgt. Niles knelt beside him and asked if he could do anything for him.

"Do you have a blanket, John? I'd like to cover this boy up; he saved us—I need a blanket."

"Yes, sir," Sgt. Niles looked around the encampment for a suitable covering, found one of the sleeping bags outside the cabin, and used it to cover Michael's body. He glanced at one of the prisoners and recognized Greg. Leaving the Governor, he walked over, and in a tone of surprise, asked, "Greg, is that you?"

"Hey, Niles," Greg said from the ground, "Would you ask this nice man to let me up, we've got a lot of explaining to do, and it's kinda hard to do it from down here with my face in the dirt."

"Niles, you know this man?" Stewart asked, gesturing with a nod for his man to let Greg up.

"Yes, Sir. This is Greg Hansen, railroad special agent from Fairbanks and a former lieutenant with the Alaska State Troopers." Niles looked at Greg as the man rose to his feet and brushed himself off. "Greg, what are you doing out here?"

"First, this is Tony Rogers, a guide from Cantwell. Over that cliff," Greg pointed. "you'll find our third man. He gave his life to save us and killed the German down there with him. RCMP Captain JP Leon. The FLQ firebombed his house and killed his family in Toronto; he wanted payback, and I'd say he got it!"

Hearing that name, Sir Whiteburn jumped to his feet and abandoned the shaken Prime Minister. Jonathan rushed over to see JP's body below the embankment and knelt as tears welled up. "Oh, JP—you had to do it your own way—didn't you?" Jonathan reached out and tossed a two-finger pinch of soft dirt over the cliff. "I'll miss you, my old friend. You're with your family now. Thank you for what you did here." Whiteburn rose to his feet, saluted his friend, and slowly returned to the PM.

EOD personnel checked out the area for explosives and found the remaining Stinger and extra missiles. The FBI Hostage Team gathered up all the weapons. Unable to land because of trees, a Blackhawk hovered overhead and dropped a box of black body bags. A National Guard medic was lowered and after ensuring the Prime Minister was unharmed except for a case of nerves, took him back up. Jonathan sent one of his agents with the Prime Minister. Other Black Hawks would soon be arriving, but Jonathan wanted the PM in a hospital immediately. When the helicopter landed at Fairbanks Memorial Hospital, a team of Canadian Secret Service and FBI agents were on scene to handle his protection. Governor Hughes opted to stick around accompanied by Sgt. Niles.

More Guardsmen, FBI agents, and State Troopers were lowered by other helicopters. Dozens of crime scene photos were taken. The governor identified Munroe and showed the officers where they had buried Senator Sterns. It took them over an hour to bring the bodies of Greg Landis, Hugo, and JP up from below the embankment. Photographs were taken of the dead bodies before they were moved. Crime scene people were part of the way in but had to hike to the cabin. They were busy for the rest of the day, photographing, collecting evidence, and diagramming the scene.

Dragged out of the cabin into the light, Munroe was identified as the man responsible for the cold-blooded killing of FBI Agent Woods and the shooting of Bob Rexault. Steve Munroe would be charged with many more murders and, of course, the kidnappings of Prime Minister Haegens, Governor Hughes, and Senator Sterns. The formal list of charges against the FLQ would take a couple of law clerks two days to type up. Courts from the two countries would have to decide who got to try Munroe first.

Guardsmen carefully dug up Senator Sterns' body, placed her into a body bag, and kept her separated from the terrorist's bodies. The bodies were moved to a clearing a short distance away big enough to handle the Blackhawks. Before boarding the helicopter, SAC Stewart walked over to where Jonathan stood "You must have known this Captain Leon quite well?"

"Yes, we worked together a lot over the years. A courageous man who went out as a Mountie; boots on and a weapon in his hands."

"Must have been a hell of a man," Stewart said. "Once we get this all unraveled, you can tell me what a Toronto Intel Captain was doing in Alaska."

"I say, let's have a chat with this Greg fellow. I'm sure it will be most enlightening."

"After you, Sir Whiteburn."

Greg was getting his hand treated and bandaged by Sgt. Niles when Sir Jonathan and Sac Stewart appeared. "Can you give us a brief rundown, Agent Hansen? We can take your full statement later, back in Fairbanks."

Greg smiled and began a brief synopsis of what they'd done since leaving Fairbanks. He didn't mention Lt. Steve Farber but spoke in great detail about JP's courage and devotion to his country. He told them of Tony's refusal to stay out of it when Greg asked him to remain behind on the upper ridge. Of how Tony had helped free the Governor and Prime Minister. As to who shot whom, Greg said he'd rather have a lawyer present to make sure he didn't step over his tongue and land Tony and himself in jail.

SAC Stewart stood with a dumbfounded expression, "And I'm supposed to go back to my bosses in D.C. and tell them an Alaska Railroad Special Agent, an RCMP Captain on vacation, and a one-eyed Nam vet turned trapper, have accomplished what we'd been unable to do? I've got satellite coverage, Black Hawks, the best Hostage/Rescue Team in the world, and the Alaska Army National Guard at my disposal, and you three men take out the entire FLQ. They won't believe it. Better yet, I don't believe it, and I'm standing here to witness it." Stewart walked to where he could use his satellite phone to call the CP and brief them.

Sir Jonathan put his hand on Greg's shoulder, "I knew what caliber of man you were when I first met you in Anchorage. You didn't disappoint me. Thank you for saving my Prime Minister's life. Sometime, when you have a moment, you'll have to tell me about your talks with JP. He was a dear friend, and I'd be sincerely interested."

When Senator Sterns' body was placed inside the Black Hawk, an American flag was unfolded and draped over her. A military salute was given by the guardsmen present. A similar display was given to JP when a Canadian flag was carefully unfurled and draped over him. A salute by Alaska National Guardsmen was offered in recognition of his bravery and supreme sacrifice.

Greg and Tony insisted they be allowed to accompany JP's body down the hill to the clearing. Several times, Greg had to help Tony make the climb down. When they got to the tracks, Tony collapsed and had to be placed on a stretcher. After checking his vital signs, an Army medic began pumping fluids into him through an IV tube. Greg climbed into the helicopter to be with him. JP's body lay beside Tony's stretcher, and both Greg and Tony wept.

Munroe had to be lashed to a stretcher and shot full of sedatives; it was the only way to get him down the hill and into a helicopter. Before leaving to carry out his duties as Governor Hughes's bodyguard, Sgt. Niles favored just shooting him, but Stewart reluctantly vetoed that option.

Munroe managed to get his mouth free of the tape and bit one of the FBI agents in the arm. When Stewart wasn't looking, the agent backhanded Munroe and knocked him unconscious. He replaced the plumber's tape with white surgical tape, sticky stuff that he wrapped around Munroe's head. When they pulled the tape off, it would take a lot of hair with it. The agent had lost a couple of Canadian friends with the bombing of the Parliament Building and felt absolutely no compassion for the terrorist leader.

Crime scene geeks from the AST crime lab took photographs of Senator Sterns' former grave and the confiscated weapons. EOD personnel removed the Stinger missiles from the area. MSgt Brady received a hardy "Well done" from Sac Stewart before flying out. MSgt Brady had saved SAC Stewart several times by locating Hugo's traps and disarming them.

A Black Hawk set down near the scene where the terrorists were killed by the bear. Photographs of the scene, the bear, and the dead cubs were taken to be used as evidence in Munroe's trial. The bodies of the terrorists were placed into body bags and transported out. There were no honors or flags for them.

Greg and Tony had the GPS position where they left the ATVs and kept that quiet for the time. They'd go back later to recover them; Greg was already planning on taking his son along to handle JP's ATV.

Orders were eventually issued from the Command Post to remove the roadblocks from the Parks Highway. Within an hour of the notification, Cantwell, Sheep Creek, and the Parks returned to ordinary busy summer mode.

Governor Hughes was flown to Providence Hospital in Anchorage for a complete check. After one night, he returned to Juneau for several days off. Sgt Niles remained at the hospital with Governor Hughes and then returned to Juneau.

Steve Munroe was transported to Fairbanks Memorial, checked over by emergency room personnel, and placed in a cell on the hospital's third floor reserved for the mentally impaired. From cuffs and chains, he was placed into a straitjacket and secured to a hospital bed. He would later be found unfit to stand trial in Alaska and Canada and spent the rest of his life in a mental ward.

Tony Rogers was given a thorough check-up at Fairbanks Memorial and transferred to a hospital room for observation. He was dehydrated and needed some potent pain medications delivered by IV. A government-assigned private security guard was placed outside his room to keep nosey newshounds at bay.

A National Guard hangar at Ted Steven's Anchorage Airport was temporarily transformed into a morgue under heavy guard. Full-body bags were placed on an 8'x 4' sheet of plywood, supported by two sawhorses. The bodies of Senator Sterns, JP, and Michael were flown to Providence Hospital and held in their morgue. Alaska State Troopers were assigned as guards.

Greg was transported to Fairbanks Memorial and treated in the emergency room for injuries to his hand and fatigue. His boss, Donald, drove to Fairbanks and looked in on him like an upset but concerned parent. Afterward, with Donald, he was escorted by FBI personnel to the Fairbanks Federal Building. Under the advice of legal counsel, he made a complete statement for the record. He had the Governor's personal assurance that he wouldn't have any trouble with the law and that he and Tony would be honored for their duty to the State of Alaska.

Greg felt pretty bad when he found out from doctors the degree of discomfort Tony was in. His right leg would need to stay immobile for at least a week. He would be transferred to the Veterans Hospital in Anchorage for additional care. Tony would be on crutches for a time, as his braces needed to be replaced for healing to occur.

Sir Whiteburn, working with AST and the Anchorage Police Department, established perimeter patrols around the hospital and on the Prime Minister's floor. It was Sir Whiteburn's duty to notify his superiors that the Prime Minister was in no shape for travel. He requested his personal physician be flown to Anchorage immediately. "The Prime Minister has survived an unspeakable ordeal. We cannot let him be seen by news services at this time." Sir

Whiteburn withheld the fact that the PM was babbling like a small child and having problems controlling his bladder.

By midnight of the 17th, news services worldwide were carrying the rescue story. SAC Stewart tried to keep it quiet until the FBI spokesperson could be on hand to release the information. Governor Hughes insisted that the report be released immediately, at least in Alaska.

A somewhat somber Governor Hughes held his first interview with the press inside the National Guard hangar with two Blackhawks involved in the rescue as backdrops. After taking several questions, his closing remarks centered on the dead terrorists, "We citizens of Alaska will not now, or ever, bow before international or domestic terrorism. Nor will we cower like frightened schoolchildren from those who hope to use fear as a weapon against us. The dead terrorists in our morgue should demonstrate to the world our resolve not to give in to terrorists' demands of any kind. This is a warning to such people. You come to Alaska with evil intent, and you will surely die for your cause. Thank you."

In a call to his ex-wife, Greg learned his son was camping with a group of church kids on the Kenai Peninsula. He disconnected the phone cord from the wall and took a long hot shower thinking about JP and the events that transpired on the mountainside. Gazing up at the ceiling, his body limp and his hand sore, he thought about what JP had said about his family. He recalled what Tony had mumbled about God moments before he collapsed and had to be loaded onto the stretcher.

Ted Stevens Anchorage International Airport
June 18th, 1:46 P.M.


An RCMP prop-driven aircraft from Whitehorse, Yukon Territory arrived at the airport and after stopping in the VIP aircraft parking area, two distinguished-looking Mounties dressed in formal red tunics disembarked and were met by Lieutenant Tanner from the Alaska State Troopers.

The Mounties, both lieutenants, had arrived to transport JP's body back to Toronto with the Canadian flag draped over his steel casket. Colonel Augustus had issued orders that Captain JP Leon would receive full honors and be treated as a hero killed in the line of duty.

Providence Hospital - 3rd Floor
June 19th, 6:41 a.m.

With enough psychiatric drugs in him to keep him calm, Steve Munroe awakened to find himself strapped into a hospital bed lashed in a thick white straight jacket. He was troubled to see two uniformed security officers standing over him with a cold icy glare in their eyes.

Once the feared leader of the Front de Liberation du Quebec, Steve Munroe was frightened. He couldn't remember what had happened to him after Janene was mauled by the bear. Though he demanded his day in court, he was deemed unfit to stand trial in Alaska and Canada, nor was he allowed to speak to news people and leave confinement. Two years later, Munroe would leap out a window and fall to his death from the sixth story of his hospital. No one claimed the body.

# EPILOGUE

Law And Disorder
In The Months To Follow

Before his death, which was ruled a suicide, Steve Munroe attempted to have a high-priced legal firm represent him. They tried to have him removed from US jurisdiction and moved to Toronto. This was denied by the US Superior Court, and Canadian authorities refused to become involved in the matter. The Supreme Court in Washington, D.C. was asked to review the case and refused.

The laborious investigation conducted by Sgt. Steve Adler and Sgt. Brady Wilkens' team, involving 1,604 man-hours, resulted in the Federal Court in Toronto issuing arrest warrants for Dr. Richard Quison, Sir Albert Bruisse, Bradley Osmire, Richard Doyle, and Richard Webster. Federal authorities froze all their banking accounts in Canada and the United States.

Colonel Augustus left Sgt. Adler in charge of the investigative team and promoted him to lieutenant. Another captain would be brought in to take over the RCMP Intelligence Division in Toronto. As for Sgt Wilkens, he elected to retire when the case was completed.

Sir Albert Bruisse was found in his den by his maid, a suspected suicide. He had taken his life with a Smith & Wesson .357 caliber revolver.

Lt. Adler apprehended Richard Doyle when he attempted to fly out of the country via a personal aircraft. Two suitcases were found in the aircraft's baggage hold containing $192,000 in large U.S. bills and another $110,000 in Canadian funds. Doyle refused to talk with investigators and hid behind a wall of lawyers. While locked up in pre-trial confinement, Doyle was assaulted and nearly killed by an imprisoned relative of a woman killed in the Parliament bombing. Returning from the hospital, he was placed in segregation for his own safety and held without bail until his trial. He was later found guilty and sentenced to 89 years in a Canadian prison.

Richard Webster died in a shoot-out with Toronto's RCMP Special Weapons and Tactics Team. He held his mistress hostage while attempting to trade her for a flight to South America. According to his mistress, a woman who would eventually appear on numerous talk shows, Webster seemed very distraught. Supposedly, he had started drinking heavily after learning an arrest warrant was issued for him.

Accompanied by his lawyers and a known radical radio reporter, Bradley Osmire surrendered himself at the Toronto RCMP Headquarters. Osmire and his lawyers were allowed in with investigators, while the upset radio reporter was told to remain in the lobby. Refusing to say anything other than provide his name and mailing address, Osmire was transported to the correctional facility and placed in segregation. Appearing at arraignment, he was remanded without bail against his lawyer's request. He would be found guilty and sentenced to 89 years in a Canadian prison.

Dr. Quison attempted to flee the country but died in a fiery helicopter crash 14 miles north of his hunting lodge. His body was later identified by an RCMP medical examiner. Also killed were the pilot and two bodyguards. Investigation showed that a bomb had detonated when the helicopter reached a certain altitude. Dr. Quison was identified through dental records and DNA. No suspects were identified in the helicopter bombing. However, it was suspected by local authorities that there was Parti Quebecois involvement. As with the first FLQ, the new group had seriously hurt the "Freedom for Quebec" movement. It was suspected that revenge was sought. The government seized Dr. Quison's private lands, along with $23,150,080.00 found in Dr. Quison's personal bank accounts in Montreal and New York City banks. As CEO of his company, Dr. Quison's assets were seized by the Canadian government and held temporarily until legal proceedings were completed. Canadian and US Governments worked out who owned what and what might be paid to the victims of the attacks in both countries. Eventually, the investigation revealed Dr. Quison's true identity; Luther Taylor, who was reported missing as a 17-year-old runaway from British Columbia. For over 40 years, he was listed as a suspect in the murder of a high school classmate.

When it was learned how Captain JP Leon died, nearly every RCMP officer on the force wanted to volunteer time in the multi-unit investigation. By the time it was finished, four provincial employees and seven Canadian federal employees were indicted for accepting bribes from the five Canadian businessmen. Nine of the 11 culprits were also charged under US and Canadian terrorism laws. Not one RCMP or Toronto Police officer was named in the indictments. All eleven government employees were identified as militant members of a secret faction inside the Parti Quebecois, led and financed by Dr. Quison. Once this was learned by the Parti Quebecois, all suspected members of the secret faction were removed from the party's membership. Several of them were later charged with crimes connected to the Toronto bombings.

Mr. Osmire's and Mr. Doyle's company and personal assets were seized and held pending the outcome of their trial for murder and fraud. Both industrial companies would file for bankruptcy and were later taken over by competitors.

It would take a room full of law clerks three days to prepare the trial's charging documents for Osmire and Doyle. A total of 945 formal charges were being brought against them for the deaths and destruction they wrought in Canada. Federal and State authorities had charges pending in Alaska. For every passenger on the train, another criminal indictment was made for terroristic threatening, and attempted murder. Both countries wanted these men to pay for their violent acts of terrorism and murder.

Using monies from the five men and the sale of their companies, the Canadian Government set up a special fund to assist the families of those killed by the FLQ, which included the victims in Alaska. Hundreds of minors would have their college tuition paid through the fund, family homes, and other expenses paid off.

Once the investigation was wrapped up, and officers returned to their home units, Colonel Augustus placed Lt. Adler in command of a new RCMP unit. Under the Intelligence Division, the new unit would be investigating various terrorist groups known to be operating in Canada. One of the first items on Adler's list was suspected Chinese involvement in Eastern Canadian politics and illegal gangs.

Both Adler and Wilkens were decorated meritoriously, after which, Sgt. Wilkens voiced his decision to retire to avoid working for the newly promoted Lt. Adler. "I love the guy, but this way, we can remain good friends," Sgt. Wilkens said during an RCMP gathering in Toronto.

Colonel Augustus retired at the end of the year, moving back to the Yukon Territory and living out the rest of his years hunting and fishing at a lodge he had purchased. Recently retired Fire Captain Whitehead would become a frequent visitor during trout season.

Prime Minister Haegens remained hospitalized for some time, leaving his office due to physical problems and turning the duties over to the Assistant Prime Minister. Sir Whiteburn and Agent Loury were decorated for their involvement in the McKinley Hotel incident. They both resumed their Secret Service duties and stayed in touch with Sgt. John Niles.

Sgt Niles remained with Governor Hughes as his bodyguard. Once every other year, Niles and Whiteburn got together for a fishing trip in Mexico. Promoted to Lieutenant, John Niles declined to retire right away. He would lead the AST White Collar Crime Unit and graduate from the FBI Academy in Washington, D.C.

The RCMP Commandant, at the request of Colonel Augustus, posthumously awarded Captain JP Leon their highest honor for valor and buried him with full honors beside his wife and children. Greg Hansen and Tony Rogers were in attendance as honorary pallbearers. JP's photograph was placed on the memorial wall at Toronto RCMP Headquarters, which also listed his many other honors.

Governor Hughes insisted Bob Rexault continue his duties once he was able. When Rexault returned to work, Sgt. Niles was on hand to push his wheelchair around and offer his old adversary a hot cup of coffee every morning. A friendship of sorts between the two men formed over their shared experience in the Alaska wilderness.

Following a lengthy interview with Governor Hughes and the Commissioner of Public Safety, Greg Hansen was invited to return to the Alaska State Troopers as the new Captain in command of the AST Major Crimes Unit. In assuming the position, Captain Greg Hansen moved to Anchorage and immediately had Trooper Bosley transferred from Cantwell to his unit. Greg returned to the church, began dating his ex-wife, and saw his son as often as possible.

Lt. Steve Farber retired early from the Fairbanks Police Department and was hired as Greg's replacement as ARR Special Agent-Fairbanks.

Out of the hospital, Old Man Taylor went back to the Reindeer Lodge and hired Sam Watterson to assist him behind the bar. Not so much a believer himself, Taylor allowed a newly appointed Pastor Tony Rogers to hold Sunday afternoon services in his place. Within a year, Tony would have a church building constructed. It became a central meeting place for dried-out alcoholics, reformed drug addicts, and burned-out Nam vets. He offered to counsel those who were still dealing with those problems. He had 13-steady members in his

AA and NA group, and the number was growing. His church, a non-denominational fellowship, was known as New Hope and a church home to 41 people.

In the years to follow their adventure against the FLQ, Greg maintained a strong friendship with Tony. The two of them would share other experiences in the Alaska wilderness.

As for the Alaska Railroad, they would spend the next nine years in civil court, dealing with 293 damage and Mental Anguish lawsuits and six Wrongful Death lawsuits, including one filed by the parents of a dead terrorist. As usual, it was the lawyers who continued to profit.

**THE END**

# ABOUT THE AUTHOR

William Casselman was raised in Southern California. He enlisted in the U.S. Air Force in 1971 to become a Law Enforcement Specialist/Military Working Dog Handler. He served the next ten years in the military and met his lovely wife, Mona Sue, at Eielson AFB, Alaska.

A Vietnam veteran, he left the service to become a police officer in Dillingham, Alaska, and spent the next twenty years in Alaskan police work. From patrolman to investigator, he has worked with four police departments and was the Public Safety Director for the City of Whittier during the tragic Exxon Oil Spill in Prince William Sound in 1989.

William, a 42-year Christian, retired as Senior Investigator for the State of Alaska gaming program. With 44 years in Alaska, he has six children and seventeen grandchildren, and great-grandchildren.

William and his wife, Mona Sue now live in rural Alaska.